PRELUDE TO ASCENSION

The Assemblies of the Living Series

a novel about first contact

Brent Clay

287

For Virginia

Prologue

"Uh, Clip?"

"I'm on it," Jason Clipper said, without looking away from his computer monitor.

None of the three men in the large computer lab had been relaxed to begin with, and now there were three rigid backs leaning forward from their chairs towards what looked to be the beginnings of a disaster.

"Talk to me," John Riley said, his eyes tracking nervously between the monitor and his friend.

"Okay," Clipper said, still not looking up. "Your cologne has a nice woody finish, but a little too sweet for my tastes. Not fond of your shirt either. Can we finish this later?"

Riley got the point. He shot a glance at the third man in the room who looked more perplexed than concerned. AJ was a guest, and about to become an unwitting accomplice. He had come to meet them for a late breakfast before leaving town. That was all. And now, as the virtual walls began giving way around them, the colossal mistake of bringing him into this highly secured room was obvious and inexcusable. *Damn!* he thought.

Clipper pulled his eyes from the computer screen for the first time in several minutes – long enough to exchange a knowing look with Riley. "Whoever this is, I think he's got us."

AJ was piecing things together. "Gentlemen?" he said, with a hint of concern, but neither Riley nor Clipper acknowledged him. Clipper had already returned to boring a hole into the monitor with his eyes, his fingers moving in fits and starts as he reacted to what the computer threw at him.

Talk about a comedy of errors, Riley thought as he helplessly willed Clipper forward. This would all come down as though he had laid awake for weeks planning every detail. It was becoming painfully obvious that the very safeguards built into the computer lab would be its downfall. The servers were locked away in a sub-basement behind doors that could repel an army, beyond his reach, and the simplest of all remedies, which was to simply turn them off. He had never even seen the physical machines. He could visualize them, tucked innocuously among racks and racks of look-alike servers, in a smoldering frenzy, mindlessly carrying out commands that would ultimately be their undoing. It would only be a matter of time. The virus would replicate and infiltrate Mayfield Hammond's computer infrastructure unabated until nothing short of a system-wide wipe and restore would…

He stopped short. Something occurred to him and it wasn't good. He searched his mind for an out, some escape from the realization, but there wasn't one. "Clip?" he said finally. "Does this lab share resources with EcoGrid?"

The impact of the question was immediate. Clipper froze, then eased slowly back into his chair, his hands lowering to his lap. Lines of terse text were still appearing on the computer screen; scrolling, stopping, scrolling a bit more, but Clipper had tuned it all out. "Gentlemen," he said, "we may not have only just made the evening news, we may have just made history."

At that, the tension that had begun filling the room over the prior few moments reached its breaking point.

AJ looked to the computer monitor. It was busy. What it all meant, he wasn't sure, but it was clear that the computer was chewing on something and applying everything it had to whatever it was. He glanced over at Riley and Clipper. They had begun rifling through a notebook, desperate for some answer that he somehow knew they would not find.

They were panicked. Plain and simple.

Without a word, AJ swung his chair around in front of the monitor, pushing Clipper slightly out of the way as he did. Surprised, Riley and Clipper looked back in astonishment, and Clipper reached out to stop him, but not fast enough. Before either of them could react, AJ typed two simple words into the computer's command line interface:

Please stop.

Part One: Gravity

Chapter 1

B rian Matthews looked out over the manicured Mayfield Hammond campus grounds from his corner office. The view from the Executive Building was impressive. As Chief Technology Officer of, arguably, the most successful and powerful business technology company on the planet, he had it all as careers go, and at the early age of 38.

The power afforded by the position went far beyond money, and far beyond the borders of the expansive campus. A simple opinion voiced by Matthews could change the fortunes of thousands, maybe more. The decision to adopt this protocol over that, this approach over another, would instantly alter the roadmaps of startups across Silicon Valley and virtually everywhere else. The reason was simple: if Mayfield Hammond did it, it was, for all practical purposes, already a standard. Smaller fish would embrace and adopt or be left out.

Years of that type of influence; not the belief, but the simple truth that his opinions, his views, his decisions shaped so much of the world, went to no lesser extent in shaping the man. Brian Matthews lived in the holographic bubble of his ideals; a world that either operated to his expectations through the tremendous efforts and sacrifice of his extensive staff, or failed to do so by the incompetence of the same. The inconvenience of unwanted facts were rarely allowed to infringe upon his laboriously constructed world of preconceived notions – a world from which all unwanted details had been swept from view.

But this might be about to change. There was a new dynamic, or soon would be. To his credit, he was troubled only because he had the foresight to see what almost no one else could. Despite his shortcomings, his success was no accident. His grasp of the state of technology and where it was headed, was unique.

Something new was coming.

He looked to the tablet lying across his knee, lifting it again to scan through the article he had been reading. This particular threat was different. Mayfield Hammond generally operated within the realms of business technology. Research and development amounted to using existing technological resources to innovate in the spaces of business, not in developing the technologies themselves. Those were the raw materials out of which business innovation emerged. But this new field of opportunity was different, and Matthews knew that opportunity was only another word for something his competitors would certainly do, and hope that he did not.

He swiveled his chair towards his desk and pressed the call button. "Anna," he said, "can you please find information for me about a man named John Riley? He finished his postgraduate in Particle Physics at USC a couple of years ago. I'd like to know more about him and how to reach him."

Anna Burns was Matthews' Executive Admin. She sat in the anteroom of his 900 square foot office, too far away for casual conversation. "Yes, Mr. Matthews, when do you need it?" she said.

"Sometime this afternoon is fine, thank you."

Matthews resumed his agitated survey of the campus. The article he had been reading was from one of the many science and technology publications he subscribed to, both in printed copy and online. It was written by John Riley, and discussed concepts related to the manipulation of gravity. *Antigravity*, to be more precise. Matthews had seen it a few days before and had let it go. In fact, hadn't even read the whole thing at first. But even though his cognitive mind had moved on, his subliminal mind had refused to drop the subject. Over the days since first spotting it – itself something of an accident as it had been published nearly two years prior – it had repeatedly returned to his thoughts, each time with greater emphasis. It had now grown to take on a sense of urgency.

What could be done with a technology that could control gravitation? he wondered. The list would not be short:

transportation, space travel, power generation, to name only a few. It would also be a green field for patents. There could be hundreds of opportunities in the space.

He pressed the call button again. "Anna?"

"Yes, Mr. Matthews," she said.

"Would you mind asking Tony Erwin to stop in to see me at his earliest convenience?"

"Happy to."

Tony Erwin had joined the company a few years prior, maybe three or four, having come in from one of the big wireless carriers where he had been a Senior Network Engineer. He was the type of person usually referred to as a 'technical resource,' and his breadth of technical knowledge was impressive. Since joining Mayfield Hammond, he had brought the now infamous EcoGrid product to life, taking it to technological heights not remotely envisioned during its formative stages. Matthews reasoned that the man was as likely as anyone in the company to have an opinion on Riley's paper.

In a moment, Matthews' tablet chimed with a notification from Anna. *Tony will appear in your office within the next few minutes. No more than 10*, it said. He placed the tablet onto his large desk and rose to retrieve a bottle of water from his private refrigerator.

Shortly, Erwin arrived as promised. He was a tall man with broad shoulders and sandy blond hair, but not necessarily athletic. He lacked executive pollish, but had the type of confidence that most people never understood or achieved; which was that he never thought about confidence. It was a distinction few people would pick up on, but something Matthews had noticed and liked about Erwin since the first time they had met.

"Morning Tony," Matthews said as Erwin entered the oversized office.

"Morning," Tony said. "What can I help you with?"

"Do you follow many pubs on science or physics? Research and all that?"

"I do," Erwin answered.

"USC is your alma mater, am I correct?"

"Yes, been awhile – graduated ten years ago."

"I found an article by a guy who graduated from there a couple of years ago. I'd like for you to read it and give me your impressions." Matthews stepped forward and handed the tablet over, which Erwin took and began scanning with interest. Matthews waited, sipping at his water, but didn't interrupt.

After a few seconds, Erwin looked up. "Seems vaguely familiar. I'd need a few minutes to read in more detail." He looked back to the tablet. "Looks like about 25 pages or so."

"Understood. If you wouldn't mind, take a few minutes to do that. I need to have a quick hallway conversation on other business anyway."

"Will do."

With that, Matthews made for the door, but hesitated before exiting. "Feel free to raid the fridge. Lots of stuff to drink in there."

"Thanks boss," Erwin said, but he was already absorbed in the reading.

Matthews returned 20 minutes later to find Erwin on his feet drinking a Diet Coke and looking out the window. "Nice view," he said, gesturing out the window with the bottle.

"Thank you," Matthews said. "You finished the article?"

"Yes, and once I got into it I recalled seeing it before."

"What do you think?"

"Short answer? I think this Riley fellow is onto something."

"Really?" Matthews said, surprised that Erwin would share the opinion without a disclaimer. "What makes you say so?"

"I did some physics in school and now do casual reading on the subject. Gravitation is one of those things that has refused to budge as far as physics go. We can create electricity, split atoms, send people into space, you name it; but we can't do a damned thing with gravity."

"What do you like about Riley's ideas?"

Erwin shrugged. "If you think about it, the concepts are almost obvious. The prevailing sentiment of science is that there are four fundamental forces, or interactions of nature; the *strong force*, the *electromagnetic force*, the *weak force*, and *gravitation* – ignoring the Higgs field. In the simplest of terms – maybe oversimplifying a bit – he asserts that the strength of a gravitational field can be modified as a function of the other three. He doesn't spell it all out in his paper – smart man – but that's the summary."

"Is it possible? If he had the chance – the equipment and resources – do you think it could be done?"

"*He* would probably say yes. I'm not so sure, but he makes a compelling case. A big part of it relies on modifying the strong nuclear force itself. That's the thinnest part in my view. The strong force is as fundamental as gravity, and way, way stronger, so I don't see where it would be easier to modify than gravitation itself. It's the basis of his hypothesis though, so he must have thought it through – he just didn't put it into the paper. Probably on purpose."

"But you think there's plausibility here?"

Erwin tilted his head in thought. "Well, I–"

"Yes or no."

Erwin hesitated before answering. "Yes."

Matthews flinched at the response. It was an unexpected reaction, like a man who had just validated something he knew to be true but hoped wouldn't be. "Two years," he said, more to himself than to Erwin. He walked to his desk and pressed the call button. "Anna, I know I asked for information on Riley by end of day, but do you have anything now?"

"Still looking into it, Mr. Matthews."

"Have you located him yet? It may be enough for now if I can talk with him."

"I don't have his contact info as yet, but should very soon. I do know that he is in Atlanta at the moment, attending a conference on—" she let off, searching her notes. "Cloud Computing."

Matthews was impressed. "Nice work. How long does the conference go?"

"Another three days after today – ends on Thursday."

"Thank you, Anna. Please make travel arrangements for me to go to the conference location immediately. Are any of the corporate jets available?"

"I'll check," she said.

Matthews looked back to Erwin, who was watching him curiously. "Listen, I'm gonna see if I can talk with John Riley today, but I'd like to get a few more eyes on this too. Would you mind pulling together a few people who might have an opinion? I'll get back to you on this tomorrow."

"No problem," Erwin said.

Chapter 2

March 14, 2023

John Riley had flown through Atlanta once before. It seemed an unlikely location for the world's busiest airport, but seeing was believing. He had not gone into the city on that prior trip – it was a touch-and-go connecting flight – but this time Atlanta was his destination. He would stay in the heart of the city and attend a conference on Cloud Computing at the Georgia World Congress Center. It hadn't been easy to persuade his employer, a small technology startup in the Midwest, to front the money, but they had.

Cloud computing was everything these days. Although far from his intended field of work, technology had become a somewhat satisfying fallback. From hosted servers, content delivery networks, serverless functions, NoSQL databases, distributed ledgers, and event-driven architectures; the field had come a long way in a few short years. It was a good time to be in technology.

All conferences – and this one would be no different – were networking opportunities as much as anything else. The rub was that Riley was somewhat standoffish. He was there for the sessions, and that was it. The *Platform as a Service* offerings of major Cloud providers were a new frontier of opportunity, and like any other goldrush, the sooner you knew and acted, the better.

The opportunities were intriguing, not in the least part because of monetary appeal, but also for the technology itself. The big Cloud providers had done more than level the playing field; in a very real sense they had shifted the advantage away from the huge companies that had dominated the best opportunities of the past, to smaller, agile firms. These platforms brought the economies of scale that were once the reserved domain of the largest and most powerful, to the smallest of upstarts that could turn on a dime in ways that their larger counterparts couldn't hope to match. The result was unbridled innovation and competition. The new game was to hatch a good idea, stand it up in a fraction of the time it would take for any of the big companies to do it, and then sell out to one of them.

By the afternoon of the first day, Riley had already decided that the trip would not be a disappointment. He had attended sessions on *big data* and *analytics*, best practices in *identity and access management*, and would shortly attend a track on application deployment strategies. In the few minutes of free time before then, he found a comfortable chair off the beaten path, extracted his electronic tablet from his satchel and began scanning through scientific and technical articles, sipping at a cup of coffee.

Per usual, he kept an eye out for anything that touched on matters of gravitation. Things like advancements in gravitation meters, new findings and theories on Dark Matter – the apparent, but inexplicable shortage of visible matter in virtually every galaxy in the observable Universe, and then general chatter.

He saw nothing particularly unusual, and hadn't expected to. Had there been, his tablet would most certainly have found it and percolated it to the top of his reading list, sparing him the need to search for it at all. No, there was nothing new that he could see. That would change soon enough, he knew, and he would be the one who changed it, but it would be for another day.

To John Riley, gravitation was one of the few remaining, interesting frontiers of physics. Not that there was anything close to a shortage of frontiers. He knew very well that humankind was far from solving all the mysteries that the grand Universe had to offer, and that his great grandchildren – if he were to ever have any – would probably have to concede the same. But gravitation was special; so pervasive and common, so directly experienceable, yet so unmovable.

Part of the intrigue was in the science of it, but another was more elusive. As yet, humankind had been utterly unable to manipulate gravity. Space stations on drawing boards used centrifugal force as a crude substitute: Spin an enormous wheel, let people walk on the inner side of its rim – feet pointing outward from its center – and who needs the real thing? That was all well and good, but it wasn't gravitation.

On the up side, all of it meant that John was on his way towards one of the only places in the Universe as he knew it, that had not already been visited by someone else. His current professional status was something of an unexpected detour, but none of it had dissuaded him in the least. He spent as many hours as he could on the subject. Every new blip on his computer screen, every new puzzle he encountered on his quest to conquer the secrets of gravitation was, to his thinking, an aspect of this fundamental property of nature that no one else had ever seen.

Of course, there was a downside as well. The cost of his education had been a compelling reason to secure gainful employment, which he had done, but in the end, it didn't change his goals. He wanted to solve gravitation, that was all; at least for now. And it could be done, he was certain of it. In the interim, it forced him to live with the uncomfortable fear that he would one day check his computer to find that someone had beaten him to it. It kept him awake at night. To his relief, as he lowered his tablet to the small table next to the chair where he sat, he knew it would not be this day. He looked up from his tablet in time to see a man he didn't recognize approaching.

"Hello," the man said over the low rumble of voices in the open concourse of the hotel.

Riley was somewhat surprised, but responded with a pleasant 'hello' in return. He expected the man to move on, but he didn't. "Would you happen to be John Riley?" the man asked.

Riley looked at him questioningly, trying to place him, but couldn't. "I am," he said. "Can I help you?"

"I hope so. In fact, there is a chance we may be able to help each other." It was an unexpected statement, and it prompted Riley to try a little harder at placing him. The man looked to be middle aged and wore a suit not typical of conference goers, but Riley had no idea who he could be.

"Really?" Riley's said, more a statement than a question.

"Could be. May I have a seat?"

"Of course," Riley allowed, shifting in his chair to a more upright position, but still wishing the man would move on.

"Thank you. I'm Brian Matthews, with *Mayfield Hammond.*"

"Good to meet you," Riley said, choosing not to be too put off by the man's sudden appearance. Conferences were exactly for this type of thing. Riley tried to guess for a moment how Matthews had come by his name. A strong possibility was that he had read it from the name tag hanging from the lanyard around his neck, but if so, he must have done earlier. Riley didn't notice him looking at it as he approached, and even if he had, the man's demeanor seemed to suggest that the meeting wasn't an accident.

"Are you familiar with Mayfield Hammond?"

Riley nodded. "Are there still people who aren't?"

"Probably not in this building, but never hurts to ask," Matthews said, grinning slightly. "I'm head of Technology and Research over there. I'd like to ask a few questions regarding a paper of yours that I came across recently. It was about antigravity. Do you know the one?"

It had been only a couple short years since Riley wrote that paper. It could seem both longer ago or more recent, depending on how he thought of it. For some reason, being raised so unexpectedly by a stranger at a technology conference made it feel very immediate. "It'll be some time before I forget that one," Riley said.

"I understand. Would you mind my asking if you're still working in physics, or are you now in technology?"

"You have to pay the bills," Riley said. "I would love to get back into physics, but the right opportunity hasn't presented itself. Technology feels something like a close cousin, so it could be worse."

Matthews nodded agreement. "Makes sense," he said. "Exposure to technology can really benefit a physicist. I wouldn't consider the hiatus a waste of time."

"I don't," Riley said.

There was a short lull in the conversation. Riley decided to wait rather than attempt to coax Matthews into revealing his intentions. The pause didn't seem to affect the man. He sat entirely at ease and surveyed the foot traffic across the large open area with passive interest. "Mr. Riley, I'm interested in learning more about your theories."

Riley didn't respond.

"Is it your belief that the technology and tools needed to produce the effects of antigravity exist today?"

Riley felt suddenly wary but pushed the feeling aside. If he were ever going to do anything with gravitation, it would require someone with resources to come into the picture, and who better than Mayfield Hammond? It's something he had known all along. An antigravity machine couldn't be built with parts from the neighborhood hardware store. If this somehow turned out to be the opportunity he had been waiting for, it made no sense to let it pass in hopes that another opportunity, about which he would know nothing more, would come along. "Yes," Riley said, at last.

"What type of timeframe? If you had the equipment, how long do estimate it would take to get to something demonstrable?"

"Fifteen months," Riley said, without hesitation.

Matthews quirked an eyebrow. "That was quick. I would have thought you'd need a little longer to work that out."

"Four years is a fair amount of time," Riley said, trying to hide his irritation at the comment. "That paper didn't happen at the start of my research, it was a summary of it. The fifteen months allows three months to assemble a team and get a project underway. The remaining twelve is to get it done."

"Of course," Matthews said. "Here it is, then, Mr. Riley. I've read your paper and asked a few of my engineers to review it for plausibility. I've also asked our *Product* team to work up concepts and a few mock business cases. I'll cut to it. I'd like for you to come to Charlotte and join our company. We'll provide the resources to enable you to turn your theories into reality if you agree that Mayfield Hammond will own the technologies and products that result from them. I don't expect an answer now."

With respect to his last statement, nothing could have been further from the truth. Matthews had rarely found it more difficult to maintain a poker face. He did want an answer, and immediately; and couldn't wait to put his legal team to work on pinning Riley down and laying claim to his concepts.

Riley sipped his coffee, feeling no urgency to respond. Matthews waited, showing no less patience. "There would be a lot to work through on the arrangement," Riley said at length. "This isn't the time or place for that, but we'd have to agree on a few things in principle, at least."

"Shoot," Matthews said.

"First ... and this will seem trivial in the broader scheme of things, but I have to ask. I would hope that my current employer could be reimbursed for the cost of this conference. Wouldn't seem right to leave them otherwise, at least not immediately."

Matthews nodded, dismissing the point.

"Second, I'll need a stake in the technology. Frankly, we both know that the potential here is on par with electricity. It could change the world just as much, and we both know that is not an overstatement. I don't want to find myself, five years down the road, drawing a physicist's salary while Mayfield earns millions from products and services based on my theories."

Dropping the second part of the *Mayfield Hammond* name was a common practice. Riley had done it without thinking and wondered for a moment whether Matthews would react. He didn't.

Matthews wasn't surprised by the demand. "That will be a matter for the attorneys and the board, but we'll be able to work something into the arrangement that's fair and equitable, I'm sure of that. If you're good to take this to the next step, my admin will reach out to schedule time for us to continue the conversation."

"I look forward to it," Riley said, for the first time feeling a jolt of excitement at what this could represent.

"Excellent," Matthews said. "How can we reach you?"

"I happen to have a card," Riley said, producing one from his pocket. "I'll give my personal email." He crossed out the work-email address on the front of the card, then turned it over to write on the back.

Matthews accepted the card and gave one of his own in return. Riley accepted it and glanced at it briefly. It was only then that he connected all the dots and realized who he had been talking with. Matthews caught the moment of recognition on Riley's face, but neither man acknowledged it.

"Mr. Riley, despite what I said a moment ago, you may be surprised to learn that I've come here with some urgency. The good news is that, I think it will serve to our mutual benefit. If you are, in fact, interested in pursuing this opportunity – and I warrant to you that it will be nothing less than I have conveyed – then I would like to move forward with extreme haste. My admin will contact you no later than tomorrow. Please do all diligence to collect your thoughts and intentions as soon as possible so we can get the preliminaries out of the way."

Matthews rose and Riley followed suit. The two shook hands and Matthews turned for the door. Riley watched him as he walked. He had a swagger, not overdone, but impossible to miss; the product of years of power and influence that had shaped a man not accustomed to inconvenience or disappointment. He didn't look back, passing through the glass entryway doors at the front of the hotel lobby and approaching a black Cadillac Escalade parked just outside. Its passenger door was opened for him by a sharply dressed man who timed the event so that Matthews could take his seat without breaking stride. The man then closed the door, walked around to the front the vehicle, and in seconds, was gone.

The unusual meeting had happened so unexpectedly and ended so abruptly, that Riley could have doubted it had happened at all, were it not for the card in his hand. He sat looking at it. It read: *Brian Matthews, Chief Technology Officer, Mayfield Hammond.*

Chapter 3

March 14, 2023

Pastor Owen Henson locked the front door of the small church building behind him as he entered just before dusk. It was a typical Tuesday evening. He walked quietly through the small foyer and into the darkening sanctuary just beyond. Horizontal light from the setting sun filtered through the west windows projecting a procession of distorted rectangular imprints onto the east wall of the large room.

Henson passed the light switches without turning them on and swung to the right, negotiating his way between pews near the back of the sanctuary. He stepped into the sound booth, which occupied a small, elevated platform near the back, and powered-up the PA system with the push of a button. It crackled to life with a pop, amplified over the house speakers, before settling into a gentle hum – a nuisance that many hours of work had failed to correct. Cooling fans on the 24-channel mixer and nearby computer began whirring contentedly, and an assortment of green and red lights glowed importantly on electronic equipment. A few mouse clicks on the computer, and soft worshipful music began to play, filling the space like a warm blanket.

He stepped back onto the sanctuary floor and made his way to the front of the room where he began pacing quietly in the space between the platform and first pew. Soon, he would be lost to himself; to everything in the room, and to everything beyond. Through the years, prayer had become a vital form of meditation for him. He could now enter this state of spiritual calm almost effortlessly, and it had become the anchor around which the chaos of his life turned.

Henson had played this scene out countless times before. Although not always in a church building, he had begun the practice of praying in this way when he was only a teenager. Now at 64, he had come to regard his prayer times – what his wife had called his *prayer life* – as an essential and indispensable part of who he was.

Tracks of soft music rolled gently forward, transitioning gracefully from one soothing melody to the next without so much as a crescendo to draw attention from his inner calm. And like the roof above his head and the walls surrounding him, the music was already fading into a muted, less tangible expression of itself; lingering on the far side of the quiet calm that was enveloping his mind.

But there was something new. It was not a thing that imposed itself upon his meditations, but more underlied them – permeated them. For year after year, Owen had entered this state of prayer within the context of a belief system. He hadn't even realized that. His notions of truth, his thoughts and insights on questions of faith and God had been guide rails that both defined and limited where his heart, mind and spirit had ventured to go. Then something changed. It didn't begin with the rejection of anything. It was quite possibly by accident that his inner-self had one day, for reasons he simply did not know, wondered for the first time whether the silent spaces of his meditations were, indeed, suspended within the cupped hands of his Christian faith.

What had begun as a mere flicker of contemplation steadily rose to a force that could not be willed away. When he first realized that this simple muse of thought had become entrenched within him – had begun disrupting his calm – he sought to encapsulate it, to earmark it as a symptom of simple weakness that could be overcome through still more prayer. But there was a problem. The decision to expunge the doubts from his mind had been made by the man who lived outside of this space. The inner corridors where the doubts had taken root were beyond the reach of cognizant reasoning. To a person who lived only within the realms of the cognizant, who knew of only the high-contrast, tactile faces of life and living, all of it would be less than nothing; nonsense. To anyone else, it would be everything that such a person would know it to be.

The transition had been slow. Week after week, month after month had passed until the questions he had once called doubts began to resolve into something more. No longer doubts, but deeper truths. He was sure of that now.

And ultimately, the course that was always going to play out, finally had. He was the pastor of a church. It was the only life he had known. He was surrounded by family and friends who relied upon him, and the steadfastness of his faith to anchor their own. He was Pastor to a congregation of men, women and children who would never guess at his struggles. And now he faced private, self-imposed questions about his own character.

He was, to his own thinking, no less a person of faith than he had ever been. Perhaps more so. He believed – deeply believed – that there was a spiritual component to life that was real, but was now forced to finally confront the realization that whether that belief be true or false, Christianity was not its explanation.

In the quiet sanctuary of the church building, he looked across the empty pews, vaguely outlined in the sparse remaining light, and imagined the faces he would see in them on Sunday.

There were many implications. Until now, they had all manifest as private struggles. But when the moment came – a moment he had seen with dread, coming from a long way off – the moment he had to finally admit to himself that he had ceased being a believer in the Christian faith, it could no longer remain private. Character and integrity still mattered. That same sense of honor and truthfulness was, in fact, the part of him that insisted he not continue to deceive family and friends as Pastor of a Christian church, when deeply within, he could no longer believe its message.

Of all the people who would be impacted, he knew that his daughter, Sarah, would feel it most. She had lost her mother only four years before, and now this. It could very-well devastate her. Sarah had come late in their lives, and the impacts of that took time to reveal themselves. Her mother being one. His own failing health being another. But she was a true believer; as strong-willed as any human he had ever met. He knew she would be fine in the end.

And now that he was finally – perhaps only within the last few moments – nearing the end of the long and difficult journey from which he had always known he would not emerge unharmed, he must begin thinking about removing himself from the church. It would take time.

How to begin? He didn't know who to ask. What an odd sense that was.

The most tangible outcome of his new – what should he call it? perspective – was that he no longer had a place to direct his prayer. If he were to give in, as it appeared he may be doing even now, to finally giving up all of his prior beliefs, then his prayer life would change. It would truly become meditation. Only meditation.

The thought was unsatisfying. Could there be something more? He had journeyed away from so much of his prior beliefs. Was there anything left among the remaining shards of his prior faith that could give higher purpose to meditation than ... what? Self-improvement? Strength? Peace?

There had to be more. There must be more. He sensed it but could not identify it. How could something as real and undeniable as truth, with depths unfathomable, be of no greater utility than understanding, or insight? Surely, the toilsome road to wisdom, the self-denial of character, the sacrifice of knowledge, could not dead-end with self.

Chapter 4

March 22, 2023

When John Riley lifted his foot to board the plane that would take him to Charlotte for his meeting with Mayfield Hammond to finalize the details of his employment, and more importantly, the rights and claims related to the work he would do on gravitation, it was the start of a new life. Among all the discussions and questions, all the events that had led to that day, it was that moment – the deliberate act of boarding that plane – that rose above all others as the point at which the life he had known and somehow expected to persist with him through all of his breathing years, had ceased. He had boarded the Boeing 737 aircraft to find his reserved, first class seat on the front row, and nothing would ever be the same again.

Riley expected, even welcomed the changes he knew to be coming, however abrupt they may be. He would relocate to a part of the country that he had never even visited, to join one of the relatively few companies that was powerful and ubiquitous enough to have become a household name. As an engineer or technical professional of any title, there was simply no better platform than Mayfield Hammond from which to engage the world.

"You must bear in mind, Mr. Riley, that what Mayfield Hammond brings to this arrangement is more than money or even resources," said Lynn Turner, Chief Legal Counsel. "The reach of the company is unrivaled. Not only will we provide to you the opportunity to pursue your theories with a freedom that few, if any other companies can; our ability to see products through to marketability is unmatched."

They had been at it for the better part of an hour-and-a-half, in a stately-looking executive conference room lost on the sprawling campus. They were talking over a mahogany table that bore a scattering of half-drained coffee mugs and half-eaten pastries. Tired as he was, Riley was determined not to let fatigue play a role in this particular conversation. Without a doubt, it was the most important of his life so far. "I see your points, Ms. Turner, and wouldn't dispute them," he said, evenly. "But there is the matter of the science itself. That is what I bring to the table. And I would argue that I am as uniquely positioned in that regard as Mayfield is to delivering all the good things that you just mentioned."

"Mr. Riley," Brian Matthews cut in, "with due respect, your theories on gravitation are just that; theories. They are wholly unproven. Even your prior Professors at USC will not vouch for them. That makes this, fundamentally, a research project – and a long shot. The salary and benefits package we're offering is more than generous. You should know that this is a Director-level compensation package, with salary and incentives pressing the upper boundaries within even that. Promising a percentage of revenue, however small, to an employee for contributions to product development is without precedent. Your request for 1% of net profits could equate to a fair amount of money someday, if this all happens to work out, but what if we fail? What if some unforeseen liability is realized as a result of this product? Are you in a position to help shoulder that burden?"

Riley was not in the least rattled. "Yes," he said, simply, knowing his response would draw more than a little ire from all present.

Matthews let out a chuckle. "You must be in possession of tremendous resources," Matthews said, with unabashed sarcasm. The comment was supplemented by a reproachful look from Turner.

"I am in possession of the science, Mr. Matthews. If there is risk, I am managing it now, at this moment, in this room. I submit that in this arrangement, it is only the manipulation of gravity itself that is without precedent."

The comment found its mark. Matthews became visibly frustrated, throwing up his hands. "Well," he said, "maybe we're at an impasse then." The remark was directed to Turner, but clearly intended for Riley's benefit. "I guess we go back to the drawing board then," he said. He looked back to Riley. "We've spoken with a couple other physicists," he lied. "You were the top candidate, but it looks like we'll have to move on."

Riley nodded and rose to his feet. "Thank you both," he said, without drama.

"So that's it?" Matthews said, forestalling him. He was beginning to lose his cool, uncharacteristically.

"You've already lost two years since I wrote that paper, Mr. Matthews. I purposely never hinted at how to put my theories into practice in that paper, or in any other written form for that matter. How much longer will you be delayed if you start from nothing with these other physicists?" He turned to leave. Then as if taken by another thought, stopped unexpectedly, appearing to ponder opposing options in his mind. He turned to face Matthews again. "On second thought, Mr. Matthews, I believe you are entitled to full transparency, so here it is: First, there are no other physicists. If there were, I would know them by name. Second, there's a good reason none of my prior professors at USC will vouch for my theories. Tell me if I'm getting warm. Your people probably told you that the key to gravitation, according to my paper, lies in modifying the strong nuclear force. They're right. That's what the paper says, but it's a cold trail. And it's no accident." He passed an openly disapproving glance over Matthews and Turner as he turned again towards the door, which spoke as much to his disappointment in them as to the failure of the negotiations.

"A half a percent," Matthews called out, exasperated, "but it'll require board approval, which is far more of a long shot than getting me to agree. You'll find that out soon enough." The look on Matthews' face betrayed that he was angry with himself for having been beaten so handily at the negotiation. Riley was a young man with very little experience; he should be happy to leave with a third of the salary he had been offered. But the facts were the facts. Matthews knew it, and Riley did too.

Riley was the single source of the secrets of gravitation. That was the length and breadth of it. How soon that was likely to change was anyone's guess, and there were undesirable consequences to any scenario, however soon or distant it may turn out to be. But for this day, Riley was it, and everyone in the room knew it, most of all Riley himself.

Turner's expression turned scandalous at Matthews' concession. She wheeled on him, but he was ready for her, holding up a forestalling hand. "I know, I know," he said. "We can't let this one get past us, Lynn."

Had he not been so thoroughly frustrated and affronted by his treatment, Riley would have behaved much differently. In fact, had hoped that the discussions would go better, but no respect had been shown to him by either Matthews or Turner. He knew that if he were the naive young man that they had both expected, he would be leaving to smiles, handshakes and slaps on the back right now, but with next to nothing to show for his theories. Instead, he watched, more than a little shocked that the two of them had taken suddenly to speaking so openly in front of him. They were irritated and bickering amongst themselves. The sight of it angered him even further, for reasons he wasn't quite sure of.

"1.5 percent," Riley said, interrupting their quarrel.

"Wait just a minute!" Matthews said, taking to his feet, anger now apparent in his voice. "We've been talking about one percent this entire conversation, you can't change that on a whim, Mr. Riley. This is not novice hour." Matthews had now abandoned all pretense of civility.

"And we had been negotiating on the pretense of honesty and trust, Mr. Matthews. It was you who changed that." Riley was now angry as well. "Be assured that contacting me to discuss anything less will be a waste of your time and mine," he said, then exited the door, ignoring Matthews' voice as it called after him.

Chapter 5

April 17, 2023

W orking through the details of the contractual agreements had not been a tidy affair, but Riley and Matthews had finally closed the gaps. Over the subsequent weeks, they had put the uncomfortable moments of that first engagement behind them, although Riley suspected Turner never would.

Matthews now carried on as though the initial disagreement had not happened at all. Since negotiations were bound to be a frequent part of the man's daily life, Riley guessed it may not have been a particularly memorable event for him, except that he may be used to them going slightly smoother. But even that was uncertain. It was entirely possible, maybe even likely, that Matthews had expected to give far more than he had. It could have all been a ruse. The good news from Riley's perspective was that it didn't matter. He had gotten what he wanted. The money was a non-trivial part of it, but to no lesser extent was the principle that he would never allow another person or entity to gain sole possession of his brainchild. He would share – that was unavoidable – but he would not relinquish. It had been his goal, and it was a goal achieved.

Riley arrived for his first official day of work at Mayfield Hammond on an April Monday morning. He entered the Information Technology building through the front doors where he was greeted by a receptionist who accepted his signature on a registry, then asked him to take a seat in an adjoining waiting area. It had taken some convincing to persuade the man that it was indeed, Brian Matthews himself who would come to collect him, but he had succeeded in the end.

When the wait for Matthews' appearance had stretched to thirty minutes, Riley contemplated approaching the receptionist to verify connections had been made, but before he could, a man he did not recognize rounded the corner and approached from the direction of the elevators. "John Riley?"

"Yes," Riley said, rising to his feet.

"Scott Riddell," the man said, shaking Riley's hand. "Sorry to keep you waiting. Mr. Matthews is detained. He asked that I show you in."

"I understand," Riley said, noticing the receptionist passing a knowing glance in his direction.

Riddell turned at once to lead Riley through the turnstiles towards the elevators. "I handle staff ops for Matthews. I'll help you get situated; employee badge, laptop computer, stuff like that. He mentioned that he plans to sync up with you at some point this morning, but we'll see what his schedule permits."

"Busy man," Riley said.

Riddell laughed. "The President of the United States is busy. The Pope is busy. Matthews is something else entirely. You'll see for yourself soon enough," he said, not unpleasantly, as he stepped into the elevator corridor and pressed the call button.

"I'll take your word for that."

"Mr. Riley," a voice called out. Riddell and Riley turned to see Matthews entering the foyer from the outer doors. He passed through the turnstiles without scanning his badge, sounding an alarm that he didn't slow to acknowledge. The receptionist hurriedly jabbed at a button on his desk to silence it, but didn't react beyond that. "Glad you're finally here," Matthews said. His tone sounded genuine.

"Likewise," Riley said, somewhat taken aback by the unexpectedly friendly greeting. A bell chimed and the doors to one of the four available elevators opened. They stepped in and Riddell selected the fourth floor.

"Scott here, will show you to your desk and the section of the fourth floor that we've reserved for your team. I think you're going to like it," Matthews said. "But listen, I wanted to catch you – and I hate to hit you with this in the first few seconds of your employment – but I think we've located some property for the equipment build-out. The good news is that there's lots of space; the not-so-good-news is that it's about 60 miles from here. The legal team wouldn't hear of anything closer. I'd like your thoughts on it as soon as you can manage it. The details were emailed to you last night." He turned to Riddell, "Scott, could you be sure John can log into his computer and access his email, first thing?"

"Will do."

"I'll take a look at the materials right away," Riley added.

"Great," Matthews said, giving Riley a friendly slap on the arm as the elevator doors opened. "We'll catch up later in the day if we can. Sometimes my schedule gets crazy, so if not today, we'll make something work in the next day or two." With that, Matthews stepped into the hall and disappeared as if he had been swept away by an invisible current. Riddell followed the encounter with a nod to Riley, as if Matthews' flyby had validated his earlier comments.

Riley was pleased with his office, guessing it to be about 140 square feet. It was well furnished with a plain, but pleasant desk and chairs, and an impressive view of the campus. By mid-morning, most of the compulsory tasks of onboarding were done. Riddell had expertly verified Riley's online access and escorted him to the security desk for a picture and badge that would allow him to roam freely across the campus.

That done, and finally alone with his computer a couple hours later, Riley sat in the unsettled office, his satchel forgotten atop his desk, and opened his email account from his new laptop computer. There were two emails in his inbox. One, a welcome message from Human Resources, and the other from Anna Burns on behalf of Brian Matthews. The subject was, *The Installation.*

The Installation? Riley wondered at the title. He opened the message and read:

> *Hi John,*
>
> *Welcome aboard! I'm Anna Burns, Executive Admin for Mr. Matthews. He asked that I mention a couple things to you and provide the attached images.*
>
> *First, he would like to adopt the codename "Springboard" for all work related to your project and reminds you that any information about the project should be shared only on a need-to-know basis. Any individuals brought onto the project must sign a nondisclosure agreement prior to any information-sharing, subject to prior approval by Mr. Matthews himself.*
>
> *Secondly, he would like your thoughts on the suitability of the property in the attached images as the location for the off-site equipment needed for Springboard. He would like this by close of business tomorrow and suggests that you visit the property today if you can manage it.*
>
> *Thank you, and I look forward to working with you.*
>
> *-Anna*

Riley clicked on the first of the attached images, opening it to reveal an aerial view of a nondescript plot of ground. It was possessed of the deeply green tones of North Carolina summers, but with fewer trees than typical for the area. He checked his watch. It was already 10:30. He looked around his office a final time, thinking of the many hours he was destined to spend there. The work ahead was mountainous, which meant the office would become his second home, and soon. Fortunately, it was not an unpleasant space. He was grateful for that.

Without delay, he hefted his satchel and made for the door.

Chapter 6

April 29, 2023

The details of Riley's employment came together in the only way they could. Mayfield Hammond would spin up a new, wholly owned subsidiary as the vehicle through which financial and patent concerns related to gravitation would be handled. Riley would receive a 10% stake in the company but remain in the employ of Mayfield Hammond proper.

There had been wrangling over what the new company would be called. Despite the tendency to want to give it a name as forward looking as its charter, the more pressing concern was to keep its work and purpose quiet. Neither could the name be too broad. A name such as *Mayfield Hammond Labs* would incorrectly imply many things, including that other research projects may run through it as well, which was not the intent. A name like that could also draw the attention of shareholders and the army of analysts who watched and reported on everything the company did. Partial ownership of the company by Riley also meant that its work would be confined, by edict of the board, and without exception, to gravitation.

The final name was *Mayfield Hammond Lift*. Matthews lobbied that the name was too revealing of its purpose but was ultimately overruled. The prevailing belief had been that the leap from the simple word "lift" to the topic of gravitation was big enough that no one would pay attention even if someone were to get it right. Matthews agreed, but also pointed out that Riley's stake in the enterprise would be an easy trail to follow, given his prior writings on gravitation. It was a glaring oversight in Matthews' opinion, but the wheels had turned anyway, and the name was ratified.

Riley's employment began immediately once the details were ironed out. The specifics were drafted in a *Memorandum of Understanding*, which the Legal department had drafted in a day. The appropriate signatures were collected from company leaders, along with Riley's own, and he was set free to begin work. The details were to be translated into contractual form over the days that followed, and Riley predetermined not to press the details. He had gotten what he wanted, and anything that did not impact the fundamentals wouldn't be worth the risks of reopening the conversation.

The realities presented themselves immediately. Riley was to produce a high-level plan that defined the goals of the project for the first 18 months. What would success look like? Would kids be roaming city streets on '*Back to the Future*-ish' hoverboards in a year, or would the team be doing well to nudge paperclips across tabletops?

Riley hoped the realities wouldn't disappoint. What a physicist may regard as tremendous progress rarely struck the typical person in the same way. The mental images conjured by the thought of manipulating gravity would naturally set a high bar, and the importance of managing expectations could not be underestimated. If the company's commitment waned, it could spell the end of the project, and Riley was determined not to let that happen.

He set to work outlining the structure of his team; the skills that were needed and the size of the staff. There would be program managers, project managers, physicists, electrical engineers, equipment fabricators, software developers and others who would help design the equipment and then build it. All of it meaning that they would need spacious facilities too.

The amount of first round funding to get everything into motion was eye-opening. On completing his draft budget, Riley was glad he hadn't known what the number would be prior to negotiating terms; it may have softened his resolve.

The only significant hitch that came during preliminary planning was the sudden realization by the Legal department that as the gravitation team undertook its work, they would generate fields of altered gravity that could range in size to a radius of more than a hundred meters. The effects would be miniscule; far too subtle for a person to notice. In fact, it would take sensitive detectors to even know the effect was there at all, but none of that mattered. Legal balked at the notion, and in a big way. There was no data on what the impacts could be to the health of any person in proximity.

At the start, the issue had seemed a small detail – one checkbox among a long list of others – but within hours it seemed to rise from the page to overshadow everything else. Riley soon realized that Legal was angling towards demanding a halt to the entire program, or more accurately, declaring it a non-starter.

It was then that Riley realized that his demands for a material financial stake in the program may have saved it. Ownership, and therefore, liability for the program would be handled by an external entity, *Mayfield Hammond Lift*, which provided a natural separation between the project and Mayfield Hammond proper. It wasn't perfect or bulletproof, but it was there. They had also, by that time, executed voluminous legal contracts placing very clear requirements on both Riley and Mayfield with respect to the program. Riley had already divulged many, but not all of his secrets as called for in those contracts, and now Mayfield must do its part. Cancelling the program would not be a simple thing.

The entire episode never shook Riley's belief that the project would go forward, and ultimately succeed. Mayfield was but one chapter – only the latest – in a story in the making for more than 10 years. By some inner confidence that could not be traced to its source, Riley did not believe, but knew success was imminent. He would break the gravitation barrier, step through the door that doing so would open, and take in *first light* of the new Universe it would reveal.

*   *   *

"So, what do you say?" Riley asked Jason Clipper.

Clipper was a childhood friend Riley had known since the age of 10. They were two of three boys who had become friends early in life, and who had stayed close from that point forward; the third being Andrew Jacobs. A year younger than Riley, and livelier than either he or Andrew by most measures, Clipper was typically first to notice an opportunity to have fun and always the first to jump in – often to less than desirable outcomes. He had been the unpredictable element in what would have otherwise been a quiet and uneventful childhood; Riley had never doubted that.

Over the years, Clipper's outgoing ways had settled into their adult counterparts. He was confident and smart, a risk taker, and above all, in possession of an innate ability to enjoy life. After high school, the three young men had gone separate ways to college. Andrew Jacobs, who went by *AJ*, had gone to Duke University to study economics while Riley had gone to USC for Particle Physics. Clipper had stayed close to home, studying Computer Science at the University of Kansas.

"Sounds interesting," Clipper said, returning his pint of Boulevard Tank 7 ale to the table. "I'm not a physicist, so not sure how I can help."

"We're going to need software to control the equipment," Riley explained. "I have a couple electrical engineers and physicists to help with the design, and we'll tap Mayfield's existing infrastructure for fabrication and vendor management, but I don't want to use their Information Technology department for the software."

"What's wrong with their IT team? I thought those guys were the best at everything," Clipper asked, surprised.

"That's not the question. I don't feel comfortable sharing the level of detail about the project that would be necessary for them to help. I want to do this with as few people as possible, and share as little about the program as we can."

"How many developers will there be?"

"That's where I'm hoping you can help," Riley said. "I would like you to come aboard, see what we're going to do and then help me build the team. Mayfield has excellent benefits, and I can get you in at a 15% increase above anything you're making now plus cost of living differential; guaranteed."

Clipper shook his head doubtfully. "North Carolina, huh?" He looked off to the corner of the room as if sizing up the prospect. "You realize that I went to KU, and even the Jack Russell I had growing up was named Toto, right?"

"Yeah, and the real Toto never had any fun until he left Kansas," Riley retorted, lifting his own pint.

"Okay, okay. Let's do it."

"Excellent," Riley said. "I think you'll be glad you did, Clip, I really do; but we've got to move fast. I mean really fast. I've got three months to get the team in motion and twelve more to meet my first round of objectives. It may sound like a lot of time, but it's not – not when you consider what we've got to do. The sooner we can get you out there the better, but you can work remote until then. How long will you need?"

"A couple weeks to start and probably a month to make the actual move. Gonna be tough leaving my Jayhawks though," he said, reflectively. "And being that close to Duke doesn't feel right. Think there's any chance they could start a basketball program of their own?"

Riley was too caught up in the prospect of getting Clipper's help to come in on the banter. "Wouldn't know," he said. "I'll make some calls to get things going on Mayfield's end."

"Sounds good. So now that we're going to be working together, tell me what we're into," Clipper said.

Riley started to speak, then hesitated. "Seems a little odd to have to say this, Clip, but all this is under very strict NDA, so it can't be discussed."

"You got it," Clipper said, nodding over his ale.

"Short answer is; Mayfield brought me in to prototype my theories on gravitation. They're providing funding in exchange for owning patents in the space, and for rights related to commercialization, productization, that sort of thing.

Clipper raised an eyebrow. "You're handing everything over to them?"

"Not everything. I have some provisions in there."

"Glad to hear," Clipper said, then followed through with his sip.

"My first-year deliverable is just to show that we can do it – that we can manipulate gravity," Riley explained. "It won't be sensational from a science fiction perspective, but it'll be enough. Once we get the basics down, everything that follows will be learning and refining."

"You're confident you can do it, then?"

"Absolutely."

Clipper whistled. "That's crazy stuff Riley, even for you. How are you going to do it?"

"We'll get into the specifics when you get out to North Carolina, but in a nutshell," Riley said, looking around the bar for anyone who may be close enough to hear. He found none but lowered his voice anyway. "We're going to change the way matter interacts with Spacetime. Doing so will have the effect of modifying gravity, but only as a secondary effect. It's not quite that simple, but it's a good enough simplification for a bar," he said, gesturing around the room.

"Fair. Sounds like heady stuff."

"A little," Riley said, returning his drink to the table.

Clipper looked at his friend questioningly, as if suddenly more interested in understanding him. "What made you start thinking about all this, Riley? Why gravity?"

Riley shrugged. "I don't know. I'm not sure there's an interesting story behind it. I just believed it was possible, so I went after it."

"I'd like to know."

Riley narrowed his eyes as if pondering the prospect of wading into a stream of cold water. "It's probably not all that unique or interesting."

"How could solving gravitation not be unique or interesting?" Clipper said, with a little incredulity in his tone.

"I don't know. The outcome maybe. That could be interesting ... the gravitation part of it, but the path to discovery itself is of the same general variety that leads to discoveries across any other discipline. The difference is only in the particular problem I decided to solve. Some people become enamored with internal combustion engines and spend a lifetime tinkering with them. I became fascinated with how the gears and pulleys of physics work together, and it led to some insights. It's really that simple."

"Just like that?" Clipper said, unsatisfied with the explanation.

"There could be a little more to it, but yeah. I've just connected some dots that hadn't been connected before. It was always going to happen; the question was only who would do it first."

"That's pretty vague, Riley," Clipper said, refusing to be put off. "Look, if you don't want to divulge–"

"No, it's not that," Riley said, seeing Clipper's minor frustration. "If you must know, my take is that physicists tend to spend too much of their time trying to understand physics – how things work and why they behave the way they do. Makes sense, right? Since that's pretty much the job description. I spent my first few years in physics doing the same. It's unavoidable. You have to learn enough about your subject to be able to contribute to it. But the things you learn only become valuable when they can be put into practice in some way. What do you do with the knowledge once you start to get a handle on it? I wanted to knock down a wall. There are a lot of unanswered questions out there, so I took aim at one of them. Mine happened to be gravity. Ultimately, though, my take is that it's one thing to understand how the Universe works, but I can't help wondering what the damned thing is. We're getting a sense of where we are within the Universe, but where is it? Every question we answer takes us a step forward. I want to be a part of it."

Clipper was absorbed in the thought. "Do you expect gravitation to answer all that?"

"No, I don't," Riley said, easily. "But they're the questions that rattle around in the back of my mind when I whittle away at the edges of physical science. I chose gravitation because it's a blind spot in a lot of ways. We can impact and manipulate all sorts of things around us, but we can't do anything with it. I want to know why, and I want to be the first one through the door. But I'm even more interested in what lies beyond the door. What new frontiers are out there that we can't see because we're blocked by gravitation, and how much closer will they take us to that bigger picture? That's what I'm interested in."

Clipper picked up his pint and leaned back in his chair. "I guess I should thank you in advance for the sleepless nights I'm going to have chewing on all this."

"I can share some pointers on that," Riley said, laughing slightly. "In seriousness, Clip, you should know that none of this stuff is in the job description. The job is gravity, that's it. Whatever gravity may be sitting on, or whatever may be next, will have to wait for another day and probably another team. Now that I think about it, though, it may be useful for you to read up on the *Standard Model of Particle Physics*. Google it. It's easy to find."

Chapter 7

April 2008

I t was early enough in the Spring that the Bradford Pears were still in blossom. Andrew Jacobs walked alone up the long incline of his neighborhood street, oblivious to the world around him. His home was down the way and around the corner, now long out of view, hidden by the tall Cottonwoods, Silver Maples and Osage Orange trees that were a bit too common to the area.

A wisp of cool air blew past him, ruffling his hair, but he hardly took notice. His gaze was fixed upon the street ahead of him and he only occasionally glanced up to see that no cars were coming. These streets were not so far into the rural country that cars were a complete rarity, but they were relatively few – few enough that the road itself was still the best place to walk.

AJ concentrated on a smooth rock sitting oddly on the road ahead of him, approaching it with practiced cunning. He had found the rock – and quite a find it was – sitting near the side of the road. It was perfect. Slightly larger than a golf ball and shaped like a partially-flattened lump of dough, it slid along the street like a puck on ice.

He wasn't in the habit of collecting rocks. In fact, he didn't have any; but thoughts were already taking shape of what a great addition it could be to his small collection of most prized possessions. He imagined the rock sitting prominently next to his microscope, the fountain pen that had been carelessly discarded by a classmate, but which still worked, his pocket knife, and his silver dollar. The silver dollar wasn't a real silver dollar; it was just a regular coin that any bank would give in change, but AJ liked the weight and size of it. Common though it was, what made it unique was that it was his. He carried it everywhere.

At this moment, though, the coin lay forgotten in his pocket. He was engaged in the practice of one of his primary skills; rock kicking. It was a habit he had picked up long ago – an acquired craft. It was one of AJ's secret vanities to believe that it was somehow, very important; other people just didn't know how to appreciate it. This inability, he was convinced, left others lacking in all of the areas of life that rock kicking had enriched in his own, and afforded him the private indulgence to believe that it made him special in some way. Not just the ability to kick rocks, but the very knowledge of how important it was. It was a lore.

Kick.

Another good one. Kicking any rock straight enough that it stayed on the proper trajectory was a skill that he took more seriously, and worked harder to perfect than anyone would guess. Smooth rocks tended to be easier to control than the oddly shaped ones, and this rock was very smooth indeed.

A car appeared at the top of the hill ahead. AJ waited patiently for it to pass before making his next kick. The car passed slowly by and the driver glanced over at him. A quick moment of eye contact passed between the two of them without leaving the slightest imprint on the mind of the driver, but which AJ immediately began pondering.

Coming to this place just in time to see him in this way, AJ thought, was probably not the coincidence it appeared to be. There was every possibility – no, likelihood – that the driver had traveled some great distance specifically for this encounter. Maybe even from overseas. Even AJ himself had no way of knowing the details. The man could very well have traveled from around the globe on some secret mission, breaking off only to verify AJ's whereabouts. AJ looked down at his clothes. *No telling who knows I'm wearing this blue shirt by now*, he thought. All the spy rings were probably sending out a flash bulletin.

Kick.

Yet another good one. Now the trick was to reach the rock in stride so that he could kick it again without slowing down or otherwise breaking his cadence. The smoother the better.

Kick.

The thought that Becky Arnold could be watching suddenly occurred to him. He was passing her house now – it was not the time to lose focus. He had to make it look easy even though it clearly wasn't. Becky's house was odd looking in some ways; brown in color, and too dark, like hot chocolate without marshmallows or cream. None of the other houses in the neighborhood were anything close to that color, but he guessed it was okay. He wouldn't look over, though. He couldn't take the chance he would be seen.

Kick.

There was no sense of time when AJ receded into his imaginations like this. It's what made him the loner he was. Others looked on and saw only a solitary 10-year-old boy walking alone on the street or tracing endless circles around some playground, but in his mind the world was full of mystery and intrigue, buzzing with intricate happenings that few could appreciate or decipher but himself.

In a few moments, excited voices drew his attention. The neighborhood kids had organized a soccer game. They were gathered in Mr. Dollard's backyard; a man who kept mostly to himself and also happened to keep an immaculately manicured house with an equally manicured two-acre field behind. The field was always neatly mowed and trimmed, and without so much as a shed or forgotten piece of lawn equipment to distract from the perfection of its suitability for organized games. Velvet green with Kentucky Bluegrass, AJ guessed that it had been placed upon the earth for no other purpose than to host soccer games.

Dollard's wife of more than 40 years had passed away several years gone. Dollard had since decided that the field could serve no better use than as a gathering place for the neighborhood kids. He didn't seem to mind the devastation suffered by the grass, but leave a Styrofoam cup behind when the game was over and there would be hell to pay. Despite the generosity, no one knew Dollard all that well. Everyone steered clear of him, in fact; and the man seemed obliged to return the favor.

AJ approached, but kept his distance. He could see that the game had not yet begun; they were still choosing teams amidst the chaotic excitement that always seemed to characterize such things. Sometimes he would join in, or try to, but only rarely. It usually didn't turn out well. The most he could ever hope for was to be the last person picked for a team – and those were the good days. More typically, team selection would digress into an argument over which had to take him.

The thought made the decision to keep walking an easy one ... that and the rock. A moment later he realized that the distraction had made him walk past it. He turned to see it standing on the road a good twenty paces behind him and vaguely wondered how it had gotten so far away.

It was the time thing again. AJ had long since determined that thoughts must somehow be fueled by time. The deeper the thought, the more time it consumed and the more it disconnected him from the world. The further disconnected he became, the further he would resurface from the point where he had left it.

A sudden surge of panic arose in him at the thought that someone could swoop in and seize the rock before he could reach it. He didn't want to look too anxious, just in case someone could be close at hand. No use in drawing unnecessary attention.

It was a good rock, and friendly too. As he approached, he realized all the more that it would be a shame to let it get away. Plus, if he did, who else would appreciate how special it was? He may be the last chance this rock would ever have to be valued as an individual, worthwhile object. The thought made him feel suddenly bonded to it in some way, as if they shared a similar place in the world. It was so compelling that he picked it up and turned it over in his hands.

It was smooth and round. Yes, he would keep this one.

Shouts again. The game had only just begun and there was already a disagreement. Was a kick out of bounds? Did someone cheat? One of the paradoxes of neighborhood games was that the very same group of kids who did not know better than to argue about not accepting someone onto their teams, had to then govern themselves with some semblance of fairness. It usually didn't work out well, but somehow, did work well enough.

AJ lifted his head curiously to see if he could catch a glimpse and was startled to find that while he had been examining the rock, two cars had approached from opposite directions to converge near the spot where he was standing. The car traveling down the street was passing slowly by while the one going uphill was forced to stop. AJ's heart leaped in his chest. The car sat 25 feet from him; big and quiet. It was Mrs. Pickering. She lived only a few houses down. The other car passed, and AJ waited as Mrs. Pickering began rolling down the electronic passenger window on her approach, eyeing him curiously.

Here comes, he thought. Sure enough, she pulled forward and stopped. She hesitated briefly, as if weighing her words. "AJ, be careful now," she said, then smiled.

AJ could only stare. The quick mental preparation he had made for the verbal lashing he was sure would come had left him unprepared for the kindness, and no words came. After a few seconds, a weak, *okay,* finally left his lips. She smiled again and pulled away. AJ watched her for a few seconds and noticed that she kept checking her rear-view mirror. He realized that she must be waiting for him to move off of the street, and so he did.

He didn't want to kick the rock anymore, but he would keep it. He slid it into his pocket and took a few steps. It was too big. He pulled it back out and looked at it again. He didn't want to carry it either. Maybe he would put it in a safe place and come back for it later. He located a good spot in the form of an open drain pipe running beneath a nearby driveway. He sat it at the pipe's opening and framed the image of it in his mind for later reference.

Perfect, he thought. He then stepped back onto the street and continued walking, never to see it again. And like the rock, thoughts of Mrs. Pickering and of the soccer game and of Mr. Dollard's immaculate field had already evaporated from his mind.

He angled off to the right towards the north where the river was. It was further away than he felt like walking, but he would head in that general direction and at least a ways into the thick woods. There was a creek there. That could be fun. There would be crawdads.

It was always amazing how fast the world dropped from view when he entered the woods. There were no subdivisions or houses between his neighborhood and the river. The intervening land was covered with dense trees that were, as far as he could tell, undisturbed from time immemorial. That was, except for the scatterings of forts and hideouts that stood as enduring monuments to the generations of kids who had gone before.

The creek wasn't far. Soon, he unexpectedly glimpsed the bright colors of small shirts and blue jeans. Someone was already there. He dropped into stealth mode, not sure he wanted to be noticed just yet, and peered through the trees.

"What do you want, AJ?" a voice called out.

It had to have been that last twig, and that was far from his best effort anyway. He stepped into full view. It was Kim Silverstein, Sarah Henson and Mary something or another. "What are you doing?" he asked.

"Finding crawdads. What do you think?" the voice said. It was Kim. She could be that way. In fact, she was always that way. Mary looked up from her hunting for a brief, disinterested moment, but didn't comment. Sarah took no notice at all. She was as preoccupied with keeping her long brown hair, which reached fully to her waist when she stood upright, out of the water as with scanning the creek bed. It was looped over her left hand. The effort looked futile from AJ's perspective, and didn't appear to be fun either.

Sarah lived only a few houses from him, but they rarely spoke to one another. There was no particular hostility or dislike between the two, beyond the general tension that was always present between boys and girls of that pre-teen age. That she was a year older made him all the less interesting as well.

At once, she stood to her feet. AJ's eyes immediately tracked to the large thrashing crawdad between her thumb and forefinger. She turned to a small bucket on the embankment and dropped it in. "That's eight," she said. Only then did she seem to notice AJ. "Wanna see?"

"Sure," AJ said, surprised to be on the receiving end of a comment that was not interlaced with some debasing undertone. He stepped forward and peered into the bucket. "Those are big," he said, with genuine appreciation.

"They're everywhere," Sarah said. "We haven't been here long." She looked off to the creek. "See, there's another one."

"What are ya gonna do with them?"

"I don't know. Throw them back, I guess."

"I'm gonna take'm home," Mary said.

"For what? What good are they?"

"I'm gonna cook'em," she said, but it was unconvincing.

"Eew," Kim said.

"I'm done. I've caught two. You can have mine," Sarah said. She plotted a couple steps up the small embankment to fetch her shoes. They were sitting neatly, side by side with her socks folded into one of them. The socks and shoes of the other two girls were scattered haphazardly nearby. "Want to walk with me?" Sarah said, hooking a shoe over her foot.

"Sure, where are you going?"

"Probably home."

"Okay."

Sarah's farewell to her friends was not encumbered with fanfare. They simply waved their goodbyes and parted. AJ felt awkward walking next to her, but it wasn't entirely unpleasant. "What is your real name, AJ? It's not really AJ is it? It stands for something?"

"Andrew. Andrew Jacobs," he said.

"Why not go by Andrew then?"

"I like AJ better. Plus, I was named after my great uncle, so it makes it easier to tell us apart."

Sarah mulled the thought for a moment and apparently concluded that it made sense. "You're a fifth grader?"

"Yes."

"Who do you have, Mrs. Campbell?"

"Brenneman," AJ said.

"Ooh, Brenny. I've heard she's mean."

"Not really. Sometimes she gives us too much homework, but she's not mean about it."

"I'm going to be in seventh grade next year. I'm going to Eisenhower Junior High."

"Cool. Are you scared?"

Sarah laughed. "Why would I be scared?"

"I don't know. I've heard it can be a tough place."

"No, I'm not scared."

They walked along the familiar streets towards their own part of the neighborhood. AJ was not practiced at casual conversation, but found Sarah to be unexpectedly pleasant to talk with.

The fascinations and interests of young boys can turn on a dime. By the time they reached the end of Sarah's driveway, the walk having taken far less time than suited AJ, he was already wishing for more time with her. The feeling didn't appear to be mutual. She turned up the driveway with even less of a parting thought than she had given her two friends at the creek. AJ watched helplessly; she was leaving. In a moment she would enter through the door of her house and that would be that.

"Sarah?" AJ called out.

She turned to face him, a question on her face. AJ felt caught in the moment. He had wanted her to stop, to spend more time with her, but now that he had regained her attention, was at a loss for something to say. He did the first thing that came to mind. He reached into his pocket and pulled out his dollar coin. "Want this?" he said, with words that embodied more hopelessness than he would have preferred.

"What is it?" She stepped forward and looked at it. "It's a dollar," she said. "Why would I want your dollar?"

"I don't know. I thought it was pretty cool. Maybe you'd like it."

There was a moment; a long terrifying moment where AJ stood in the balance between humiliating rejection and the simple acceptance of a simple gift. It wasn't like he was asking her to be his girlfriend. The coin wouldn't mean anything, even if she accepted it. But something he could not quite discern, something that shouldn't be, but somehow was important and meaningful, hinged on what Sarah would say next. Each passing second exponentially heightened the sense of it.

It was AJ's first taste of what all men innately understood in life: that the opposite sex had the inexplicable power to lift a man or shatter him with the simplest of words. Finally, she reached for the coin. "Thank you, AJ," she said, then turned for the door without looking back. He watched her hair dance across her back as she crossed the drive and ascended the stairs to the door.

She had accepted his dollar, and he was both dumbfounded and mesmerized by it.

Chapter 8

May 29, 2023

Shelter house six at the Shawnee Mission park had been the gathering grounds for church picnics from the beginning. Deeply wooded, with a gentle brook that passed beneath a wooden walking bridge before trailing away into the dense growth, it was easy to forget that a major interstate highway was only a few minutes away.

By the time AJ arrived, everything was in full swing. It was a crowd of familiar faces, most with names not forthcoming. Walking onto the grounds, he saw the usual group of people – ladies mostly – standing in the shelter house making arrangements for the lunch buffet that would probably begin soon. Per usual, Linda Stricklin, the General Manager of the church, stood at the center of it all. She was pointing at something, while several of the other ladies standing nearby peered intently in the same direction. AJ took in the scene for only a moment before altering course, swinging a little further to the right. Whatever it was, he didn't want to become entangled in it.

He spotted two of his friends at the horseshoe pit further down the hill and headed in their direction. Ken Hadler and Randy Baehr were both in their late twenties like him, but married, and with toddlers already in the house. Ken was busy driving a pole into the ground when he noticed AJ coming. "AJ! The man, the legend," he said.

AJ barked a laugh. "You ladies gettin' along okay or do you need some manly help?"

Ken's head popped up and he feigned looking around expectantly. "Have you seen one?" he said, then returned to his hammering, hardly missing a beat.

"We're gonna get a tournament started after lunch," Randy said. "Want to play?"

"Absolutely," AJ said. "I haven't played horseshoes in years." He looked around the area. "Need help with anything?"

"No, we're about done here. I do think the pit could use a little breaking in though," Ken said. He pointed to a tree that stood nearby. "The shoes are over there." AJ went to fetch them. When he returned, Ken tossed the hammer to the side of the pit and stood erect, knuckling his back.

"You two go ahead. I'll catch the winner," AJ said, extending the four horseshoes.

Only then did AJ notice that in the few seconds it had taken to retrieve the horseshoes, Ken's demeanor had changed. He seemed suddenly distracted, and his next words were no less cryptic. "I have a hunch," Ken said, ignoring the horseshoes and peering up the hill towards the shelter, "that you won't have the time."

AJ's brow furrowed. "What? I'm here all day," he said.

"Yes, I'm beginning to think so too," Ken replied, even more cryptically this time, a grin now crossing his face.

AJ turned, following Ken's gaze up the hill in search of the reason for the change. It took only an instant to find. Sarah Henson was walking down the incline of the hill straight towards him. He groaned, drawing chuckles from the other two men.

Sarah closed the distance in seconds and on arriving, spared no time for pleasantries. "If you're not too busy," she said, looking disapprovingly around the pit and then to AJ, "I could use some help setting out the trash bins. There are six of them. They all need liners." She had the look of a Sunday School teacher who had caught a student passing notes.

"Uh–" AJ began, but was cut short, which wasn't an uncommon occurrence around Sarah. Especially for AJ.

"Unless you have other pressing matters to attend," she said, gesturing towards the horseshoes. AJ had already forgotten he was holding them. He looked blankly at his hands as if he had no idea how they had gotten there.

As the moment teetered awkwardly, Ken reached for the shoes, which AJ gave up reluctantly. "We'll take good care of these for you," he said, then turned away. If he was trying, he was doing a bad job of hiding his amusement.

AJ watched him go, baffled by the bewildering speed with which a perfectly good moment had been crushed. It took no time at all for him to realize that there was nothing to be done. He passed a final forlorn look around the horseshoe pit before nodding dumbly to Sarah in acceptance of his fate. "After you," he said. Ken and Randy were no help at all. They stood at the side of the pit, grinning from ear to ear.

"The bins are in the back of that white truck up there," Sarah said, pointing towards the lot. "If you could bring them down here, I would appreciate it."

"Righteo," AJ said, fighting back his irritation. *Why had she chosen me?* he wondered. But just as quickly, decided that he shouldn't be unwilling to help and collected himself. "I'll be glad to," he said. "Be back shortly."

"Good, me too," she said, then started back toward the shelter.

Sarah walked only a few paces after the two parted, then despite herself, looked back after him. AJ strode up the hill without a care in the world. She smoothed her skirt and then checked her shoes. By the time she looked up again, he had disappeared onto the lot. She craned her neck, absently checking an earring, and spotted him passing between cars.

As if only then realizing that she had stopped moving, she glanced around reflexively to see if anyone was watching. It appeared for a moment that Linda may have been looking in her direction from under the shelter, but just as quickly the woman became occupied with some unseen task and melted into the crowd. Sarah lifted her chin, her normal sense of pride returning, and resumed her stride.

In the lot, AJ found that the trash bins were the stackable, 32-gallon type. He could manage only three at a time. He brought them down, but Sarah had not yet returned so he went back for the last three. On returning again, he found a roll of liners on the ground, but still no Sarah. He unstacked the bins and inserted a liner into each one. Finished, he looked up to find her talking with Linda under the shelter canopy. She held up a forestalling finger and headed toward him. He waited as she approached, surprisingly content to have something constructive to do.

"Thank you," Sarah said, once in earshot. "I think we could use a couple over there on the far side of the shelter, another two over here on the near side and–" she looked around, "I don't know, I guess we can put one by the horseshoe pit and another by the children's play area."

AJ nodded. "Will do," he said, setting off immediately with two barrels in tow. He chanced a look back and saw that Sarah hadn't moved. She was still looking at him. "Is there something else?" he said.

Sarah stammered for a moment but recovered quickly. "There's a lot to do AJ. I'm sure we can use more help after you've finished with this, if you don't mind."

The horseshoe pit beckoned, but AJ resigned himself to the possibility that he wouldn't be able to play for a while. Maybe not until the tournament began after lunch. "Of course," he said, then turned to resume his chore. In no time he was pulling the last of the bins towards the horseshoe pit. Ken and Randy had started a game.

"You're a better escape artist than I gave you credit for," Ken said, peering over the horseshoe in his hand, poised to make a throw. He tossed it.

AJ watched it sail through the air. It wasn't close. He then spotted another horseshoe, apparently the one Ken had thrown only a moment before, no less than four feet from the pole. "I'm kinda new to all this," he said. "The goal is to hit the pole, right?"

Ken shot a look at him. "Funny. Your turn is coming." He stepped aside, allowing Randy to take up position for his own toss. Ken watched with marginal interest. "Did Sarah already cut you loose or did you run?"

"No, still on KP," AJ said. "Just had to bring this trash bin down here." He jostled it for no good reason. "Apparently she has more for me to do. Not sure where she went, though. I'll have to track her down again."

"Shouldn't be too hard," Ken said, gesturing up the hill again. Sure enough, Sarah stood under the canopy looking straight at AJ, hands on hips in her signature disapproving pose. Ken shook his head empathetically. "Randy and I will sacrifice a small animal to the gods on your behalf," he said with a pitying sigh, then slapped AJ on the back to set him on his way. "Good luck," he said as AJ started back up the hill. "Domestication is a tough time in every man's life."

The too-familiar sight of Sarah's scrutiny brought a brief resurgence of reluctance to AJ, which forced him to spend the short walk from the pit to the shelter house performing the mental exercise of regaining his 'glad to help' state of mind. By the time he arrived, he had mostly succeeded.

Sarah didn't wait for him to reach the shelter before making her next request. "See those table linens over there?" she said as he stepped up, pointing to a neatly folded stack of disposable tablecloths. "We need to—" she began, then stopped. "Oh, thank you for handling the trash bins, by the way."

"Don't mention it," AJ said. He was already eyeing the tablecloths, the next task taking shape in his mind. He counted them and then began counting the tables. Sarah watched for only a few seconds before becoming visibly impatient. Apparently, she expected him to be a little more attentive.

For a moment, the infraction appeared to be enough to renew her general disapproval of pretty much everything he did, but to his surprise, she bit off whatever comment she was about to make. When she did speak, her voice was pleasant again. "There's a bucket with a washcloth over there," she said, pointing to the far corner of the shelter without looking away. "If you could fill it with soapy water and wipe down the tables before putting the tablecloths on them, that would be an immense help."

AJ had counted twelve tables. "They'll take a while to dry. Maybe I should just wipe them down first and spot-wash the ones that need it. Most of them don't look bad."

Sarah glanced at the tables and nodded. "Good idea," she agreed, then smiled.

AJ did a double-take at that. *The woman is actually pretty when she lightens up*, he thought. He allowed his eyes to linger on her for a moment longer, then said: "Fair enough. Is there a place to get water around here?"

"There's a spigot up by the rest rooms. We'll have to make due with cold water, but it should be fine."

"Good. Well, I'll just get to it then." He motioned to leave, but something in her expression suggested she may have more to say. He hesitated uncertainly. When she didn't speak, he said: "Right then. I'll be back in a second." But he took only a few steps before hearing his name again. He turned, the bucket swinging to a stop in his hand. "Yes?"

"AJ, when we eat later–"

"AJ!" an unseen voice called out. "Can you give us a hand?"

Some men were hauling picnic tables towards the shelter from the playground area, and one of them had noticed AJ. "There are a couple more tables down there that we need up at the shelter," the man said, pointing. "Can you help me grab one?"

"Un, sure, no problem," AJ said. "Be there in a sec." He turned back to where Sarah had been standing, but she had already slipped away and disappeared into the crowd under the shelter.

*   *   *

Linda had been noticing Sarah's growing preoccupation and frequent dissatisfaction with AJ for some time. In some ways, it looked like an odd sibling animosity except that Sarah and AJ were in no way related.

Over time, Sarah had found increasingly creative ways to show her discontentment with almost anything AJ did, but the man hardly ever seemed to take notice. If other people behaved like rudely-awakened cats in response to Sarah's ... assertiveness, with growls of protests and raised backs; AJ was more like a bag of beans. He would absorb anything she dished out, and then just topple over into the other direction.

Clearly, Sarah didn't know what to make of him. She had silently moved away to the far end of the shelter where she stood watching AJ finish moving the tables. When the men finally parted, her eyes followed AJ to the water spigot as if none of the others had existed.

Linda had watched the whole thing.

Sarah was cute, that was never a secret, but Linda had never been able to figure her out. As always, her long brown hair was the first thing anyone would notice about her. Today it was gathered into a loose knot at the base of her neck, somehow intertwined with a white linen cloth, before flowing down her back, clean and shining, nearly to her tiny waist. Linda was sure that she would pick up a subtle hint of lavender if she drew much closer.

There was something about that hair. She had never seen it out of place. Linda thought that, somehow, if Sarah were caught in a gusting wind storm with a dozen other women, all of their hair would become hopelessly entangled except for hers. Sarah's would somehow ignore the wind and refuse to leave the curves of her body.

She continued her appraisal of the young woman. The bracelet on her arm was delicate and petite, like the woman herself; golden and tasteful, and a match with her single-pearled necklace and earrings. White sandals with clusters of sequins, a denim skirt that reached almost to her knees, and a light-colored green and blue cotton blouse completed her appearance. It was an outfit of the sorts that middle-aged women fondly remembered wearing in their earlier years but could now only enjoy vicariously through younger women like Sarah, or resent in the few middle-aged women who could still carry them off.

There she stood, watching AJ as if he were the only remaining human being in the world. Linda almost felt sorry for her. *The girl needs to get it together*, she thought. Sarah seemed to have so much of life figured out. She was confident, smart and pretty, and by all measures at the start of a promising road, but she clearly knew nothing about men.

Linda followed Sarah's gaze to AJ. He was a good looking young fellow too, and she could imagine that the two would make a good couple. But when it came to the opposite sex, he was, by all accounts, as dimwitted as she was. *They need help*, she decided at once.

AJ was washing out the bucket. Not many men would bother to do something like that, and it was somehow, yet another subtle hint of how lost he was. Linda gave Sarah another look and then focused back on AJ. *How could a guy that age not notice this chic?*

Linda stepped forward, approaching Sarah from behind. "AJ is a nice enough guy, isn't he?" she said. Sarah looked up, surprised and caught off guard, but collected herself quickly. She passed a final glance in AJ's direction before answering, concluding that she hoped he wouldn't 'dilly-dally' around for too much longer before getting the tables ready. Linda decided to press the matter a bit. "Have you talked with AJ much?"

Sarah shook her head a little too hastily. "I find that I can only take the man in small doses."

"Yes, I–" Linda began, but didn't know how to complete the sentence. She decided to start over. "I always thought he was pleasant enough," she said. The statement earned a grunt from Sarah. It wasn't much to work with, and Linda began to realize that the whole thing could be a bigger challenge than she had thought. She decided to pull back, at least for now. "Anyway," she said. "We'll be ready to start lunch pretty soon. I think most everyone who is planning to eat with us is here by now."

"Okay," Sarah said. "I'll see if I can light a fire under AJ." It didn't look to Linda like doing so would be an imposition for her.

Within a half-an-hour, the parking lot was nearly full. Sarah had helped AJ with the last of the tablecloths, and from a distance, Linda saw that at least a few civil words had passed between them along the way. At a minimum, they had managed to be in proximity of one another for more than a few minutes without Sarah stalking away.

Shortly, the Pastor appeared. Linda hadn't noticed his absence until seeing him approach from the walking trail. He worked his way through the crowd, exchanging words along the way, and then raised his voice. "We're so glad each of you has joined with us for this time of fellowship and wonderful food," he said. Then, without further elaboration, bowed his head to pray. "To whomever we may be indebted for this food and the peacefulness of this day, we are grateful."

It seemed an odd prayer. Linda looked up and saw that Sarah had done the same. Sarah eyed her father quizzically, but few other people, if any, appeared to have taken notice.

The food lines moved along for more than twenty minutes before tapering down. After filling his plate, AJ took a seat with Ken, Randy and their wives, and lighthearted conversation sparked to life at once. Sarah sat a few tables away, near a group of women whose conversation carried forward without acknowledgement of her. She sat quietly, her gaze passing in AJ's direction often, her eyes reflecting unmet expectation. Another avalanche of laughter emanated from AJ's table, causing her to shake her head almost imperceptibly.

She picked up a paper napkin and began folding it absently, lost in thought. In a moment, she placed it back onto the table and rose. Her best efforts to hide her trepidation as she approached AJ were not convincing, but no one was watching. "AJ?" she said, on reaching him. He looked up at once. She was grateful not to have been forced to speak up again. Even so, her sudden appearance had silenced the table. "Can I have a word with you?" she said.

AJ looked at once around the shelter and then to the food lines for what Sarah may be about to ask him to do. "Uh, of course. What can I help you with?"

"I'd like to talk with you for a second. Can you come with me?"

Sarah felt the eyes of the others at the table heavily upon her, but she didn't look back at any of them. For reasons she wasn't sure of, she felt a kernel of resentment for the group, but forced it down.

"Absolutely," he said. Then to the group at large, "I'll be back in a few."

Sarah led him away from the shelter. The silence between them stretched long enough that AJ began worrying that something may be very wrong. Clearly, this was not about another chore.

They eventually reached the walking trail, but she didn't stop until the shelter was obscured by thick trees. By this time, AJ had completely disconnected from everything else. Sarah was upset. Vulnerable. "Are you okay?" he asked.

She turned to face him. "I–," she began, but seemed at a loss for words. Standing so close to her, facing her, AJ caught the familiar, faint wisps of lavender and realized again how small she was. She couldn't have been more than 5' 2". At 6' 1", he looked down at her with growing concern. "I was hoping," she said, "that we could sit together for the meal."

AJ somehow knew better than to offer that she could have joined him at the table with Ken and Randy. As terrible as he was with women, even he knew better than that. But search as he may, he found no words. The two of them looked at each other for a long moment. It was as if he was seeing her for the first time. "I'm going to help clean up," she said abruptly, then stepped around him. She walked away without looking back. AJ found no words to ease the moment. He watched helplessly until the trees obscured her from view.

Chapter 9

June 4, 2023

Since the church picnic and Sarah's surprise announcement the week before, AJ's world had been a different place. He had not heard from her since and made no attempt to reach her.

Instead, he had spent the week trying to rethink his feelings towards her – from start to finish. He had heard a saying once, that a woman would search a lifetime for the right man, but a man would settle for the first woman to pay attention to him. The prospect of turning a complete about-face in his relationship with Sarah – such that it was – all because of one comment made him leery of becoming the personification of that particular anecdote. He didn't like the thought of it.

The LED clock on the nightstand showed 5:48 AM. He sat staring at it for a long moment, then took to his feet and headed for the bathroom. Twenty minutes later he was behind the wheel of his truck, driving through the predawn darkness, still not sure of where he was going. He left the radio off and fiddled with the thermostat to warm the cab. Even in early June, the morning hours could still be chilly. Scarcely a moment later, his phone rang, startling him. He looked at the display to see that it was his mother, Alice. "Hello?" He answered quietly, as if not to disturb anyone in the empty truck.

The voice on the other end was groggy. "Are you okay? I saw you leave. Is something wrong?"

"Sorry mom, I didn't think about worrying you. Just couldn't sleep, that's all. I think I'll get breakfast or something." She spoke again, and he answered, "No, no. I couldn't have you getting up this early, but thank you. No, I'm just going to have breakfast and coffee somewhere and take it easy before heading to church. Love you." She made a final comment, and AJ hung up the phone.

At once, he decided that pancakes were in order and began planning a route to the IHOP a few minutes away. Traveling the empty streets at such an early hour on a Sunday, he quickly found himself about to pass the church. On the spur, he turned onto the lot. His truck made its way towards his regular satellite parking space where he stopped. The truck was finally warming up. He turned off the headlights and sat there in silence, the engine idling.

He was not used to eating so early, and the thought of it was beginning to sound a little less attractive, he realized. Not sure of what to do, and already second-guessing his decision to leave the house so early, he began thinking about Sarah. It would be two and a half hours before church would begin, which would lead to the inevitable encounter with her.

He sat staring into the darkness. The corn in the field to the east of the church stood knee-high. The first hints of an azure sunrise were beginning to touch the eastern sky. A car drove by, its headlights carving a small swath from the darkness ahead of it. He watched it pass by.

A gust of wind swept a swirl of grass-clippings across the lot, and a moment later more headlights came, this time appearing in his rear-view mirror first. The car became visible out his driver-side window as it drove on to the east, and he watched until its red taillights disappeared down the road.

He couldn't help wondering where these people could be going so early on a Sunday morning. To work, most likely. This odd, quiet side of the town was something he didn't see often.

More headlights appeared. He watched, lost in thought, expecting them to pass. They didn't. To his astonishment, the small car – a white Ford Focus – slowed and turned onto the lot. It was Sarah. He couldn't have been more surprised. He was not ready to see her, not yet. And he instantly realized that it made sense that she would arrive at the church early on a Sunday. As obvious as it was in hindsight, the possibility hadn't occurred to him, and now he was trapped. The car moved slowly up the drive and he hoped for a fleeting moment that she wouldn't see him. The possibility seemed to gain promise as the car continued to move towards the church, but then, halfway up the drive, it stopped unexpectedly. It stood motionless for long seconds until AJ began wishing with earnest that he had gone for the pancakes. The moment stretched on, and the car did not move. It sat as a cloud of condensation from the exhaust built up behind it and slowly dissipated on the unusually cool morning.

There was no seeing into the darkened windows to make Sarah out, but he tried anyway. Still, she waited. *Great*, AJ thought. *She'll think I did this on purpose, and they'll be no convincing her otherwise. She'll probably be creeped out and that will be the end of that.* He couldn't remember being more frustrated with himself.

He realized that the best he could do was simply leave, but as he reached for the shifter, Sarah's car started slowly forward. AJ's hand froze on the lever, and his heart began pounding with renewed vigor. Exasperated with himself, and not for the first time in the last few seconds, he decided to let her park and get into the church building before leaving. He had little doubt that she would not welcome his company alone in the church at such an odd hour.

To his astonishment, though, as he watched, the car rolled past the front doors of the church without slowing and rounded the corner, approaching him. It looked for a moment like a stalking cat. The feeling of being trapped overtook him again.

Nervously, he rolled his passenger window down to talk with her, but instead of doing the same, she parked her car a couple of spaces away and got out. By the time she reached the truck's door handle, AJ had almost closed the window again, but not quite. On noticing, and realizing that he had apparently expected her to stay in her own car while the two of them attempted to hold some semblance of a conversation shouting across the parking lot, an exasperated expression crossed her face that was all too familiar. It lasted for only the briefest moment before dissolving away. That in itself was something of a surprise.

Without a word she pulled the door open and a burst of cold air followed her into the cab. She took the passenger seat without speaking, and the two of them sat in a silence that was somehow, not entirely awkward. As AJ struggled to catch up with the moment, the sweet smell of her perfume reached him, and not for the first time, he noticed her long brown hair, which, even in this light, shone invitingly.

She was beautiful.

She seemed to be struggling with what to say, and AJ waited, not sure of what to say himself. When she finally did speak, she did so without looking at him. "I don't always know what to say, AJ. And I don't always know what to do." AJ started to speak, but she went on as if she hadn't noticed. "I know I've been an idiot and I'm sorry."

To AJ's surprise, the dome light came on again as Sarah opened the door to get out of the truck. "Sarah, please don't go," he said. His words stopped her halfway out of the truck. She lingered over the threshold for a moment as if unsure of what to do, then sat back in the seat. She looked over her shoulder at him, the dome light still on, before closing the door again. "I don't either," he said.

Relationships are like any other living thing. They are most vulnerable during their fledgling moments. Something in AJ understood that the next few minutes would decide whether anything could or would take shape between them. Oddly, he was not entirely sure of how he felt about either prospect, or whether one was ultimately better than the other. One thing was certain, he was in the midst of a life-moment, and he knew it.

The look on her face told him that she knew the same. Silence passed between them unnoticed until she spoke again. "I grew up in all this. I'm 27, but I've never been away from home. I work here," she said, motioning towards the church. "I'm the only daughter of a protestant preacher, and I have a reputation for being hard-headed." She laughed quietly. "That may be a cute trait for a little girl, but not at my age. I have a Master's in Divinity, and even that I earned by correspondence. I've lived my whole life in a very small world. I didn't plan it, it just happened."

AJ continued to look at her in silence. He had never seen her come close to letting her guard down even though he had known her since childhood, and now hoped that he wouldn't say the wrong thing. Whether the two of them would become something more or they wouldn't, wasn't the issue. He just hoped that nothing he said or did in the coming few minutes would hurt her. The sight of her uncertainty and vulnerability made his heart reach out … and not necessarily in a romantic way – more in a caring way. He felt a sudden, unexplainable and unexpected impulse to protect her somehow, to shield her. And then, all at once, he realized that he could love her, or maybe, that he already did.

As the thought unfolded in his mind, it was like his heart had taken a deep breath, maybe for the first time in his life. He no longer saw Sarah, or the truck, or the church. There was no awkwardness, no nervousness – just a moment of realization that a part of him that had been lifeless for a long time – maybe always – was stirring.

He returned to himself to see that Sarah was still watching him. Her face had softened, had changed somehow, as if she had reached a conclusion of her own. "I know you have a lot to do," AJ said. "Will you have lunch with me later? After church?"

There was a long pause. AJ could see that she was thinking deeply. It was almost like she had tuned him out. Finally, she said: "I never get out of here before 1:30 or so. I have to count the offerings and record everything on the computer. If that's not too late–"

"I'll wait," AJ said.

Chapter 10

January 8, 2024

I n 1936, a group of Caltech graduate students began a series of experiments involving small alcohol-fueled motors. They were collecting data for a graduate student and aeronautical engineer named Frank Malina whose goal was to develop a sounding rocket capable of carrying data-gathering equipment to the edge of space. It was dangerous work; so dangerous in fact, that he and his small group of helpers were dubbed the *Suicide Squad* and eventually forced to take their experiments, which sometimes failed in spectacular fashion, to a safer location away from campus. They settled at a seasonal river canyon about six miles to the northwest in the San Gabriel Mountain foothills of Pasadena. Now, nearly 100 years later, the site is home to the *Jet Propulsion Laboratory*.

For scientists and engineers, it is a celebrated piece of land, upon which many of the best and brightest set their sights from their earliest childhood years when the hopes and dreams of most top achievers flicker to life. Lynn Burton was one of them.

Lynn had been a Senior Investigator on the *Gravity Recovery and Climate Experiment* mission with NASA until its end in the mid-2010's. GRACE, as it was better known, had collected highly detailed data on variations in the Earth's gravitational field. When the European Space Agency had launched GOCE, its own *Gravity Field and Ocean Circulation Explorer* mission in 2009, Lynn had become involved. The teams shared data, insights, and techniques, producing increasingly accurate views of the Earth, seen not in terms of visible light, but its gravitational field.

The resulting images were odd to say the least. When the data was depicted in colors that portrayed the highest field strengths in the high-frequency colors of blues and violets, and the lower strengths in the lower frequencies of reds, and then extrapolated that data to artificially render the Earth's shape in terms of density, the resulting image was of a withering tomato with odd colorings that were not entirely appealing. It was like the earth had been stripped of its outer clothing to reveal its naked form, with less than complementary results. In fact, there was a tangible sense that looking at the image was to see the Earth in a way that, if it were a living thing, would easily amount to a trespass of privacy.

The data was oddly informative to fields of science that were not entirely obvious either. Climate Change being one, but insights related to Earth's surface stability, atmospheric profiles, and freshwater runoff were among a long list of others.

Burton had been careful to have his information in order – organized and concise – before soliciting Cynthia Reynold to come for a look at what he'd stumbled upon. She was a friendly-enough person, but busy, and not given to wild leaps of faith or unfounded conjecture. Reynold had served as Principal Investigator on more than one high-profile NASA mission, and as a group, PI's were a peculiar breed. Reynold's favorite line, probably less in practice than reputation, to be fair, was 'show me.' It just wasn't wise to put anything in front of her that was half-baked or founded on guesswork.

"Here's the deal," Burton said. "I noticed an anomaly about a week ago and then did some back-checking. As far as I can tell, it started around three months back. It was weaker then, but it was definitely there." He pressed a few buttons on a keyboard causing two images to appear, side-by-side, on a computer monitor. They depicted the same region near the east coast of the United States. He then began zooming in until both were centered at a location to the southwest of Charlotte, North Carolina. On first glance, the images appeared to be identical. Burton leaned forward and indicated two discrete positions on the screen, the same location, as it appeared in each, then waited without comment for Reynold to draw her own conclusions.

In a moment, she spotted the oddity for herself. She leaned in for a closer look, her eyes narrowing. "Well, hello there," she said. "What might you be?"

The image at left showed the area as light green, but in the other, a highly-localized, perfectly circular area of lower apparent density was rendered as a radial gradient that tapered from a yellowish color at its edges to a deep green at its center. Reynold's eyes passed between the two images for several seconds before standing erect to face Burton again. "You're saying this is a recurring anomaly?"

"It is, but it's hit and miss on what the frequency is, since it's a matter of timing for when the surveyors happen to be overhead. I've caught only a few events. And, I've artificially enhanced the effect in the images so it's easier to see. The actual effect is very minimal."

"I'd like to see the data," she said, then checked her watch. "I've only got a few minutes. Have you looked at what the acceleration differences are?" In terms of gravitation, *acceleration* being the measure of the intensity of a gravitational field.

"I have," Burton said. "The elevation is only around 750 feet, so the typical acceleration for the area is around 9.798 meters per second. But get this," he said, as if what he was about to say was extraordinary. "The center of this ring is..." he leaned forward to read from a notebook lying open on the desktop, "9.783867. That's a delta of .014, which is about 80% of the difference between what's typical for the area and the average at the North Pole."

Reynold whistled. "That's significant," she said.

"Absolutely," Burton agreed. "And it's clearly artificial. I don't know how it couldn't be. Look how perfect the circle is." Reynold looked back at the image as if weighing the possibility but didn't comment. "And something else is interesting here, too," he said. "I'd bet whoever's doing this, thinks that they won't be detected."

"Why do you say that?"

Burton swiveled his chair to face her. "Think about it. To get this far would require money, expertise, equipment, and lots of it. And it didn't happen overnight. Whoever has done this has gone to enormous expense, and nearly as much effort to keep it quiet. You and I both know, secrets like this aren't kept by accident. Frankly, I think they're taking a measured risk. They know they can't do this without the possibility of being seen, not with GOCE up there, but they're stuck, because there's no way to hide it. So, at the end of the day, they move forward in the only way they can; they rely on *obscurity security* and hope for the best."

"It's not working out too well for them," she said.

"No," Burton grinned, "but they had no options. The only possible alternative would have been to go mobile – to do their tests at different locations, but it's not likely that the equipment – whatever it is – can be moved easily. The diameter of this field is only a couple hundred meters – two football fields, end to end. To call that a needle in a haystack is an understatement, considering the surface area of the earth. They must've thought they wouldn't be discovered. It would be like noticing a particular piece of dust in a gymnasium."

"And yet, you did"

"Yes, I did. This particular piece of dust happens to be in my backyard."

"That's right, I forgot. Charlotte?"

"Rock Hill, but close enough."

Reynold looked back at the images. "If they're trying to be covert, why wouldn't they time the events to when there are no observers overhead?"

"Good question. Is it possible they don't know about them?"

"Not likely."

"Maybe it doesn't matter in the end," Burton said. He raised his hands as if at a loss for a better explanation. "Damn, and I thought we knew everything that was happening in this field. Hell, we are the field!" Despite the fact that Burton had spent weeks looking into this, something about Reynold seeming to take the discovery seriously drove the implications further home. For the first time, its potential importance began to occur to him, and he could clearly see that Reynold was thinking it too. There were questions about the technology, of course; but the people responsible for it, their motives, and the potential impacts to every person on the planet were of no lesser interest. Only then did he notice the butterflies churning in his stomach.

In the rather cramped quarters among millions of dollars of advanced equipment ranging from supercomputers and lasers to gravity wave sensors, the two sat in silence, pondering. "These guys can't be academia," Burton said, at last. "We'd know all about it if they were. This is a private affair, but who?"

Reynold knew at once that she had to find out.

Chapter 11

January 29, 2024

Already far later in the evening than even Jason Clipper was accustomed to remaining at work, he sat in the half-light of the vacated Mayfield computer lab staring at a monitor. The usually-well-lit corridors, offices and cubicles beyond the lab were obscured in shadow, silent and ghostly, making exit signs hardly noticeable during the day stand out like red sentinels. It was a sight that many in the company never saw.

The lights in the lab where Clipper sat were never fully extinguished. Two of every three fluorescent fixtures inset into the ceiling were dark. The reduced light, the myriad of blinking electronic panels and never-ceasing cooling fans had long-since lulled him into a sense of timelessness. It was late, but familiar.

It was also fun, in that odd way that work can sometimes be. Of all the problems Clipper thought he may encounter in his professional life, antigravity wouldn't have even made the list. It wasn't magic. He saw that now. In fact, the underlying principles were almost simple. The base mechanisms and behaviors that acted in concert to bring about the effect where less so, but even those he was now beginning to grasp.

It was a matter of *nuclear dilation*, as John Riley called it. In the first days of the project the term was as obtuse as a mud puddle, but clarity had begun to emerge, and Clipper now saw that it was simple enough to be genius. Even if it hadn't worked, it would have been a hell of an idea, but the craziest part was that it did ... and well.

Almost all of the mass, and therefore, weight of an atom is concentrated within its nucleus. The extent of the *gravity well* created as an atom presses into spacetime, however small, is a function of that mass. The more nucleons – protons and neutrons – the atom contains, the heavier it is and the deeper it goes. The effect is also cumulative. The more atoms that coalesce in a given area, the deeper the gravity well they create.

There are forces at play within the nucleus that determine how closely knotted together the nucleons within them are. It is a matter of balance between the *color charge*, which holds all of the pieces and parts together, and the *electromagnetic charge*, which works to push them apart. Because the color charge is many times more powerful than the electromagnetic charge, the natural state is for the nucleons to be clumped tightly together.

When that balance is changed, the nucleus responds correspondingly. As the electromagnetic charge is increased, it begins to counteract the attractive force of the color charge, causing the protons to separate. The impact is that the nucleus becomes less dense, and its corresponding gravity well becomes shallower as a result; meaning the atom weighs less even though it still contains precisely the same amount of rest mass.

So, the final solution is not about antigravity as it's usually envisioned, where the gravitational field of the earth itself is somehow altered directly – although in technical terms it could still be thought of in that way – but in diffusing a targeted body of matter, essentially making it more buoyant. Clipper had read Riley's paper on it several times before getting the principle, but once he did, he became an instant believer. He knew it would work.

Not everything had been as it appeared. Clipper had been looking at a particular anomaly for hours; staring at image after image, attempting to find subtle nuances that distinguished one artificially-modified gravity field from the next. It had been exhausting, but gratifying. Over the previous weeks he had progressively tweaked and restructured the data he had collected, leveraging the *Unity* gaming engine to render three-dimensional models of the gravity wells.

His latest improvements introduced shades of color to indicate apparent stresses on the spacetime fabric. The result was that each experiment was now recorded and compiled into images, which depicted spacetime as a spatial collection of data that could be inspected virtually – from any vantage point – and to an enormously high degree of magnification. In truth, Clipper had found the image processing work to be nearly as gratifying as the science.

In the early days, back when Riley had first been brought aboard as the technical team lead of a then-unknown and highly secretive new project – which was created and eventually staffed just for him – the experiments were elaborate affairs. It was still mostly theory then, even to Riley. Especially to Riley.

There were more than a few things up in the air during those early days. Riley was a smart enough guy, there was no doubt about that, but could he lead? Beyond this was the oddity of Mayfield Hammond's decision to fund the science in the first place. Sure, there were obvious commercial applications for the products that could be based on the technology – if it was ever perfected – but even the most optimistic of people could not deny that the time it could take to get there may be measurable in decades. Even the most patient of investors were usually not that patient.

All of that was neither here nor there at the moment, however. Jason placed his already-cooling coffee mug on the edge of the desk in front of him, his eyes passing between two large computer monitors that stood like billboards upon the desktop in front of him. He bore as perplexed an expression as his face could muster, even though he didn't realize he was doing it. Having stared at endless logs for days, it was now clear that something was wrong, or at a minimum, unaccounted for. With a grunt, he began scrolling through the logs of data yet again, his frown renewing as he leaned forward.

Gravity prints, as they had become known, were a late development. It had been understood early on that when the gravity units pumped enough highly focused, precisely channeled electrical current into a clump of Caesium, the curvature of local spacetime changed. It was imperceptible to anything but the most sensitive of equipment, but it was real; predictable and repeatable. What had taken more time to realize was that the events were never quite the same. The impacts to spacetime – the spacetime fabric itself – were not identical. The differences were minute, but undeniable.

With considerable time and effort, Clipper had undertaken the task of tuning the sensors to more accurately detect the changes and eventually to record them. It was like taking sequences of snapshots of the shape of spacetime itself and recording them digitally, like three-dimensional images. The result was that every time a gravity field was modified, the entire event was captured in the form of voluminous mounds of data. In much the same way that an audio recording of a four-minute song may occupy many megabytes of data, a single exhaustive gravity print could consist of three to four hundred gigabytes of data – even more if the event was especially long or used more power.

Capturing so much data in such a short span of time was no small feat either. No single computer in the lab had the ability to capture the data in real time – that is, in the time it took for the event to actually transpire. Even the three supercomputers in the heavily secured sub-basement of the building could not manage it. The problem was not a matter of processing power, but bandwidth. When the gravity machines were activated, even for a moment, the sensors arrayed in a circle around them produced such enormous and rapid bursts of analog data that there was simply insufficient bandwidth to capture it all. Oddly, had the lab been slightly less advanced, the solution may have been easier to achieve.

Everything was digital now. There were no massive reel-to-reel tape recording machines so common to the computer labs of the past, which could have captured the real-time events as native analog data easily and completely. Had there been, the events could simply have been recorded, then played back at slower speeds for processing into a lossless digital format.

There certainly were tape backup machines in the building, used precisely for their named purposes, but they were no longer a typical part of any modern computer lab beyond that simple use. Clipper had mentioned that he would like to gain access to some of those machines, but had no success.

The effort was exponentially more difficult without taped recordings, but Clipper had finally made it work. His solution, after many hours of around-the-clock work that had swollen to absorb his weekends for the prior two months, was to stream the bursts of analog data to a dozen individual computers at once and allow each one to capture slices of the event. Once the work was finished, Clipper found that he was glad it had turned out the way it had. Although having the taped events in analog form would have been far easier, and even better in some ways, processing each one would have taken hours. Now, when an event took place, he had the results in minutes. It also made it easier to enhance the software. He could now run tests and make alterations in shorter cycles, rather than always working against previously recorded and laboriously slow tapes.

Having only completed his parallel recording programs a few days before, and continuing to make improvements as he saw the need for them, he had already glimpsed more from the events than even he had expected. Indeed, each print had measurable and distinguishable characteristics – almost identities of their own. In general shape, each was fairly similar to any other, but only in the same way that one human hand may be similar to another – roughly the same shape, but uniquely identifiable nonetheless.

The gravity prints were the same. There were slight differences in the spacetime curvatures, and even in the texture of the surfaces of the curves – if they could be called surfaces. They were always there. Initially perplexed, then distracted, and finally obsessed; Clipper had burned hundreds of hours of his own time to find an explanation. To his dismay, the answers were proving stubbornly elusive.

At first, he had been certain that the differences must be due to inexact test data – meaning the energy pulses that drove the machines must have been inconsistent in some way. This was true, of course, but not to the degree he initially suspected. When a test event was scheduled, it was always carried out by a computer, which could repeat any command with accuracies far more granular than the margins of error he was seeing. Even when using the lowest quantities of energy possible, and for the smallest measurements of time, 10 milliseconds or less, the images were distinct.

After several days of languishing beneath the near incomprehensible mounds of raw data, Clipper had been forced to realize something that, in hindsight, should have occurred to him much earlier; that spacetime itself, the spacetime canvas upon which the imprints were painted, was more dynamic than he realized. The experiments never produced identical results because spacetime was more fluid than he had suspected. It changed continuously, even if the changes were small enough that it took an enormous degree of resolution to detect them.

To Clipper's dismay, this discovery had been largely dismissed as insignificant by virtually everyone on the team save himself and, perhaps, Riley; whose interest was less than enthusiastic. Still, if he could have chosen who would have had even marginal interest, who better than the team lead?

Turning the gravity units on produced the prints and turning them off again caused spacetime to snap back to its prior shape. That was the way of it. The default shape was almost, but not quite perfectly flat, given that the earth itself stood deep within the gravity well produced by its own mass.

Scrutinizing the seemingly endless mounds of logs and their incoherent rubbish by the screenfuls, Clipper's eyes had long-since begun to weary. The blur stealing across his vision with increasing regularity was a reminder that he had already been at it for too many hours. But, like a teenager who wanted just ten more minutes at his video game before giving up for the day, Clipper had found it difficult to pull himself away from the mystery.

He turned in his chair and reached for the keyboard. The console displayed a simple interface into which parameters for the tests could be entered. In the early days, all of this was done manually, but now it was barely more complex than sending an email. He began to type:

- *Duration: 4000 milliseconds*

- *Ingress duration: 500 milliseconds*

- *Egress duration: 500 milliseconds*

- *Watts: 5000*

- *Volts: 220*

- *Amperes: 22.727*

- *Execute at: now + one minute*

- *On display as: Springboard*

- *Go*

Clipper checked his watch, then out of habit, looked up at one of the large, network clocks mounted on a nearby wall. They agreed, of course. As soon as he submitted the request, wall panels arrayed around the lab displayed a countdown.

jclipper – Springboard – Field generation: 23:47:00 (-60)

A new wave of fatigue rolled over him that made clear to him that he was past the point of diminishing returns. The day was spent. He would finish this last test, then go home.

His eyes tracked back to one of the gravity prints from a prior test, still displayed on the computer monitors. There was something there – something odd. He had to get to the bottom of it, but it wouldn't be today.

In a moment, one of the computers behind him began to beep an alarm – a local proxy for the machine it monitored and controlled at the Installation 60 miles away. It was soon joined by another, then another. It took time for the meaning to seep into him. He turned to see that although the test had finished as programmed, the recording equipment was still going, collecting dead-air. It was quickly filling the storage space on the servers.

Something had gone wrong. Stopping the recordings was supposed to happen automatically. He took to his feet and began individually shutting down the recording software on each of the computers. It wasn't the end of the world, but could easily turn into a real mess. The Linux operating system that these computers ran on did not run out of storage space gracefully. They could all be corrupted. The thought was not a good one. He silenced the alarms and hoped for the best.

He definitely wanted to go home now, but needed to be certain that he hadn't created a problem from which recovery could consume much of the following day. On examination, it looked like he had dodged a bullet. He mounted additional disk storage space for his computers to use, then waited as his software compiled the raw data into viewable form. It took nearly 30 minutes. The unusually long video that resulted looked to be inconsequential.

At the start, the typical gravity well appeared, then faded away as power to the gravity machine tapered back down to zero watts. Blankness followed for several more seconds as the video ticked forward, showing only a flat cross-sectional plane. He expected to find nothing. So much so, in fact, that his finger hovered above the delete button. The only thing that kept him from trashing the whole thing immediately was the amount of time he had invested in generating it.

The coffee mug sitting forgotten on the table in front of him now contained only a splash of cold coffee, a lingering artifact from earlier in the evening. Despite that, he absently picked it up and finished it off. His face twisted into a grimace at the cold, stale coffee, and he looked into the cup as if it had betrayed him. He checked his watch. 1:38 AM.

Rising tiredly from his chair, he reached for the keyboard to log out, but something caught his eye. A distortion; fleeting, but unmistakable passed over the screen. *Was it static?* While he had been fidgeting with his coffee cup, the video had reached its end and automatically looped back to the beginning. He focused on the screen with renewed interest and waited as it played again.

The timer counted silently upward. The gravity well appeared. Disappeared. Then nothing. The terminal showed only a flat plane for several seconds – as still as a photograph. Maybe he had imagined it. Seven seconds. Eight Seconds. Nine. It rolled to 12.

There it was. Something rippled across the screen. He pressed the spacebar and the video stopped. If it was a glitch, it had been captured within the data itself.

The timer showed 14 seconds. Taking the mouse in hand, he pulled the video thumb marker to the left across the timeline to 12 seconds. He kept moving; 10 seconds, now 7. Slowly, he pulled the timer forward, watching intently as the frame counter, which reflected his position within the video, climbed back upwards – back to the position where he thought he had noticed the distortion.

It was still there. A set of ridges appeared on the otherwise smooth image at precisely 12.3776 seconds. He sat back down and zoomed in. Striated bands crossed the plane in three adjacent frames. They didn't pass over the field like ripples on water; instead, they simply appeared in place, lingered for three frames and then disappeared.

Chapter 12

January 31, 2024

Cynthia Reynold stepped into the lab at the JPL early in the morning to find Lynn Burton already hovering over his computer terminal, the coffee cup on the cluttered bench to his left nearly empty. "Are you early, or very late?"

Burton grinned. "I didn't stay the night here, if that's what you mean. May as well have for all the sleep I got." He scooped up the coffee cup, took a drink and paused for a moment. "Any insights?"

"No insights, but a *next step*," Reynold said.

"I'm all ears."

"I spoke to Porter."

"And?"

"And, he's intrigued. He wants to know who this is. He's already reached out to Aarav Kumar, out at LIGO, and approved travel for the two of us to go snooping around."

"Nice," Burton said. "Something new for my resume."

"So it is."

"When's this going to happen?"

"That's the question. In Porter's words, somewhere in the neighborhood of a week ago yesterday works best."

"That's a highly unusual timeframe for anything around here," Burton said, sarcastically.

"Can you make it?"

"I can. I'll just need time to book travel. I assume we'll go together?"

"Yes, but no need. Arrangements have already been made. Porter's admin took care of it last night. We leave this afternoon. Itinerary is in your email inbox."

"Perfect," Burton said. "I don't know how old the Google Maps images are for that area, but I couldn't find anything useful. The lat/long is 34.873318, -81.839827," he said, referencing a piece of paper from a nearby table. "So, it's out there a ways. I know the rural areas don't get updated all that often, so there's nothing particularly odd about that. And no street view is available, either. Going out there is probably our only bet."

"Agreed. I looked too – couldn't turn anything up either. We'll fly out to Charlotte this afternoon, get a rental car and stay at the Hilton near the airport tonight. That'll allow us to get an early start in the morning."

"Perfect," Burton said, rising to his feet. "I'd better get going then," he said, heading for the exit.

Reynold looked after him. "Our plane doesn't leave for nine hours."

Burton didn't look back. "I'm going home to get some rest," he said. "I lied. I've been here for 28 hours."

Chapter 13

January 31, 2024

Two days after capturing the striated bands on the gravity prints, Jason Clipper found that he couldn't dismiss them from his mind. He certainly had other work to do, and lots of it; but something about this mystery pressed him to keep pondering causes. No computer glitch he could imagine would manifest in such a strange way. Any typical interference would almost certainly have a less structured, more random appearance.

He had initially suspected an error in his own imaging software, or more specifically, the data he fed into the 3D modelling engine, but the following night, through repeated testing, he was able to prove that it was not. Furthermore, the pattern was reproducible – a discovery he found a bit unsettling.

The sequence was always the same: turn on the gravity machine, let it create a gravity well, turn it off, and the pattern would appear in just under seven seconds without fail.

He was baffled.

It was now Wednesday morning – another early one, and likely to stretch into a late night. But it was by his own choice, and that made it tolerable. By 8:30 AM, Clipper had already been in the lab more than two hours when a higher-than-usual buzz of activity began taking shape around him. The EcoGrid OS team had moved into the lab to begin another battery of pre-release tests, which Clipper knew would run for most of the day.

He broke away from his images for a sip of coffee, and passively scanned the room. Six or eight 'Grid' people were in a huddle. He was not surprised, but interested nonetheless, to see that Tony Erwin was among them. In his brief and intermittent contacts with Erwin since joining the company, Clipper had already decided that he was one of the most talented engineers he had met. He would like to have talked with the man, but this was clearly an inopportune time. On days like today, Erwin would occupy the vortex of a frenzy of activity. The chaos had yet to form around him on this particular morning, but a low-pressure system was clearly taking shape.

"Mind if I take this chair?" A woman's voice said from over his shoulder, startling him. He swung around to see one of the EcoGrid System Admins, Melissa Ulrich, looking down at him, her hand already resting on the back of a nearby chair.

"By all means," he said.

"Thank you," she said, already pulling the chair towards a neighboring computer. Clipper watched her go, but she stopped unexpectedly, returned the chair to its original position, then sat down. She eyed Erwin warily. "On second thought, I think I'll give Tony a couple minutes to get things set up," she said hesitantly, still looking in Erwin's direction. Clipper watched her but didn't respond. In a moment, Melissa looked over at him, as if to verify he was still there.

Clipper realized he had missed his cue. "So, all of this is a pre-release acceptance test for EcoGrid?"

"It is. This one is a full point release – going out with a whole new threading model. It's proving to be nearly as hard to test as it was to build."

Clipper whistled. "I'll bet."

"We're already three weeks behind, and every time we try to get a complete suite of testing done, something goes wrong. I'm afraid Matthews is about to call in the headsman." She laughed, somewhat disquietedly. "I wish that were more of a joke than it is."

"A new threading model, huh?" Clipper repeated. "Sounds serious. What brought that on? Just a general performance enhancement?"

"I wish it were. No, it's actually more serious than that. We are, unfortunately, learning that deviousness is not unique to human beings. A few months back we started seeing modules in production stealing cycles from one another – it's threatening to crash some of the installed economies." She looked suddenly much more serious, shaking her head yet again. "No, this one is a big deal."

"Wow, this is embarrassing," Clipper said.

"What?"

"I have no idea what you just said."

"Really? I thought you gravity guys were the technology elite around here."

Clipper chuckled. "Hadn't heard that one, god help us. No, the truth is that I just haven't had the chance to learn much of anything about it."

"Oh, it's fascinating," Melissa said. "It really is. It's worth looking into when you find the time."

"It's on my to-do list as of now."

Melissa smiled, then looked over at Erwin again as if sizing him up. Apparently satisfied with what she saw, she went on. "This particular release is primarily going out to keep our backsides out of the fire."

"In what way?" Clipper asked, intrigued. "I don't know what you mean about economies."

"You weren't kidding then. You really know nothing about it?"

"Sorry," Clipper replied, a bit sheepishly. "I've been told that honesty is one of my weaknesses."

"You should work on that," Melissa said. Clipper smiled, but she went on without noticing. "EcoGrid is different from any other software or operating system in, well, in history. It really amounts to bringing together all the algorithms that constitute an artificial intelligence platform and weaving them together into an operating system."

Clipper raised an eyebrow. "No kidding?"

"Seriously. The concept is simple. The idea is that when the OS is installed on any hardware – it could be a cloud segment, some legacy distributed system, or an airplane – it sets up a virtual economy. Any new components that are then installed on that hardware have to enter into, and compete within that economy."

"Sounds novel," Clipper said.

"It is. The OS is a government. It doles out resources to modules and processes based on their relevance and contributions to the common good, which it determines. But it goes far beyond that. It really tries to be capitalistic. Meaning, it enforces trading policies and ensures that what you might think of as civil services don't fail."

Clipper was confused and not doing a good job of hiding it.

"I'm sorry, I'm boring you," Melissa said, apologetically.

"No, really, I'm very interested."

She appraised his expression for a moment, searching his face for any signs of irony, then proceeded. "For instance, say we installed EcoGrid on an airplane – no, let's go with something simpler like a car. Under the older paradigms, the software would have been tailor-made for that specific model of car. All the systems, subsystems, components – you name it – would be specifically designed to control all the aspects of keeping the car working. With EcoGrid, the end goal is the same, but the way it's accomplished couldn't be more different." She turned her chair to face Clipper more directly. "Let's say that instead of building an enormous, customized system to control all the different functions of the car, you instead created a framework that governs components – any component. So, if you build, for instance, a component that controls the fuel system, you create it with the ability to negotiate with the framework according to the rules it enforces. It must first register itself with the framework in much the same way that a business may register with the state to open shop. Once the component is recognized, it enters into that economy."

"How does that play out?" Clipper asked. "I mean, what if the fuel system isn't playing by the rules? It would be bad to shut it down during rush hour because it defaulted on its taxes, right?"

Melissa allowed a grin. "You're seeing some of the issues right off, but they're really not unusual, or particularly difficult for that matter. In the same way a real government identifies essential functions like defense and civil infrastructure, and then ensures they remain in operation, the fuel system would be recognized as an essential service too. It would not be allowed to fail and couldn't be denied necessary resources to function, but it would certainly trigger the controller to begin looking for a new vendor."

Clipper was getting it.

"But then, let's say that your car registers itself with the city of Charlotte," Melissa went on. "In that case, the city-wide EcoGrid economy would have a broader view – a bigger perspective of things – of which your local car-hosted economy is only a part. The municipal controller can experiment with traffic light patterns to gain efficiency by, for example, monitoring the amount of gas purchased from local filling stations. It can then use the data as a multiplier in determining the impacts of traffic flow changes. It may even take the average duration of your commute, which is volunteered by your car because you opted to provide the information in exchange for a discount on fuel or a break on your taxes, and use it to strike a balance between the benefits of fuel savings and any possible increases in overall drive times."

"Holy smokes," Clipper said. "I had no idea."

Melissa was laughing, "That's a pretty typical response. Let me tell you that if you find this stuff even marginally interesting, trust me, you owe it to yourself to look into it more – these are very simplistic examples. They get much more intriguing."

"Wait a minute," Clipper said. "You're trying to recruit me!"

Melissa smiled. "Why, I would never!" She said, feigning a Southern accent.

Clipper laughed. "All that sounds like some darn cool stuff. Ever worry about the controller itself misbehaving?"

"Not really, the controller is managed by us, so we are the final authority."

"It all sounds amazing," Clipper said. "When this gravity work slows down, I may have to talk with you more. But I've gotta tell you," Clipper said, nodding a sidelong glance in Erwin's direction, who was looking more troubled by the second. "I don't envy you today."

"Me neither," Melissa said, suddenly appearing more somber as she looked at Erwin too. "From the looks of things, this may be another long one." She paused a moment, then shrugged. "Anyway, I suppose I'd better get moving, but first, I'm wondering what protocol that is." She gestured towards Clipper's computer monitor.

Clipper gave a start. "Excuse me?"

She was studying the image. "I've never seen–" she paused, leaning forward. "Huh, that's pretty interesting. What are you working on?"

Clipper looked at the image and then back to Melissa. "What do you mean, protocol?"

"It's an odd way to render the data – it's banded like some sort of analog signal, but squared as if it's a low-bandwidth digital signal."

Clipper frowned, then looked back to the image sharply. "What makes you think that? Why a protocol and not just some other strange image?"

"Oh," Melissa said, seeming almost surprised by the question. "Look at the edges. The pattern is reversed. The bands on the edges are mirrors of each other."

Clipper rubbed his forehead, and in a few seconds, found himself laughing quietly.

Chapter 14

February 1, 2024

Riley's morning began with the chime of his mobile phone. It was a message from Jason Clipper: *I have something to share with you. It's kind of urgent. Starbucks at 7:30?* Riley stared at the words. They set his mind in search of possible issues, especially related to Springboard, but nothing occurred to him. He typed into his phone: *Yep.* Then set it back on his nightstand.

The Starbucks drive-through window was in full stride by the time he arrived an hour later. A precession of minivans and SUV's snaked around the side of the building, with the last of them barely nosed onto the lot. As Riley pulled in, Clipper wheeled in behind him in his Mustang GT. They parked side-by-side.

"Glad you could make it," Clipper said, getting out of his car.

"It wasn't an easy invitation to ignore. What's up?"

"Let's get inside and I'll tell you all about it."

On entering the lobby, Riley realized with some relief that the frenzy at the pickup window was only thinly reflected inside of the building. The rather small seating area was mostly empty. "What'll you have?" Clipper asked as the two of them approached the counter. "It's on me."

"Grande Latte, thanks," Riley replied. "I'll grab us a couple chairs."

"Make it three," Clipper said, almost dismissively before turning to the counter to order.

Riley, who had already leaned into his first step, stopped with a stagger. "Who else?"

"Uh–" Clipper began, but at that moment the young man behind the counter asked for his order. "Hang on," he said. Then, as if just remembering the electronic tablet he carried, extended it towards Riley. "Would you take this to the table for me?"

Riley took it without a word. Shaking his head and still pondering the question, he turned at once to find that he recognized a woman sitting at one of the tables as Melissa Ulrich, one of the Network Admins from Mayfield. Riley didn't know her, per se, but knew of her. He guessed she was a couple years older than himself. She was petite and pretty, with a resident thoughtfulness upon her face, as if continuously drawn by some forlorn memory. As far as he had known, Clipper and Melissa were not all that well acquainted either. On seeing him, Melissa motioned him toward a chair with a smile. Clearly, she had known *he* was coming. He stepped forward and, feeling oddly awkward, pulled out a chair to sit.

"How are you, Melissa?" he asked airily.

"I'm good, you?"

"Good." He settled into his seat, placing Clipper's tablet onto the table in front of the empty chair to his left, and looking up, took in Melissa's full appearance for the first time. Her gaze had fallen upon him with a cool intensity he did not expect. She somehow communicated a sense of presence that wasn't entirely typical: alert, smart and perceptive. Suddenly unsure of what to say next, he gestured towards the counter where Clipper stood waiting, "So, Clipper roped you into this ... whatever it is too, huh?"

"I guess that's what I'm about to find out." She smiled.

"Fair enough, that goes for me too."

The woman sat there, the picture of self-possession. Her light brown eyes were clear and pretty, as was her shoulder-length brown hair. Any person who had not made her acquaintance could be forgiven for underestimating her intelligence, but her reputation in that regard was well known. Riley recalled a conversation in which a colleague had summed her up by simply saying, "That Melissa, she's no dummy."

Well put, Riley thought.

Now that he thought about it, something else had always stood out about her as well. Despite the relaxed dress code in the IT department on the campus, which applied to her as well, she always dressed nicer than the bare minimum that seemed to suit most other engineers – men and women alike. She generally wore a nice blouse with a thin gold-wound chain necklace and slacks. Today was no different. She seemed in a good mood, too, and in a moment, Riley found himself wondering why he had never taken the time to get to know her better.

"So," she said, "how's gravity these days?"

Riley laughed. "That's a good question. Probably better for the wear than me. And you? How's EcoGrid?"

She grinned pleasantly. "Same."

Within a few seconds, Clipper appeared with two drinks. He sat them on the table and disappeared again to fetch his own. Without hesitation, as if grateful for something to distract from the moment, Melissa and Riley each took up their cups and sipped. Clipper returned and sat, but before he could speak, Riley spoke up, "Well my friend, you've got our full attention. The suspense has been a good diversion from my typical Thursday, even if there's nothing more to it."

Clipper looked Riley in the eye over the rim of his coffee cup, then sat it down, leaning against his ladder-backed chair. "I have good news, I've done all of this for far more than just suspense." He opened his mouth as if to continue but stopped suddenly. "The two of you have met, right?"

"We have," Melissa said.

"Okay, good." He paused for a moment, tilting his cup on the table, studying it as if it held the secret to what had suddenly become a difficult problem. "I guess I'll just come out with it." Riley noticed Melissa incline her head. Clearly, she was as intrigued as he was, and just as much in the dark. Riley wondered if her day had started with a text message too.

"In a nutshell, I need your help," Clipper said. He looked to Melissa and then to Riley, making eye contact with each of them. "And," he went on, "you probably need mine too; or, at least you do," he said, gesturing towards Riley.

"I have no doubt you're right, Clip. Can you be more specific?"

"I can." He picked up his tablet and continued talking as he tapped on the screen. "Melissa and I ran into each other in the lab last Wednesday," he said. "I was looking at gravity prints. I'd noticed an anomaly that I had not been able to understand – some kind of noise in the data. It was an accident that I saw it all. That anomaly happened to be on the display screen when Melissa stopped by, and now I'd like to show it to you." He sat the tablet on the table so both Melissa and Riley could see it. Melissa nodded in recognition.

"Did you know," Clipper said, directing his comment to Riley, "that just under seven seconds after each gravity test, something disrupts the field surrounding the area?"

Riley's eyebrows furrowed, and he shook his head almost imperceptibly.

"I'll take that as a 'no,'" Clipper said. "I've been chasing my tail on this for three weeks. I'm embarrassed to say that I did not recognize this as anything but noise until you saw it last week," he said, gesturing to Melissa. "Like I said at the time, honesty is one of my weaknesses." Melissa looked mildly surprised but didn't comment.

Riley reached for the tablet, "do you mind if I have a closer look?"

"Not at all," Melissa said.

He picked it up. "You've verified that this isn't a glitch in your software?"

"I have," Clipper said.

"How about the equipment? Could this be some sort of energy fluctuation that happens as the machine powers down?"

"Good question," Clipper said. "The answer is, no, not in any way I've been able to determine."

Riley's demeanor shifted into one of intense interest. "There's structure here," he said after a few seconds. "How long has this been happening?"

"Not sure. I only caught this by mistake. I introduced a minor bug into my software during the last update. It caused the recording to go long. It's happened on every test since, so my guess is that it's been happening all along."

"This happens every time? Each time we run a test?" Riley said, lowering the tablet.

"Every single time," Clipper confirmed. "At exactly the same point with respect to the end of the test."

"Seven seconds?"

"Closer to 6.5, depending on where you start counting, but yes."

Riley raised the tablet again, then lowered it back to the table. "Have you tried reducing power to see if there's a threshold where this stops happening?"

Clipper shook his head. "This is all I have so far."

Riley nodded as if reaching a conclusion. "Two things. First, I'd like to find that threshold. Second, I'd like to look closer at the signal itself."

"Agreed," Clipper said. "To that point; Melissa, would you mind repeating what you thought this looked like when you first saw it last week?"

Melissa made to speak, but Riley spoke first: "It's the first of a three-step communications handshake."

Melissa paused. "That's what I thought, too," she said.

"Would you be willing to look closer? See if you can determine which protocol it is?"

"Probably TCP," Melissa said, "but I'll take a look."

Riley looked back to Clipper. "Has this been shared with anyone?"

"Only the two of you."

"Good. Let's keep our cards close to the vest on this until we understand it better," Riley said. He looked back to Melissa. "Are you good with that?"

"Of course," she said, "but remember, I'm not NDA'd on Springboard."

"I understand. This is just a question of the signal. It's not Springboard."

"Good enough."

"Listen," Clipper said. "Let's give ourselves a couple days to do our work, then reconvene at my place. I'll make dinner. How about Saturday at 6:30?"

Riley and Melissa looked at each other. "Sounds good," Melissa said, with a look of being not that unpleasantly surprised. "But, unfortunately, I have to work on Saturday. Will Sunday work?"

"Yep, see you then."

Chapter 15

February 1, 2024

"This is a nice car," Burton said. He had been fiddling with the dash, pressing every button and twisting every knob until nearing the boundaries of Reynold's endurance. He had insisted on driving when they picked up the rental car, and Reynold now saw that it was for the best. If he were left with nothing better to do than sit idle in the passenger seat as they drove through the countryside, there was no telling what the man would have found to occupy himself. It could only be a matter of time before the novelty of the unfamiliar car would begin to wear away, so she diverted her attention to the landscape and rode along in silence.

"That's one thing you never fully appreciate from maps," he said; "the hills." Reynold didn't respond. Burton looked over at her appraisingly for a moment, then settled back into driving. They had been on the road for nearly 90 minutes. "We're getting close," he said.

Reynold checked the GPS. "About ten miles," she said.

"So, you can speak." Reynold passed a brief, incredulous look at him in response, but didn't answer, and Burton wisely chose not to press the point. He drove on for another fifteen minutes, then unexpectedly rolled the car to a stop. "This is interesting."

"GPS says it's only a quarter mile ahead, why are we stopping?" Reynold asked.

Burton pointed out the window. "What do you make of that?"

At first, all Reynold could see were trees. Even though it was winter, many of the trees in the area were not deciduous, which meant it was still a challenge to see for any distance. But they had just crested a hill, so the view had opened up marginally. She saw nothing for a moment, but then, there it was. "What is that?"

"I think … it's a drone." Burton said.

"Why would someone be flying a drone out here?"

"Good question. And if I didn't know better, I'd say that whoever is flying that thing doesn't know what he's doing. It's not military. That's a consumer, remote-controlled drone, plain and simple – and it's weaving like a drunken sailor."

"That is so odd," Reynold said. "At least we know we're not alone out here. Let's just drive by at first, and then come back if it looks clear."

"You got it." Burton started the car rolling slowly forward. The trees began to thin, revealing a large black SUV sitting at the entrance of a gated property. "There's a woman standing in front of that truck," Burton said.

"And she's got a remote in her hand."

"Yep. She's flying the drone, and she ain't good at it." Burton said, then let out a chuckle. "That's hilarious. She's spying just like we are, only she had the wherewithal to plan ahead."

Reynold shot a sidelong look at him. "Funny," she said, then her eyes widened. "Wait, she just saw us. Keep moving. Don't look." It was of no use, of course; Burton couldn't help himself. He looked over as he drove by to see a solitary woman looking back at them with wide eyes. What the woman couldn't see was that behind her, the drone had begun drifting to the right as soon as she looked away, and in the time it took for them to pass, had already slanted into an irredeemable dive. Burton drove, checking his mirror nervously, but Reynold had fully pivoted in her seat to watch. "Oh my God. She lost her drone. It crashed!"

When they had driven far enough to be out of view, Burton stopped the car to turn around. There was no place to turn off and the country road was narrow, so it took several attempts to maneuver the car into the opposite direction. By the time they drove back far enough for the property to come into view, the SUV was already heading in the other direction. Burton stopped and waited until it was gone from sight, then pulled into the entrance where it had been. There was a sign on the closed gate. It read, "Mayfield Hammond. No Trespassing."

Chapter 16

February 4, 2024

"hat is it?" Clipper asked.

Riley, Clipper and Melissa sat in the living room of Riley's apartment scanning the images of the striated bands from the latest gravity print on their phones.

"It's a strange duck, that's what it is," Melissa said. That drew a curious look from Clipper, but he didn't comment. "May I use your TV?" she said to Riley.

"Of course."

She reached for the remote and turned it on, then tapped her phone a few times. The image appeared. Without missing a step, she pointed. "It's got the unmistakable appearance of an electromagnetically transmitted digital signal, but there is no attenuation at all. No delay attenuation or distortion or noise. It's pristine."

Clipper looked uncomprehendingly at the screen. "I'm not following."

"See how perfectly squared off the parallel bands appear? How perfectly spaced and even in height?"

"I do," he said. "Looks like any textbook digital signal I've seen."

"Exactly, and that's my point. It's too 'textbook.' If you know about how data physically moves through unguided media, you'll know that there are realities around how a signal behaves ... and particularly, the ways in which it eventually and inevitably degrades ... none of which are reflected here. Digital signals never look like this in reality – only in textbooks."

"Okay. How should it look?"

"Sloppy. Rounded at the corners, and if delay distortion comes into play, unevenly spaced. Unless you're receiving a signal from very close proximity to a transmitter or repeater, any signal starts to break down – it degrades over distance. So, unless the sender is right under our noses, this signal makes no sense – for this and other reasons, by the way."

"Other reasons, like what?"

They both looked to Riley, but he was now ignoring the image on the TV and had returned to looking at his phone. He seemed to have tuned them out. Melissa's eyes lingered on him for a moment before going on. "It's also perfectly aligned with our plane; meaning its path of propagation happens to align perfectly with our viewing angle. And weirdest of all, it's not an electromagnetic signal. You're the experts, but it looks to me like the spacetime fabric, as you call it, has been coerced into assuming this shape. If this were an actual electromagnetic–"

Clipper broke in. "You mean radio wave, right? An electromagnetic signal is the same as a radio signal?"

"Radio waves are a form of electromagnetic radiation, but yes, close enough. If it were one, it would be impossible to capture like this. It would be traveling through the field at the speed of light and physics would dictate that you couldn't just take a side-view picture of it in flight. The truth is that this doesn't even look like a real digital signal, it looks like an illustrative depiction of a signal, like it's not really passing through the field, but being projected upon it in some way."

"Okay," Clipper said, trying to level-set the conversation. "It's a cartoonish, electromagnetic look-alike, projection of a signal. What do we take from that?"

"It's a communications handshake," Riley said, unexpectedly breaking his silence. "Somebody wants to talk, but probably not with us. Whoever it is probably doesn't know we're seeing it at all."

"I'd have to agree," Melissa said. "But who has the technology to see it?"

"Who indeed?" Riley agreed. Both Clipper and Melissa looked at him. He was lost in thought, and only then did they realize what this could mean to him. If this were real, and it looked to be beyond dispute, then someone had beaten them – beaten Riley – to conquering the riddle of gravitation, or at least, pushing and prodding spacetime in a way that would have the same effects.

"This has to be military," Riley said, finally. "We've been keeping an eye out for new patents around gravitation. There aren't any."

"That could be explained by the Invention Secrecy Act," Clipper said. He looked to Melissa. "I didn't know about it until I became involved in gravitation with Riley, but it's there for this very purpose: to protect secrets. There could be patents that haven't been made public yet."

"That's possible," Riley allowed, "but not likely. Whoever is doing this has been at it for a while, given how long it must have taken to refine the technology to this level. These guys are working with surgical precision and we're still banging rocks together. There would be tell-tale signs by now – and I would have seen them. If nothing else, there would be a gaping hole where the patents should be, pointed to by an array of lesser, but related ones. No, that's not it," he said. He had started to say something more but stopped and gave a perplexing sideways look towards the screen as if something had just occurred to him. "Why this?" he said, more to himself than to Clipper or Melissa. "Why this artificial binary sequence?" He looked at Clipper. "Your characterization was good. This is a cartoon."

Riley lapsed again into a trance of thought, and Clipper and Melissa fell silent, watching. Melissa was new to all of this, but had already realized what Clipper had witnessed for most of his life; that when Riley set his mind to something it was only a matter of time. Within moments, Riley had tuned them out so completely that it felt as if they were no longer in the room with him.

Eventually, after long minutes, Riley began nodding slowly to himself, his eyes searching unseeing around the room. He took a deep breath. "This is very likely military. It's not smart or safe to fiddle with it any further."

Clipper and Melissa looked at each other. It wasn't the reaction they expected.

"You're suggesting we stop with gravitation or the signal?" Clipper asked, somewhat in disbelief.

"Not gravitation. There is that small detail we call our jobs – and that decision is owned by Mayfield, anyway. No, the signal. We should refocus our energy on gravity wells and keep moving."

Clipper had taken on an incredulous smirk by now. "And what? Hope it goes away and that it's not the tip of a really big iceberg that will put a hole in our boat? At a minimum, we have to tell Matthews about this, right?"

"I'll handle that part."

Chapter 17

February 5, 2024

The next morning, Melissa found Clipper sitting alone in the lab. It was early, as usual, and empty except for a couple of individuals at the far side of the room, immersed in their own concerns. Clipper saw her coming and swiveled his chair to face her, sipping a cup of coffee.

"Have you seen Riley yet today?" she asked, pulling a chair forward to sit.

"It's a little early for him, but he did text me. He said he needed to head to the Installation to check on the generators and that it would probably take most of the day."

"Interesting," she said.

"Yes, interesting," Clipper agreed.

"Listen," Melissa said, "I don't have the history with Riley that you do, but what do you make of his reaction last night?"

It was a question Clipper expected. "I know Riley very well. Better than he realizes. I'll tell you what I really think, if you want to know."

"I do," Melissa said, passing on the opportunity to point out that she had just asked the question.

"Riley is the smartest man I've ever met, and I suspect he's smarter than most I haven't. If you spend much time with him you'll start to see it, you just will. But you also have to know something about the *kind* of smart he is. Working in technology, you and I are used to people saying we're smart because we deal with computers and logic and ones and zeros, but the way most people think of us is that we're smart at the techy stuff, but very much, not smart at anything else. That's what a geek is, you know?"

"I do," she nodded. "We're propellerheads – we see the technology but never the big picture."

"Exactly. Well, Riley, he's not that way. He's not a geek. He's not an idiot with an IQ of 190. He's smart in every way. His reaction last night was not subtle. He knows something he's not sharing, but the way he handled it was not Riley-like. If he doesn't want you to meddle in something, he'll phrase his intentions in a way to make you lose interest or put something else in front of you to lead you to where he wants you to go. He made a feeble attempt at that last night with the whole 'military signal thing,' but I'm not used to Riley making feeble attempts at anything. Something got to him last night. Maybe it was just the blow of thinking someone snatched the prize of gravitation from him, but something tells me there's more to it than that. He connected some dots and didn't like what he saw."

"Okay," Melissa said, as if Clipper's explanation jelled with her own. "I agree with all of the above. So, what do you think he saw?"

"Not sure," Clipper admitted, "but I'm working on how to find out."

"Well, I think I see part of it," she said. "It's just one piece, but could be a significant one."

"Really?" Clipper said. "What do you know?"

"First, I think that when Riley was kind of thinking aloud and said something about, *why the cartoonish image?* he connected the first dot. There is only one reason to produce such an image – if we call it that – and that is to get someone's attention. This signal is purpose-designed to draw the attention of anyone who has the technology to see it, and Riley realized that last night."

"That makes damned good sense," Clipper agreed.

"What do you think a man like Riley would do with that realization?" she said, smiling slightly.

Clipper began nodding slowly, the meaning becoming clearer. "He would start figuring out how to respond – to let the sender know that he had seen it."

"Bingo," Melissa said, allowing her grin to transform into a full smile.

"And," Clipper said, now joining the line of reasoning, "wouldn't you know that suddenly there's something at the Installation that requires his attention today. He must have realized that he's been sitting when he should be running. Someone is sending messages but hasn't yet received a response, and now he feels a sense of urgency to give them one." Clipper took another sip of coffee, thinking. "Do you think he really believes it's military?"

"Don't know," Melissa said. "I'm not sure the answer would change his reaction much. If this is military, showing he can see what they're doing will get him noticed, but to what end? I think he's so passionate about gravitation, he's willing to take the risk of revealing himself to whoever this is because he'll want to know what they're doing. What better way to do that than to simply reply to the message?"

"I think you're right on all counts," Clipper said. "Pretty good for a girl."

Melissa rolled her eyes, "Thanks, that means everything to me. So what do we do?"

"We let Riley know that we know what he's up to, and that we want to help."

Chapter 18

February 5, 2024

Matthews sat on the leather settee in his office sipping at a bottle of water. It was 9:30 in the morning, and he had another thirty minutes before his next meeting.

Vacuums of time like this – even thirty-minute ones – were a rarity, and he had come to appreciate them with the same relish he'd had for an entire day in his earlier years. He scanned through his Twitter account, glancing over the stream of posts until one in particular caught his eye. It read, "Antigravity coming soon?"

He was leaning forward before he knew it. There was no link to any external article, so he navigated to the homepage of the person who had posted it. Most of the tweets on the page seemed random, but there were intermittent references to gravitation, and finally one with a link to a science-based discussion forum. Matthews followed it.

There was little activity on the thread. Just a few scant sentences, and it was beginning to look inconsequential until he noticed a particular string of statements. "I've heard Mayfield Hammond is up to something. Can't confirm," it said. That was followed by a, "Me too," and finally, the most jarring remark of all: "It's more than a rumor."

"Anna!" he called out. He hadn't pressed the call button this time.

In a moment, his admin appeared in the doorway, somewhat startled. "Yes?"

"Can you please get Erwin in here right away?"

"I can, give me a few minutes."

By the time Tony Erwin arrived, Matthews' blood was boiling. Without a word, Matthews handed the tablet to him. "Know anything about this?"

Erwin scanned the device quickly. "News to me."

"How about any of the people who posted the comments? Recognize any of the names?"

Erwin looked back to the tablet. "I don't."

"Damnit!" Matthews said. "Riley's contract is specific on this. If the man has been talking, it'll cost him."

Erwin was hesitant to speak. "Hard to imagine Riley saying anything. He didn't talk much even before he came to us."

Matthews took in the words. "Someone on the team, then?"

"Don't know, boss. I gotta say, even that's hard to fathom, but I can snoop around a little."

"Do that. Can you find out who these people are?" Matthews pointed to the tablet.

"May not be easy. A lot of people use anonymous accounts with made-up user handles. I'll get back with you later in the day if I find something."

"Thanks, Tony. Anything would be appreciated." Tony turned to leave, and Matthews followed him through the door. "Anna, could you please gather the ingress/egress logs of the lab for John Riley and Jason Clipper over the past 90 days?"

She stammered slightly. "Yes, but not sure how to find them, so it may take a while."

"Check with Corporate Security, they'll fix you up. I need this right away, so let me know if I need to help move this along."

"Okay," she said, nodding.

She disappeared through the door, and within 90 minutes, the report was in his inbox. He was surprised to find that Clipper had been logging even more hours than Riley over the past three months. They were averaging between 55 and 65 hours per week, with a couple spikes above 70 by Clipper. There had also been a significant uptick in visits to the Installation over the past three weeks. He hadn't asked, but it was a good catch for Anna to think of checking that too.

Chapter 19

Clipper had been to the Installation, where the gravity field generators were located, several times. It was a long drive, but not a bad one. Far away from the city, among dense deciduous trees and steep hills and curved roads, it was the kind of terrain his Ford Mustang GT seemed built for.

The Installation was unremarkable in most ways, but not all. The region was not known for its flat open spaces, but this location was generally level, and with fewer trees than typical for the area. Four small-to-medium sized buildings stood near its center that a passerby would find curious and difficult to explain. There was some concern with that, given that it could lead to questions and rumors about the place. Mayfield's leadership had wondered how to handle that and decided the best policy was to show as much transparency as possible to avoid unnecessary speculation that could lead to even more unwanted attention. The final solution was to put a sign at the entrance of the drive that simply read, "Mayfield Hammond. No Trespassing. For information please visit *mayfield-hammond.io*." Of course, there was no further information to be found on the site, other than mention that the location existed and that it was indeed a Mayfield property. The website's analytics showed that only a small trickle of individuals actually went to the trouble of looking for information each month, but so far no significant interest had been generated.

Clipper pulled into the drive and flashed his employee badge at the automated security gate, which opened by lifting away to the right. He was one of only a very few people with access to the facility. Riley's solitary Toyota Matrix was parked near the largest building.

The Installation required no full-time personnel to operate. In fact, it was purpose-built to that effect for safety reasons. A maintenance crew came in every so often to refuel the generators that powered the facility and to monitor the health of the equipment, but beyond that, it was Riley who spent the most time here.

At the time the facilities were constructed, there was much concern on the part of Mayfield's Legal team related to the safety of the tests. They were adamant that no one was to be allowed on site while the equipment was in operation and went so far as integrating the field generator systems with the badge access system. If anyone was shown to be on premise, as determined by whether they had checked in but not checked out, it would not operate. Visitors were also prohibited. Anyone who was not an authorized employee was simply not allowed in, and it had been made abundantly clear that any employee who broke those simple rules would be subject to dismissal.

Concerns around safety had since been largely put to rest, but the policies lingered, and no one pressed to change them, least of all Riley who saw them as a way to keep unwanted employees from invading the place. When Riley was on site it was usually because he was modifying or tuning the equipment in some way, which meant that there were no tests being conducted anyway. It was conveniently overlooked, however, that as part of those tunings he often activated the equipment manually for test purposes. That meant he ended up sitting in the middle of the gravity fields just the same. It didn't concern him in the least, but he made a point never to mention it.

Clipper entered to find Riley on the floor behind the largest of the two field generators peering into an open panel. It was a large, odd-looking machine. It had no visible moving parts, but touted the impressive appearance shared by all advanced electronic equipment that had lofty, but not well-understood purposes.

At its center was an odd tower, bearing resemblance to a Tesla Coil. It was about eight feet tall and rose improbably from the floor, surrounded by a ring of seven smaller, paneled boxes with a look and shape reminiscent of residential central air conditioners. The "air conditioners" were called *balancers*, and the tower in the middle was the actual field generator itself. It was a remarkable piece of work that Clipper admired each time he visited, mainly because he knew that regardless of outward appearances, the technologies embodied within the machine probably had more in common with a bicycle than a Tesla Coil.

The smaller generator – the first to be built – was largely prototypical, and housed in one of the small neighboring buildings. It stood about 52 inches in height – just over four feet – and had only four balancers of proportionally smaller size. The most it could muster was an almost immeasurably small disturbance in the surrounding gravitational field, but it was enough to prove the concept, and doing so had been a major and critical milestone for the project. Despite its comparatively primitive design and capabilities compared to the newer, larger one, Riley still tinkered with it and insisted it remain intact.

Riley looked briefly up from his work to acknowledge Clipper as he approached. "Took longer for you to get here than I expected," he said, looking back into the panel. He was tinkering with something outside of Clipper's view.

"Why do I feel the impulse to call you Victor Frankenstein every time I see you in this place?" Clipper asked.

"That would be far too difficult for me to guess," Riley said. His tone belied that he wished Clipper would go away but knew he wouldn't. Apparently getting cooperation from whatever he was fiddling with, Riley closed the panel and leaned back against a nearby balancer. "Okay, out with it," he said.

"You should let Melissa and I help with this. Credit where credit's due, Melissa saw through this before I did, but I think I would have gotten there myself soon enough."

Riley studied Clipper, first to determine whether they were talking about the same thing, and then to think about what his answer would be. "There's some risk here, Clip. I have no reservations for my sake, but I don't want you or Melissa to take a fall with me if this leads to trouble."

"Understood. I can't speak for Melissa, but I, for one, have no qualms on this. So what if it is military? What are they going to do? We aren't breaking into anything, we're just acknowledging their message."

"True. From that perspective this isn't all that risky. What we find when we actually respond successfully could change that, but for now, agreed. The bigger risk at the moment isn't the sender of the message, but Mayfield. Think about how a response will play out, Clip. We'll use Mayfield Hammond's equipment, intellectual property and facilities to respond to a message from an unknown and possibly hostile sender, whose intentions are entirely unknown, without the knowledge or consent of management. Have I missed anything?"

Clipper quirked an eyebrow, acknowledging the complications. "Good points, all. Then why not get their consent?"

The question struck a chord with Riley; it was clear from his reaction. Clipper realized on seeing it that it must have been something he had been wrestling with since the night before.

"That's where I'm stuck, Clip. I don't have a good reason, except that once we do, this whole thing gets away from us. All the questions you can imagine will follow. Who is the sender? Do they already have all the patents? Are we chasing the solution to a problem that's already been solved? And last but not least, this is no longer a technical issue and therefore no longer the concern of Riley or Clipper. They may very well corral us back into our pens with these machines and cut us out." He chuckled ironically to himself. "Amazing how quickly things change. Just yesterday, that was all I wanted."

"Why do you want anything different now, then?" Clipper asked.

"I've thought about that, too," Riley said, "and the answer is simple. I'm following the trail of gravitation, and this is its latest turn. This signal has now become part of it. That's all."

"I won't dispute that," Clipper said. He saw the quandary. After only a moment's hesitation, he said: "Okay, apology is better than sacrifice. Let's do it. You need my help, end of story. You've got me in most ways, Riley, but I'm a code-slinger and you're not, we both know that." Code slinger being slang for a crack computer programmer. Riley smiled at that, and for a brief moment it was the two of them sitting on their bicycles at the age of 12 conjuring the nerve to knock at the door of Hollie Otts.

"If you're up for it then, I am too," Riley agreed. "But the least you could have done was show me the courtesy of getting here sooner. I've been waiting for two hours."

"I was a little slower reading your mind than usual this time – needed an assist from Melissa."

"Yeah, well, sharpen up," Riley said, rising from the floor. "I've given it some thought, and I think next steps are somewhat obvious. We can't match them for control, so the only thing we can do is send pulses back to them. Think about it, even though they're miles ahead of us in the technology, what we're doing is at least good enough to have gotten their attention; which, in itself, is something of a riddle to me."

"And," Clipper said, finishing the thought, "if our menial abilities are good enough to make them want to talk with us, then they'll work with us when we try."

"I think so," Riley said, but then his face grew dark again. "That's not all, though. If the only purpose of this signal is to get our attention, then we have to ask the corresponding question."

"Which is?"

"Why? Why would they want to talk to us? They're clearly – I would guess – years ahead of us. What's the one thing we can do, the one thing we can tell them that they don't already know?"

Clipper pondered the question, but the answer was not forthcoming.

"They want to know who we are, Clip," Riley said, answering the question for himself. "And the next question is where we really start getting to the deep end of the pool: why would they want to know that?"

Clipper's face was now somber as well, but it lasted only a moment. "No idea," he said. "Let's find the hell out."

"Okay, then," Riley said, bringing the discussion to an unceremonious end. "We've already got a system that turns the gravity machine on and off, let's make a way to do it in a mechanized way. Can you modify the software so we can power it up and down in a timed sequence?"

"Sure, it'll be trivial," Clipper said.

"Perfect. Then let's take a closer look at the signal pattern. It's basically made up of a series of ridges with flat peaks and troughs. Some peaks are narrow, some are wide plateaus, but the troughs are the same. Let's find the narrowest plateau in the overall pattern and treat that as the smallest unit of measure – that'll be the bit duration. That smallest unit will correspond to one tick of a clock. The fastest speed that we'll able to talk will be a function of the shortest pulse we're able to carry off. If the fastest we're able to create a minor gravity well and shut it back down is one second, then the amount of time it will take for us to echo back the entire signal we received will be one-second times the number of ticks it will take to retrace the pattern from end to end. The ridges will be on and the troughs will be off. Do you follow?"

"I do. Piece of cake."

"I'm hoping we can do better than one second per pulse, though," Riley said. "The faster, the better."

"The limitation won't be the computer or the software, but the amount of time it takes for the pulse to be generated and shut back down."

"Agree," Riley said. "I think we can speed that up by reducing power. For a typical test, we currently ramp up to about 5000 Watts, and we take about a half second to get there so we don't overamp the equipment. Then it takes another half second to ramp back down. Let's do some experiments to see how low we can go on wattage before we stop getting a response. Then, we can shorten the ramps correspondingly."

"No problem," Clipper said. "Most of the system is written in Java, with some of the hardcore pieces in C++, but the parts that control turning the machine on and off are just simple scripts. I used *Python* for almost all of it. And the specifics of each test are already configurable, so finding the minimal baseline on power and matching that to an optimal power ramp will be trivial as well."

"Very nice," Riley said. "How long?"

"Give me a couple days."

"Okay, I'll do some math on the Wattage. My guess is that it's a pretty sure bet that the amplitude of the bands, as a percentage of the amplitude of the overall gravity wells we've been generating will be the same percentage we can come down to." He saw that Clipper wasn't following. "In other words," Riley explained, "I think we can cut power to where the depth of the gravity well is no deeper than the height of the peaks in the signal."

Clipper nodded comprehension. "Makes sense. Essentially, we'll match bandwidth. I'm guessing we'll land at about 10% of the well-depth we typically use."

Riley nodded. "Sounds about right."

"Okay," Clipper said. "I have a few things to get done today, so I won't be able to look at this until tonight, or maybe tomorrow night." He suddenly looked around the space and then scanned the gravitation machine. "What were you doing here, anyway? Something I can help with?"

"No, thanks," Riley said, casually. "Just checking some things out."

Chapter 20

February 9, 2024

AJ and Sarah had plans for dinner, but she was running late at the church. It wasn't unusual. AJ had learned the routine well enough over the seven months that he and Sarah had been dating that he gave it little thought. He had never appreciated how much work a small church could demand, and it wasn't always about counting the offerings. Sarah and her father spent as much time cutting grass, painting classrooms and cleaning bathrooms as anything else. He had added himself to the rotation where he could, but there was always more to be done.

AJ unlocked the church door with a key Sarah had given him for just such occasions and stepped inside. There were voices coming from the sanctuary. He entered to find Sarah and her father sitting on opposite sides of the main aisle, at the end of two adjacent pews, talking, with two vacuum cleaners standing nearby.

Sarah smiled at AJ as he entered. "Sorry I'm late," she said. "We had a bit of a mess in here ... a youth group mishap last night."

"Sounds fun," AJ said.

"I'm sure it was for the kids."

AJ chuckled. "Looks like whatever it was, you got it." He eyed a large wet spot in the aisle.

Sarah looked back at it too and seemed pleased with how it had come out. "Anyway, give me a few minutes to freshen up. We just need to put all this away first." She gestured to the vacuums and cleaning supplies.

Owen spoke up. "Not necessary. I got it."

"I'll help," AJ said.

Sarah didn't take much convincing. She said a brief thank you, then disappeared into the office area.

Owen had never been particularly open with AJ. It was something AJ had finally gotten used to, so he no longer made an effort to start up a dialogue when he was in proximity of the man. In the early days, it was hard not to take the silence personally, but he had finally reasoned that it was just the way Owen was wired.

They each grabbed a vacuum and handful of cleaning supplies and hauled them to a utility room through a side door behind the platform. AJ noticed that carrying the vacuum was a bit of a struggle for Owen, but it took only a couple of minutes. AJ found his way back to the sanctuary afterwards, and took a seat on the back pew, careful to walk around the spot on the floor.

"Thanks, AJ," Owen said.

"Happy to help."

Rather than leave, AJ was surprised when Owen took a seat across the aisle from him. He sat down and looked in AJ's direction. "How are you doing?"

AJ tried not to look too surprised. "Good, good," he said, attempting to look more casual than he felt.

"Glad to hear. Looks like you and Sarah are getting along well."

"I think so, yes," AJ said.

"Glad to see that. I didn't like how single-minded she'd become about this place. She needed something else to devote time and energy to. There's always something to do, someone who needs help, something to fix or clean up. Sometimes, you just need to get away from it for a while."

"I can imagine," AJ said. There was a brief silence. AJ wasn't sure what came over him, but he ventured a question. "None of my business, Pastor," he said. "Sarah tells me that you're considering resigning the church."

Owen raised an eyebrow. He seemed unsure of how to respond for a moment. "Yes," he said, finally.

"I'm sorry to hear it," AJ said, already thinking about the penance he would have to pay for the mistake.

"I'm afraid it's inevitable now," Owen said. He seemed to size AJ up for a brief second, then nodded to himself, as if reaching an inner conclusion. "I don't blame Sarah for confiding in you. It'll impact her more than anyone; but, she's a tough one. She'll come out better for it in the end. She doesn't see that yet, but I do."

"I think you're right. She will, but it'll be struggle for a while."

"I suppose you're wondering why," Owen said.

"Frankly, yes, but wasn't going to ask."

"Short answer; maybe it's just time. Long answer; I'm not really sure."

AJ was surprised by the comment, and Owen saw that it had raised more questions than answers. "In the end, AJ, the quandary for me is that I am no longer able to deliver what this congregation wants."

AJ noted that he had used the word *wants*, instead of *needs*. "I don't understand. In what way?"

"Faith is a deeper and trickier subject than meets the eye. When you devote your life to it, you should be prepared for the possibility that you may eventually learn that your earlier, less mature notions of it start to thin out. The absolutes of youth rarely translate well into the wisdom of age. That's not only true of faith, by the way."

AJ nodded. "Have you abandoned your faith, then?"

"No, I haven't. In fact, if anything, I hope I'm seeing more clearly now than ever." Sarah came back into the room. AJ noted that she must have brought a change of clothes. On seeing her, Owen paused. "I don't want to keep you," he said.

Sarah was pleased to see the two talking, so she took a seat on the pew in front of AJ. "We're in no hurry," she said, passing a glance at AJ to confirm.

"Not at all," AJ replied.

At that, Owen picked up where he had left off. AJ got the sense that the man had something to get off his chest. "Let me put it this way," Owen said. "In the Old Testament, things were clear regarding the written word. God told the people of Israel to adhere to the Laws of Moses in no uncertain terms. He reiterated the point when Joshua took over after Moses' death."

AJ nodded.

"But what about the New Testament? There was no command to write any of it. Even Paul said that faith was taught by tradition."

"2nd Thessalonians," AJ interjected.

"Yes. So, in the Gospels – the first four books of the New Testament – we see that Jesus and the disciples went around preaching the Word of God, but that was before the New Testament was written. Do you agree?"

AJ nodded again.

"If Jesus wasn't preaching from the New Testament writings – since there weren't any – then the only scripture available to him at the time was the older writings. It seems safe to say that if Jesus had been repeating the words of Moses and the prophets, he wouldn't have gotten any one's dander up at all. He would have essentially been doing the very same thing that the religious leaders themselves were doing. He clearly had a different message, but what was it? What 'Word of God' is the New Testament referring to?"

AJ didn't have an answer.

Owen said: "I think Jesus thought that a simple message of love and forgiveness could get traction, and that it would be the means by which the Old Testament law could truly be fulfilled. His one true commandment was to love God and treat others as you wish to be treated. Israel would be reconciled to God because it would become a house of brotherly love, forgiveness and forbearance. Salvation by grace wasn't about getting to heaven, it was about the redemption of a people while they were here on earth."

Both Sarah and AJ were without an immediate response. "I've never thought about it quite that way," AJ said, "but none of it contradicts the overall message."

"No, it doesn't," Owen said, "except that it tells me that salvation is about changing your own behavior; to be forgiving, to love others and to treat them well. The disciples were able to teach the 'Word of God' before the New Testament was written for a very simple reason, which was that the message itself was simple. That also tells me – and I wouldn't try to convince you or anyone else to take my views – that the entirety of Christianity is exactly what Jesus said it was: love others as yourself. By that you are reconciled to God. More than that, it tells me that the struggles of the early church, the harshness of the Old Testament, and even the teachings of the Apostles and Paul's Epistles, were only ways of getting all of us to see that simple message. I believe there is a spiritual component to this life, but the stories and claims of Christianity are not its explanation, beyond that one simple truth. The rest of the teachings of Christianity are no longer my focus ... the prophecies, the judgement, the doctrines. They're interesting, but in truth, all I want is to see if there is a way to know God by following the one commandment Jesus gave, which is why I can't be pastor of a Christian church and at the same time, be true to myself and the people who come here."

AJ looked off and away in deep thought. In a moment he inclined his head. "Makes a lot of sense," he said, almost to himself.

Sarah's eyes shot to him. Her expression was surprisingly disconcerting. She regarded him for a moment, then looked back to her father. "I'm sorry, dad, but I still don't see the issue. There is a lot at stake here. What are you going to do? What am I going to do if you walk away from everything we've worked so hard for? And I think it's fair to include myself in this. I have a Master's in Divinity, dad. Divinity!" She began rifling through her purse for a tissue, which she found and then used to wipe her nose. "I know I should have thought ahead – that I should have made my own way rather than always depend on you, but I didn't. I just never dreamed that anything like this was coming." She laughed pathetically. "I'll be lucky to get a job at the corner grocery store." Her breath caught for a moment before she could continue. "It's big, dad. It's big for everyone – all of us. The board of this church won't exactly hoist me onto their shoulders and parade me around the building when you resign. Sometimes I think they'd burn me at the stake if they could."

"That's not true, Sarah, and you know it," Owen said, gently. "Poison is a much cleaner solution."

Sarah laughed reluctantly. "Oh, you made me laugh. Dang it," she said, exasperated. "This time we can't laugh our problems away."

"I'm not sure I agree, Sarah. Sometimes you can't know what the right thing is. All you can do is sidestep the things you know not to be. Maybe it will mean something if I tell you what my hopes are in all this," he said, his demeanor suddenly becoming visibly lighter. "I hope that by seeing my mistakes and correcting them rather than hiding from them or pretending they aren't there, I'll discover a better way: that these are birthing pains of a new, good thing – not the death throes of what has been. We can't know what it is, what it looks like, even what to call it until we see it, but we're about to see it. I'd like to believe that, Sarah. It just seems right to me."

AJ's heart went out to her. He could see that her father's consoling words were not finding their mark. *I'll take care of you*, he wanted to say, but couldn't. It just wouldn't fit.

The Pastor's voice brought him back. "Let's get to the bottom of what we have, Sarah. Let's step back and look at what we have rather than what we want to insist we have. Once we get to that, we'll know what our options are." He reached out and touched her arm. "We'll be fine. I mean it." Sarah was clearly not soothed by any of it. He signed. "Maybe it was ill-advised of me to bring all of this up."

Sarah looked down at her lap as if wishing the entire world would go away. While her eyes were averted, Owen passed a knowing look to AJ, as if the situation itself completed his point. AJ only nodded.

"I don't understand this. I just don't, and mom wouldn't have either," Sarah said, in a statement that seemed like the boiling over of what had begun as a private thought.

"I'm sorry I've upset you, Sarah, but your mother did understand," Owen said. "You should know, just as she did, that the very same desire to know the truth, to be honest with others and myself, and you, that brought me into the ministry in the first place, is now pressing me out of it. I have been driven all my life by the search for truth. Honestly, I don't even know why. I can't explain it, and never could. But I won't be a fake, and I won't be dishonest."

AJ decided to take the opportunity to let the two of them continue in private. "Sarah, why don't we do dinner on another night?" he said.

She didn't look up. "Okay, maybe that would be best."

AJ nodded again to the Pastor, then left without saying anything further.

Chapter 21

February 10, 2024

Emerging into the afternoon sun for a late lunch, AJ noticed a white car parked next to his truck at the far end of the lot of the home improvement store where he worked. It took only a of couple seconds to realize it was Sarah. He squinted. Small though she was, her form was clearly visible behind the wheel. He picked up his pace. She was looking into her lap and didn't notice him until he had almost reached the car. She smiled tentatively on seeing him and AJ opened the passenger door.

"Hey! This is a surprise," he said happily, but it took only the briefest moment for him to realize that something was wrong. "Is everything okay?"

She hesitated, struggling against some unseen pain. "Not exactly," she said. "AJ, I'm very sorry, but I'm afraid I have to tell you something."

All traces of the grin that had accompanied AJ to the car vanished. He got in and closed the door. "Are you okay? Did something happen?"

"I'm so sorry, AJ, but I don't think things are going to work out between us." It took a moment for her words to find footing. He looked at her blankly, his mind searching for alternative meanings of her statement. There weren't any. "AJ, I'm sorry. You heard my dad last night. Things are about to change for me in a big way, and right or wrong, I've built my life on that church; faith – all of it. Now my dad, who was the one who brought me into everything to start with, is – I don't know – giving up. When I heard the two of you talking last night I knew you were having the same doubts. That would make two people – two important people in my life – turning away from something that is too big a part of mine to ignore."

AJ only partially heard her, now looking out the windshield in disbelief. It was amazing how only a few words could change the world – and in a matter of seconds. He became numbly aware of the mundane happenings around him. The sun streaming in through the window, a mother and child making their way towards the doors of the store, a contrail slowly unfolding itself across the blue sky drawn by an airplane too distant to see. When he returned to himself, Sarah was silent. Her eyes glistened with unshed tears, but she appeared resolute. He took a deep breath. "You've thought this through?"

"I have," she said. The words were not entirely convincing, but they were convincing enough.

"Fascinating," he said, sarcastically. "Well then, I guess that's that. It didn't occur to you to talk with me about it first? To you, it's best to throw our relationship overboard as a precaution?" She didn't respond. "Good, that. Better safe than sorry, right?" An edge had come into his tone, unbidden, but there was nothing he could do about it. He grunted and returned to his survey of the lot.

"You have no way of knowing, Sarah, how well all of this fits with what I have come to expect from this world." He shook his head almost imperceptibly, then looked out the window at nothing in particular again. "You are under a lot of pressure. I'm sorry for that, but here's some advice for posterity: when you find yourself in a tight spot, the answer is not to sever ties with people who care about you." He paused, looking into his lap. "I don't know, maybe you've made the right choice. When it comes to faith, I don't know where I am, you're right about that." He gave her a final sidelong glance. "I hope you've thought this through." Then, more to himself than to her: "I knew better," he said, then opened the door and got out.

"I'm so sorry, AJ," Sarah said. She may have said more, but whatever it had been was cut short by the door closing.

At that moment, AJ wanted few things in life more than to get away from her but didn't want to look too flustered in doing it. As smoothly as he could, he sorted through his keyring, opened the door of his truck and got in. He wheeled away without looking back.

An unexpected clarity came over him. In a matter of seconds, he knew what he would do.

Chapter 22

February 13, 2024

Writing the pulse sequencing software was even easier than Clipper had expected. The system was already designed to allow gravity tests to be executed on demand, and even supported configurable parameters for all the values, including power and duration. Building a Python script to execute commands in sequence amounted to only a few lines of code. He had thought about the problem throughout the day and realized that completing the simple modifications could take as little as a few minutes.

He was seated in his usual place in the lab, putting the finishing touches on the small script when Riley entered and pulled up a chair.

"How's it going?" Riley asked.

"Pretty good. The script itself is trivial. That part's mostly done. Now I'm looking at the bands themselves to map pulses to the signal. I've made it so we can express the values as a series of ones and zeros, where zeros are the troughs and the ones are the plateaus." He opened a paper notebook sitting on the table. "I drew this earlier," he said, pointing to a diagram. It showed a horizontal line broken by a series of right angles so that it looked something like the crenelated top of a castle battlement. On the sections of the line that formed the top of the crenels, Clipper had written a *one*. In the opposite sections, within the crenels, were *zeros*. "Now I'm just trying to get the sequence right."

"No need, I've already done that," Riley said. "It's a string of sixteen octets. The first four and the last four appear to be control numbers. I think the middle eight must be synchronization and acknowledgement bits." He laid a tablet on the table. "Here's what I came up with. The top line is their signal translated into binary form. I put the hyphens in to make it easier to read. The bottom line is the same value in hexadecimal format, so it's a little more manageable."

1111 0000 1100 0011-0000 0000 0000 0001-0000 0000 0000 0000-1100 0011 0000 1111

F0C3 0001 0000 C30F

"Ah, perfect," Clipper said, picking up the tablet, relieved that the tedious work had already been done. "This'll speed things up. If they're always going to use octets, then it'll be easier if I make this script capable of using them too. It'll save us typing and we'll be less prone to mistakes."

"Agreed," Riley said. "Notice that the first four octets are the reverse of the last four, at a binary level."

"Yes," Clipper said, "makes sense. Those must be boundary identifiers for the overall data packet."

"That was my guess as well," Riley said. "They probably also denote the type of record it is – the type of data it contains. Like I said, this appears to be a synchronization request; just a very simple one."

Clipper said: "That would mean that the first number after the starting marker is one, and the second octet is zero – probably where the acknowledgement bits go. Do you want to respond with the exact value they sent, or since this appears to be a sync request, go ahead and increment the acknowledgement bit?"

"I'm guessing they'll expect us to increment, but I'd like to start by just repeating the same value back. See what happens," Riley said.

"You got it. Give me fifteen minutes to modify the script to handle the hex values. After that, we'll be ready to give it a whirl. How about the power? What should we drop to?"

"This won't be super scientific, but from what I can tell, I think we should be able to drop to about 10% on power, just like we discussed."

"Okay," Clipper nodded. "And if we drop the ingress and egress durations correspondingly, we'll go from 500 milliseconds to 50, both ways."

"Maybe," Riley said. "but let's see what happens if we take the duration down to zero milliseconds. My guess is that the natural latency between pulses will be enough to delineate each value. If it works, that'll get us to ten octets per second improvement on throughput. That break in power will have the effect of producing the troughs for us."

"You don't want any delay between the octets, then?" Clipper asked.

"I don't think we'll need them, since we're ramping up and down like we are. Our signal will be rounded – more sinusoid – but I think it'll get the job done. I'll leave you to get the mods finished," Riley said. "Want anything to drink?"

"Coke Zero," Clipper said, without looking up from the terminal.

Riley left to get the drinks, and when he returned, found Clipper leaning back in his chair talking casually with Melissa, who had taken a chair next to him. The sight of her made him smile. He approached. "I was about to offer something for you to drink, too," he said to her, "but I see you're covered."

She was holding a refillable water bottle, and held it up slightly. "Thank you anyway, but I'm good." Riley handed the Coke Zero to Clipper, then took a sip of his own Diet Coke.

"Have you brought Melissa into the loop on what we're about to do here?" Riley asked.

"In fact, I have, and you should know that she was impressed with your conclusions that this is a type of very elementary sync request. And also feels, by the way, that we should increment the acknowledgement octet to one."

"You're right," Riley allowed. "I'd just like to try the other way first as an experiment."

"You're the boss," she said, as if she didn't hold a strong opinion either way. "But, how come?"

Riley inclined his head. "In a nutshell, I want to know whether this pulse approach will work the way we want before actually sending a correct acknowledgement. If we're wrong, and sending the response as a series of pulses doesn't work, then we may see a full acknowledgement for each pulse we send. You know what I mean? If we send thirty-two pulses and then after seven seconds we start seeing a flood of thirty-two signals back, it'll mean that they didn't recognize the individual pulses as a group that belongs to one message. If, on the other hand, we send all thirty-two and receive only one response, then the sender at least understood that the pulses were part of the same message."

"Or they may have acknowledged only the last one," she added. "Clever, but wouldn't you know the same either way?"

"Probably," Riley said, patiently, "but, this will separate the questions very clearly. This will just keep things clean. We'll take it one step at a time." He turned to Clipper. "Am I to conclude, Mr. Clipper, that you are taking your ease because you have completed your tasks?" Riley said, lightheartedly.

"Indeed, sir, I have." He motioned towards the computer terminal. Riley looked to see that the appropriate command was already entered. All that remained was to start it going with the press of the enter key. "Fire when ready," Clipper said.

"No time like the present."

"Righteo," Clipper said, pressing the enter key. Ones and zeros, the binary form of the hexadecimal values he entered onto the command line, streamed across the terminal in a burst. It took about three seconds. They waited the additional seven seconds, the typical interval between a signal and a response, to see if anything would come back. It did. "Looks like we have an answer, per usual," Clipper said. "And appears to be only one – not 32. Good news. It'll take a couple seconds for the imaging software to render the gravity print, then we'll be able to see if anything has changed." Clipper typed terse commands into the terminal and in a few seconds the image appeared. All three leaned in for a closer look at the striated bands.

"Hard to tell visually like this–" Melissa said, mostly to herself. "Looks the same."

"Agreed," Riley said. "Clip let's send back the following: F0C3 0001 0002 C30F. That's their last sync value of two with a new acknowledgement value of one."

"On it." He keyed in the new command, then looked to Riley, "Send?"

"Let fly."

Clipper set about the task with practiced ease. The few seconds ticked by, as before, as the many complex wheels turned to carry out the commands. It involved work on behalf of the computer in the datacenter in the subbasement of the building, plus sending the instructions 60 miles to the Installation to be carried out by the gravitational field generator. It all worked flawlessly, as it always had. Within a few moments a new image was on the screen. Clipper moved the playhead marker back and forth along the image timeline, searching for the return signal at its typical place. "The hell?" he said.

"What is it?" Riley asked.

"I don't see a response."

"No response?"

"None. This is the first time – ever – that I haven't received one after a gravitation event."

"Any chance we've dropped the power enough that we're on the lower edge of their ability to receive? Maybe they barely caught the last transmission, and this one was too degraded by the time it reached them. Let's trying increasing power by 25–"

"What's everyone looking at?" an unexpected voice said from behind them. The three, who were now huddled towards the computer terminal in rapt attention, stood erect, startled. It was Brian Matthews. No one had seen him enter. "Something exciting, I hope. Sure looks that way."

The moment stretched for an awkward few seconds before Riley spoke. "Good morning, Mr. Matthews. How are you?"

"Couldn't be better. You?"

"We're fiddling with the power levels on the gravitation machines. We've been running at about 5,000 watts, now we're coming down to about 10% of that to see what happens."

Matthews demeanor remained cheerful but seemed a thin veneer over deep suspicion. "Ms. Ulrich, I hate to stand on protocol here, but I wasn't aware you were NDA'd on Springboard."

Melissa was clearly caught off guard, but Riley intervened. "This is my doing," he said. "We learned by chance while the EcoGrid team was here doing some tests a few weeks ago that Melissa has expertise in wave propagation. She's helping us tune the gravity fields. My mistake not to bring her under NDA. I'll do so now, if you approve."

Matthews looked at Riley and Melissa warily before answering. "Of course," he said, as his eyes drifted towards the display. He looked for a moment at the screen without speaking, which a few seconds before, would have shown the striated bands of the prior, incoming signal. Riley didn't look, and tried not to show the relief he felt that the bands had chosen this time to stop coming in. He hoped Clipper and Melissa could keep it together as well. "Learning anything?" Brian asked.

"It's early," Riley said. "We just did our first test a few minutes ago. It occurred to me to see what might happen if we created a series of gravity pulses in succession. We haven't had a chance to look at the results. I don't expect anything super interesting on that front, but an easy thing to try, so I thought we would."

"Sounds interesting," Brian said. "Let me know if anything turns up. Have a good one." He looked away from the image and scanned the three of them again before turning and walking away without further comment.

"Thanks, you too," Riley said to the man's back as he strode across the lab floor. Riley then turned back to Clipper and Melissa. "Let's continue. If we break off now, it'll look worse than it already does." Both nodded and returned to peering at the image. "So, did something go wrong?" Riley asked.

"Verifying now," Clipper said. He was typing at the keyboard. Strange text covered the screen. "Logs show that the signal went out okay. I can't imagine that it wasn't received. It always has been."

"Can you take us to the exact frame where we should have seen the response?"

"Sure," Clipper said, moving the mouse pointer over the image and dragging the playhead into position. In a moment, he started shaking his head slowly. "We're empty, boss. Signal is gone."

"Let's try again," Riley said.

"Increment the acknowledgement octet before sending?" Clipper asked.

Riley thought about it, then looked to Melissa. "What do you think?"

"Technically, we're still trying to acknowledge their last signal. I say we stay with the same value."

"Agree," Riley said. "Let's just send the same string back to them, but with 25% power."

Clipper made the adjustments and sent the command. They waited. No response.

"Damn!" Riley said. "Were we recording per usual?"

"Always," Clipper said.

"Okay. Let's take a closer look, but later, not here."

"Copy that," Clipper said, with a glance at the door where Matthews had left only a few seconds before.

"We'll talk later. Figure out where to go next," Riley said. He turned for the door and Melissa followed. He hadn't necessarily expected that, but seeing it, said: "Well, you're officially NDA'd on Springboard; or will be as soon as we can get your signature."

"Yeah, I'm excited," she said.

"And, I appreciate your help on this. Would you be up for dinner as a thank you?"

"That sounds good," she said.

Chapter 23

February 13, 2024

P astor Henson's white Chevrolet pickup truck was sitting under the church canopy as usual, with two other cars parked against the curb behind it. One had to belong to Linda, AJ guessed, but the other he didn't recognize. He wheeled his truck around the lot and into the nearest spot.

It had been a long time – years, in fact – since he last felt the now-familiar sting of love's disappointments. The sense of loss that persisted even when the cognitive parts of the brain were occupied with other things; an aching tooth settled into a recliner at the edge of the mind, licking its thumb and leisurely turning the pages of its magazine, but refusing to leave.

It had weighed more and more heavily on him of late, that his life had not taken the shape he had expected it would by now; in his late twenties. His two best childhood friends had gone away following school and were now, as far as he could tell, rising stars at Mayfield Hammond. *Mayfield Hammond!* The company was a household name. And here he was, manager of a lumber yard at the local home improvement store. He had never meant for that to be a permanent, or even marginally long-term vocation. He took the job as a stop-gap, as something to bring in money while he decided what really to do with his life. The problem was that it had been a year-and-a-half and he was still here – and nothing seemed to be taking shape at all.

He had allowed himself to become distracted. It was so clear to him now; he had begun to settle into life, but it was the wrong time for it. He must first shape his life into something better suited for the long haul before settling into it.

Sarah's break-up had almost instantaneously jolted him into the gritty realization that his idle plans, his expectation that life would somehow resolve itself into a coherent path all by itself, was wrong. He couldn't expect the opportunities of life to present themselves on a menu, from which he could choose roast beef and cheddar, or turkey and Swiss, a blonde and a ranch or a brunette and a townhome. He had a Master's in Economics from Duke. He was upwardly mobile. The time had come to get started.

Despite the fresh pain, his rational mind knew that what he had – all this time – been afraid to admit could be love, was probably 80 percent emotion. Yes, he probably did love her, but not as much or as deeply as his heart was insisting in its pathetic, shuttering whine at this moment. He would have to endure the ebb of his feelings as they slowly, painfully bled out from him, but they eventually would. And once the emotion of it was under control the kernel of true love – the part that could live on within him for years if he was stupid enough to allow it – could begin the long process of pearlizing into something he could live with.

He needed to grow up, to put his education to work, and the time was now.

It suddenly occurred to him to wonder what his parents would think when he told them that he was going to move away, to start something new. Probably, that it was about time. Wow, how embarrassing. His parents had probably been waiting for him to do something real for over a year. He saw that now.

Well, it was time, and he would do it.

AJ walked into the unlocked church foyer with the key to the front doors in hand. He would drop off the key and take the remainder of the afternoon off from work. It occurred to him to wonder about Sarah's timing as he entered the thankfully-empty sanctuary. Why had the woman chosen lunch rather than telling him later in the day, after work?

The answer was irritatingly simple. It was the earliest opportunity. She had probably made her decision the night before and couldn't wait to close the loop on their relationship. The thought of it made him angry anew. He felt a flush of embarrassment at having spent so much of his day thinking about her. While he had been pondering their relationship and fretting over what was in store for her at the church, she was probably watching the clock, anxiously waiting to eject him from her life.

He made his way towards the office area where he was sure the Pastor and whoever else was in the building would be, and walked in to find Linda Stricklin on the phone. She gave a somewhat startled look on seeing him, then smiled and motioned for him to sit. She had no way of knowing, of course, that that was not a prospect for him.

"Yes, I know," Linda said into the phone, chuckling. "I know!" she said again, louder this time. AJ laid the church key on the desk next to her and then pointed to the door, to let her know that he was leaving and didn't need to talk with anyone. When Linda saw it, her face formed into a question as clear as if she had spoken it aloud. "Hey, can I get back with you in a few minutes?" she said into the phone. "Someone just stopped in. Yes, that'll be fine. Bye." She hung up.

"You don't want the key anymore?" Linda wore the puzzled expression of a person who had just witnessed someone finding a $100 bill, then throwing it away.

"I no longer need it," AJ said, searching for a way to get out of the building without being pulled into a long discussion, or even a short one.

"You never know when it will come in handy. You may as well hold onto it," she persisted.

"Well, the truth is that I'm making plans to move out of the area. It'll be a few weeks, but I'm starting to make a few changes now," he said, then started for the door, forcing a non-convincing smile.

"What's going on, AJ?" a voice called to him from behind.

AJ turned to see the Pastor standing in the doorway of his office. "Hello, Pastor. I was just telling Linda that I'm making plans to move away."

The man paused a moment before speaking. "Really," he said, rhetorically. He had a disconcerting way of looking into a person that gave appearances that he already knew everything he wanted to know, and that his audible questions were a formality he endured for the sake of whoever he was talking with. AJ stood looking back at the man, determined not to let the searching gaze rattle him. "I'd sure like to talk for a moment, if you can spare the time," the Pastor said.

A voice in AJ's head objected irritably to that. It was just what he did not want to do. The request was a fair one, he knew, but that was not enough to make him want to accommodate it. "Oh, I'm sorry Pastor," he said, regretfully, as if unseen pressures precluded the possibility. "I really need to get going."

The man held his gaze. "I wouldn't want to make you late for anything AJ, but if you could, just a few seconds to help me understand what you're planning would be appreciated." The man was stolid. By appearances, always self-possessed, always in control, and with the capacity to grasp and process the world in a measured, methodical way. It was like he forced the world to slow to his pace rather than the other way around, and somehow, forced anyone around him as well. He was doing it now.

AJ would not give in, he told himself, but in a moment considered changing his mind. The silent voice was still there, angry and trapped, demanding that he leave, but AJ ignored the impulse. The Pastor looked concerned – possibly as concerned as AJ had ever seen him. He would give the man a few minutes. Nodding, AJ started toward the office without speaking. The Pastor stepped out of his way as he entered and then closed the door behind them. The clicking of the latch had barely faded before the Pastor spoke. "AJ, I hope this isn't because of our conversation last night. You can imagine the tough spot that would put me in."

"I'm sorry Pastor, but in fact it is. Sarah caught me in the parking lot as I was leaving for lunch and ended our relationship." The Pastor's expression revealed that the news was not what he expected. He opened his mouth, then closed it again. AJ went on. "For what it's worth Pastor, nothing you or anyone else said last night was even the least bit upsetting to me. Not your plans, or the reasons for them. But Sarah apparently sees things differently."

"Well, I don't quite know what to say AJ. This was my fault. But as someone who obviously knows Sarah very well, I must tell you that she is prone to rashness. I would be very surprised if the two of you couldn't patch things up, if you gave it a little time."

That possibility had not occurred to AJ. The breakup seemed to have such finality to it that he hadn't stopped to consider whether it really was. "Maybe you're right." AJ said, pausing to give the notion a moment of consideration, but then, as if a switch had been thrown within him, he set whatever he had been thinking aside and moved on to a new subject. "I've got to tell you, Pastor; there is something of a parallel between you and I that I hadn't noticed until Sarah broke things off with me. It may be thin, but it's there." AJ stopped himself and looked around the room, "Can we speak freely here?"

The Pastor shrugged. "One of the few requirements a Pastor has is a confidential place to talk. He may not always have a congregation, or even new shoes, but a place to speak privately, that he will."

AJ nodded, but lowered his voice just the same. "If I heard you last night, you basically said that the experiences and lessons of the last twenty years of your life have produced a man who is no longer a fit for the life he has built for himself. You haven't abandoned anything; the time has simply come for you to pull together your life experiences, the things you've built, the influence you have gained, and form it into a platform that you can now climb onto and stand upon. It is a new station, a new plateau for you. It's your new life. To stay where you are, to refuse to move on would be to ignore the potential of where all that you have gained could take you. Here's the parallel. I'm a young man who has spent a fortune on education, but I have yet to put it to work. I'm not particularly worried about that, but I have collected and built some platforms of my own. Honestly, Pastor, I'm not sure if I fell in love with Sarah or not. I think I did – it certainly feels that way. But if nothing else comes of it, her breaking up with me did – and in a very few minutes – wake me up. I had come to see this church as a second home. It's odd really, I'm not even all that social with the people here. But think about it," he lowered his voice almost to a whisper. "You are leaving soon anyway, if I heard you right last night. And–" he stopped as an unexpected catch in his throat cut off his words, "Sarah is already gone."

The Pastor regarded him in silence for a long moment. "AJ, I don't want to pry into your personal life, or Sarah's, but could I ask about the reasons she gave?"

"You could probably guess. She said that I appeared to share many of your doubts about the faith. She said that having two people in her life with doubts like that was not something she could afford. That's the way I heard it, anyway."

The Pastor looked around the room thoughtfully, as if searching for something he had already searched for unsuccessfully countless times before. "I'm afraid your relationship with Sarah may be the first of many casualties, AJ. I'm sorry it spilled over onto you."

"Don't be. I was headed here. Nothing has happened that wasn't always going to happen. If Sarah doesn't have room for me, all the better I find out now."

"No hard feelings, huh?" the Pastor asked.

AJ raised an eyebrow. "Well, my head is doing better than my heart at the moment, if you must know. She's your daughter, so I guess I should watch how I say this, but she got me pretty good. I'll just leave it at that."

"Fair enough," the Pastor said, then grunted. "The girl's head is filled with concrete."

An unexpected silence filled the room after that. A short one, but deep. The kind in which the underworld of normally-unnoticed sounds like creaking floorboards, pencil lead scratching over paper, and the babbling of coffee pouring into a cup, opportunistically steals into the world of noise. A clock from somewhere over AJ shoulder ticked loudly and he briefly reflected on how rare mechanical clocks were anymore – working ones, anyway. If any person would be likely to have one, though, AJ supposed it would be the Pastor. He also knew, without looking, that the clock would be set to the correct time. Something like that can say a lot about a man. Mechanical clocks don't stay on time or keep running by themselves – not for long. AJ found it interesting that the Pastor took the time to maintain it, and for reasons he couldn't quite pinpoint.

Some things are tools of self-discipline and others are products of it. AJ found himself musing over the question. Did the man wind the clock as a way to keep himself sharp, alert, and methodical; or did he do it because he was already all of those things? AJ began, inexplicably, suspecting the former; that the clock was a chore – self-imposed, but demanding. The man was forced to remember it, to maintain it, to keep it alive – it had become a hard-point in his life, a hinge of some kind around which other parts of his life swung reluctantly, perhaps even in protest. Suddenly, AJ knew – how, he wasn't sure, neither why he should care enough to give it a second thought – that the Pastor hated the clock. Family heirloom or not, and regardless of what cherished memories may be attached to it, the Pastor now secretly hated it, but just the same, could not part with it.

AJ collected himself and pushed thoughts of the clock away. He wasn't sure how his mind had managed to conjure so much from so little. It was stupid. No, it was Sarah. She had him off his balance. "Whether what you say is true or it isn't – about Sarah maybe changing her mind," AJ said, "I don't think I can wait."

The Pastor didn't respond, and AJ leaned towards the door as if to leave, but the clock reasserted itself. He stopped. He could see it now. Sure enough, it was old-looking, just as he expected – maybe it was too loud to be new. Some kind of dark wood, ornate, with a large white face, aged to a look of yellowing paper. A mantle clock, perhaps. It had endured some mishap in its past. Part of the decorative wood that scrolled down its right side had been chipped – quite badly, once you noticed it. Repairs had been undertaken, but they hadn't aged well – not as well as the rest of the clock. They probably looked fine at first. "How often do you wind the clock?" AJ asked.

The Pastor didn't answer immediately. He quirked an eyebrow inquisitively, like a person measuring the intentions of an opponent who had just made a deceptive move during a game of Chess. "Every morning," he finally answered without elaborating.

"How about Saturdays?"

"Saturdays too."

AJ nodded thoughtfully. "None of my business, Pastor, but I think you should leave the clock when you embark on your new life. Free yourself from it."

AJ left the office, the Pastor watching him blankly as he went. He said another goodbye to Linda, too, as he passed. He had noticed that she never made her return phone call, and wondered vaguely whether the Pastor's office was as private as he believed.

AJ headed out of the church for the last time. If he ever returned here, he thought, it would not be as a member of the congregation. In a few days, the taillights of his truck would pass beyond the last outlying hills of Kansas City proper, and he would never call it home again.

Kansas City would, indeed, stop being his home soon, but for reasons far different than he could ever guess.

Chapter 24

February 16, 2024

Melissa's apartment was on the second floor. Riley ascended the two half-flights of stairs in the waning hours of the Friday evening daylight and approached to find a simple, but tasteful welcome mat outside the door with a potted plant to one side. It was a warm, and fitting sight to who he knew Melissa to be.

He knocked at the door, which opened momentarily to reveal Melissa in stylish blue jeans that sported several factory-worn spots on the legs where white threading was visible, some torn completely so that parts of her skin were visible beneath. Not overdone, just a balance of fashion that he immediately found unnerving. A mauve colored t-shirt with a large Mackinac Island logo across the front, worn over a long-sleeved gray shirt, completed the outfit.

She was even more beautiful than he had realized, which was something that had not escaped his notice even before this. Riley quickly realized, with more than a little embarrassment, that the sight of her had left him speechless. Her smile was the finishing touch to a picture that he could not have found more captivating, and he could only hope that his mouth hadn't been agape while he had been lost in the grip of the spell she had unexpectedly cast over him. Her smile, however, made it as clear as if she had spoken the words aloud that it was to no avail. She had seen it all. Her eyes reflected the subtle but unmistakable fact that she had read every thought that had passed through his feeble mind. Abandoning all hope of dignity, he shook his head almost imperceptibly, only once, as if trying to find the words to describe a work of art. "You're wonderful," he said.

The statement gave her pause, and her eyes turned playfully inquisitive. "Thank you, Mr. Riley. I happen to think the same about you."

"I can't imagine why," he said, recovering. "But, I'll take it."

"Will you come in?" she asked.

"Love to."

Riley could have described the apartment before seeing it. It was a reflection of Melissa to the finest detail. Spotless, first and foremost. Understated. And in the tones of white and off-white colors that gave the space an airy sense of endless sunny Spring afternoons. Riley shortly became disgusted with himself as his mind went involuntarily in search of an explanation for Melissa's not already being in a relationship. She was gorgeous, unencumbered, self-reliant and… gorgeous. No explanation was forthcoming. He shook the thought.

"Your place is very nice," he said. "I'm now officially embarrassed for every moment you've spent in mine. But," he said, looking around, "there's no way I'll be able to keep pace with you on that front, so I'll go ahead and forfeit now."

"You have a nice place, John," she said with customary courtesy, but the point bore no further deliberation.

"Thank you for the charity," he said, smiling. "I don't know if you have anything specific in mind for dinner. I have reservations over at Nelson's Steakhouse, but it's about an hour out." he said, checking his watch.

"That sounds very good," she said. "How about a glass of wine then? We'll head over in a while. It's only about a fifteen-minute drive from here, I think."

"Perfect." Soon, they were sitting comfortably at opposite ends of the white sofa, facing each other with shining glasses of Riesling white wine in hand.

"Thanks for the invitation to dinner, John. I've been looking forward to it."

"My pleasure," he said. "I'm glad you and Clip had the chance encounter in the lab. Otherwise, this may never have happened."

"Me too," she said, with her natural grace. "I've had more fun over the past few days than I have in, I don't know how long. Getting to know both of you has been fun and the gravitation work has been fascinating." She looked at him thoughtfully for a moment, then to her wine glass. The moment lingered pleasantly. "This is it, isn't?" she said, almost reluctantly. "The moment we start to learn whether we have anything in common other than the shared interests of work."

Riley inclined his head, acknowledging the point. "I suppose it is. Let's see … so far, I like the wine." He then glanced again around the apartment, "and you're a fantastic decorator. And we agree on what makes a good place to eat on a first social evening."

"Not bad," she said. "You're better at small talk than I would have guessed."

"Thanks. For what little practice I've had, I'm rather pleased myself." He smiled again, and she grinned thoughtfully, as if working this new, previously unseen lighter side into her overall impression of him.

"So you and Clipper grew up together?"

Riley nodded, amused, as if mention of Clipper immediately brought a host of good memories to mind. "Yes. He and I and another guy named Andrew Jacobs, who we call AJ, all grew up together. It was an unlikely group in a lot of ways, but we hung together through the years. I'd say the three of us are as close to brothers as you can get. We literally had a secret handshake."

Melissa laughed. "Oh, I would love to see that."

"Won't occur," Riley said, with unconvincing finality.

"Okay. I'll let that go – for now," she said, grinning mischievously. "I'd love to have friends like that. I've had friends over the years, but never anything that turned long-term or sisterly in any way."

"Sorry to hear it," Riley said. "I take AJ and Clipper for granted anymore."

"Where is AJ now?"

"He's back in Kansas City – a suburb of Kansas City, actually. He went to Duke out of high school. Walked out with a Master's in Economics, then went back home. He's not sure what he wants to do, I think."

"With a degree like that from Duke, he can do anything he wants, I would guess."

"No doubt. I think that could be part of what made him go back home – to take a breath before stepping into his career. He knows his options are wide open. As a matter of fact, Clip just told me that AJ is planning to head our way for a visit soon. You'll get a chance to meet him if you want."

"I'd love to," Melissa said.

"So, where did you grow up?" Riley asked.

"Here," she said. "My folks live about ten minutes from here. My dad was a Software Architect for a big part of his career. He's Director of Software Development at a company over town right now, and my mom is an Executive Admin for one of the VP's over at Bank of America."

"Interesting," Riley said. "So, how about you? What are your aspirations?"

"Good question," Melissa said, taking a sip of wine. "I don't really know. In the near-term, just to do well I guess. Mayfield suits me for now. The EcoGrid work is fun."

"Sounds like a good place to be. You may be more content by nature than me," Riley said. "I have a bad habit of strategizing through every moment. Not particularly for career advancement; maybe more to just make sense of everything."

Melissa's expression turned playful again. "Am I to understand that you are strategizing against me at this very moment?" Melissa's words seemed to surprise even her, and Riley suspected that if she could take them back she would. Being too late for that, she waited expectantly for him to respond.

Riley regarded her thoughtfully for a long moment. "I suppose I am," he said. "But, of a rarity, my strategy is not to figure you out or even to understand you, but to enjoy being with you and hope that you enjoy being with me."

"Wow, you are good at this," she laughed.

"Who knew?" Riley said, then laughed as well.

She hesitated in a moment of contemplation as if deciding whether to share something more. "Not sure what would be good timing for this," she said, "so I think I may as well come out with it early on. I married my high school sweetheart my junior year of college," she said, suddenly more serious. "It lasted four years. We went our separate ways about three years ago."

"Sorry to hear that."

"It's okay, I just wanted you to know. Regardless of where the road ahead may lead – even if it's to nowhere, I wanted to get that out onto the table. The good news is that it didn't go bad in any catastrophic way. Randy is a good guy. It's not like the whole thing is some horribly dark episode of my life. We just realized after a few years that we had made a mistake. No kids. No ties. We decided it was for the best."

Riley nodded. "My only hope would be that you're happy with your decision."

"Oh yes," she said. "It was a good thing."

"Well, I have no past," Riley said. "No relationships of consequence, unless you count Clip and AJ, which I don't," he laughed. She did too.

"Really? No relationships of note? None?" she pressed.

"Is it a requirement that the feelings were mutual, or that the woman knew I existed? If not, then I have a long and impressive list to share; Jennifer Lawrence, Scarlett Johansson, just to name a couple."

She was laughing again. "Sorry, John, I'm afraid that won't do."

"Rats," he said. "Then, no, not really. Nothing that was ever serious – at least not for her. I had a high school sweetheart too. College sent us in opposite directions. She met someone and ended up marrying."

"Sounds painful."

Riley shrugged. "At the time, yes. I think it was for the best in the end."

"Okay. Turnabout is fair play," she said, redirecting the conversation back towards a lighter path. "What are your aspirations?"

"Wow, two tough questions in a row," Riley said, shifting in his chair. She only sipped her wine patiently. "That question could have a few answers, I guess. There's probably a 'first date friendly' version – I'll shoot for that. In a nutshell – although I'm not sure I've ever thought of it in these terms – I think I may have spent too much of my life looking at the wrong things. Had I stayed with what I would think of as more typical interests and questions, I would probably have been content to move along professionally, living a good life, storing up for a nondescript future of comfort and leisure. Instead, the things that caught my attention as a young man were the parts of the world that we knew least about. Where are we? Where did it all come from? How does the Universe work? You know, all the typical geeky questions. And they're not philosophical, by the way, not for me. They're physical. I wasn't content not to at least try to answer some of them, not that I'm making bold predictions about doing so. In the end, that has a lot to do with where I am, what I do, and where I hope to go. I spend a fair amount of time reading, keeping up on things. And, I like to cook."

"Cook, huh? Me too. Anything in particular?"

"Not really," Riley said. "I like Italian. Seafood. I don't do a lot of red meats but enjoy a good steak now and then."

"Well, there's a common interest," Melissa said, tipping her wine glass towards Riley. "I enjoy cooking too; and I would probably describe my tastes the same way. I also like afternoon drives, mainly out to small towns. I'll stop and look through antique or consignment shops here and there, eat at a cafe I've never been to before, and just enjoy being away from everything. I tend not to buy antique furniture, but I make little finds to use in my decorating." She motioned to a picture on the wall. "I found that picture at a place outside of Lauren? No Laurel? Laurel Hill last year. Five dollars. My most recent find," she said, turning in her chair, "was that vase. I found it a few weeks ago. I was out by Norwood, east of here. It was a big spend. Thirty dollars. The lady wouldn't come down a penny."

Riley nodded appreciably. "I haven't done many antique shops, but sounds fun."

"Yeah, well, another thing you find in consignment shops is books. If you like James Patterson, Danielle Steel, John Grisham, Stephen King; you know, any of the mainstream writers, you'll find hardcover books that go for twenty-five dollars, new, in like-new condition for fifty cents each. They're everywhere."

"No kidding."

The dialogue continued, eventually turning away from the 'what's your favorite color' questions of early relationships to the relaxed and comfortable conversations of living. They made their way to the restaurant and, despite the crowd, were seated without much delay due to their advanced reservations.

"Good thinking on calling ahead," Melissa said as they were escorted through the press of humanity in the entryway, and further into the quieter recesses of the large dining area where their table stood waiting. Seated, Melissa reflexively folded her cloth napkin onto her lap. "I won't press you, John," she said quietly, starting the conversation onto yet another new thread, "but I can see that you're worried about the signal."

He didn't respond at first. "I am," he said. "It may have been – without exaggeration – the most unexpected surprise of my life."

"Is it something that could cause an issue for your work? Is that what's worrying you?"

"Unfortunately, my thoughts on all of it are still half-baked. I have a couple theories on what's going on, but either way, the game has changed. The only way I know of for anyone to have made that signal is by the very technology I thought we were pioneering. Whether it ends up being the military or the North Charlotte chapter of the Freemasons, somebody out there has figured this out. Nothing I can do will change that. Moving ahead as if this hasn't happened, or isn't real, won't work either. My only goal at the moment is to understand who's doing it, and then I can think more about what it means. Until then, I'm flying blind."

"I said I wasn't going to press," Melissa said, "and I won't. I'll stop asking questions any time, just say the word; but you do know more about who this could be than you're sharing. Am I right?"

Riley leaned back and looked off and away as if the topic was a difficult one. "I've been at a loss for the most part. That's an honest answer." He looked back into her eyes. "I absolutely don't know who it is. What I will say is that some possibilities have occurred to me that are," he paused, in search of the right word. "Let's say, intriguing."

"But you won't divulge?"

"For reasons that could, if I'm outlandishly correct, become apparent soon."

"For what it's worth," she said, "I've wondered whether Matthews has another team already looking for ways to put your concepts to work on other things. Is it possible that we're picking up another Mayfield team?"

"That's a good thought," Riley said. "My only question then would be how they got so much better at it than us?"

"Yes, you're right," Melissa conceded. "It's not very likely."

They finished the evening on lighter topics, and by the time they said goodbye at Melissa's door the prevailing sentiment was that the evening had been a good one. Riley walked the short distance to his car and decided that it was time to upgrade from his Toyota Matrix to something with a little more power, and also more hospitable to any possible country outings that could present themselves in the weeks ahead.

Chapter 25

February 17, 2024

Riley and Clipper had been discussing the communication problem for only a few minutes before Melissa arrived at Riley's apartment. She tapped at the door, but didn't wait for a response before letting herself in. Amused, Clipper took a mental note to watch the two a little more closely, but knew better than to even look in Riley's direction at that moment. It would be too easy for Riley to guess what he was thinking.

"Hey guys," she said, clearly in a good mood. She was carrying a small grocery sack and made straight for the island counter in the kitchenette where she began unpacking its contents. "I have bowtie pasta, extra virgin olive oil, white button mushrooms–" she said, naming each item as she sat it on the counter.

By this time, Riley and Clipper had risen and walked the few paces to join her. "This is wonderful," Riley said. "What did it come to?"

"Don't be silly, this is my treat," she said. Neither Riley nor Clipper pressed the point. Sometimes it's best to know when to accept a kindness.

"Looks like whatever it is, it will be amazing," Riley said. He gestured towards the end of the counter. "We have a nice Cabernet ready to uncork when the time is right. We'll give it about 30 minutes to breathe."

"Going to be a great evening," Clipper put in, as he walked over to inspect the wine. "Very nice Bordeaux. Nicely done, Riley."

"Okay," Melissa said, "Riley, if you could start up the grill. I need a nice sear on the chicken. Clip, we need to halve the olives and slice the mushrooms. I'll get the pasta going, then start on the onions and zucchini."

"You got it," Clipper said.

"This is my mother's recipe. She called it Spicy Chicken Pasta, and it was my favorite growing up. Takes about 30 minutes, maybe a little better."

"Can't wait," Clipper said.

"Makes two of us," Riley said, before disappearing onto the balcony to start the grill.

Each one set to their tasks. The promise of good food and wine among friends made the mood light, and Clipper was a little surprised at how quickly Melissa had come to feel like part of the family. It had always been Riley and AJ. It was the three of them. Now, AJ was apparently getting serious with Sarah, who Clipper thought he may have remembered vaguely from some prior point in their childhood; and despite whether anything may or may not be happening between Melissa and Riley, Melissa was fun and easy to be around. She seemed a natural addition.

Riley went to stand next to Melissa at the counter once the food was ready to be served. "This dish has good color," he remarked as she spooned hearty portions onto three lemon-yellow plates.

"Thank you. My mom always thought about that kind of thing. In this recipe, it's the bright red tomatoes that give it that extra pop, so you have to add them in late, so they don't lose their color. The yellow dishes are perfect for accentuating the effect too, so that's an added plus."

"I'll see to the wine, then," he said, and headed off to uncork the bottle.

The conversation stayed light as they ate, with many kudos about the meal and wine passed along the way. Afterwards, Clipper insisted on cleaning up. The two protested customarily for a moment, then acquiesced. They sat on the couch in the living room, sipping wine and chatting casually.

Once Clipper had finished and rejoined them, wine glass in hand, it was Riley who raised the subject that was the ultimate purpose of their gathering. If it had seemed unfathomable that the signal could simply disappear, and that it would be the end of the story, it was for good reason. It hadn't. It had only changed. Dramatically changed.

"This signal is much denser, more granular," Melissa said. "Compared with the prior signal format, it would translate to a much lower bit-duration. But that's a relative thing – the speed – so it really makes no practical difference."

"Except that it's a hint that they want us to go faster," Riley said.

She nodded.

"What's most interesting is that they've started changing amplitude as well," Riley said.

The three of them sat studying the image. Where the prior signal could have been compared to a zoomed-in view of a vinyl phonograph with unevenly spaced ridges of varying widths – maybe something like Saturn's rings – this one had evenly spaced ridges, all of the same width, but with different heights. It was much denser as well. Several of the new ridges would fit into the same space as only one of the narrowest ridges from the prior format.

"They've moved to Amplitude-shift keying," Melissa said, raising her hand palm-up as if cracking a puzzle on Wheel of Fortune. Riley nodded thoughtfully.

"What the hell is that?" Clipper asked. "And even more importantly, I'm not entirely comfortable trusting a person who would know that."

Melissa grinned, but moved on. "It's a way of packing more data into a digital signal. With the prior signal, we translated the plateaus and valleys into ones and zeros. They were the only two values we had to work with. Binary. The narrowest possible width of a ridge was the bit duration – meaning it told us where one value ended and the next began. To assemble them into meaningful data, we had to line them up and understand that it took several of them to make a single recognizable value. The *synchronize* and *acknowledgement* data in the last signal, for example, was made up of eight bits each. It was only by understanding that, that we were able to know how to increment the acknowledgement bit in a way they understood." She pointed at the screen, elbow on knee. "This way allows several bits to be packed into one bit-duration by keeping the width the same, but varying the height of the plateau. Each distinct height represents a specific value. So, where before we could interpret only ones or zeros, this way allows the amplitude – the height of the plateaus themselves – to represent multiple bits." She turned to Clipper, "If you imagined that I had a bunch of sticks with different lengths; say, one, two, three, four and five inches in length, and I wanted to transmit a value of five, I could just use the five-inch stick. The old way, I would have to use three markers; a one-inch stick, the zero tab, and another one-inch stick."

"Right," Clipper said, "In binary, five would be 1-0-1, because each digit is equal to twice the value of the one to the right of it. That makes five the same as 4 + 0 + 1."

"Exactly," Melissa said.

"So," Clipper went on, "the length of these new *ninja* bits translates to the same number of the old bits that had to be side-by-side, as if they were stood up on their sides, vertically?"

"Pretty much," she said. "The amount of data they can cram into the signal will amount to the number of distinct amplitudes – or signal heights – they can create."

"Shouldn't be hard to figure that out," Riley said. "We look for the greatest amplitude and divide by the lowest."

"That'll do it," Melissa agreed, "assuming the amplitudes ramp up in equal increments, which I would guess they will."

"True," Riley said. "I'm also guessing we'll find eight distinct values. Even though we're not binary anymore, it will make each bit-duration a clean octet just the same."

"So," Clipper said, "I need to modify my scripts to not only send a sequence of pulses like it does now, but also to be able to independently adjust the power for each pulse, so we can change its amplitude?"

"I don't think so, actually," Riley said. "We're going to have to get a little more sophisticated. To come even close to this, we'll need to bring a modulator into the mix. Instead of powering up and down in rapid succession, which I don't think the equipment could do well, we'll leave the power on, but modulate the throughput to achieve the different amplitudes."

"You realize what's happening here, right?" Melissa said.

"They're leading us," Clipper said, seeing where Melissa was going. "They're dropping breadcrumbs."

Riley nodded meaningfully. "They see us, and now they know we see them. It could go any direction from here." He turned to Melissa. "Melissa, Clipper and I have been talking about where to go from here on the signal. I don't know how much he shared with you, but however we look at this, there is some risk."

Melissa looked back but didn't comment.

"You've been instrumental in deciphering what's going on with this – in figuring out what the anomaly is and what it could mean, so to me, that entitles you to make your own decision with respect to continuing with us from here or stepping out. Either way, it's all good."

The question was clearly not as easy for her as it had been for Clipper, and she took a contemplative sip of her wine before answering. "I'm a little nervous, I'll admit, but," she shook her head as if she didn't like her own conclusion on the matter, "I don't think I could live with myself if I gave up now."

"I understand," Riley said, "but you don't have to think of it that way, really. At least from my perspective. Clipper and I are going to pursue this, so one way or another, we're going to find out what's next, and you will too."

"Yeah, I know, but it wouldn't be the same, would it?" she said.

"Maybe not," Riley allowed. "But, how important is that? In my opinion, if you have any reservations, they are worth–"

Melissa cut him off. "We all have reservations, though. Am I right?"

"I guess we do," Riley admitted.

"How about we take this next step, then," she said. "We figure out how to acknowledge this new signal and then reassess? The takeaways from that could be enough to change everything, including our minds – even yours – on whether to leave this thing alone, notify Mayfield, or who knows what?"

"Fair enough. Is that your decision then?"

"Yes, it's my decision."

Riley studied her for a long moment before speaking again. She held his gaze, but Clipper saw that she never accomplished her intent of convincing him of her resolve.

"Melissa–" Riley said, tentatively, but she cut him off again.

"I'm good, Riley," she said. "I'm good. If you're waiting for me to convey a sense of complete confidence, it probably won't happen. Not today, anyway; but I've thought about this, and I want to take the next step with you."

Clipper wondered briefly if there could be double meaning in the statement, and knew Riley caught it too, but neither acknowledged it in any way Clipper could see. Clipper suspected that if he himself had not been present, the conversation may have taken a different turn at that point, but he would never know.

"Okay then," Riley said, nodding, "next steps, then." He took another sip of wine and set the glass on the end table. "We have a few things to do. None of them are particularly complex, but they'll take time. Good thing is, we have the right skills between us."

"Melissa, tell me if you agree with Clipper and I on this. We're going to control amplitude using a modulator. I don't think our equipment is well suited to doing it any other way."

"From what I know, makes sense," she said.

"Okay, so here's what we need. I already started looking at where and how we can install a modulator onto the system. In fact, Clip, that's what I was doing when you came out to the Installation on Monday. Next, we'll need to write a computer program that allows us to control it. What I'd like to be able to do is change the signals on-the-fly. Meaning, we decide what pulses we want to send, and the amplitudes required to do it, and the computer interacts with the modulator to carry it out. I want to be able to change them on demand, including speeding them up or slowing them down, or you name it."

"Wait a minute," Clipper said. "How could you have known we'd need a modulator then? We were still working with the old format at the time."

"I'll admit I didn't expect the format to change, but I knew, even then, that the way we were generating pulses had to be improved. We had to have a modulator. It's simple."

Clipper eyed him warily. "Okay, when I figure out whether you're snowing me, I'll let you know. In the meantime, unfortunately, this could get a little tricky. We'll need a controller for the modulator, but it won't be able to sit on the company network."

"Agreed," Riley said. "I've already realized that, too. We'll need to insert the modulator between the field generator and its own controller, and then have another computer that controls only the modulator out of band. Because of the safeguards built into the computer systems, we won't be able to be on premise at the Installation during these test runs either, so the modulator controller will have to be accessible remotely. We'll just need to lock it down from a security perspective."

"I think you're right," Clipper agreed. "The path of least resistance is probably to install a Raspberry Pi as an IoT device and hook it to a mobile phone on premises at the Installation, so we can use a carrier network to talk to it. Is there a decent signal out there?"

"Usually. Shouldn't be a problem," Riley said.

"So how far did you get on Monday? Did you actually install a modulator?" Clipper asked.

"No, I was just looking for the right place to install one."

"And did you find it?"

"I have a couple candidate locations," Riley answered. "I don't think this part will hold us up."

"Cool, so do you have one?"

"Unfortunately, no," Riley said, "but I have ordered one. You should be able to go ahead with writing the software, and we'll test it out once the modulator arrives."

"Got it," Clipper said.

"For my part," Melissa cut in, "I think the initial response is fairly simple; we just repeat back what we received like we did before with the old signal. We convert it to ones and zeros and amplitude-shift them into the new format, and all this plays out pretty much the same as before. If we can come up with a way to respond on-the-fly, it could save a lot of time going forward."

"Agreed. We have a plan, then," Riley said. "The modulator is supposed to be delivered within three business days, which should be Wednesday. Clip, how long do you need?"

"I'll be ready by then. I have a couple Raspberry Pi's to work with. Once we have the modulator, I'll need another day or two to integrate with it."

"Sounds good," Riley said. "If you let me use one of the RP's, I'll get it hooked to my cell phone and start installing the IoT libraries that will allow us to talk to it."

"Righteo," Clipper said.

"Why not just sit a wireless hotspot out there?" Melissa asked.

"That would work," Riley said, "but the hotspot would broadcast its own 2.4 or 5GHz signal. That's not likely to interfere with the field generator, but would stick out like a sore thumb to the systems crews that monitor the site. If I tether the RP to the phone, the phone will still send its own signal out over the carrier network, which could also be detected rather easily, but only if someone is specifically looking for it. I don't think anyone will, so it's less likely to be noticed."

"Makes sense," Melissa said.

"What do you say about meeting at Starbucks on Tuesday morning for a checkpoint?" Riley asked.

"Works for me," Melissa said.

"7:00 AM?"

"Perfect."

Chapter 26

February 19, 2024

The Starbucks was most pleasant during the early morning hours. As a rule, the conversations were quieter, the sun a little kinder, and the air more pleasant than later in the day. It made for a peaceful start.

Clipper was the morning person of the group, that despite being something of a late person as well. He had been seated for only a few minutes when Melissa approached, coffee in hand. "I would have ordered something for you," he said, "but wasn't sure of your tastes."

"Oh, thank you," she said. "My tastes are simple. Medium blend with cream."

"Noted."

She smiled, and her eyes passed over the lobby door. "Am I to conclude that our illustrious Mr. Riley is not given to 7:00 AM meetings? This was his idea, right?"

"It was, but I gave up trying to decipher the man 15 years ago."

She laughed pleasantly. "This is all ... odd," she said, taking a seat. "Here we are, forming our own covert operations club. Feels a little like being 12 again, only with more to lose than three days of telephone privileges with my giggly friends."

"I'll have you know that Riley and I are fully capable of reverting to the 12-year-old versions of ourselves, but we are not giggly. That is final."

Melissa smiled again. She had the tired look of someone who had spent hours languishing over options without reaching a satisfying decision, and in the end, resigning herself to wherever the current may take her. Clipper was worried about her but didn't know what to do about it. He wished she would step away for her own sake, but had no way of communicating that in a way that would reflect his true motives; which were that he simply didn't want her to get into trouble if the road they were travelling led in that direction.

Clipper said: "Riley has been on a quest of his own making for his entire life. Truth is, I'm not sure anyone really knows or understands him."

Melissa's countenance transformed at that. "Is he a good man?"

"Oh yeah. Absolutely a good man. But after all these years I'm not sure how well even I know him. He sees deeper into things than other people – me, anyway. I used to think it was a matter of being guarded, private; but now I know that he simply goes to places where others can't follow. If you haven't seen that part of him, you will."

Clipper read Melissa's expression and became worried that he was giving her the wrong impression. "Listen, just half-baked thoughts, don't take them too seriously. Odd as it sounds, I don't think I could respect anyone more than I do Riley. Funny thing to say about a person you should think of as a peer, given that we grew up together."

"No, I'm glad you shared that," Melissa said, seeing that Clipper was beginning to doubt himself. "I have seen traces of what you're talking about. He's intriguing."

Clipper nodded. "When you're with Riley you can't help noticing that he's never fully in the room with you. There's always some other place that he seems to be coming from. It's like he has his own virtual model of the world, and he takes in everything that happens around him, internalizes it, and then applies it to that model. Say something funny and I'll laugh. Riley will too; but then he'll reconstruct the entire world in light of it. That new piece of information – that little event – however trivial, will tumble through his model and change everything along the way, and before it's all over, he'll connect dots that seem as far removed as hushpuppies from spaceships. But the outcome, whatever the connecting of those dots mean, will matter in ways that only he appreciates. Even if he shares what they are, it doesn't work, because he sees them in light of that larger model, and the rest of us can see them only in light of our own. It is what it is. You may have a better model than mine, so you may have better luck than me. In fact, I'd be surprised if you didn't. Come to think of it, I'd be a little surprised if the coffee cup you're holding didn't. Either way, that's how I've come to think of Riley."

Melissa pondered his words, in no hurry to speak. "You have a knack for self-abasement, Mr. Clipper," she said, finally. "But insights like that don't come from coffee cups."

"Maybe not," Clipper said, and then became thoughtful again. "You should know, Melissa; that Riley lives in a state of deep thought. It seems that he's never in the room with you because he isn't. Maybe you have the power to change that in ways that AJ and I never could," he said, taking a chance on giving her a meaningful look, "but I suspect a big part of that will require a willingness to go with him to places none of the rest of us can."

"I must be far more transparent that I realized," she said.

"No. Just more of my coffee cup wisdom. You never really stood a chance," he said, grinning.

"Seems I'm being carried aloft by fate, then. Either way, I'm not sure Riley has had a glimmer of thought about me, except with regard to how I've played into all this."

"I wouldn't want to unnecessarily torture my prior analogy," Clipper said, "but I will say that there is no way that Riley's *world model* hasn't been heavily reconfigured by your appearance. In the name of self-preservation, though; that's as much as I had better say."

She grinned again. It was always pleasant when she did. "Understood," she said, then looked to the cup of coffee in her hand as if suddenly embarrassed.

Clipper saw a glint of sunlight reflected from a car as it pulled onto the lot. It was Riley. "And here he is. He's had all night to think about everything. If there's an opponent out there on the other end of this, whoever it is has already lost – they just don't know it."

In a moment, Riley entered. He bypassed the counter an approached. He had an insulated coffee cup already in hand. "Morning," he said, sitting down. "Sorry I'm late."

"Not to worry," Clipper said. Melissa didn't speak, but looked at him appraisingly. Seeing that, Clipper knew he had better get the conversation going. He wouldn't want Riley to realize that he had been the topic of conversation. It was too late. Riley looked pleasantly to Melissa and then back to Clipper in a, 'is there something I should know' kind of way that made Clipper have to concentrate on not shifting in his chair.

"Well then," Riley said without preamble, "any luck on the modulation program?"

"Ready to test," Clipper said. "How's the Raspberry Pi?"

"Same. I've been tracking the modulator. It's in transit, but still a day out."

"No worries," Clipper said. "Are you available to give the Raspberry Pi a try later today? We can at least get some of the kinks worked out while we wait."

"Yep, stop by after work. We'll see how it goes."

"Okay, I'll–" Clipper began, but cut short. Seeing his surprised expression, Riley and Melissa turned to see what he was looking at. Brian Matthews had entered the store and approached the counter. He didn't appear to see the three of them. "This is something new," Clipper said, under his breath. "I've been in this store more times that I can count. I've never seen Matthews in here."

Matthews placed his order and waited by the counter, shortly becoming preoccupied with his mobile phone.

"I'd have to say the same," Riley said.

In a few moments, Matthews had his coffee, and to their surprise, made immediately for their table. Clipper hadn't noticed him look in their direction to even know they were there, but here he came. "Good morning," he said, lifting his coffee for a sip. "Another pleasant surprise. How's EcoGrid coming?" he said to Melissa, in particular.

"So far, so good. Thread patch finally went out the door."

"That was a big win," Matthews said with a grunt. "A lot going on." He looked around the store as if only then deciding to get a fix on where he was, then took to rubbing his chin. "How is it that you came to get mixed up with these guys?"

Matthews knew the answer, and Riley knew he wouldn't have forgotten. "Our paths cross here and there in the lab," Melissa said, not missing a beat.

"I see. Mayfield can make it tough on all of us, we're all so locked down on one secret project or another. Sometimes it's nice to get away and remember we all aspire to have personal lives too."

Melissa nodded. "Very true."

"Anyway, the three of you have a good day, I'd better get moving," he said, offering a friendly wave with his free hand as we walked away. No one spoke until he had left the lobby.

"That was ... interesting," Clipper noted.

"And no accident," Riley added.

"What do you mean?"

"It just didn't feel like a chance meeting."

"Then what was the point of it?" Melissa said.

"I think there is only one possible answer for that. I'm not sure how, but he's gotten wind of what we're doing. If we're going to do something, we may not have as much time as we thought." He looked to Clipper. "You still in?"

"More than ever."

"Okay, come over to my place as early as you can tonight. Let's get this thing moving. Melissa, this part of things won't require your help, but you're welcome to come too."

"I'll be there," she said, but was still puzzled by Matthews' visit. "I don't get why you said Matthews' stopping in here wasn't a chance thing. Why not? What makes you say that?"

Riley looked for a moment like a man who had been asked to explain why water was wet. "Think about what he said. He asked how you knew us, then made a point of how important it is for us to keep quiet about the secret projects we're on. And–" he said, pointing out the window. "See that coffee cup sitting on top of the trash can outside the front door?" Both she and Clipper turned to look. "That's the coffee he just ordered." He made a half shrug. "Maybe he didn't like it."

Chapter 27

February 20, 2024

The tangle of wires, circuit boards, mobile phones, keyboards and computer terminals littering the floor of the room looked like a mess that could have no possible meaning or value. Riley and Clipper were huddled in the middle of it all, peering at a scattering of black windows displayed across one of the terminals. Fragments of terse and seemingly meaningless text appeared in each one; some stationary, others scrolling, stopping, then scrolling again all on their own.

They didn't hear the front door, only Melissa's voice, soft and tentative, coming from the doorway to the room. They turned to greet her, but the expression on her face put anything they may have said on hold.

"What's wrong," Riley asked, immediately concerned.

"I'm off the EcoGrid project," she said, rubbing her forearms absently. A silence trailed her statement, filling the room. A 'W' formed on Riley's lips, the start of a question that refused to be asked. "As of tomorrow, I'm on production support," she said. She stepped into the room and leaned heavily against a wall. "I'm sorry guys, but I think this means I had better step away from our little adventure too."

It was amazing how quickly the air in the room transformed. It would be a big blow to Melissa's career. "I'm sorry, Melissa," Riley said.

She nodded, looking down, but it lasted only a moment. She looked back up as if garnering her courage. "Time to suck it up."

Riley had risen to his feet. "Can I get something for you to drink? All this can wait," he said, gesturing to the mess on the floor.

"Thanks John, no. I'm going to go home and think things over. I can't let Matthews rewind the clock on my career like this. I'm not sure what to do, but I have to start thinking about it."

Riley nodded, clearly wishing for a way to help and knowing there was none – at least not this evening. She would need time. "Melissa," he said, drawing her eyes. "I'm sorry."

"This was my doing," she said. "You all but kicked me off the team and I refused to go."

"That's not how this unfolded," he said. "It's just not." She nodded again, her momentary rise of confidence seeming to have already ebbed away. "Can I walk you to your car?" he asked.

She nodded again.

Clipper watched the moment unfold with a hollow ache in his stomach. He wished he could cross the room to give her a hug, and that it would somehow make everything better. He had no romantic feelings for Melissa, but the pang of hurt he felt at her unexpected setback made him realize how fond he had become of her; like the protective instincts of an older brother for a younger sister, although he had no idea whether he was actually older than her or not. "Maybe it would be better if you weren't alone for a while," Clipper said. "I didn't have much time to devote to this tonight anyway, so I may as well be on my way."

"Oh, no," she said. "Really, I'm leaving."

"I understand," Clipper said, but made his way towards the door, just the same. "Melissa, I'm sorry too, and I think I speak for Riley as well, in saying that we are at your disposal. Just yell." A moment later he was outside, crossing the parking lot to his car. He was determined not to spy on the two, but also noted that by the time he drove away from the lot, Melissa had not yet appeared in Riley's doorway. That was a good thing.

Inside, Melissa's resolve to leave was also waning. Within a few minutes, she and Riley had found places on the sofa. "There's a pervasive silence to life," she said, unexpectedly. "A sadness. Do you see it?"

Riley watched her for a moment. "I'm not sure I do," he said. "At times like this; maybe."

"Oh, I see it all the time. Just me, I guess."

"In what way?"

"It's not important and probably makes no sense," Melissa said, now giving appearances that she regretted saying anything, and wanted to drop the subject. Maybe she was rethinking her decision to stay.

"Okay. I won't press," Riley said, "but I'd like to hear your thoughts if you're willing to share them."

Melissa teetered on the edge of moving on. She looked penetratingly into his eyes in that way she had. "From what I can see, John, you live in your world of physics. Your mind spends its time there. I won't deny that you see deeper into, I don't know, reality than I do – deeper than anyone I know. I'm embarrassed to say that if there were an alternate space that I tend to live in, it's in the vacuum of life where all the things we should be doing, thinking, undertaking on behalf of the people we care about, should be, but aren't." Riley tried to understand. "It's not a big deal," she went on. "Not sure why I brought it up."

Riley was weighing her, she could clearly see it. She looked back at him like a person who suddenly realized that she had wandered onto a stage in front of a crowd of people and wanted nothing in life more than to escape back to obscurity.

When he didn't speak, Melissa pressed on, as if the only way out was through. She shrugged to convey the trivialness of the subject. "There are people I care about," she said. "My mother, for instance. Her health isn't good, and I'm worried about her. She's living a happy life and we spend a lot of time together, but somehow, it's not enough. I find myself wondering about all the moments that, when one day she isn't around anymore, I will wish I had made better use of. But it's artificial, isn't it? It has to be. There isn't enough time in the day, or even the appetite for the meaningful moments we all think should be important enough to stop us in our tracks, but that never do. There is some part of us that knows there are things of paramount importance that we should make more time for, but somehow they're not important enough to act on. It's everything, really. The meaningful things are always shouted over by the demands of life."

Riley had taken to nodding slightly. "Those are the undertones, the undercurrents of life."

Melissa's eyes reflected a recognition that made her face rise. "For me, the whole Randy-thing; the marriage, the divorce, was not about the same things for me as for him. There was something he needed, a space that was important for him that I couldn't fill. The best I was able to understand about what he needed from life was that he liked to have fun. He wanted to be out doing things – experiencing things, but even when I went with him, there was always something missing in his eyes. I was doing them, but he was living them. They fed something within him that was important, even critical, that despite my best efforts, I could not appreciate on the level he did. It was unfulfilling for him. I couldn't connect with him at the level he needed me to. I tried, because I saw it even then; but I couldn't become the person he needed me to be. At the end of the day our marriage left too many things lacking. On my side, there was a different, but similar miss. A misalignment that he didn't see, and which meant very little to him, but was where *I* felt the vacuum. I always believed that if we could at least recognize where we were coming up short for one another, it would be enough for us to begin to build upon. It wasn't."

"That's a big part of it, isn't it?" Riley said. "Life? Being with someone requires the willingness to understand the needs of that other person, and being willing to make the investment to meet them in the places that matter to them."

"Yes," Melissa said, "but it takes two. You can decide you're willing to pay that price, but if you find that the other person isn't, then … it just stops."

"Melissa, I know this isn't the time for me to start flooding you with apologies and regrets. I'll spare you that. I understand that you may need time to sort this out, and that there's a real possibility that you won't be able to separate me from the whole of it. If you find the need to step away from me as part of stepping away from the rest of this, I won't make it difficult for you."

She looked at him searchingly. "Don't make it sound so easy."

"I don't mean to, believe me. Maybe I'm just used to playing the role of the person who gets left behind."

"I don't want that to happen, Riley. We haven't known each other for long, I know, but I've been afraid since the start that what looks like it could be a good thing wouldn't last. Whatever happens with work, or this signal, or even gravitation, I hope we both give each other a chance."

"I am more willing to do that than I could put into words."

"Me too," Melissa said.

There was a slight pause. "I can order in Chinese," Riley said. "I think this would be a good night for a quiet evening and movie."

"That sounds wonderful."

Chapter 28

February 21, 2024

AJ rolled into Charlotte at close to 4:30 on a Wednesday afternoon. He had made arrangements to stay with Riley for a few days, then shift to Clipper's for the second half of the visit. After a depressing night at a roadside hotel the night before, and the persistent ache of his dismissal by Sarah, the sight of his two friends would be a welcomed sight.

Knowing Riley and Clipper would be at work, he drove first to Riley's apartment to get the effort of finding the place out of the way, then back to a Starbucks he had passed only a couple blocks before. He ordered a *triple venti latte* and settled into a cushioned chair with a paperback book in hand. He texted them both to let them know he was in town. His phone chimed with responses within seconds; first from Clipper, then Riley. They would be about an hour. Riley offered that AJ could pick up a key to his apartment from work, which was only a 10-minute drive, but AJ decided to forego the effort. The drive from Kansas City had been almost exactly 1000 miles and it felt good not to be behind the wheel for a few minutes.

Sarah had been in the habit of sending occasional texts to him. Having just read texts from Riley and Clipper, he reluctantly scanned for anything from her. There was nothing, and hadn't been since she broke things off with him. No emails either. With a sudden resolve, he realized it was time to begin the work that had brought him to Charlotte. He would stop looking back, stop hoping for any chance Sarah would return, and start thinking of what was next. He had entertained moving to Charlotte for several reasons; Clipper and Riley being two. Charlotte being the second largest financial center in the nation being another, but getting over Sarah was the biggest of them all. The time to start was now.

His immediate goal was not to allow his personal upheavals to overshadow the time with his friends. He opened his book, *Executive Power*, by Vince Flynn, and began to read. The next forty-five minutes passed quickly as the novel did its work. When he received the expected text from Riley saying he would be home within fifteen minutes, AJ rose, tossing his finished latte into the waste bin, and set on his way.

He wheeled onto the lot of the apartment complex slightly before Riley, who arrived minutes later in a white Toyota Highlander SUV with 30-day tags. "What's this?" AJ said as Riley exited the vehicle.

"Hey my friend," Riley said. "Just got it. I needed a little more power for the hills around here."

"Looks like you got it. Nice," AJ said, approaching and giving the vehicle more scrutiny. "Thanks for having me, Riley. I hope the timing isn't bad."

"Nonsense. How was the trip?"

"Felt a lot like going back to school. I've made that run more times than I can count. This time it was a hundred miles shorter, so that part was pretty good."

"I'll bet," Riley said. "Clip's on his way. We've cleared some time from our calendars."

"Don't let me get in the way of anything," AJ said, already surprised by how much better he felt at the sight of his old friend.

"No worries. I picked up some steaks last night. We'll get the grill going. Clip's bringing some beer. Sound okay?"

"More than I could say. I'd offer something, but I'll have to settle for treating you guys next time."

"You know better than to worry about that," Riley said, leading AJ towards the apartment.

As predicted, they were joined by Clipper within minutes. He entered the apartment with a brown paper bag, which he sat on the island in the kitchenette before turning immediately to AJ. "How's it going my friend?" he said.

"Couldn't be better. You?"

"Same. Life is good." Clipper began unloading the contents of the bag into the fridge, announcing as he went. "Sam Adams Boston Lager, George Killian's Irish Red Ale, Michelob Amber Bock, and Budweiser. It's a work night, so some of this is for posterity; and sorry ladies, nothing light on the drink menu tonight. What'll it be?"

"Boston Lager sounds good," AJ said.

"I'll have something in a few," Riley said, on his way to the balcony to start the grill.

Clipper turned to the fridge and feigned looking around. "Don't seem to have any of those. Afraid you'll have to settle for something else."

"Okay, okay. Make it a red, then."

"Admirable choice, admirable choice." Clipper opened the bottles and handed them over. Riley took his, raised it to his friends, then headed for the patio door.

"Thanks Clip," AJ said. "Been too long guys."

"Indeed it has," Clipper agreed.

"So, is it true you're thinking about getting out of Moab and coming over here to Canaan with me and Riley?"

"I'm thinking about it. I've lined up a couple interviews."

"That'll be a slam dunk, I would guess."

"Hope so. Time to get serious about my student loans. I round to the ten-thousands, you know."

"Ouch," Clipper said.

"Duke. What more is there to say? So, how have you guys been? Anything going on?"

"Work, mostly."

"You're gettin' along okay over at Mayfield Hammond then? How is it?"

"Not bad. Lots of hours lately, so you'll be a good diversion."

The evening progressed through the meal and a few beers to find the three of them lounging in the living room, the television playing a movie, unheeded, on the big screen as the conversation turned from reminiscing, to the present, then to outlooks.

"I just got distracted by things at home," AJ was saying. "Sarah was an unexpected complication, but it seems to have worked itself out. Now it's time to get serious about getting my career started."

"Listen, AJ, I'm sure the Sarah thing stings a little now, but it's for the best," Clipper said. "Take that from a career bachelor."

"I will, and with a grain of salt," AJ said, but Clipper ignored the gibe.

"Did Sarah go to school with us?" Riley asked.

"No. Blue Valley."

"Okay. She sounds familiar. Anyway, that's tough stuff, AJ," Riley said sympathetically in response to AJ's redress of his storied relationship with Sarah.

"How are you and Melissa getting along?" Clipper asked Riley.

Riley smiled, a little surprised by the question. "How many of those have you had?" he said, pointing to the Budweiser in Clipper's hand.

"Hey," Clipper said, "AJ has been forthcoming about his romantic adventures, I thought we may as well push you into the ring as well."

"Okay. Pretty good, if you must know. We've been out a couple times." He decided not to bring Melissa's setback into the conversation.

"She's a gal from work," Clipper said to AJ, then made a show of winking conspiratorially.

Riley shook his head. "AJ, if you haven't noticed, Clipper is still, uh, Clipper, I'm afraid." They all laughed.

"To that end," AJ said, "how about it Clip? Any ladies on the line?"

"I have no intention of forfeiting my God-given freedoms. There's never 'one on the line.' I just enjoy time with the ladies and leave it at that."

"Is that a fact?" AJ said incredulously. "Sounds like famous last words to me."

Clipper grunted.

"AJ," Riley said, changing the subject. "Are you serious about coming to Charlotte?"

"I don't know. I'm not dead-set on it, but it's not a bad option."

"I haven't been here long myself, but I've made some decent connections. I could put in a word for you at Mayfield if you're interested."

"Appreciate that, Riley, but let me see how the interviews go and take it from there."

Chapter 29

February 28, 2024

It had been a while since AJ last sat through an interview, but he knew it had gone well. So well, in fact, that he was not surprised in the least to find an offer letter in his email inbox a few mornings later. The formal letter made the decision to move to North Carolina suddenly more real. Accepting the job would change everything. His family ties would thin out abruptly and considerably. Kansas City would no longer be home, it would now be where he was from. And it would force the part of him that clung to the hope that Sarah would return to admit that she never would. That was no small thing.

On the up side, it would reunite him with his childhood friends. But even there, as much as he liked the idea, something about the notion gave him pause. Maybe it felt too much like going backward in some way. He knew it wasn't, but it was still a thought he didn't like. Regardless, the offer letter was now in his hands, which meant the exercise was no longer academic. Either he had come to North Carolina to start a new life, or all of it had been a charade and colossal waste of time.

He started the day with a visit to the neighborhood Starbucks – a routine that had transplanted across the country rather nicely. He parked his truck and looked out the window for a long while before getting out. The thought of calling Charlotte home was a little difficult to get his arms around. It was a fine city, no doubt; it just seemed foreign somehow.

Something else bothered him, too. For some reason, this morning – this day – seemed to tremble beneath a canopy of uneasiness. He guessed it was his chronic loneliness. Sarah was gone. She didn't want him. Nothing else, not even the thought of moving away from his parents – as much as that weighed on him too – came close to the burden that placed on his spirits. For a moment he reconsidered going in at all, the only thing keeping him from driving away being the inconvenient question of where he would go once he did.

He went into the Starbucks and ordered a latte with an oatmeal-raisin cookie, then stood checking email on his phone as he waited. A murmur of conversation filled the space, indistinguishable from its Kansas City counterparts. When the latte and cookie were ready, he turned to look for a seat, and his eye was drawn immediately and unexpectedly by the lines of a familiar face looking in his direction.

His mind seemed unable to accept what he saw, and nothing in his thoughts could piece together an explanation that made sense. It was Sarah. She sat looking at him, as real as the floor he stood upon. The two locked eyes for a long moment before AJ regained his feet. By the time he reached her table he had already considered ignoring her, putting on airs of not being surprised or rattled, or even confronting her with anger, but in the end, he simply took a seat across from her, leaving all pretense aside. "What–" he said, but didn't know where to take the statement.

"Yes, I'm here to see you," she said without preamble.

"How did you know I'd be here?"

"I didn't, actually. I spoke with Clipper earlier, he wasn't hard to find. Your mom had his number. He agreed to help me make connections with you this afternoon, but this is easier. I should've known I would have a good chance of running across you here."

"What can I help you with?" he asked, still perplexed, and becoming guarded.

"I had to talk with you, and I realized it wasn't a conversation we could have over the phone. Will you talk with me?" she asked with unfamiliar vulnerability.

Surprised by the question, AJ was not sure how to respond. "What? Of course. Of course I'll talk with you. Is everything okay?"

"I hope so." She shifted in her chair, looking towards her lap, then back at AJ. "I'm sorry AJ, but you were right. When things happen in life that aren't what you want, you don't start by cutting ties with the people who care about you."

"You've come all this way to apologize?" AJ asked, already having the sinking feeling that she was here only to explain why she had done what she had.

"No. I'm hoping you'll forgive me, and that you will give us another chance." She said the words and then fell silent, holding his gaze as if waiting for a jury foreman to pronounce a weighty verdict. AJ hesitated, expecting her to say more, but she didn't. She only looked at him without moving, her face expressionless.

He leaned back in his chair heavily, the bizarre implications of the moment finally finding traction in his mind, and for some reason, he found it difficult to look in her direction. Finally, he said, "Sarah, it was a surprise, even to me, how fast I fell for you. It was stupid of me, but I couldn't have done anything different. It just happened." He gave her a moment to respond, but she didn't. "This past week has been tough," he said, meeting her gaze. "I came all the way out here for a singular reason, Sarah, to start finding my way out of the hole your leaving left me in. I've hoped beyond hope that you would have a change of heart, but I don't want to relive that again. Not ever."

"I'm sorry," she said. "You're right. I didn't do any of this right."

"You want to get back together, then? Is that what I'm hearing?"

"Yes, I do. Very much," she said simply.

There were no other words in the world that AJ had hoped to hear more over the past week, and it seemed surreal, almost unbelievable that he was hearing them now. "I don't know what to say," he said, finally. "Of course I want to get back together, but—" He hesitated.

"What AJ? What is it?" she pressed.

"I don't know. I won't ask for guarantees," he said. "I know there are no guarantees in life. Maybe I would just hope that you'll be more considerate of me if we give this another chance and it ends up not working. This was hard on me, Sarah. I won't dwell on it, but it turned my world upside down. I don't want to feel that way again. Not ever."

She nodded, wordlessly. "What I did was unfair and juvenile, AJ. I hope you will at least forgive me for that, even if nothing works out between us from here."

He nodded. "So where does this leave us?" he asked.

"If you will give me another chance, AJ, it means we start over."

"Okay, Sarah. I would like that more than anything in the world."

A tear slipped from Sarah's eye. She looked again to her lap, then back to AJ. "I love you," she said. "I do."

"I love you too," he said, quietly.

For the first time, the faintest smile touched Sarah's delicate face. It wasn't joy or even happiness, but the look of a person returning home after a long absence and seeing deeply into the hidden recesses of all that it meant. They sat in the quiet stillness of the moment, separate and apart from the noise and chatter around them until Sarah spoke again. "This is real, right?" she said. "We're back together again?"

"Yes, we are. We're back together," AJ said. And before his eyes, Sarah's smile began to emerge from the weight of all prior concerns to again reflect the sunlight deep within her, her eyes brightening as if waking from a bad dream.

Without a word, she stood to her feet, walked around the table and bent to kiss him. The kiss was a short one, but tender, and when she pulled away, AJ's eyes lingered on hers questioningly. "I'm going to go home now," she said. "We can talk about where we go from here when you return. Whether it's Charlotte or Kansas City doesn't matter. I just want to be with you."

"Please stay," AJ pleaded.

"I think it's best if I go now."

"Are you in a rental car? I can take you to the airport."

"Thank you, but I have a car," Sarah said. "If it's okay, let me just go back now. We can both collect our thoughts."

"Okay," AJ said, slow to accept the request.

She smiled again, knowingly. "Remember the commitment you've made to me here, Mr. Jacobs. I'll be waiting."

AJ watched her go, and before he knew it, his eyes were glassy with tears. He stood to leave, a different man. Neither of them were even remotely aware of the sequence of events that such a simple conversation would set into motion.

Chapter 30

March 10, 2024

"Doesn't matter how long your vacation is – a day, a week, a year – before you know it, you're looking back at it."

That earned a nod of agreement from Clipper, who was sitting on the edge of his living room couch in mid-bend to fetch his second shoe. "You can still stay here in Canaan if you want. You haven't declined that job offer yet, have you?"

"Not yet," AJ said. "I tend not to unnecessarily close doors."

"Good thinking," Clipper said, pulling his sneaker onto his left foot with a hooked finger. "Didn't take long for that gal to throw her net over you again. I hope she doesn't decide to throw you back once she has you flopping around in the bottom of her boat."

AJ was a little surprised at how vocal – and direct – Clipper had become on the whole Sarah ordeal. "What, you don't like her?"

"No, actually I do. In fact, I'm impressed. She's a little out of your league, and you should know I'm feeling uncharacteristically generous right now." AJ gave a grunt, but Clipper forestalled, holding up a hand. "No offense, she's out of mine too. I just know what women like that can do. They can toss a man aside like a spent tube of lipstick."

AJ couldn't dispute the point. "So I'm a fool, what difference does it make? I decide I don't want to be this woman's fool, and what, the next one will be different?"

"Got me there," Clipper said. "Maybe you're right. It's inevitable, but that doesn't make it pretty. Maybe what I'm really trying to say is that freedom is a valuable thing, and it has the bad habit of not coming back once you give it up. Sarah's amazing, so this is a very awesome thing – don't get me wrong there – just be sure you think it through, that's all."

"Thanks Clip, I hear you." The thank you was a little harder to muster than AJ let on.

"So, this still the day?"

"I think so," AJ said. "I need to get back and figure things out."

"What about the job offer?"

"I sent an email yesterday afternoon telling them I was entertaining a few options and that I'd get back within the week."

"No need to unnecessarily close doors…" Clipper repeated. "Listen, I'm meeting Riley up at work. We've got some things to do, and our only good window is this morning. There won't be any distractions on a Sunday. We'll be a couple of hours. How about an early lunch before you go?"

"That'll work for me. I'll get the truck loaded, then give you a call."

"Done." Clipper grabbed up his keys, fetched a Diet Coke from the fridge, and was gone.

*   *   *

Riley's SUV was already parked on the Mayfield Hammond lot when Clipper arrived. Clipper swiped his badge at the side doors and entered the building. It was cloaked in its usual off-hours shades of gray. He eventually found the lab and entered to find Riley already pecking at a keyboard, squinting at a monitor. "Morning. What's up?" Riley said as Clipper approached.

"AJ's pulling out today."

"Is he going to be able to make lunch?"

"Yep." Clipper pointed to the computer monitor. "What's going on here?" he asked, dropping his notebook and badge onto the table.

"Just doing some tests on the modulator."

"How's it looking?"

"Solid. Do you have your new scripts ready?"

"Yep. I've got 'em out on the Amazon cloud. I'll just have to pull them down from my S3 bucket. It'll take about a minute." *S3* being shorthand for Amazon's *Simple Storage Service*.

"Okay, give me a couple more minutes," Riley said absently, still typing. In a moment Riley nodded to himself, apparently satisfied with what he was seeing. "Okay, I think we're good here." He pushed away from the monitor in his rolling chair, and Clipper wheeled around to take his place, immediately beginning to type.

Clipper unleashed a flurry of keystrokes, and in a moment, pushed back to face Riley. "Here's what I have. There are a few scripts. The first one is preprogrammed to play back what they sent to us, unchanged, just like we did on the first signal. The second – assuming we're right about the placement of the acknowledgement data under the new format – will send the same signal back with the *acknowledgement octet* incremented. Again, that's exactly what we did on the first signal. From there, the third script will allow us to send arbitrary data. It'll encode anything we want to send, so we can talk, even on-the-fly, if it comes to it. The way it works is that we can put whatever we want into a file, and then feed the file into the script to be sent out. That'll allow us to modify the file content however we want as we go."

"Perfect," Riley said. "All of this will be recorded, just like before?"

"Yep, it's automatic. But here's the cool part – still under development – so not 100% reliable as yet, but I made a run at getting the scripts to automatically decipher the pulses into octets. So, whatever we get back can still be compiled into the images we've been using, but it'll also take a stab at translating the pulses into numeric values that'll be easier for us to work with."

"Really?" Riley said. "Analog to digital translation is not an easy thing. How could you pull that off so fast?"

"Anymore, you can find open source software for anything. I found some oscillation software that can pick out the sine/cosine ratios from the amplitudes of a signal if you can get an image formatted in a way that it can understand. From there, the math wasn't all that bad. I just had to associate the ratios with discrete values. The hardest part was manipulating the images. I had to do some fancy rotating and cropping, and crank the contrast through the roof, but I finally got it to work fairly well."

"Impressed," Riley said. "Can't wait to see it in action. What does it do with the data?"

"Writes it to a file. The other catch is that the data is going to be in binary format, which means we won't be able to view the raw form of it. So, the last thing I did was make another simple utility that *base-64* encodes it, so we can look at it. It may not be useful, but it was easy to do, so I figured, why not?"

"I like it," Riley said. "Let's do it then."

"Righteo. Without further ado." Clipper pressed a button on the keyboard. "One away," he said. They both watched the computer screen as the seven-second interval ticked by. "And there's seven," Clipper said. "And, we have incoming data – compiling." The compilation step kicked in automatically. The raw data was transformed into three dimensional images, and a moment later, Clipper brought up the results. "Too bad Melissa isn't here. She's way better at this than either of us."

"True," Riley said. "But there's no way I'd have her here for something like this. We're way over our skis as it is."

Clipper nodded but didn't respond, already squinting at the new image. There was a lot of data, but both he and Riley knew where to look. "Cool, the incoming response is unchanged. Just like our first go-around."

"Good," Riley said.

"And," Clipper said, typing more at the keyboard. "Here are the files that contain the data we just received, converted to binary form, and then the binary data retranslated into base-64. The 0934 in the file names is the time the data was captured." Riley looked at the screen:

> *clipper$ ls incoming*
>
> *incoming/data-0934*
>
> *incoming/data-0934-base64*

"Nice," Riley said.

"Okay, moment of truth," Clipper said. "Send the acknowledgement?"

"May as well. If we weren't going to follow through, it would have been far easier to decide that weeks ago."

Clipper pressed a few more keys. "Two away," he said. They waited the seven seconds. Then longer. Clipper went to looking through the compiled gravity prints, and in short order, began shaking his head. "How 'bout them apples?"

"What?"

"They must have changed the signal again. There's nothing. It's gone."

"Again?" Riley was clearly surprised. "Try resending."

"Okay," Clipper said, "didn't work the first time they changed formats, but may as well." More keystrokes. "Done." But the next seven seconds were no more productive. Nothing appeared.

"Where's the logic in that?" Riley said.

"What do you mean?"

"I just mean that, I get why the first signal was there. It was to grab our attention. But if the second signal format was to lead us to improving our stuff so we can do a better job of sending and receiving data, why break that into three steps? If they really have changed to yet another format, then it'll have to be a lot different than this second format, otherwise, what's the point? Why not just leap from the first format to the final form?"

"I'm with ya," Clipper said. "And I'm tired too. I may need to take a breath before tackling the next one – if there is a next one. I sure as hell don't see anything in the data though – even at full zoom." He manipulated the latest image on the screen, shaking his head as he did.

Clipper's mobile phone rang, interrupting the conversation. "Ahh, that's AJ." He picked up his phone. "Yo. Yes. Sounds good. We're about done here anyway. Where do you want to meet?" He paused. "Good enough, we'll be out in a couple minutes then." He hung up the call. "AJ wants to get going a little earlier than he planned. He's waiting outside in the lot now. He dropped by to say goodbye, but I figure we can grab a late breakfast before he heads out. That sound good?"

Riley was still not over the disappointment of losing the signal yet again, but nodded in acceptance of the finality of it and rose to his feet. "Absolutely," he said, taking a deep breath. They made for the side doors and emerged onto the lot.

AJ was parked in the nearly-empty lot a couple spaces from Riley's SUV, and he stepped out of his truck as they approached. "Hey guys, sorry for the change of plans. It looks like it might rain, and I thought I'd just make an earlier go of it."

"Don't blame you," Clipper said. "Hey, it was great seeing you. I hope you come out and join us. It's not a bad town."

"If you decide to," Riley said, "you can stay with me for as long as you need until you find a place. I can give you some pointers on where you may want to live depending on the part of town you end up working in."

"That goes for me too," Clipper said. "You have time for a late breakfast before you hit the road?"

AJ scanned the sky, which had the appearance of imminent rain, but he shrugged as if it didn't matter. "Of course," he said. "Lead the way, I'll follow."

"Ah, damn," Clipper said to Riley. "I left my notebook and badge in the lab." He felt his pockets. "And my keys."

"I'm the absent-minded one of the group," Riley said. "Don't be angling in on my turf."

AJ realized at that moment, how much he would miss his friends, but there was nothing to be done. At least, not for the moment. He turned and began walking to his truck.

"No need to wait out here," Riley said.

"Yeah, come on in with us," Clipper said.

"It's not a problem," AJ said. "I can wait out here. Wouldn't want to get you guys into trouble."

"Nonsense," Clipper said.

They entered the building and made their way to the lab, Clipper leading and making straight for his notebook and keys lying on the table where he had left them, Riley and AJ a few paces behind. Clipper reached to pick them up, then did a double take at the computer monitor.

"Uh, hello!" he said, dropping the notebook and keys back onto the table and easing slowly into his chair, his eyes never leaving the screen. Riley noticed and broke off, walking around to look for himself. On seeing what Clipper had seen, he dropped into his chair and leaned forward, deep concern creasing his face.

It looked odd to AJ, but he didn't comment. This was where the two worked. They would handle whatever it was. He averted his gaze and looked around the lab, amazed at the work environment his friends had landed in. *Impressive* wasn't the word for it. From the outside, all of the buildings on the campus were impressive, but he would never have guessed that the likes of this lab would be in any one of them.

"Uh, Clip?" he heard Riley say, followed by, "I'm on it," from Clipper. AJ's eyes focused on the two for a moment before resuming his nonchalant survey of the lab. There were large display screens arranged at intervals on every wall, and dozens of workstations. He imagined working in such a place, but knew that he never would. Even if he were to join a place like Mayfield Hammond, he would be relegated to the standard ranks and file of the very types of cubicles he had always dreaded. No, he would be lucky ever to see anything like this, even as an employee.

"Whoa!" he heard Clipper say, and his eyes tracked back to his two friends.

"What?" Riley said.

"Editor just went wonky for a sec. Looks like we're back. Hang on."

Despite some part of him clinging to the assumption, even the expectation that whatever Riley and Clipper were doing, must fall well within the realms of the typical for them, something in their tone was hinting that it could be more. AJ found himself slightly nervous, and ready to be out of the building.

"Whoever this is, I think he's got us," Clipper said.

That was clearly not right; and certainly not expected. Something was wrong. AJ knew very well that he was already doing the only thing he could to help, which was to stay out of the way. He walked a few paces in the direction of his two friends, but kept his distance. They were both looking at a notebook. Despite himself, AJ took a chair and rolled forward, leaning in for a closer look. He wanted to stay out of the way, and also knew that because he was an outsider, he was not meant to see whatever was happening on the computer, but concern for his friends compelled him forward just the same. He inched to the left and saw the screen, upon which scrolled row after row of terse text. A good six feet away, it was too far to read, but he could tell just the same that it was of the type of technical-looking computer language that only the most skilled could make sense of.

The two were still talking. AJ couldn't hear most of it. In a moment, Clipper leaned back in his chair, and for the briefest of moments, AJ hoped it meant good news. Clearly, it was not. "Gentlemen," Clipper said in a resigned voice, "we may not have only just made the evening news, we may have just made history."

AJ's stomach curled into a knot. His eyes scanned over the two of them. Clipper's eyes remained fixed on the computer monitor, but Riley was looking directly back at him. His expression said everything. It showed concern, fear and regret. The monitor was still moving: text, and more text kept coming. AJ didn't know what was happening but knew it was bad. Very bad. Clipper swiveled in his chair, facing Riley and AJ with his back now to the monitor. He opened his mouth to speak, but never got the chance. AJ dug his heels into the carpet and propelled himself towards the keyboard. He stiff-armed Clipper aside, and before a protest could be mounted, typed two words into the keyboard.

Please stop.

The relentless shower of text that had been spilling down the computer screen abated at once. Riley's mouth was agape, and Clipper looked, disbelieving, first at the screen, then to AJ. The silence that followed lingered, and then lingered more.

Riley was first to speak. He pointed to the exit. "AJ, you need to go. You weren't checked in, so there's a good chance no one will know you were here." He didn't mention the near-certainty that he would appear on surveillance, but hoped it wouldn't come to that. This wasn't a break-in, so why would anyone bother? And there was still a chance that AJ's quick thinking – however incredible it was that it appeared to work – may have stopped this before it had gone too far.

Riley's mobile phone rang, startling the group. He looked down to see that it was Brian Matthews. "That didn't take long," he said. He pointed to Clipper and AJ, and jerked his thumb towards the door to hurry them along. They took to their feet and disappeared down the hall.

Chapter 31

March 10, 2024

Riley picked up the line: "John here."

"John, it's Brian. Corporate Security just called. They said something just happened up at the lab. Is it you?"

"Yes."

"They're pretty pissed, what's going on?"

"You'd better get up here," was all Riley could think to say.

There was silence on the line. "Is it serious?"

"I hope not, but there is that chance."

"John, we're four days from another major patch to EcoGrid. Whatever this is had better not impact that." Riley didn't respond. "John, tell me we're not impacted."

"I don't know. Just come in and I'll tell you what I can," Riley said, then hung up the line.

Clipper was back in the lab within a couple minutes. "AJ was a little shaken," he said, "but he's on his way home. What did Matthews say?"

Riley shook his head as if there could be only one answer. "There was a good ... I don't know ... twenty seconds there, where it looked like we may have dodged a bullet. That's no longer a possibility." Clipper took the words stoically. He fiddled with the back of one of the chairs, his eyes lingering on Riley, before getting a good grip on it and pulling it back to sit down. "*Corp-Sec* called Matthews," Riley explained. "Whatever we did was enough to light them up."

"Damn. Didn't take long."

"No. Seconds at most. Matthews is on his way in. This won't be pretty."

Clipper leaned back in his chair and began swiveling back and forth, then took to looking around the lab. "I feel a little like fish in a barrel."

"Only a little?"

"I'm gonna grab a Diet Coke. Want anything?"

Riley was a little surprised that Clipper would be thinking of something to drink at a moment like this, then realized the idea wasn't bad. "Same for me, thanks."

Clipper was back within a few minutes and they sat resignedly in the lab chairs, sipping at their soda and waiting. "Can you believe the turn of events that put AJ in here with us?"

"I was just thinking the same. Hindsight, hindsight," Riley said. "I should never have brought the man in here."

"It was both of us, and that's that. I couldn't count how many times the three of us have been in hot water together. Somehow, I thought those days were behind us for good."

Riley grunted. "Yeah, well, apparently not. I just hope no one notices he was with us."

"He's never been here before, so there's no record of him in the system, and he didn't sign in today."

"There is the matter of surveillance," Riley said.

"True, but you and I are here. There's no one else to look for, so why would they even look at the videos?"

"I hear you," Riley said, not placated in the least. "It's a worry, that's all. At least no one else was here." Clipper knew he was referring to Melissa.

The hallway lights came on and Matthews appeared, accompanied by a man and a woman Riley didn't recognize. Matthews entered the lab and looked around before approaching. He was well into his rant by the time he reached the midpoint of the room. "Corp-Sec, here, seems to think we have a significant breach going on," he said, indicating the man and woman who followed him in with a thumb over his shoulder. "What's the story?"

"What's the nature of the breach?" Riley asked.

"Let's start with you telling us what the hell you've been doing?" Matthews demanded, his voice already rising. "I've been following you guys for the past three weeks. Not close enough, apparently. Rumors about this project have been out on twitter and half the science forums on the internet!" He passed a menacing look at both of them, which was particularly effective, given that it was clearly not an act. The man was livid.

"You're John Riley, and you're Jason Clipper?" the woman who had accompanied Matthews into the lab asked.

"Yes," Riley said, and Clipper nodded.

"Mr. Riley, I am Deb Harris, Director of Network Security. This is Bill Garcia, a security expert on my team. A short while ago, a burst of information was routed from one of the servers on the private network directly to the internet. That was followed by a series of outgoing messages, which my team is now investigating. The problem is, none of that should have been possible. There is no line of sight from the lab subnetwork to the outside, not in either direction. At least two firewall modifications were made to make that possible, and the changes originated from this lab within the past 35 minutes."

Clipper was shaking his head. "I can't see how anything we did could have done that."

"I'll grant you that," the woman said, "not sure myself – and I do this stuff for a living." Riley was surprised by the admission, but knew it was a simple statement of truth. "It happened," she said, "that much I know. My first guess is that you inadvertently let something in – a virus, but it had to be a hell of a virus to do something like this. Is this the terminal you were using?"

"Yes," Riley said.

She pulled up a chair and started reading the text on the screen. Shortly, she was shaking her head in bewilderment. "What the hell were you two guys doing?" she said, in a tone that conveyed confoundment more than anger.

Riley regarded her for a moment, then directed his attention to Matthews. "Brian, you are right; we have been up to something." Matthews expression foretold his intention to pounce on whatever the explanation was, but he didn't speak. "We made an interesting discovery a few weeks ago. You've seen the gravity imprints that Clipper generates from the tests?"

"Of course I have," Matthews said, his anger still very much apparent, and only barely in check.

"Okay. What you haven't seen is that seven seconds after we perform any of those tests, we get anomalous patterns on the output. We thought it was noise at first, but were eventually forced to conclude that it's not. Someone out there is using the same technology we're using to generate Gravity Wells, only they're using it to communicate." Riley left off and waited for comprehension to register on Matthews' face. When it did, he seemed unsure of which, among an avalanche of questions, to ask first. "The hell? Someone beat us to gravitation?"

"It looks that way, yes."

"Who?"

Riley motioned around the lab with an open hand. "Brian, you are, at this very moment, standing chin-deep in our attempt to find the answer to that question. That is the length and breadth of it. Everything we've been doing here this morning, and for the past six weeks has been an attempt to identify the other party."

If Matthews was going to say more, it was cut short by the appearance of three more men at the entrance to the lab. They entered and stopped just inside the door, beckoning Harris to join them, and both she and Garcia did so. A conversation ensued that was not short on body language, conveying a steep escalation in anxiety. Harris began looking around the lab as if it were a sinking ship that was beyond saving.

Seeing that, Matthews turned back to Riley and Clipper, asking with forced civility: "What are we into gentlemen?"

Despite everything, Riley felt the need for measured disclosure. "We attempted to communicate by replicating a signal we received several weeks ago," Riley said. "We analyzed it until we understood how it was formatted, recreated it, and sent it back. Our version was much cruder, but it was enough – the remote party appeared to understand it. Once we achieved that, the remote party changed formats. My guess was that the first format was a breadcrumb, intentionally designed to get our attention, and the change was to lead us to improve our ability to communicate. Not sure why, to be honest. But, we studied it, made the mods on our end to mimic it as best we could, and responded again this morning. You're seeing what happened next."

Over Matthews' shoulder, Harris nodded sharply and turned to approach again, the four men in tow. "Mr. Matthews," she said. "We are, in fact, dealing with a virus as suspected. All activity seems to have ceased for now, but for the few minutes it was active, it burned up the wires. We had simultaneous traffic going out over the internet, and there was copious data coming and going over the dedicated connection between the lab and the Springboard property. We're looking at the data itself to see what was sent and received. The good news is that, as far as we know for the moment, no Mayfield Hammond proprietary information was divulged, nor any customer data compromised. Neither does there appear to have been sabotage or vandalism. The problem is this: as I said, the virus somehow reconfigured part of our local area network to gain access to the internet from our secure data centers."

"How is that even possible?" Matthews said.

"That is the question, isn't it? We're efforting it now. In the meantime, we have a couple visitors who would like to talk with you." She looked to Riley and Clipper. "Sorry gentlemen, this will have to be a private conversation."

"We'll be in the breakroom," Riley said.

Harris watched as the two walked away. "Any worry that those two are a flight risk?"

"No," Matthews said. "They could have left anytime this morning if they were going to."

One of the men spoke without waiting for an introduction. "Mr. Matthews, I'm Martin Moore, Deputy Director of Information Assurance with the NSA."

"NSA?" Matthews said, surprised. He looked around the room as if he had missed something. His eyes lingered for a moment on Harris, but her expression conveyed that she was equally perplexed. "Let's keep in mind, shall we?" Matthews said, reflexively, "that this is a lab environment we're talking about here. No customer data has been compromised in any way, nor is there any risk of that happening. And, no other sensitive information is housed within the lab that could be of relevance to anyone else, save our competitors."

"Thank you," Moore said, "but that's not what brings us here today."

Matthews pressed ahead as if Moore hadn't spoken. "Regardless, the activities of this lab are a matter of corporate concern. This lab has no–"

"Mr. Matthews, if I may," Moore said, breaking in. "I believe I can clarify the confusion."

Matthews shot a final look to Harris, but she could offer no help. "Okay," he said gruffly, his tone implying that his forbearance wouldn't last long. "I'm listening."

"Are you familiar with the LIGO Scientific Collaboration programs? Gravitational wave detection and all that?"

Matthews' eyes narrowed. The connection between Springboard and anything having to do with gravitational research were immediately clear. "In fact, I am," he said, looking again around the room, "but before you continue, Mr. Moore, I suspect that this conversation may lead into topics that are under strict NDA here at Mayfield Hammond. Can we have this conversation separately?" Matthews knew of LIGO only because of the cursory research he had done on the physics of gravitation at the start of Springboard.

Moore considered the question for a moment. "I see no particular issue with that, except that these men already know everything about the points I need to cover. Nothing about the proprietary work of Mayfield Hammond is necessarily germane for the moment. In fact, there is every chance that we will share more information with you, than we will ask for in return."

Harris spoke up. "Brian, I've been NDA'd on Springboard since the start, so I'm already aware."

Matthews considered her for a moment. "Fine," he said, then gestured for Moore to continue.

"Thank you. I'd like to introduce Aarav Kumar," he said, gesturing to the man next to him. "He is a Research Leader on the LIGO program. I think he will do a better job of describing the issues at hand than me."

"Thank you, Mr. Moore," Kumar said. "Mr. Matthews, I would like to explain a few things that will help you understand why we are here. It'll take only a few moments, I assure you." Kumar paused for a response, but Matthews offered none. "LIGO began back in 1997. Our charter was, and is, to detect gravitational waves. It was several years before we found anything, but what is not commonly known is that in 2004, a series of anomalies were picked up that were never publicized, and never explained. The anomalies manifested as gravitational disturbances – almost too faint for notice. The source of them was never found. With today's technology, we now know that the disturbances were actually a sequence of ultrafine gravitational pulses. Back then, the best we could do was take note of them as indistinguishable noise. Yet, even beyond that, and perhaps even more peculiar than the disturbances themselves, was the incredibly odd timing of them. To understand how and why, you have to know a little about how LIGO works."

"There are actually two very large LIGO detectors – laser interferometers, as they're called – and they're separated by 2,000 miles. One is in Hanford, Washington and the other in Livingston, Louisiana. The facilities are separate for a few reasons – interference cancellation mainly – but one benefit of the design is that, because gravitational waves travel at the speed of light, the difference between when the two interferometers detect the same event can say something about the direction of its origin, among other things. The shape and size of the detectors themselves – being, as they are, in the shape of a large 'L' – give us the ability to determine directionality without requiring that there be two facilities, but the two acting in concert affords to us much greater accuracy than could be achieved with only one. It's just another bit of information that adds to the story."

Matthews shifted impatiently in his chair, but didn't interrupt.

"Now," Kumar went on, "when the anomaly occurred in the early 2000's, the clocks at the facilities were capable of accurately pinpointing the time of any given event to within about ten nanoseconds – maybe a little under. In terms of how fast a gravitational wave propagates, that translates to an accuracy of about twelve meters. In other words, it would be possible for us to know the location of a wave at a specific point in time to within twelve meters. We had, of course, not had the opportunity to see that in action as yet, but that was our capability. As measurements go, it wasn't bad."

"Okay," Matthews said, in a tone that conveyed his general impatience.

"The odd timing of the event amounted to this: both facilities detected the anomalous event at precisely the same time – again, to the extent supported by our clocks. And I might add that for purposes of the issue at hand, we can consider that accuracy to be fully precise. It seemed a strange coincidence. Logic tells us that if the two detectors picked up the same event at precisely the same time, then the source had to be somewhere on a perpendicular plane between them. Do you get my meaning? It would tell us that the wave had to originate from a location pretty much exactly the same distance from both of them – directly perpendicular to an imaginary line drawn between the two detectors."

"I see the point, but I'm not following. Where is this going?" Matthews said, his patience beginning to wane.

"If you will please forbear a moment longer," Kumar said. "I believe that you will not find this dialogue to be a waste of your time." Matthews considered a moment, then nodded, gesturing for Kumar to continue with an extended hand. "Thank you, Mr. Matthews. So, both facilities recorded the time of the event, and it appeared to happen at precisely the same instant. Let me now say something more about the accuracy of our clocks. It will bring further clarity to the astonishing nature of what we found. A nanosecond is to one second, what one second is to nearly thirty-two years. At an accuracy of ten nanoseconds, we were at the equivalent of what one second would be to more than three years. When I say that the events were detected at precisely the same moment, that is quite literally, what I mean."

"But something else was wrong. The anomaly did not propagate as a wave in any way that we could understand. You see, the shape and purpose of the interferometers is that as a wave moves over them, it crosses the large 'L' shape of the detectors, giving us the ability to understand its properties as it moves along. But that didn't happen. It was more as if the anomaly was projected upon the detectors. It did not move across them, it simply appeared and then disappeared. Notwithstanding that we could not explain the behavior – even to this day, in fact – it also robbed us of the ability to pinpoint a source direction. There we were. As if detecting such a strange anomaly was not enough, there was the added strangeness of its behavior and characteristics, which we also could not understand." Kumar shook his head almost fondly at the recollection of it. "But, the good news is, the Earth turns. We kept our eyes open and watched to see if it would happen again."

"And it did?" Matthews guessed.

"Yes, it did; 10,405.4 seconds later, or about two hours and fifty-four minutes. The disturbances, to the extent of our ability to judge at the time, were identical to the first, so we quickly set about comparing timestamps. To avoid unnecessarily complicating the conversation, it is enough to know that at the rate of the Earth's rotation, that should have produced an appreciable difference in the aspect of the detectors in relation to the source, regardless of where it may have been. If we assumed that the source had not moved appreciably in relation to us, but that we had as a result of the Earth's rotation turned away from it, the result would manifest as a difference in the time of detection between the two facilities. But alas, there was again, no difference – the anomaly was detected at precisely the same time at both locations."

"Then the source must have aligned with the Earth's axis," Matthews said. "If it were due north or due south, then the rotation of the earth in relation to the source would not change."

"Astute observation, Mr. Matthews," Kumar said. "That could very well have been the explanation were it not that the two facilities are positioned at an offset of roughly 45 degrees from a direct north/south bearing. Assuming for a moment that the source of the anomaly was either directly north or directly south, there would be a delta of about two milliseconds between timestamps at each facility. The amount of time is, of course, less than what it would take for a wave to pass directly from one facility to the other, because the anomaly would overtake them, let's say, diagonally."

"This is all very interesting," Matthews said, apparently having exhausted his patience. "May I assume we're nearing the point?"

"Indeed we are," Kumar said. "There is yet another possibility that could have explained the timing peculiarities. Can you guess what it might be?"

Harris spoke before Matthews could. "That the source was either from a satellite in geosynchronous orbit, or somewhere on the ground."

"Correct," Kumar said, appearing to enjoy the discussion. "Again, if we consider the imaginary line between the two facilities, and the perpendicular plane between them with which the source must be aligned, there is no reason we should not look to locations upon, or even within the Earth as the source. So we did. It was easiest to discount the satellite possibility. We need only inquire of our friends at various space agencies. And, as expected, there were none."

"None that were disclosed to you," Matthews said.

"True, there is a chance that some secret satellite was in orbit that we were not privy to. Even if that were the case, and what a strange case it would have been for such a satellite to have been perfectly positioned with respect to our detectors, we have since been able to definitively rule out the possibility. We then diverted our attention to potential ground-based sources. We began by looking for candidate locations along the path where our perpendicular plane would intersect the surface of the earth, but found nothing. Our search for subterranean sources also yielded nothing. Failing that, we had only one remaining option; and apologies, I do not intend to patronize, but would you like to guess what that final option was?"

"Mr. Kumar is it safe to conclude that along with your activities at LIGO, that you may also be a Professor at some extremely fortuitous university?" Matthews asked.

Kumar laughed, but Harris spoke before he could respond. "You needed a third detector," she said.

Kumar's face lit up, and he pointed to her with a pleased smile. "Right again."

"And this third detector has been built?" Matthews asked.

"Yes. It has been available to us since 2007, but we didn't build it. The third detector was built by the French and the Italians. Not for the specific purposes underlying this discussion, but to their benefit, nonetheless."

"Virgo," Matthews said.

"Yes, Virgo. It's a Michelson Interferometer located near Pisa, Italy, and operated by France, Italy, the Netherlands, Poland and Hungary."

"So, all you need now is the anomaly itself."

"Yes, indeed. I must confess, it has been a painful span of years in that respect, Mr. Matthews. But, I am pleased beyond measure to say that we have finally, again, detected the anomaly."

"Really," Matthews said, with genuine interest.

"Yes," Kumar said. "Beginning just over six months ago." He stopped talking and waited for Matthews to connect the dots. It took only a moment.

Chapter 32

March 10, 2024

"I hate to disappoint, Mr. Kumar," Brian Matthews said, "but as you know, Mayfield's forays into gravitation began only a year ago, and as you yourself have pointed out, we only began seeing success within the past six months. We were not around in 2004 to have had anything to do with the anomalies at that time."

"That is a fair assertion," Aarav Kumar allowed. "Forgive me, but I happened to have overheard the final words of your conversation with one of the men here in the lab a few moments ago."

"John Riley. That was John Riley," Matthews said. "He is Research Lead on gravitation."

"I should very much like to meet him at some point. My guess is that he will confirm that the latency he sees between carrying out his tests and the appearance of what he calls, *the signal*, is not actually seven seconds, but on average, 6.4247 seconds."

"Okay," Matthews shrugged, "let's say that's correct, what difference would it make?"

"My point," Kumar continued, "is that your gravitational tests are triggering a response from some unknown source, and it is the same as we saw back in 2004. At that time, something else triggered the anomalies. We don't know what it was, but the response itself – the content of the anomalies – are identical to what your teams are seeing now. Or, at least were up to a few days ago. There has been some change, which has only been noticed very recently."

Matthews was incredulous. "A while ago you told me that the state of your technology at the time – in 2004 – was not good enough to see into the details of the anomalies – that you could only detect them as gravitational disturbances. How can you know they are the same?"

"True, at that time the disturbances were opaque to us, but we were able to capture them in analogue form with a great deal of accuracy."

"I'm not convinced," Matthews said, defiantly.

"Mr. Matthews," Kumar said, "say that I were holding a complex object in my hand, perhaps this computer keyboard," he said, pointing to a keyboard on the table. "If you could not see me or the keyboard, and I were to use a flashlight to project the keyboard's shadow onto a wall, you could capture the shape of that shadow with great accuracy. Even without having seen the details of the keyboard itself, you could then know with fair certainty if another shadow, say as projected over a shoe, were of the same object or not. If you were then able to finally see the keyboard itself, it would be possible to project its shadow, again, onto the same wall and know with reasonable certainty whether it had been used to produce the shadow you saw before. You could then extrapolate differences between the keyboard and the shoe, or a coffee cup, or a key, or anything else. The analogue of the signals being seen today are an exact match to those captured in 2004 to a degree of confidence that I am prepared to declare as conclusive. In structure, they are indeed, identical; and you should know that our equipment is able to capture far more than a simple shadow."

"All of this is still full of holes, Mr. Kumar," Matthews said. "My guess is that if your systems are reporting that some event is being detected all over the planet at the same time, the fault is in your equipment. I find it unlikely that someone is transmitting gravity-based signals from the center of the planet."

"Yes, we reached a similar conclusion."

Despite himself, Matthews was unable to hide a resurgence of agitation. "Gentlemen forgive me, but I have responsibilities to this company. We are faced with a security breach with unknown implications. As fascinating as all of this is, I am sitting when I should be running. I need to assess the situation and stop the bleeding. Instead, I am detained in discussions on intriguing, but intangible riddles."

"I understand your frustration," Moore said, his voice carrying the relaxed intonations of a man accustomed to power, and who was at that very moment, exercising it. His demeanor made the imminence of the conversation plain to everyone in the room. "Mr. Matthews, I agree and understand that your primary concern is to assess your situation. Be advised, that the most relevant information you will need to do that effectively can be found nowhere else but here. I wish there were a more concise, shorter way to convey it, but I'm afraid, as imperfect as it is, this is the best we can do – and the best *you* can do."

Kumar's eyes lingered on Moore for a moment, as if to be sure he was finished speaking before restarting the discussion. "Your assertions are logical, Mr. Matthews," he said, "but we have rechecked our systems many times, I assure you. As contradictory as it may seem, the systems of physics do not necessarily contradict what we have learned about these signals."

"So you're calling them signals now?"

"It is a recent development for me, but yes; since we discovered and began monitoring the activities playing out between this lab and the remote source. But with regard to speed limitations of gravitational waves, I can easily clarify. Recall that I have indicated that the disturbances do not travel as waves; they seem to appear and disappear in a stationary way. I cannot claim to fully understand everything about them as yet, but I do know that we are not detecting some far away event as I originally assumed – not directly, anyway. The signals themselves are the events. To clarify, I'm afraid I must resort, yet again, to another analogy. And in appreciation for your patience, you should know that we then will be able to draw our final conclusions and clarify our requests of you."

"I'm listening," Matthews said.

"We know that through the medium of air, the average speed of sound is about 340 meters per second. At that speed, within this room, there is no appreciable difference between the time you hear my voice and when Ms. Harris hears it. For all practical purposes, it's instantaneous. But if we imagined that my voice were somehow able to carry around the world, a person standing on the shores of France would not hear my words for several hours. Yet, we know that it is possible for such a person to hear them within milliseconds. How is that? Must we break the laws of physics? Must we find a way to increase the speed of sound waves? No. You and I know the answer already. The sound is first converted into a form that can be transmitted over another, faster medium, and then reproduced at its destination as sound waves. The person in France will never hear my actual voice, he will hear only a reproduction of it. No, Mr. Matthews, my suspicions are that the sender of these signals is very far away, indeed. In fact, so far away that if the method of transmission was as gravitational waves, we would not receive them for years, even if they were to come from our closest cosmic neighbor. Yet, we can now know with certainty that the signals are not many years old for one very simple reason, and one that I would never have guessed in 2004; and that is because the activities of your team are prompting them. We had assumed, since first detecting these anomalies, that we were probably witnessing the remnants of an activity that occurred far in the past, and that they had reached us from a far distant place. The signals could have been millions or even billions of years old, as far as we knew. Now, we know that we were wrong. Each gravitational test here at Mayfield Hammond is met with an almost-immediate response; within 6.5 seconds. If we perform a few simple calculations, allowing time for the remote receiver to receive and respond to the signal, it would tell us that the distance to the remote sender is approximately 3.2 seconds at the speed of this unknown medium, and that whatever that speed ultimately is, it is much greater than light. We know this because, if the medium were gravitational waves, we could easily calculate the distance to the source at roughly 1.5 times the distance of the moon. There is nothing at that location."

"So, you're now claiming that something is going faster than light?"

"Yes, but it is no contradiction to my prior statement. This could be a matter of advanced uses of quantum entanglement, but we do not think so at present. Instead, we currently suspect that something is propagating faster than light, but not through the mediums of spacetime. In the same way a person who knew nothing of radio waves could correctly assume that instantly hearing a distant voice must involve some secondary medium that is much faster than sound waves – which we would now know to be electromagnetics – it appears we should now begin applying similar logic to the puzzle before us. Whatever the ultimate answer, it will not be magic. It will only be a new awareness of an existing medium about which we happen to have no current knowledge or understanding. You must bear in mind that the speed of light, as a cosmic speed limit, is based upon, and encapsulated within the physical laws of spacetime itself – relativity, which happens to be our primary interface with the Universe around us. But keep in mind that those laws, and the principles of mass/energy equivalence that ultimately spell out its limitations of speed, are themselves defined by, and contained within that system. If there is, indeed, another medium of which we are only now coming into knowledge, that medium is certain to have its own laws and behaviors that are as different from those of relativistic physics, as electromagnetism is from sound vibrations. At present, we only know that this new medium is capable of interacting with spacetime because at the apparent endpoint of the signal, the underlying message is translated into spacetime interference as spacetime curvature."

"The signal Mr. Riley speaks of, is of the very same nature as what was detected in 2004. Only now, we are better equipped to understand them, and your team has already done much work that we could not have done alone, since we have only the means to detect, but not create gravitational interference. You see, even though the actual gravitational testing has been carried out on Mayfield Hammond properties, we have been, from our labs, able to see and monitor the activities – I would venture to say – even better than your team. I suspect that the equipment that generates the gravitational interferences are also equipped with an interferometer, otherwise Mr. Riley and his team would not be able to measure their own progress. I would also guess that your interferometer is no more than one or two hundred meters in length; whereas, each of the LIGO facilities has two detectors, set at right angles to one another, at four kilometers in length."

"Our detector is optical, and only 30 meters in length," Matthews corrected. "Believe me, persuading a revenue-driven, publicly traded company to build something as expensive as that was a feat in itself." He grunted as if considering a deep irony. "If we hadn't been able to book it as a capital expenditure, it probably would never have happened." He looked back to Moore. "Gentlemen, I'm not sure where all of this leaves us. What do you need from me?"

"This is it," Moore said. "The implication here is that the signal we're receiving is not natural – there's someone on the other end and we need to know who it is."

"Aliens?" Matthews said.

"The real McCoy."

"So, what do you want?"

"We want to talk with them, and we want to use your lab to do it," Moore said.

"That will be impossible," Matthews said. "You've seen what this virus was able to do in just a few minutes. It apparently wasn't content with a simple *hello*. It took off at a dead run, making itself at-home by reconfiguring our network and who knows what else? If we start it back up, how do we know it won't take the sudden notion to reconfigure the entire internet?"

"Mr. Matthews," Kumar said, "I suggest we isolate the lab by cutting all connections to external systems before attempting to resume communications."

"Out of the question!" Matthews said, his irritation returning with a fury.

"This is now a matter of national security," Moore cut in. "We will either leverage this lab by your leave, or unfortunately, be forced to seize this technology to build up our own capabilities. If we are forced to that course, we will also require immediate and indefinite cessation of all activities at this location. Are we clear?"

"There it is," Matthew said, his demeanor turning instantly sour. "So, there's the punchline. We have significant investment in these facilities, and in the resulting intellectual property, Mr. Moore. I'm afraid this will not be that simple."

"I understand your predicament."

"Do you?" Matthews said. "I don't think so."

Moore said: "Even if you're right, Mr. Matthews. Even if I am the personification of all your worst stereotypes of the government, believe me when I tell you that this is no ordinary circumstance. There is only one path ahead of you. Only one."

Chapter 33

March 11, 2024

AJ was tired. The drive back from North Carolina had been long and filled with troubling thoughts. Prospects of relocating to Charlotte for a fresh start had been upended by Sarah's unexpected reentrance into his life; and the oddity of his last few moments with Riley and Clipper in the lab had stayed with him like a bad dream. Whatever had happened there had clearly rattled his friends, which had in turn, rattled him.

In the wake of it all, returning home felt strangely awkward. It was definitely time for a change. Every new turn of events, however small or large, only solidified that reality. The new question was how Sarah would figure into that change. It had all seemed very simple for the few days between his and Sarah's breakup and her sudden reappearance. He would have simply found a job in Charlotte – probably with Bank of America – and made a move. It was still a possibility, except that he must now make sense of where Sarah would play into the picture.

Pride was no longer a part of it. The time for games and positioning and hurt feelings was past. He would reach out to Sarah first thing in the morning, and the two of them would talk things out.

He didn't pull into the driveway upon arriving home. He rolled to a stop on the street out front and sat in the truck for a long moment before getting out. A car he didn't recognize was parked across the street, a few houses down. When he finally looked towards his own house he was not entirely surprised to see his mother, Alice, standing in the doorway. Nothing ever seemed to escape her notice. She must have heard the truck rolling in, odd hour that it was, and come to investigate.

AJ hefted his small overnight bag and made his way to the door, leaving the larger bags for morning.

"Everything okay?" his mother asked quietly as he approached, holding the screen door open. She was a worrier.

"Yep," he said, then felt a little guilty for not being more forthcoming.

"I didn't expect you until tomorrow," she said.

"I didn't want to bother finding a room, so I decided to push through," he said, honestly.

"I've been worried about you AJ. Is something going on?"

Something in her tone, the honest and deep concern that only mothers seem to know, gave him pause. He had been acting strangely, there was no denying that, and his mother deserved more than a simple, *I'm okay.*

"Sarah broke things off with me last week and it made me start thinking about getting my life together. Truth is, I went to Charlotte to visit Riley and Clipper, but also to see about maybe moving out there."

The expression on his mother's face was hard to read. She didn't respond immediately, but a concerned look overtook her that pulled at AJ's heart. "I'm sure that you and Sarah can work things out."

"You're probably right. But, I had a couple interviews out in Charlotte and I think an opportunity may present with Bank of America."

"Why Charlotte?"

"I don't know, really. When Sarah called an end to everything, it made me want to start over – go somewhere fresh."

"Kansas City isn't big enough?"

"It is," AJ admitted. "And there's a little more to the story. Sarah flew out and met me there. She wants to reconcile. Now I'm not sure what to do. I'm going to talk with her tomorrow."

That bit of information seemed to put Alice a little more at ease. Perhaps because she saw the whole thing blowing over. "Well, glad you're home," she said, as if the point had been neatly tied off. "Get some rest."

"Thanks mom," AJ said, leaning over to kiss his mother's cheek before climbing the stairs to his room. She disappeared into the shadowy hall towards her own bedroom without another word.

*   *   *

The knock at the bedroom door was unexpected. AJ opened his eyes to a room fully bathed in light, and Alice calling his name with hushed urgency. Startled, he rose clumsily from his bed and made for the door. "What's wrong?"

"Some men are here to see you," she said, clearly alarmed.

"Me? Who...? What do they want?" he asked, confused. "Are they with the church?" It was all he could guess at the moment.

"I don't know, I don't think so," she replied, still hushed.

"Okay, give me a sec."

"Did something happen while you were away?" his mother persisted.

"What? No, nothing," he said, honestly; but in the moments that followed her leaving the doorway, as he rushed to get around, the events of the week began coming back. It took only a few moments for the lab to return to his waking memory. The recollection hit him in the pit of his stomach.

Hastily dressed, he descended the stairs to find his mother and father talking with two men in the foyer. Through the opened front door, he saw yet another man standing on the porch, and a fourth at the end of the drive. It was like a dream. Dark suits, neckties, shiny shoes; the full-on, Hollywood government agent personas – it was all there.

"Mr. Jacobs?" the first man in the group said on seeing AJ descend the stairs.

"Can I help you?" AJ asked, trying hard to show confidence.

"Sorry to disturb you unannounced like this. I'm Special Agent Michael Britt, NSA," he said politely. "We've come into knowledge of a specific event that happened over the weekend, and we're hoping that you can provide additional information."

AJ had read enough spy novels to know that the "Special" designation in the man's title meant that he was not only empowered to make arrests, but also to engage in criminal investigations. Reeling from the suddenness of it all, and part of him clinging to a thread of hope that this could be a mistake, or better yet, a bad dream, he rubbed his forehead to clear his confusion before answering. "Okay, uh, sure. Come on in," he said, motioning the man towards the living room.

The agent made no effort to move. "I'm afraid we'll need to speak confidentially. You'll need to come with us," he said.

"Why?" AJ asked, surprised.

"We need to speak confidentially," he said again, without further elaboration.

"Alice and I can leave if necessary," AJ's father put in.

"Unfortunately, that won't help us," Britt said.

Before either of his parents had time to speak again, AJ stepped forward. "Am I under arrest?"

"You are not under arrest," Britt responded, "but we're hoping you'll cooperate by answering a few questions for us."

Something in the way the scene was playing out made AJ realize that if he wasn't under arrest now, he soon would be if he didn't go along. Thoughts of riding alone in the back of a strange car, not knowing where he was going, how long he would be, or what was about to happen to him could only be better if he were not under arrest to boot.

"All right then," AJ acquiesced. "Will we be long? Should I bring anything?"

"That won't be necessary," Britt said, motioning towards the door.

AJ knew the pleasantries were a formality, and not something he would test. He had no doubt that this no-nonsense group of men and women could quickly revert to more ... direct behavior in an instant. AJ would not give them a reason for that. If there was a question of civil liberties or rights or anything else, it wouldn't be settled here. They would have to wait.

Walking down the driveway from the house, wrapped in the surreal haze of disbelief, AJ spotted four cars he did not recognize, one of them being the car he had seen the night before. They were unmarked, full-sized sedans. Special Agent Britt showed him to the back seat of the nearest one, closed the door, then took the front passenger seat without a word.

As they drove away, AJ glimpsed a man standing to the side of the house as well. If they had been watching the back, he knew, it meant they had considered him a flight risk. They had probably been there all night. It made him begin wondering how deep this rabbit hole would go.

A few minutes later, they were headed north on Interstate 35 towards downtown Kansas City, Missouri. AJ watched resignedly out the window as he passed the familiar landmarks of his hometown, trying to maintain self-control.

Thinking more about his predicament, he began gravitating towards the notion that for what would likely be many long hours of waiting and questioning; less would be more. He would not speak unless spoken to, show any more concern than he could manage, and certainly not panic.

No sooner had he settled on that course, than it was put to its first test as the car caught the Interstate 635 cutoff rather than continuing into downtown. Ten minutes later his suspicions were all but confirmed when they crossed the Missouri state line and caught I-29 north. They were headed towards the airport.

He looked down at his arm, happy to see that in the strangeness of the morning, habit had prevailed, and he had not forgotten to don his watch. It was an odd comfort, but likely to help him manage the passage of long hours that undoubtedly lay ahead. He had remembered his mobile phone as well. That was a larger comfort, but he also suspected that it would be separated from him at some point soon, whereas the watch would not.

Even so, the thought that they would take him away from the city hadn't occurred to him until now. It certainly wasn't the first unforeseen event of the young day, he mused to himself. When they arrived at the Kansas City Municipal Airport 20 minutes later, AJ was not particularly surprised when the car bypassed the roads he was familiar with and made its way to what he guessed to be a VIP area, bustling with unfamiliar activity.

The car wheeled among a series of tan-colored metal buildings with enormous gaping garage doors, and eventually emerged onto the tarmac where a private jet stood waiting. There were no markings on the plane to indicate who owned or operated it. It was a moot point, of course. The NSA was the NSA. Although AJ did spot the words Gulfstream G650ER in small gray lettering near the nose of the aircraft. He had always wondered what it would be like to ride in one, but this was not the way he wanted to do it.

The car rolled to a stop, and he was politely but firmly corralled onto the airstair of the plane without explanation. As he entered the threshold, the first real sensation of – not fear, but anger – set upon him. He could not imagine the need for such secrecy now that he was in custody, whether formally under arrest or not; and hoped someone would be forthcoming with an explanation soon.

Stepping onto the plane felt odd. AJ hadn't known what to expect, certainly not that a small plane would be filled with row after row of seats like its larger commercial counterparts, but the elegance of the interior was remarkable.

AJ counted only nine individual tan leather seats in the main cabin, one of which being set off by itself at the rear. A man in a dark suit was sitting there but didn't stir on AJ's entry. The remaining eight were arranged into groups of four, facing each other to create two separate sections, which were separated by a couch stretched along the port side, and across from that, a long wooden bar. A solitary man sat in the group of chairs towards the aft of the aircraft. On seeing AJ, he stood and warmly gestured for him to take a seat.

"Good morning, Mr. Jacobs," he said.

"I'm in high hopes that it is," AJ said, "and please call me AJ."

"Of course. I am Martin Moore, Deputy Director of the IAD, with the NSA."

"I'm sorry, IAD?" AJ asked.

"Information Assurance Directorate."

If it hadn't been clear already, that title was enough to clinch the question of whether all of this was related to Riley and Clipper and the lab. It most certainly was. In spite of it, AJ was more than a little surprised at how calm he felt. It's odd how a sense of calm can take the place fear, once a fear is realized. It's no longer a question then. With the question out of the way, it becomes a matter of dealing with it. That transition took only moments to occur for AJ as he took his seat.

"I can't help saying, Mr. Moore, that this morning has unfolded something like a Hollywood movie for me."

Moore grinned slightly at that, but only for a moment. "If it's any consolation, the morning has been similar for me."

AJ heard the door of the aircraft closing behind him and glanced back to see that Special Agent Britt had silently taken a seat in the forward section. AJ turned back to Moore to find him studying him intently. The odd admission from the Deputy Director was difficult to understand, but the look on his face seemed to convey a sense of puzzlement that corroborated it.

"AJ, most people – civilians – don't have a good understanding of how the NSA works," Moore said, without preamble. "I'd venture to say, most don't know anything. Even so, perhaps you could guess that most individuals who are interviewed by the NSA are not escorted via private aircraft in the company of a Deputy Director."

AJ had no response to that, so Moore continued. "There is still a chance that everything can go back to normalcy, for both of us, but you should know that we are perched precariously against a very real possibility that they won't. Not ever."

AJ was becoming confused, and the direction the conversation was quickly taking was doing little to calm his apprehensions. "Is there a chance you've got the wrong man?" AJ asked. "You seem to be describing possibilities that are outside my typical purview, to put it mildly. I work at a home improvement store."

The plane had begun taxiing, and shortly, the windows darkened to become opaque. They were the type that could transition from transparency to opacity instantly and automatically. Moore didn't take notice. "There is no chance, AJ," he said, simply. "Let me tell you about my hopes for this morning."

Something about that statement was deeply unnerving to AJ. Maybe it was partly because Moore had jumped right into things with few pleasantries. It was possibly the most unnerving part of the morning so far, which was no small thing. His voice suddenly dry, AJ only nodded.

"AJ, you will have your doubts. You will be convinced that I am manipulating you, and in some ways, maybe I am. If I ask for your trust, it will have the opposite effect. So here's what I ask of you. I ask that you bear with me. That you believe that I am looking for the truth. That you prepare yourself for many long hours of questions that are not designed to incriminate you, but only to bring clarity."

The plane took to the air, and despite the general numbness that enveloped AJ's mind, he noted how much more acceleration he experienced than on any commercial flight he had ever been on. Moore seemed fully desensitized to it. He sat watching as AJ's reeling mind struggled to grasp the moment.

True, AJ had never been interviewed by the NSA, but he knew that Moore must be telling the truth about one thing: this was clearly not typical – it couldn't be. He was flying in a private jet with the Deputy Director of some part of the NSA he didn't know existed – if the man was to be believed anyway. The plane seemed to lend credibility to Moore's story. But still, it defied explanation. Any explanation. There was no calamity, risk, threat, fear or event

AJ could imagine that would lead to the need for the NSA to pluck an unremarkable 27-year-old out of bed in the mid-west, and whisk him away to; where? he wondered.

"Are you taking me back to Charlotte?" AJ asked.

"Yes," Moore replied.

"To the lab?"

"Yes."

"Why? Are Riley and Clipper there?"

"They are; and the why of it, you will understand soon enough," Moore said, some of the formal nicety now absent from his tone. "But, I must now insist that you answer a few questions for me. We'll be in Charlotte in just over an hour, so we should make good use of the time."

"Okay," AJ said. As far as he knew, there was nothing about the events in the lab that he could shed further light on than what Riley and Clipper must have already done. This was a waste of time, and the NSA should know it. If something big had happened, AJ understood that the NSA would certainly want to talk with him, but not in such a dramatic way. He had been a bystander, and Moore must know that by now, so why the drama?

Moore began his questions.

"You studied economics at Duke University and earned a Master's?"

"That's correct," AJ answered.

"Should it seem odd to me that you are now working as a supervisor at a local lumberyard?"

"Maybe," AJ answered. "It's a question I've been asked more than once." He was not particularly interested in elaborating further.

"I would have guessed that with credentials like yours, you would be gainfully employed at a financial institution of some sort, or perhaps at a large corporation by now."

"That will come soon enough."

"I see," said Moore. "You've known John Riley and Jason Clipper for how long?"

"Most of my life. Clipper from when we were about 10 years old, I'd guess. Riley, longer. We went to elementary school together."

"You are close?"

"I guess so. We've been friends all along."

"Why did you go to Charlotte this past couple weeks?"

AJ did not want to make Sarah any part of this. He had no way of knowing whether the NSA knew Sarah had come to Charlotte, but he wasn't going to volunteer it. AJ had visited Riley and Clipper, it was that simple.

"I am thinking about moving out there. I actually applied for a couple jobs before going, and interviewed with Bank of America while there."

Moore nodded as if the information corroborated some of what he already knew. "I see," he said. "And I presume that the presence of John Riley and Jason Clipper were factors in your selection of Charlotte?"

"Yes, and that Charlotte happens to be something of a financial hub. Not necessarily common knowledge to people outside of the vertical."

"I see," Moore said. "How would you characterize John and Jason?"

AJ shrugged. "A couple typical guys, I guess. Except Riley is brilliant. He's probably a genius. Physics. Clipper is witty, funny, but also smart; just not in the particular way Riley is. If you talk with them, you'll see my meaning shortly. Well, maybe not the funny part, given the situation."

Moore offered a small smile. "Understandable. How would you characterize yourself?"

"Not a genius, and probably not funny."

Moore grunted. "Back to your prior point, AJ, about why the NSA should be interested in you. Your point is a valid one. Why would the NSA go to this much trouble for a person who looks to be as typical as yourself? Why are you on this plane?"

AJ knew he could answer by pointing out that Moore would know better than he possibly could, but also knew that it really wasn't true. AJ understood the question, and Moore had not asked it to be cute. "Believe me, that has been the underlying theme of my entire morning. I wish I knew."

"And you don't?"

"Let me clarify," AJ said. "I think it's safe to say that I'm here because of what happened on Sunday morning in the computer lab at Mayfield Hammond. But I'm destined to disappoint you there. In fact, I'm guessing that there are hours of frustration ahead of me – and you – as you refuse to believe that I am being as forthright and honest as you are claiming to be right now. I don't know much about what happened. I truly don't know. I was there, but Riley and Clipper had not told me anything about what they were doing, or why. And I never asked."

Moore sat in thought for a long moment without speaking. He seemed to be wrestling with what to say next. "I can almost guarantee, AJ, that you will not disappoint."

"Sounds ominous," AJ said, somewhat surprised by the statement.

"It may be, actually," Moore replied, surprising AJ even further. "We need answers, and not only from you. We have found ourselves at a place and time where we need to understand something – something that could be big. I don't think you're purposely hiding anything, and I don't think your motives are bad, but parts of the story that may seem trivial to you, could be more important than they appear. So as I ask my questions, please think of them in that way. Help us understand what happened yesterday to the best of your ability. Please."

"And what did happen?" AJ asked.

Moore hesitated. "That's a fair question. I can only guarantee that you will know everything you need to know before the day is through, but the story needs to unfold in the right way – in the right sequence. I'm guessing you'll agree with our approach once we get to the lab."

"Are Riley and Clipper okay?" AJ asked, suddenly alarmed.

"They are."

"Okay then," AJ said, spreading his hands as if conceding to the arrangement, "how can I help?"

Chapter 34

March 11, 2024

AJ didn't know how fast a Gulfstream could fly, but it was clearly faster than a commercial airliner. In just over an hour, they were on approach to Douglas International, and minutes after that he found himself in the backseat of another non-descript sedan heading east on I-85 through Charlotte.

In no time, they arrived at the familiar lot on the Mayfield Hammond campus where he last saw Riley and Clipper only the day before. It felt more like a week. The lot was full of cars, and cordoned off but for one entrance where a small contingent of men and women stood wary guard.

Looking around, AJ was amazed to realize that the other parking lots were empty, at least the ones he could see. It was a Monday, and on any other day, he assumed, they would be filled to capacity. Whatever had happened was apparently enough that the entire company had closed for business, or at least, the employees had been told to work from home.

AJ struggled to grasp the gravity of the situation. It just kept getting bigger. The upheavals of the day had not ceased to crescendo since his first breath, and now that he was here, onsite at

Mayfield Hammond, he realized that only now was his day truly about to start.

He was ushered into the building, which was a flurry of activity. AJ was not immediately taken to the lab, but routed through hallways and corridors that quickly made him lose track of where he was. Finally, he was shown into a large conference room where a dozen or so people either stood or sat chatting in small knots. As he entered, he saw a spread of sandwiches, chips, cookies and cans of soft drinks on a side counter.

He was also startled to see Deputy Director Moore in the room. That was a hard one to figure out. AJ wondered if he had flown in from the airport by helicopter or simply been a car or two ahead of him on the drive in. Of the mysteries that lay before him, however; that one didn't hold his attention for long.

Moore was deep in discussion with another man who looked to be in his early fifties; also in suit and tie, and with the hardened look of someone long acquainted with authority. AJ soon became disconcerted as the man's gaze began to wonder frequently in his direction.

"Mr. Jacobs," a woman's voice came to him from over his shoulder. "Please help yourself to something to eat if you'd like. We'll get started shortly." The voice belonged to a middle-aged woman, who was pleasant enough, but clearly all business. She gestured towards the food counter with a smile. "Afterwards," she went on, "please take your seat here." She motioned towards a paper nameplate bearing his computer-printed name sitting on the conference table.

The table formed a horseshoe with the open end pointed towards a large-screen display at the end of the elongated room, which was currently showing the seal of the NSA with its stately looking eagle holding a skeleton key in its talons. Looking around, AJ saw similar nameplates on the table in front of each chair, including two across the room that bore the names John Riley and Jason Clipper. Neither of the two were in the room as yet. By this time, AJ was so saturated with the twists and turns of the day that he gave it little thought, choosing instead to take a mental break and concentrate on eating.

Only a couple of bites into his Turkey Club, Riley and Clipper did enter, apparently also under escort. They noticed AJ immediately and both grimaced at the sight of him. Something told AJ that attempting to approach them would not be a good idea. That same insight seemed to occur to them as well. After a brief exchange with the same woman that directed AJ to the food counter, both Riley and Clipper did the same.

The woman soon brought the room to order. "Please take your seats, we'll begin momentarily," she said. The room fell to a hush almost immediately, but for Moore and the other man, who didn't acknowledge the request at all.

"Let's please start with a round of introductions and then we'll get to our agenda," she began, but was immediately cut short.

"Skip introductions. Let's get to it." The name in front of the man read, Jeff Ward. AJ figured he was an important person by Moore's demeanor towards him, but the nameplate gave no title.

"Okay," the woman said. "I would like to at least point out that Director Jeff Ward and Deputy Director Martin Moore of the NSA are here to help with the discussion." She motioned towards them with an open hand. "We have a lot to cover, but our agenda is fairly simple." Pushing a button on a handheld remote, the screen at the end of the room switched to a simple outline.

- *Introductions*

- *Opening comments from Director Ward*

- *Situation assessment*

- *Risks*

- *Opportunities*

- *Action items*

- *Next steps*

"Thank you all for coming," the woman said. "I am Natalie Briggs, Staff Ops for Director Ward. I'll be facilitating the meeting. As you can see, our goal this afternoon is straightforward. We'll effort to understand what has happened, assess risks, opportunities and plan next steps. As Director Ward indicates, we will forego introductions."

She turned to Ward. "Sir, do you have any opening comments?"

Ward's gaze fell immediately upon AJ, where it lingered for a short moment before shifting back to Briggs. He then began scanning the room as he spoke. "The events of the past two days have been a surprise," he said. "What began as a matter of breach of corporate protocol was soon discovered to have implications to national security, and now, potentially to global security. I want to be clear that anything and everything spoken in this room, that transpires in this building, or is in anyway connected with the events in question will be regarded with secrecy, of which no higher provision exists."

AJ exchanged meaningful looks with Riley and Clipper at that, but quickly looked away so as not to draw attention.

"The individuals in this room shall constitute the core of a team that will remain singularly focused on understanding and resolving issues and coordinating activities." He gestured back to Briggs. "Please proceed."

The lights dimmed, and the display was updated to depict a timeline. Briggs began speaking with admirable confidence and clarity.

"About six weeks ago, a team of engineers led by John Riley," she motioned briefly towards him with a backward wave of her hand without turning fully in his direction, "discovered anomalous readings in data collected from research experiments on gravitation here on the campus and at a satellite location approximately 60 miles from here. The detailed information was compiled and rendered graphically as you see here." Another slide appeared showing the grid patterns of gravity wells that were all too familiar to Riley and Clipper. It was a gravity print.

"This distorted grid shows curvature upon spacetime itself, as artificially produced by equipment designed for Mayfield Hammond by John Riley. The non-flat appearance of the grid is a visual depiction of gravitation. In other words, this image represents artificially modified gravity – a feat that, to our knowledge, has never been achieved before. The short experimental tests are usually no more than five to eight seconds each in duration. Although the experiments have been underway, in various forms, for nearly a year, it was not until six weeks ago that an anomaly related to the experiments was noticed."

Briggs clicked the remote again and another slide appeared showing a similar grid, mostly flat this time, but with small ripples covering it from one end to the other.

"It was discovered, by accident in fact, that approximately seven seconds after the conclusion of each experimental iteration, further distortion can be seen playing across the fields as shown in the still frame here. Initially mistaken for incidental interference, further scrutiny by Jason Clipper and team led to the understanding that the interference has structure, and furthermore, that the duration of time between the conclusion of the experiments and the appearance of the anomaly was exact for each occurrence to the extent of our ability to measure. Again, that duration being just under seven seconds."

"Detailed analysis reveals that the patterns contained within these captured events are identical, one to the next, and exhibit characteristics consistent with communication handshaking. In simple terms, when mechanized systems establish contact with one another, they undergo a series of steps to establish the terms that define how they will exchange information. For the most part, regardless of the particular protocol in play, the steps to establish the rules of engagement are fundamentally the same across modern systems. This one follows a three-way handshake similar to that employed by TCP, which is the underlying communication protocol used for the internet. The three-way handshake includes a synchronization request initiated by the originator, a synchronization acknowledgement from the receiver, and a final acknowledgement back from the originator."

AJ found himself spellbound by the revelation of what Riley and Clipper had been doing while he, to his astounding embarrassment, had been virtually idle from a professional perspective. Riley was clearly even more than the genius AJ had long suspected him to be.

The meeting continued for another two hours as milestone events from the prior weeks were slotted into a timeline – a story that culminated into their present situation. AJ had known none of it, and was by now somewhat impressed with the discipline Riley and Clipper had shown in not revealing any of this to him in the nearly two weeks he had been in Charlotte to visit.

"19 days ago," Briggs continued, "Andrew Jacobs appeared in Charlotte. He stayed first with John Riley for a period of six days, then with Jason Clipper. On the 7th day of his stay, he was visited by Sarah Henson who flew in from Kansas City on the evening of February 27th, met with Mr. Jacobs the following morning at a Starbucks near the hotel where she had a room, and returned home later that day. At this time, Sarah remains a person of interest, but is not considered an accomplice."

AJ's heart was pounding by the time Briggs' final words about Sarah were spoken, and he applied all of his fortitude to not reacting. Thankfully, Briggs rolled forward without further comment, and no other attention was drawn to Sarah's visit. Still, AJ had to wonder whether Sarah had been approached by the NSA and how much, if anything, she knew about where he was, and what was happening with Riley and Clipper. Gauging by how little he himself knew, she could scarcely know much at all, even if they had contacted her.

Mention of her name also brought to mind that he had planned to spent time with her today. The two were planning to

have a discussion this very afternoon, which AJ had looked forward
to very much. It would have been about now, he realized. He looked
at his watch. It was nearly 4:00 PM; 3:00 PM Kansas City-time.

That realization, and the swirl of unfathomable events of the
day – still well beyond his ability to order into any similitude of
sense – filled him with sudden despair, which quickly turned to
anger. He tuned back into the monolog of the meeting, which hadn't
stopped and showed little signs of doing so anytime soon.

"...the physical layout of the facilities and computer systems
are a logistical challenge from a security perspective," Briggs was
saying.

"Excuse me," AJ interrupted, raising his hand slightly.

Briggs stopped and looked to him flatly.

"I'm sorry, Ms. Briggs. To say that this day has been
unusual and unexpected for me would be an understatement without
precedent, probably in the history of humanity. I do not want to
strike a disrespectful tone, but I am exhausted and dumbfounded,
and request to be excused so that I may rest and apply myself to
putting the world back together again."

AJ could sense Riley and Clipper's eyes boring into him,
but didn't look in their direction. Instead, he found and held the
gaze of Director Ward. He was suddenly past caring what the
calculating cast of Ward's expression could mean. The room stood
suddenly silent and frozen as all eyes swung wordlessly to Ward,
including Briggs', whose hands were laced over her stomach as she
stood waiting for a response.

Ward was clearly not a man accustomed to feeling rushed
by anything. He looked searchingly at AJ for a long moment, but
oddly, didn't appear angry or in any way aghast at AJ's interruption.
Instead, he sat looking at AJ as if reappraising him. AJ held his gaze
as the silence drew on, and for a moment only the two of them were
in the room.

"We will adjourn," Ward said, at length.

Surprised by the response, Briggs hesitated for a second before speaking. "Very well," she said, "when would you like to reconvene?"

"TBD," Ward answered, still looking at AJ. "Mr. Jacobs, could I have a moment?"

It was clear, although AJ hardly took notice, that the premature end to the meeting was a welcomed respite for everyone. With little hesitation, the group rose and shuffled out without looking back, although some glances were thrown in his direction. He didn't particularly notice Riley or Clipper leaving the room, as he and Ward were still somewhat locked in the throes of a visual standoff.

In a moment, the room was empty but for the two of them, Briggs being the last of the others to leave, closing the door behind her. Ward and AJ sat across the room from one another without moving.

"I would apologize for the way this day has unfolded for you, Mr. Jacobs, were it not that it hasn't been particularly kind or fair to any one of us."

"I can see that," AJ said," which is why I think I just spoke for all of us who were in this room in saying that we need a break."

"And I can see that," Ward conceded, "but sometimes we have to deal with what life hands to us, don't we?"

AJ nodded.

Ward hesitated, taking AJ in for another moment. "Answers to your questions are forthcoming, to the extent we have them," Ward went on. "In fact, you just brought their disclosure to an end for now; but it was well enough. If you would like to be shown to your accommodations, I am happy to oblige. But if you would like to cut to the chase, as I suspect you would, I'll take you to the lab where you and John Riley and Jason Clipper were yesterday morning and show you what has caused all of this." He waved his hand as if in reference to the whole of the events in question.

Of all the things Ward was likely to say to him, this was probably the most unexpected and unlikely. *Why? Why again, would he be shown this level of special attention?* The jet, the Deputy Director, and now the Director himself.

"I can guess what you're thinking, Mr. Jacobs. You will have your answers in 30 minutes if you come with me."

Chapter 35

March 11, 2024

A lice lifted her phone, knowing the call she was about to make would shatter the calm of another life as hers had been. She and Peter had watched the government car wheel away with AJ more than 10 minutes ago, but it was only now that the last two of the five cars had finally left.

"They were making sure we didn't follow," Peter said.

Alice's gaze remained fixed out the window, but she didn't respond. She watched the cars drive away without comment, then dialed the phone.

The tentative voice of Sarah Henson answered. "Hello?"

"Sarah, it's Alice. We need to talk right away. Can you come to the house?"

There was a slight delay. "Yes, is everything okay? Is AJ okay?"

"We don't know," Alice said, honestly.

"Is he hurt, did something happen?"

"He is not hurt, Sarah. And I'm sorry to be cryptic in this way, but you will need to come here. We must talk immediately. I can think of nothing that could be more important for either of us."

Within what seemed only seconds, Sarah arrived and was calling for Alice from the entryway. There was no knock at the door.

"We're in the study," Alice answered, her voice muffled through the twists and turns of the house.

Sarah quickly made her way through the corridors to find Peter and Alice looking at a computer monitor standing atop a dark wood desk in the center of the room as if staring down a clever and untrusted opponent.

"What happened?" Sarah asked, fighting for control.

Alice drew her eyes from the computer. "We were awakened this morning by several agents from the NSA. They took AJ away."

"The NSA?" she said, incredulously, stammering to place the name. "The National Security Assoc..., no Agency?"

"Yes. They claimed something happened in Charlotte while AJ was there visiting John and Jason but gave no details. They escorted him away for questioning, but we don't know to where or for how long, or even what they're looking for."

"Have you talked with John or Jason?"

"No," Alice said. "We've tried calling. No answer from either one of them, their phones go straight to voicemail."

"What are you going to do?" Sarah asked, her voice quivering slightly.

"We're Googling the NSA, trying to find someone who can give us information."

Sarah took up her mobile phone to join the effort. Her fingers danced across its surface with practiced efficiency. The room was at once quiet as the three took to the task of mining the internet for information. It was only seconds before Sarah broke the silence. "Oh my god!" she said. Her tone was almost a panic.

The statement set Alice and Peter bolt upright. "What? What did you find?"

"It's in the news," she said, her voice doing little to mask her anxiety.

Peter was on his feet and moving towards the living room television in an instant. He grabbed up the remote and turned it on. "Where did you see it," he asked.

Sarah was looking at her phone in disbelief, slow to answer. "It's... everywhere," she said, her voice trailing.

Alice and Peter had been so absorbed in trying to learn about the NSA, that neither one of them thought of the possibility that there could be something related to AJ's circumstance in the news. Peter turned to CNN. At first, he didn't know what to make of it. It was an aerial view of an office park, clearly taken from the vantage of a helicopter. Peter looked down at the remote as if to change channels but was forestalled by Sarah.

"Wait, that's it," she said.

"What?" He looked to her, then wheeled back to face the television. He saw it almost immediately. The names of John Riley and Jason Clipper appeared impossibly in the caption at the bottom of the screen. There was no mention of AJ, but it was enough.

Alice was weeping by now. The images on the television were final, unyielding confirmation that what had begun as a scary intrusion into their lives that morning had risen to manifest their worst fears. Whatever this was, it was not going away. She knew as she watched the television screen, that something new had taken residence in their lives, and they were only now at the start of whatever it was.

Chapter 36

March 11, 2024

Director Ward guided AJ through the halls of the Information Technology building, usually called the *IT building*, to the point where he gained a recollection of where he had been the day before. The lab would appear on the left shortly. The glass door to the large room was held open by a man who offered no further acknowledgement as he and Ward passed through.

"You recall all of this, of course?" Ward asked.

Unlike the day before, the lab was now fully lit. "I do," AJ said. "It's even more impressive when you can see it." The attempt at levity was not acknowledged.

"Good. I'd like to level-set before we look at the computer terminal where all of this happened. Please, have a seat." He motioned towards a small table nearby. They sat, and he placed the electronic tablet he had been carrying upright so they could both see it.

Ward swiped across the screen and it lit up to show a vaguely familiar string of text. "This is a reproduction of what the computer terminal displayed yesterday when yourself and Mr. Riley and Mr. Clipper were here in the lab," he said. "It's a transcript. If my understanding is correct, Jason was the primary driver?"

"Yes," AJ said, not taking his eyes from the small screen. "He was sitting at the terminal as Riley and I watched."

"Good. That is my understanding. I'm not sure how much you gleaned from the meeting we just left, but the distortion Ms. Briggs made repeated reference to was, in truth, a mechanized initiation of communication."

"Yes," AJ said. "Someone was trying to talk with Riley and Clipper electronically."

"Not exactly, but essentially, yes; someone was trying to communicate with them," Ward said. "You may be even more intrigued to know that Mr. Riley and Mr. Clipper knew that. In fact, the events of yesterday had nothing to do with gravitation, per se, but were an attempt by both of them to acknowledge and communicate back with whoever this was."

AJ shook his head in bewilderment and Ward nodded as if acknowledging what AJ must be thinking.

"Mr. Riley and Mr. Clipper's attempt at communication was met with an invasion into Mayfield Hammond's computer systems by a 3rd party. It essentially installed a virus into the datacenter, which proceeded to replicate and enhance itself until it had full control of everything – nearly."

"Nearly?" AJ said. "So Clip was able to shut it down?"

"No, Mr. Jacobs," Ward said, "he didn't shut it down. You did. You shut it down."

After a moment of thought AJ understood his meaning. He recalled typing 'please stop' into the terminal and being astonished, as they all were, that the system seemed to acknowledge and comply with the request.

"Do you recall what was shown on the terminal after you typed that request?" Ward asked.

"I was out the door shortly after that, but I think it responded with a prompt to continue."

"That's correct," Ward confirmed. "Many events have played out since then. Among them that Corporate Security became involved – alerted by alarms and safeguards built into the system. Corporate Security then notified Mayfield's senior management, and then the FBI. The FBI pulled in the NSA, and by early afternoon this building had become the buzz of activity you see now. The good news is that what Mr. Riley and Mr. Clipper did not know was that the lab can be automatically and physically isolated if a breach is detected, which is what happened. Fortunately, that safeguard worked remarkably well."

"Everything was contained, then?"

"Yes," Ward said. "So far as we can tell."

"Okay," AJ said, instantly relieved.

"But let me show you what happened next." Ward swiped again at the tablet, which had gone dark while they were speaking. The screen relit, and Ward carefully inched the text down to show the next line. "Once we verified that the datacenter was truly isolated, we decided to say *yes* to the prompt – to let the virus continue whatever it was attempting to do. This was about 6:30 PM last evening. So," he said, gesturing to the tablet, "here's the prompt: *Continue?*" When Ward saw that AJ had read it, he nudged the text down a little further to reveal the next line. "And here's our response: *Yes.*"

He leaned back and looked at AJ with what, for some unknown reason, reminded AJ of a car salesman about to close a deal. "Would you like to guess what happened next?"

"I…, have no idea," AJ said.

Without further comment, Ward revealed the next statement. It read; "Is Andrew Seymour Jacobs present?"

AJ read the line, and then again, his brow furrowing in disbelief. Ward answered his unspoken question before he could ask. "It's not a joke and it's not a trick, Mr. Jacobs."

"But, this has to be a–"

"Mistake?" Ward cut in. "In what way? What kind of trick or joke or mistake could this be?"

Ward looked to the tablet then paused as if momentarily distracted by some inner thought, then shrugged. "So, there we were. We talked it over. It took two hours to decide how to respond. First, we knew we needed to talk with you. Second, we decided that we had been asked a simple question, and that we should provide a simple answer – so we did."

Ward revealed the next few lines of text. It showed that a response of 'No' was entered into the computer, which was followed immediately with another prompt: 'Please locate Andrew Seymour Jacobs. Is Andrew Seymour Jacobs present?'"

AJ's next words were almost a protest. "But no one even knew I was here. I had never identified myself. Riley let me in, but I never showed any ID or scanned into any electronic systems. It has to be a–" but he trailed away, not knowing how to complete the statement.

"Frankly, we don't know how you were identified either," Ward said, simply.

"Who then? Who is this?" AJ asked, almost in shock.

"And so we arrive at the crux of the matter," Ward said. "We don't know who it is, but we do know who it isn't." His gaze suddenly became searching again. He peered into AJ's eyes as if the next statement were a threshold that, once crossed, could not be undone. "Mr. Jacobs, this message did not originate from anywhere on earth."

Chapter 37

March 11, 2024

AJ blinked confusedly.

"You heard me," Ward said.

"Are you sure, how do you know?" AJ knew the questions were ridiculous as soon as he had spoken them. He made to apologize, but Ward waved him off.

"Don't worry. The questions are natural."

Ward sighed, showing the first outward signs of how tired he must be by now. "Anyway, you're up to date; on the big rocks, anyway."

"How long have Riley and Clipper known all of this?"

"They don't. From their perspective, the communication amounted to the disappointment that someone had beaten them to gravity. As far as we know, they never suspected that the 3rd party could be extraterrestrial. Who would? But now that you're here we can take the next step."

"To see what happens when we respond that I'm present?" AJ said, completing the thought.

"That's correct. There was some debate about whether you needed to know the full details. The truth is, I don't think it was absolutely necessary, but it was my call to bring you into the loop. If all of this is true," Ward gestured around the room, "if we really have made *First Contact* with an alien race, I choose that there will be no deception in the exchange; I will, at every turn, consider how history will look back on this day, and the parts we all play in it. No one with a role as major as yours will be an unwitting accomplice. The *need to know* circle will remain extremely tight, but for those within that circle, information will flow."

AJ was impressed by that. "Thank you, sir," he said.

Ward only nodded in response.

"The nature of my role is unknown then," AJ said. "Could be that whoever this is, is waiting for my go ahead only because I was the one who asked them to stop. Once I give it, I may drop from the picture altogether."

"In fact, Mr. Jacobs, that is the prevailing theory. There is the question of how the 3rd party could have known it was you who entered the request to stop. Beyond that, honestly, there are few reasons we can think of that you, as an individual who was present only incidentally, could have any greater significance to them. But, however this bears out for you, it's worth mentioning that the fact you were asked for by name, whether it leads to anything more or not, has placed you into the history books. You were the first man to actually speak to an alien intelligence, and that's not trivial."

It was something to think about, but in comparison with what the next few hours could hold, felt strangely empty. "I agree," AJ said, "about my role in this. It'll probably end when we respond, but I'd like to stay and witness the event if it's okay."

"I see no problem with that," Ward allowed.

"Thank you. Are there any working theories on how they knew it was me?"

Ward shrugged. "The working theory is that the virus identified Mr. Riley and Mr. Clipper from the badge access system, which recorded that they were on premises when they entered the building. We're not sure how the connection to you was made, but expect to know soon."

"How? By asking?"

"No need. We have a complete capture of what the virus was doing behind the scenes as Mr. Clipper interacted with it on the computer terminal. As the virus grew and became more sophisticated, it began reaching out; first, further into Mayfield Hammond's computer systems and then out onto the internet. We have a complete record of the queries it transmitted, to where, and the information it received in return. Amazing stuff, really, and I have never used the words more fittingly. It pulled in information at an increasing rate, which it used to supplement and further build itself up. What started as a download of only a few megabytes quickly began learning and reshaping itself. By the time you halted it, it was well on its way to becoming a staggering piece of AI software. If we do nothing else from this point, the information we already have will keep our teams busy for years."

"The virus is a Trojan Horse? It wasn't a living alien entity, but the virus itself that remotely and autonomously began doing all this on its own?"

"It's looking that way," Ward said. "The virus was gathering all the information it could, and turning it into intelligence. Scary as hell."

"To put it mildly," AJ agreed. "The datacenters are now isolated, but what about the access it had before that? Could the virus be out in the wild?"

"It could, but we don't think so. It appears that the virus was gathering information, but made no attempts to replicate itself. If it did, we're done." Ward said, fatalistically. "But hopefully, our current understanding will hold. We're physically isolated now. There are literally no physical connections that the virus can use to get out. We've removed all wireless instruments from the building, and we're even on backup power – detached from the power grid. It's possible, after all, to communicate even over electrical lines. I didn't know that before yesterday, but apparently, it's not unusual. X10 protocol, they call it. If we can do it, these guys sure as hell can."

"When are we going to respond, then?"

"Tomorrow morning."

"And Riley and Clipper, will they be brought into the loop?"

"They are as we speak. This was going to be disclosed in the briefing that Ms. Briggs was giving back in the conference room. We cut that short, so Riley and Clipper are being brought up to speed now."

"You know," AJ said, thoughtfully, "once we restart this thing, it'll continue to build itself, and based on what we saw yesterday, it won't waste any time."

"We know, believe me," Ward said. "But like any other living thing, it can only grow if it's fed. This thing feeds on data, and we control that now. Our computer team thinks the virus will realize it has been contained almost immediately after we restart it. The hope is that it'll adapt by requesting information. When it does, we'll give it only what we're willing to share."

"Does all this mean that the aliens are using Riley's gravity contraption as their communication conduit?"

"That is precisely what it means," Ward answered.

"And Riley didn't know these callers were alien?"

"Correct."

AJ realized that following the line of reasoning could incriminate Riley and Clipper, so he left off. But if Riley really was fooled, then being contacted by an alien race wouldn't be the only remarkable event of the past few days. He was always about the big picture. He never started anything without having the end in mind.

Chapter 38

March 12, 2024

D irector Ward sat with AJ for several minutes after briefing him on the situation, but eventually rose and disappeared to other matters. He had shown more patience and forbearance than AJ could have expected from a man of such weighty position.

The day had been one to unravel the most stolid of nerves, and sitting suddenly alone at the small table, AJ felt the weight of it beginning to settle in. His list of woes was long. The nature of his interment with the NSA was top of mind, and far from clear. He had not yet been arrested, but knew he was not free to leave either – even if he had wanted to. And as unbelievable as it was, he wanted to stay.

Underlying that was the sense of loss at not being able to share the day with Sarah, and more importantly, to better understand where the two of them stood. Considering everything, that one should seem trivial, but it didn't.

Then there was anxiety around the safety of Riley and Clipper. Maybe that was the top concern after all. The risk of criminal charges of some sort or another being levied against them was real and scary, and he wondered if they realized it.

And finally, there were his parents – especially his mother. AJ knew she would be somewhere drowning in a flood of anguish, but that anguish would build quickly into a fury that would not be easily contained once started. His biggest fear was that they would start spending money on legal assistance, and that's not where their hard-earned retirement savings belonged. He had to talk with them soon, period.

Yet, even with all of this, there was still something else, and it took only a few moments of inward searching to find it. He wanted to be part of this; whatever it was. If his role was to be brief and largely symbolic, it would be no small thing, but now that he had seen the possibility that there could be more, he was not sure how he would come to grips with the disappointment of being handed his hat. He would have no leg to stand on, he knew, if it came to insisting that his presence would somehow be relevant to what would follow once he had played his small role in restarting the virus.

While thinking on this, Riley and Clipper entered the lab under escort of a man who looked to be cut from the same cloth as Agent Britt. He had a blocky stature with thick arms clearly discernible beneath his suit coat, and a deliberate self-assuredness that suggested the unnerving likelihood that his build and stature were the product of more than long hours at the gym.

Once inside the lab, he spoke briefly with Riley and Clipper, then broke off and exited without looking back. AJ watched him through the glass-paneled wall as he took only a few steps to the far side of the adjacent hall and turned to wait near two other men who also appeared to be standing sentry.

One of those men, AJ did not recognize, but the other was Agent Britt. AJ had wondered what had become of the man and now realized that he had probably never been free of him. Standing side by side, the three looked like action figures standing on a shelf, waiting to be noticed and carried away by an eager youngster with aspirations of becoming one of them. It was amazing, how little AJ knew about the world those men must live in.

The appearance of Riley and Clipper added to AJ's anxiety rather than settling it. The two stood for a long moment near the entrance of the lab as if unsure of their freedom, then made in his direction.

Their expressions betrayed that they were unsure of what AJ's response would be, and AJ knew they would have discussed scenarios. *If he's pissed, we'll do this. If he's afraid, we'll do that...* It was just the kind of thing they would do.

"This is novel," AJ said once they were within earshot.

Riley and Clipper exchanged glances, but apparently, the statement was not enough for them to know which scenario they were into.

Recovering, Riley made to speak, but Clipper beat him to it. "Hey man, didn't mean for all this to happen."

At once, AJ decided they deserved a little grief. "All this?" he said. "You saw the predawn wakeup call and the flight across the country, and the waterboarding, but what, you didn't see the eventuality that there could be Diet Coke, but no Coke Zero in the breakroom?"

"Waterboarding…?" Riley broke in, instant concern crossing his face.

AJ rolled his eyes and tilted his head in that, 'you're an idiot' kind of way.

"Okay, had that coming," Riley said, sheepishly.

"So, what do you guys know?" AJ asked.

"Not sure, really," Riley said. "We were told that we're caught up on everything but have no way of knowing for sure."

"Doesn't really matter," Clipper put in. "It's gonna go the way it goes. Unless they haul us out of here, we'll find out soon enough."

"True," AJ agreed.

"Christopher Columbus, Neil Armstrong and Andrew Jacobs," Clipper said, shaking his head. "Damnation."

AJ could see that the sentiment was real.

"Oh, no," Riley said. "Two of those names will eventually fade to obscurity. Only one will be remembered 1000 years from now." Both he and Clipper looked at AJ with sincere incredulity.

AJ wasn't sure how to respond, so he skipped forward. "Seems we're all up to date then."

"Indeed it does," Clipper agreed.

After a short pause, AJ scanned the room as if only then recalling where they were. He gestured futilely around the room as if to take in the whole of the situation. "What the hell, guys?"

"Before you go on," Clipper said, "you can't fault us for not guessing our caller wasn't exactly local."

"Well, it sure as hell is a good thing he, or it, wasn't, otherwise we'd all be downtown finishing up our mugshots about now," AJ said, a little more frustration in his voice than intended.

"You're absolutely right, AJ," Clipper said. "You're right." He held up a placating hand. "All we can offer now is that we're not. We're not downtown. And as boneheaded as any or all of this may have been on Riley's part, the only thing we can offer – and fortunately for us, by the way, it's the only thing that really matters – is that we're here now, and this is what it is." That earned a silent, 'Clipper will be Clipper' smirk from Riley, but he didn't add anything.

Riley checked his watch. "Ms. Briggs just told us that they're not going to restart the virus until morning. They want everyone fresh for a long day."

"Do you think they'll let us leave?" AJ asked.

Riley shrugged. "Yes and no. They're putting us up at the Marriott over in Concord."

"Under escort, I'm sure," AJ added.

"I would not guess otherwise," Riley said.

"Well then," AJ said, leaning back and making something of a show of searching the ceiling, and then scanning the room. "This is something for the history books." The meaning was received immediately. They were most certainly being watched and recorded.

"I had no idea what you guys were doing over here," AJ went on. "Gravitation, huh?" He chuckled, "Riley, gravity is something every creature on this planet has shared for 4.5 billion years, and then you come along and start fiddling with it."

"I'll try not to break anything."

"Thank you for the reassuring thought," AJ said. "At least you're not splitting atoms."

Chapter 39

March 14, 2024

Riley, Clipper and AJ had been instructed to meet in the hotel lobby at 7:30 AM the following morning. They sat over a table of bacon, eggs, toast and coffee while their security escorts stood sentry by the dining area entrance. The enormity of the day swamped the need for conversation. The three were subdued, but found the energy to eat heartily nonetheless.

They had been strictly forbidden to talk about anything related to where this day was destined to go, and that left little to fallback to in the way of subject matter that seemed even remotely interesting in the shadow of it.

After extended minutes of silence, Clipper finally spoke. "Come on man, I mean, really, when do these guys take a break?"

"I've seen them rotate in and out. Bathroom breaks, that sort of thing," Riley said, but not with much interest.

"Have you guys had a chance to talk to anybody?" AJ asked. "My escort was kind enough to relieve me of the burden of my mobile phone yesterday morning."

"And there was no phone in my hotel room either," Clipper added. "There was a jack on the wall, but that was it."

"I just know there are people out there wondering what's happening," AJ said. "It may seem like a detail to us, but I can guarantee our families won't see it that way."

Riley had taken to pondering the issue. "It's not a tremendous stretch to let these people know that if they are really interested in keeping this quiet, better to settle the nerves of our families before they start making unnecessary noise."

"That makes sense to me," AJ agreed. "It won't do any good to ask these guys," he said, nodding towards the guarded exit. "They're under orders, and that'll be that. I'll raise it with..." He broke off, suddenly realizing that they had unintentionally angled toward the very topic they had been forbidden to discuss. The realization silenced them all at once.

"Let's be about it, then," Riley said, and the three of them rose to leave.

By the time they arrived at the campus 20 minutes later the sun had risen beyond the milky stages of early dawn to an almost artificial vibrance. It was a beautiful day, befitting, AJ surmised, the historical significance it would serve, regardless of outcome.

The parking lot was even more a buzz of activity than it had been the prior day, making the possibility that all of this could still be revealed as a hoax that much less a possibility. There were many people – physicists, scientists, analysts, network engineers and the like – who would have, by now, peered far into the enigmatic events of the past several weeks to know with certainty whether it could be or not. If it were a hoax, they would know by now.

There was also the notable addition of two Bell UH-1Y Venom helicopters, nicknamed Super Huey's, sitting in an adjacent lot. A large truck, Army green in color, with a radio dish antenna mounted above and behind its cab was parked in the grass near the northeast corner of the building. Thick cabling snaked out of the back of the truck and into the building through a ground floor opening where a window had once been. Plywood now took its place with an opening at its lower-left corner to allow the cabling to pass through.

Agent Britt opened the door of the large SUV and motioned them towards the door. AJ could clearly hear the sound of a generator emanating from the radio truck, and his gaze lingered on it as they passed across the lot to the door of the building. Britt displayed a badge as they approached the south entrance, and the small knot of men and women nearby parted wordlessly to allow them through.

They tracked among vacant cubicles and offices to find Ms. Briggs standing near the elevator corridor. She greeted them graciously, and AJ quickly realized that she had been waiting there to intercept them. "Good morning," she said.

The formal suit she had worn the day prior was now replaced by a light tan blouse and blue skirt that reached to just below her knees. Still very much business appropriate, but less stuffy than her attire of the day before, AJ thought the change was good. He had found her an attractive and pleasant person, but not necessarily personable. That side of her, he surmised, was reserved for family and friends, and for unexplainable reasons he entertained a momentary fascination with her, wondering what the more casual side of her would be like. It was hard to guess.

"Mr. Jacobs," she said, drawing him away from the thought. "Mr. Ward would like a word with you prior to assembling in the briefing room." AJ exchanged glances with Riley and Clipper at that, surprised at first that they would not be included. He would have to get used to the notion that his role in all of this, however large or small, short or lengthy, was fundamentally different than those of his friends. He nodded, trying not to look too nervous at the prospect, and allowed her to lead him away, Agent Britt in tow a few paces behind. Riley and Clipper's gaze lingered upon him for a few moments before turning to the elevators.

Briggs and AJ found Ward in a small conference room a short stride down the hall. AJ entered to find him leaning back in a rollaway chair, absorbed by whatever he was reading on his electronic tablet. Unlike Briggs, Ward's attire was, if anything, even more formal than it had been the prior day. He wore a black suit with red tie and polished shoes, appearing completely at ease – his jacket unbuttoned and laying loosely open – but for the deep concentration on his face. On seeing AJ, he set the tablet aside. "Mr. Jacobs, good morning. Are you rested?"

"Good morning. Yes, thanks," AJ said, returning the pleasantry not entirely truthfully. Briggs took her leave with another of her gracious smiles, leaving he and Ward alone; Agent Britt having taken up watch a few paces up the hall.

"Glad to hear," Ward said.

"You?" AJ asked.

"Excellent. Big day," Ward said. If there was any sarcasm in the response his demeanor didn't reflect it. "Listen," he went on without further preamble, "I wanted a word with you prior to joining the rest of the team in the briefing room. We've had an army of analysts working up scenarios and contingencies since Sunday evening, thinking about things that might happen once we restart the virus. It's common practice – something we do anytime we have the benefit of knowing ahead of time that we're about to step into something. This scenario is somewhat unique, to say the least, so there's a little more guesswork than usual, but most everything else is standard."

"Okay," AJ said, the now familiar sense of anxiety overtaking him again. It was not a welcomed feeling but couldn't be helped.

"These analysts are sharp," Ward continued. "You'd be surprised what they can, and have done. On more than a few occasions, we've had hostiles believe they were acting spontaneously and even randomly, only to step directly into scenarios we had already anticipated and worked through in detail. It never ends well for them."

Having been exposed, however briefly, to the world of the NSA and other government agencies with their enigmatic ways, AJ was beginning to realize how pitifully futile it would be for almost anyone to attempt to oppose them. They were exhaustively thorough, measured and relentless. He imagined terrorists toting weapons that the best efforts of their own governments could not manufacture, and without the rigors of training and discipline that only such a government could understand, taking up arms and attempting to outwit them. It just wouldn't work. Couldn't work. Already, if he were pressed to summarize the whole of his experiences of the past three days into one statement, it would be that he hadn't known what he hadn't known. And despite that, he knew that he had seen, even now, only the most superficial face of something that was larger and deeper than he would care to guess.

Ward, on the other hand, was speaking to him from the deepest possible understanding of all of it, and AJ was only now beginning to appreciate that. The short span of four feet that physically separated the two of them in the small conference room deceptively masked the miles by which they were separated in virtually every other regard. The realization made it seem all the more remarkable that Ward would spare five seconds to speak with him. Yet, here they were.

"You should know that there will be several individuals from the NSA and FBI in the briefing with us," Ward said. "There are some strong personalities in there and they're going to be present in the lab with us when we restart the virus. You should understand that regardless of what you're asked to do, or by whom, you will look to me for final approval prior to any action. Is that clear?"

AJ hesitated a moment before acquiescing with a simple, yes.

Ward kept speaking. "Some of these individuals have years of training, and years of experience commanding, manipulating, intimidating and even deceiving. If you feel your resolve begin to slip, take a breath, look to me and we'll get things back on track. Are we clear?"

"Yes," AJ said.

"You're going to do fine," Ward said, rising to his feet. "Let's get to it, then."

Chapter 40

March 14, 2024

AJ followed Ward numbly through the halls, glancing back at one point along the way to see Agent Britt following dutifully. It was an unexpectedly reassuring sight, although AJ knew it shouldn't be. In any scenario, in any situation, Britt would not act on AJ's behalf, but on those of his superiors – the people he worked for. Still, Britt's had been the first face he'd seen on the roller coaster ride that had been the past three days, and the only one that had remained constant through it all.

The briefing room was large. Unlike the smaller conference room of the prior day, this one had theatre seating, a much larger screen, and room for 50 or more people. Very much utilitarian in design, without frills, and not even particularly comfortable, it was nonetheless an effective space for its purpose. The NSA symbol was not on display this time. It wasn't hard for AJ to guess the reasons for that, given that the FBI would also be in attendance.

Rather than Ms. Briggs stepping forward to begin proceedings, it was Director Ward who moved to take position behind the small podium to the right of the screen. "Thank you all for coming, let's please be seated," he said. "We have a relatively short window of time here, so we'll need everyone's undivided attention and participation." He waited a moment as the room fell first to a hush and then to relative silence.

"Our Situation Analysts have been working extended hours since Sunday to discover and anticipate the possible scenarios that could play out once the virus is restarted. We'll cover those in brief over the next 90 minutes. From there, we will take a short break, and then a subset of this room will convene in the computer lab to proceed with the restart. It has been nearly 48 hours since the request for Mr. Andrew Jacobs was issued by the virus, and there is some concern that we may already be in a timeout situation. The hope, clearly, is that we are not. Our analysts have strongly urged that we not persist much longer before responding, lest we risk losing contact."

Ward looked to his left to find a younger man, sloppily dressed in faded jeans and t-shirt, donning a beard that was badly in need of grooming. AJ guessed that the disheveled look was due to the time and effort of the past three days, but somehow suspected that they were not the full explanation for his appearance.

"Mr. Ryan Meyer is team lead of the Situation Analyst chapter we've engaged for this particular scenario. He has distinguished himself on multiple occasions and was requested by name for this assignment by Deputy Director Martin Moore. He will brief us now."

Ward extended a hand in Meyer's direction, prompting him to rise and approach the podium as he himself slipped away to take a seat on the side wall. It took only a few seconds for Meyer to succinctly demonstrate his general awkwardness. He seemed unsure of whether to bring his coffee to the podium, decided he would, but then struggled to manage it along with his open laptop, ragged notebook and pen. After a moment of indecision, he laid his notebook on the chair where he had been seated. The pen immediately rolled to the rear of the chair and dropped from view, and would have been followed by the notebook had Meyer not reached for it in time. But the cost of saving the notebook was spilling a large quantity of coffee onto the chair and his shoes.

Meyer stood for a moment in what must have been anguished embarrassment, until Ms. Briggs stepped wordlessly forward to assist. Her intervention was effective and immediate. She handed her own pen to Meyer, which he took with dumbstruck gratefulness, then bent to wipe the coffee from his shoes with a cloth that seemed to appear from nowhere. She then stood erect and faced him, focusing him with a reassuring smile. It was over before it started. In seconds, Meyer was installed at the podium, and Briggs was back at her seat as if nothing had happened. AJ watched with more than a little fascination as she nodded to Meyer from the front row, somehow imparting confidence through the space between them.

All eyes were on Meyer as he stood without speaking, his hands grasping the edges of the podium as if to steady himself. Finally, he pressed buttons on his laptop computer and the large screen behind him responded, lighting up to display a simple list.

"Thank you, Director Ward," he said, his reedy voice sounding even younger than his appearance. It was a marked contrast to Ward. "Uh, we've divided our contingencies into four categories based on how the virus may react once restarted," he said. "As you can see here," he gestured to the screen, "they are *hostile, aggressive, cooperative* and *defunct*. The ordering reflects the prioritization we placed on each of them during analysis, but not necessarily the order of anticipated likelihood. Our expectation is that, once restarted, the virus will exhibit traits of the aggressive and cooperative personas. This is based on two primary observations. First, as it relates to the aggressive, we noted that the virus, during the few minutes it was active this past Sunday, pressed its host computer to full capacity until halted by Mr. Jacobs. On the cooperative persona, clearly, the virus has chosen to abide by Mr. Jacobs request to cease activity. That behavior contributed heavily to our expectations with respect to triage scenarios. There could hardly be a more direct indication of the willingness of the virus, and by extension, the remote party, to cooperate. We find this very encouraging."

"In brief, and at the highest level, any of these behaviors will be met in the following ways; hostility with containment, aggression with management, cooperation with cooperation, and defunctitude with scenario recreation."

He took a sip of coffee. "With the help of the computer technology group, we have implemented countermeasures for most hostile contingencies. These include physically isolating the computer data center here on the Mayfield Hammond grounds, and at the Installation, by removing wireless equipment that could potentially be commandeered by the virus. Some equipment, at both locations, has also been wrapped in RF shielding to further prevent the possibility that the virus can go wireless."

"Excuse me, Mr. Meyer. RF shielding?" The question came from a woman in the mid-section of the room.

"Yes," Meyer said, clearing his throat. "Radio Frequency shielding. We've wrapped the datacenters in a copper mesh that blocks all incoming and outgoing radio transmissions."

"And you're sure it'll work?" she pressed.

"The shielding, yes, Mrs. Statham," Meyer said. "The particular shielding we used has been successfully employed on many prior occasions and retested by our network team for this particular scenario."

A new voice cut in. "Am I correct that as this virus runs, it uses the gravitational equipment to communicate back with the remote party? Won't the shielding block that?" The questions came from a man sitting near the back of the room, but before Meyer could answer, the first woman, Statham, cut back in, seeming somewhat agitated at the interruption. "I'm hearing words like 'hostilities' and 'aggression.' There also seems to be ambiguity around what the shielding gives us. Are we not 100% confident in our ability to contain?"

"Good questions," Meyer said. "I believe I can address all of them with a few further clarifications." He pressed more buttons on his laptop and a diagram appeared on the large display screen depicting the primary data center on the Mayfield Hammond campus, along with the Installation some 60 miles away. "In fact, we do have some exposure due to the physical layout of the properties. This diagram," he said, gesturing to the screen, "depicts the physical properties involved. This is the computer lab here on the campus grounds." He walked over to the screen and indicated the location with his hand. "It's located in the sub-basement of this very building. And, here," he walked a few paces to the right, "is the Installation, as it's known, roughly 60 miles to the southwest of us. Because communication with the remote party requires equipment from both properties to work in concert, and because there is no direct, hardwired connection between the two, there is no conventional way of ensuring that the virus will be unable to break containment over the wide span that separates them."

"Then it is clear to me that this exercise cannot continue," Statham interjected, her voice agitated. "Not until–"

"Please allow Mr. Meyer to continue," Ward said, intervening from the side of the room. Statham fell silent, less out of deference to Ward's authority, it seemed, and more out of confusion at the unexpected interruption.

Meyer looked to Ward, back to Statham, and then to Ward again before continuing. "Yes, well, we have taken steps to mitigate these risks by soliciting help from the military," he began, somewhat tentatively. "We have commissioned an Airborne Early Warning and Control system – a Grumman E-2C Hawkeye aircraft – for these purposes." He pressed another key on his laptop computer and a new, modified version of the prior diagram appeared. This one portrayed the same two physical locations – the Mayfield Hammond lab and the Installation – but with an icon representing the Hawkeye aircraft between them, complete with its distinctive saucer shaped antenna looming above its wings. Icons of trucks, also with dish antennas mounted at their tops, were visible at the both locations. Lines connected the trucks with the aircraft to represent the radio signal that would pass between them. "This system," Meyer said, "will allow secure communication between the lab, here in this building, and the Installation. Because Mr. Riley had used a cellular phone to control pulse modulation on the gravity machine itself, a relay has been installed inside of the building that houses the machine, and the signal is now rerouted to the communication vehicle via physical cabling."

"How do we know this will be secure enough?" Statham asked, seeming to look for reasons to be dissatisfied with any solution. "What will keep someone from intercepting that signal?"

Ward leaned forward from his chair and smiled. "Mrs. Statham, I can say with confidence that if there is any breach in our containment efforts, it will not occur with this system. The signals passed between the Land Mobile Radio Systems as they're known, and the Hawkeye aircraft are highly directional and highly encrypted. They are, to say the least, military grade. No better, more secure systems exist."

Statham was clearly unhappy with the answer but seemed at a loss for anything further to say.

"Thank you, Director Ward," Meyer said, then continued. "An added benefit of this arrangement is that as data is transmitted across the wire, we will route a copy back to another computer in the data center here on premises for analysis. The aircraft will arrive in position at 10:30 AM local time, which is about 45 minutes from now, and remain in our employ indefinitely."

"How long can it stay up there?" Statham asked.

Ward intervened again. "That information is classified, Ms. Statham, but suffice to say that it will be at our disposal for as long as necessary."

Ward nodded for Meyer to continue, which he did without delay. "As for the hostile scenario," he said, "the final option is to power down all systems. Fortunately, we have good reason to believe that the scenario will not manifest. Even so, we have rehearsed the contingency and will remain at the ready throughout. As for whether the RF shielding will interfere with communication between the gravitation equipment and the remote party," he said, nodding to the man at the back of the room who had asked the question, "the strong expectation is that it will not. The underlying signal, if you can call it that, does not travel over an electromagnetic medium, and therefore, will not be affected. Any further questions before moving to the aggressive scenario?"

They had burned 40 minutes by the time all questions were put to rest, but Meyer had stood his ground and answered them all without further need of support from Ward or Briggs. AJ was impressed by how well he had collected himself; rising from an embarrassing first few moments to commanding the platform with as much fortitude and confidence as his young age and nasal voice could allow.

"Oddly," Meyer said, moving into the next portion of his presentation, "even as the risks associated with each persona taper down as we move from hostility, through aggressiveness, to cooperative, and finally to defunctitude; the range of unknowns increase correspondingly. Meaning, if the virus becomes hostile, it will be easier to anticipate what could happen and how to respond.

However, if the virus is cooperative as we hope and expect, our ability to anticipate what can happen is low. That is not a bad thing. If we manage risks, as we undoubtedly will do, we will be free to interact and learn more about the remote party without the intrusive concerns of security unduly impacting us."

"And finally," Meyer said, "I'd like to talk a little about the computer systems themselves." A new image appeared, showing a table upon which sat a solitary computer screen and keyboard. "This is a live feed from the computer lab. We've trained a camera on the computer terminal where communication with the, uh..." he stammered to find the right word. "...Remotes occurred. We can route this video feed to anywhere we like, such as we have done here. The computer itself – that is, the computer whose output is shown on this display screen is not a conventional computer at all. It is a virtual server, which is significant for a few reasons that I'll briefly cover now."

Meyer lifted his laptop from the podium for everyone to see. "Most of us, I think, are familiar with the idea of operating systems. Operating systems, or OS's, provide the means by which the applications we're familiar with, such as word processors and spreadsheets, are able to leverage the underlying hardware. In this case, a laptop computer. Mine uses Windows, which provides a convenient visual environment that masks the complexities of dealing with the hardware of the laptop itself. The most common operating systems, from a consumer perspective, are Windows, which is produced by Microsoft; OS X, produced by Apple, and Chrome OS, by Google. Even our phones use variations of them. The most well-known of those are iOS and its chief competitor, Android. These are produced by Apple and Google, respectively.

These operating systems are tailored for consumers. They're easy to use and offer pleasant visual and multimedia experiences. But, when it comes to more industrial computers, such as those that run behind the scenes in the data centers of large companies and laboratories, there is yet another operating system that is something of a *de facto* standard, called Linux. It is a more utilitarian operating system, concerned less with a polished user experience, and more with providing the tooling needed within the domains of business and industry. Incidentally, even OS X – the operating system that runs your Mac computers – is a derivative of Linux, but enhanced for a consumer market. Anyway, these backend, industrial strength machines aren't usually referred to as computers – they're usually called *servers*. It's semantics, really; they're all computers, but the server label provides a loose classification that helps clarify the computer's purpose and role. Linux servers are generally used for tasks that require no direct user interaction, like calculating payroll or serving out web pages, collecting and collating data; or performing other industrial tasks like controlling robots or, as it happens, gravitational fields."

"So, why am I sharing this?" Meyer asked, rhetorically. "As the computer industry evolved, technology was developed to allow entire operating systems to be treated like programs. That means a physical computer can serve as host to multiple running instances of an operating system, each one behaving as though it is a single, conventional computer. Virtual servers as they're called, can be spun up and shut down at will, limited only by the capacity of the underlying hardware. That's what we have here," he said, motioning again to the screen. "The terminal here is showing the output of a virtual server, running on a physical host computer situated in the lab of this building. The output from this server could have been easily routed directly from the server itself, removing the need for the camera, but we have decided not to tamper with it in any way. The low-tech alternative was to simply put a camera on it, which we did."

"Now, note the window on the upper left that continuously updates itself with numerical data. It's extremely fortuitous that Mr. Clipper opened this window and left it running. It is the output of a utility program that is a standard part of the Linux operating system, called *top*. It shows a tabular list of processes running on the server, sorted in descending order by the amount of resources they're consuming. When we re-engage the virus in a while, we'll keep close watch on this window to see how hard the virus presses the computer in terms of resource usage, and we'll also be able to see any new processes that it spawns along the way. The hope is that this window will give us the information needed to monitor the goings on without connecting to the server via more typical means, such as opening a remote telnet or secure shell session. Again, this is because we're trying to preserve the environment that the computer is running in, along with its state, so that we introduce as few new variables into the equation as possible."

"As you can see, the server is virtually idle at the moment. According to Mr. Riley and Mr. Clipper, the server was at full capacity this past Sunday. It will be telling to see what happens once we restart."

As the 90 minutes of scheduled meeting time drew to a close, Ward retook the podium. The questions and concerns of the audience had abated towards the end. Once security and safety had been addressed, those in attendance began to show more willingness, even excitement for events to actually begin.

"There are two final items of import that we must cover," Ward announced. "First, in the hallway outside of this conference room, a list has been posted with designations for each and every individual on premise. They describe where each individual is expected to take up station during the activities of the day, along with roles and responsibilities for each. Printed copies of the postings are also provided on a nearby table. Please keep a copy on your person throughout the day and instruct your subordinates to do likewise. The document also includes instructions outlining emergency plans. Please see that your teams, as well as yourselves, review in detail. Any person whose name is not on the list should report to the desk in the front lobby of the building. Any closing comments or questions?"

"I still think this is an unnecessary; indeed, unacceptable risk." It was Statham. "It is not only yourself that you are putting at risk here, Mr. Ward," she said, her confidence and voice rising as she spoke.

"Ms. Statham, perhaps you can help me better understand your perspective," Ward replied, calmly. "We have already learned two very important things about the remote party. Would you agree?"

"I don't agree. To what specifically are you referring?" she asked, defiantly.

"Obviously," Ward said, feigning surprise, "one, that they – whoever they are – are indeed out there. And two, that they now know we are here as well. Are you suggesting that by ignoring these facts, by simply powering down our devices and pretending that they are not, we will return to some fictional place of ignorant safety? That approach has never worked well for us."

"Let me be perfectly clear about what I'm suggesting: I will move that the men who brought this upon us be prosecuted to the full extent of the law," she said with a demanding voice, almost yelling by now. "There is no shortage of laws or regulations that have been broken here. And you, and others in this room, are continuing to press boundaries into areas about which you know nothing."

Ward kept his composure. "Ms. Statham, the Universe did not change this past Sunday, we only learned something new about it. Whatever change is about to happen, it will be on our part. We, as inhabitants of this world, must act on what we've learned; it's not a choice. It never is. The only way to manage the safety and security of our homes is to know what's out there and to understand it. In that respect, there is precisely nothing special about this situation. Frankly, I am confused and somewhat concerned to hear of these views from you."

Chapter 41

March 14, 2024

Without question, arriving at the computer lab in preparation for restarting the virus was the most surreal moment of AJ's life. The computer terminal where he,

Riley and Clipper had sat the prior Sunday, only two days before, was as it had been when last he saw it.

That didn't hold for the surrounding area. Space had been cleared away to make room for three more chairs, forming an arc to one side with printed name tags on each. One for Jeff Ward, Information Assurance Director, NSA. Another for Executive Assistant Director of Science and Technology, Frank Boswell, FBI; and the last for Executive Assistant Director of National Security, NSA, Margaret Statham.

Behind the three chairs was another, solitary chair, already occupied by Lead Situation Analyst, Ryan Meyer; and finally, behind him, four more, occupied by his team of analysts. All other equipment and chairs were either gone or moved aside. A video camera had been trained upon the terminal, its output showing in real time on five large screens aligned at intervals along the lengthy back wall. Knots of people were gathered in front of each one, most in deep discussion.

AJ was transfixed by the sight of his own name replicated across each screen; the final line of text reading, 'Please locate Andrew Seymour Jacobs.' And then, 'is Andrew Seymour Jacobs present?' It was a dizzying sight. There was nothing to connect the happenings of the past two days with anything prior in his life. This new event had risen from nowhere to displace and push aside everything else, and as yet there had been no time to make sense of it.

The room had not yet come to order. AJ noted Director Ward, Deputy Director Moore and Assistant Director Statham off to themselves, deep in conversation. AJ scanned the room for any person he thought might be Frank Boswell, the FBI's Science and Technology Assistant Director. If he was in the room, he didn't stand out in any way AJ could identify. Had he been, he would likely have been with Ward and Statham anyway. AJ was at a loss to imagine any other issue that could be pressing enough to keep him away. Perhaps a personal emergency, or maybe he was occupied with someone higher in the chain of authority than even Ward and Statham. AJ hoped it was neither.

Ms. Briggs was also in a discussion. She stood near the computer terminal with its odd clustering of chairs, talking with another person AJ hadn't recalled seeing before. They were reviewing a printed paper, which he guessed to be a copy of the agenda for the day. At once, she nodded as if reaching a conclusion and stepped forward to the center of the room.

"Attention please," she said, loudly, but the request was ignored. She hesitated a moment, then spoke again, louder this time. "Excuse me," she said, "your attention please." A few heads swiveled in her direction, but the request still went unheeded. "This room will now come to order!" she said, finally, with a forcefulness that took AJ by surprise. This time, all eyes tracked in her direction, even Ward's and Statham's. "We have matters to attend and I expect that each individual in this room will immediately and professionally respond to all requests. Any person unable or unwilling to do so will be excused without discussion."

The room was immediately beset with an awkward hush, but Briggs plowed forward without delay. "From this moment, all sidebar conversations that are not directly and immediately relevant and impactful to matters at hand will cease. The defining characteristics of the afternoon shall be calmness, quietness and alertness; and each and every individual will be about his or her assigned duties without distraction."

At that moment, another well-dressed man AJ had not seen before, but immediately suspected to be Assistant Director Boswell, entered the room. He scanned the gathering briefly, located Ryan Meyer and made in his direction without acknowledging anyone else. Even as an outsider and newcomer to the fray, AJ thought the move felt political. Ward, Moore and Statham, having cut short their conversation at the prompting of Ms. Briggs, closed the distance to join them. Boswell acknowledge the three with a nod as they approached.

In a few moments, and in what looked like practiced unison, the group turned unexpectedly in AJ's direction. It took a moment for AJ to realized that he had again found himself the center of unexpected attention. It felt oddly like being recognized by a cast of characters in a movie who stopped in mid-scene to look out of the television screen at their audience. Shaking the thought, he stepped forward to join them without waiting for an invitation.

"You are Mr. Jacobs, then?" the newcomer said, once AJ had neared.

"I am." AJ said.

"Frank Boswell," he said, taking AJ's hand.

"Science and technology?" AJ asked.

"That's correct." He answered, with a slight narrowing of his eyes.

"I saw your name on the chair," AJ said, sensing Boswell's question.

"Mr. Jacobs, I have been detained and unable to be on premise until now," Boswell said. "As Executive Assistant Director of Science and Technology, FBI, I would like to discuss your involvement–"

Both Ward and Briggs drew simultaneous breaths, undoubtedly to challenge the assertion, but Ward won out. "Mr. Jacobs, please allow Assistant Director Boswell and I a few moments to–"

"No need," Boswell said, holding AJ's gaze. "I don't want to delay events unnecessarily."

AJ knew where this was going and was disappointed that on an occasion as important as this, political infighting was even possible. Ward, clearly not the type of man to back down, had just taken a sideward step to round on Boswell when AJ spoke, surprising the group. "Assistant Director Boswell, with due respect, I have spent the past two days being briefed on the goings on here and how the events of the day are expected to unfold. Frankly, I don't know enough about government agencies to know which has ultimate jurisdiction here, so unless I am told otherwise by someone I recognize, such as Director Ward or the president, I have no choice but to do as I have been instructed hereto."

Boswell began to speak, but taking AJ's words as a cue, the group had already begun to disband leaving him with no one to hear except for Statham. Her presence, it became immediately apparent, was not enough to satisfy him. She stood facing him, but Boswell's eyes followed AJ as he crossed the room.

Not about to allow Boswell another attempt at commandeering the room, Briggs spoke again to the group at large. "Proceedings will begin in 10 minutes," she said, with a raised voice. "Please be sure that you have made necessary preparations for your duties and that your support teams are at the ready."

Ward stepped up to the three chairs, repositioned one of them slightly, then turned to face the room, his hands resting on its back. "Heads up everyone," he said. This time there was no need for a second call. His presence exuded a confidence that permeated the room, which AJ found reassuring. Oddly, in that moment he seemed far less intimidating than Briggs, projecting the persona of a high school basketball coach addressing his team prior to a big game. He scanned the room, making eye contact with virtually every individual.

"We're going to put events into motion in just a moment," he said. "You should know that each of you in this room is here because you have the trust and confidence of your superiors and peers. We have no way of knowing what will happen once Mr. Jacobs signifies his presence. Could be nothing, could be crazy; we just don't know. What I do know is that we'll roll with whatever it is and we'll handle it. It's what we do. If it should turn out to be nothing, be assured that not one moment of your time, not one detail of preparation made over the past 48 hours has been a waste. This came to us, and we have done diligence, it's that simple." He gestured towards AJ. "Mr. Jacobs will be at the computer and will act on my instructions throughout. Mr. Riley and Mr. Clipper will sit opposite to Mr. Boswell, Ms. Statham and myself. Ryan Meyer and his team will be positioned to our immediate right to advise on scenarios and responses. They will be the conduit of communication between the core team here," he said, gesturing to the seats positioned in immediate proximity to the terminal, "and the extended team across the room. That will go in both directions. If you notice something, think of something, have something to report, please bring it to the attention of Mr. Meyer's team. They will assess and advise appropriate individuals as needed. Questions, comments, concerns?"

The room stood in suspended silence, which Ward allowed to extend for several moments. No questions came.

"Good," Ward said, with a nod that conveyed a sense of finality. "Thank you."

Ward turned to take his seat and AJ followed suit, taking his own directly in front of the display terminal. He noted Boswell and Statham approaching and was somewhat surprised, pleasantly, that neither of them had attempted to assert themselves during Ward's address.

AJ faced the terminal. It seemed far more imposing than it had the last time he saw it. It had transformed from a simple display screen, into a window to the Universe itself. It was where he, Riley and Clipper had inadvertently made history on Sunday, and were now poised to make even more.

A transparent plexiglass cover had been placed over the keyboard. Ms. Briggs stepped forward and lifted it away, handing it to another woman who had stepped up beside her. The task complete, both stepped away without fanfare. Ward leaned forward in his chair. "Mr. Jacobs," he said, "please respond to the prompt by typing, yes."

AJ extended his hand towards the keyboard and pressed the keys one at a time with his index finger; 'y-e-s.' "Press enter?" he asked.

"Yes."

Chapter 42

March 14, 2024

A J pressed the 'enter' key and the lines of text in the window moved up unremarkably, leaving an empty black space at the bottom. The *top* reporting tool that had been dutifully refreshing the status and metrics of the virtual server for the past two days was true to its task, showing a total of 55 processes running on the server, all but 2 in a sleep state.

Nothing unusual.

Much more happened on a computer than people would typically guess, even when the computer looked to be completely at rest. In fact, they were never completely at rest. The vast majority of processes, sometimes called *threads*, on a computer are usually concerned with background chores that a user doesn't know or care about. Of those, most are idle for the lion's share of the time. It was no different for this server, virtual though it was. In this case, the active processes were accounted for by the two windows on the screen; the one that hosted the reporting utility itself, *top*, and the other where the virus was running. All others were devoted to compulsory housekeeping functions.

"No material change in resource usage," Meyer announced after a few seconds, monitoring the output in the *top* window. "Active processes, 2. Inactive processes, 53. Load, .04%. Data traffic between the lab and Installation, 0."

The room stood motionless as long seconds began to tick away. Hours of anticipation, 48 hours of around-the-clock preparation had been replaced with pungent immediacy. It had begun. They – and unknowingly – the entire world now waited in the *no man's land* between responding to the prompt and waiting for its reply. At 60 seconds, Meyer spoke again. "Active processes remain at 2. Load, .03%. Still no data moving, traffic at 0."

More seconds slipped by. The 2-minute mark came and went. On approach to 3 minutes, the vacuum of silence that had overtaken the room showed its first signs of degrading. Ward turned in his chair to look at Meyer who shrugged helplessly. Already, it felt more like 20 minutes.

Then at once, Meyer's eyes flicked away from Ward to the terminal. "Load, 3%; traffic, 0. Could be nothing. Sometimes idle processes wake up to do tasks, then go back to sleep. We'll see if this holds." He waited several more seconds. "Load increase to 7%; traffic 0," he called out again.

And then, somehow unexpectedly, even though every person in the room had been anticipating it for days, they saw what they had been waiting for. A new prompt appeared.

"Resume?" it said.

A ripple passed through the room. Not an audible or excited one, but something that moved silently along the edges of perception. A collective intake of breath. Meyer turned to his team. "Prompt is *resume*," he said. "Not *continue*." There were nods of acknowledgement, but the significance was lost on everyone but them. The cursor blinked serenely at the bottom of the terminal, waiting for a response.

Ward looked at if for several seconds before speaking. "Mr. Jacobs, please respond, yes."

AJ complied, again typing the letters one at a time, extremely careful not to press any unintended keys. Finished, he looked to Ward. "Press enter?" he asked.

"Yes," Ward confirmed.

The response was immediate. "Load 45%, traffic 0," Meyer said, followed immediately by; "load 72%, traffic, 0." It kept climbing. "Load 87%, traffic, 0. Active threads, 4 – delta is plus 2."

The output of the performance monitor showed that the server was already beginning to feel the load, a reality that seemed at odds with the steady state of the cursor in the virus window. It persisted for several minutes as the computer became pressed with greater and greater computational loads, Meyer calling out significant changes as they happened. Within a few minutes, the server was pegged at 100%.

Meyer leaned forward to speak to Ward, Boswell and Statham. "Keep in mind that the server was at 100% on Sunday as well, but at the time it had access to a relatively small slice of the host computer's full processing power. Since then, we've shut down all other virtual servers and devoted everything to this one. We're now at 100%, but the virus is consuming about 15 times the processing power as before. It's a stout platform, so whatever it's doing is intense." He then leaned back to announce status again. "Load 100%, traffic remains at 0."

Meyer turned to his team. "It hasn't sent any data anywhere, and it hasn't received any either. I would have expected it to phone home by now."

Ward had noticed as well and was already beginning to get anxious. "Mr. Meyer," Ward said, "please contact the Hawkeye and verify that, as yet, no data has been received. I want to know that everything is working as expected."

"Copy that," Meyer said, and then nodded to his team, passing the order along. "Check the radio truck too," Meyer added, but by the time he had turned back to face the terminal, things had already changed. "Belay that," he said. "Load 100%, traffic, outbound 2.6MB." The number had changed and was continuing to grow. "4.8MB and rising; 7.1MB, 9.3, 11.6, 14.2." It increased steadily, until eventually leveling off around 28MB. "Outbound traffic holding at 27.6MB, inbound at about 100KB, probably due to protocol overhead."

Meyer leaned forward to talk to Ward, Statham and Boswell again. "There's a seven second latency built into the communication round-trip," he said. "We should see a burst of incoming data at any time." In a few seconds, it came as expected. "Active threads 5 – delta is plus 3 from start state. Load down to 84%. Outbound data no change. Incoming, 1.1MB."

Meyer turned to his team again. "Ankur," he said, "please check with the datacenter and verify that incoming and outgoing data is being captured as expected. Let's get eyes on it immediately. Status and first impressions in 3 minutes."

"Copy," the man said in a heavy Indian accent. He checked his watch then set to typing at his laptop computer.

The team had become fixated on the operational metrics of the server. That no direct output had yet appeared on the terminal was not an immediate concern. They were getting data and lots of it, and that was more than enough. But then something did appear; a single period.

"A period?" Boswell said, perplexed. "What does that mean?" he asked Meyer.

"It's a message without content. It's telling us to sit tight – letting us know that it's working. Think of it as the simplest of all progress bars," he said, then returned to calling out status. "Active threads 8 – delta is plus 6 from start state. Incoming data–" He stopped, blinking as if having trouble believing what he saw. "Incoming data 16.62GB and rising," he said. He looked to Ward, then back to the terminal. "18.2, 20.6. Data traffic has jumped by orders of magnitude." He spun back to his team. "Ankur, make sure we're getting this. I'm worried about bandwidth. And please verify the numbers are correct – this is way more data than expected. I don't see how our setup can support this type of throughput."

"Copy," Ankur said again.

The number grew to 34.6GB before stopping. It took only a few moments. Another period appeared to the right of the first on the screen. Meyer turned to Ankur, whose eyes were locked on his computer screen. "We have it," Ankur said. "Bandwidth not an issue. Apparently, they're throttling the data to a level we can handle, but it's coming in as fast as we can receive it."

Meyer gave a thumbs-up and turned back around.

"Data is binary," Ankur added.

"All computing data is binary. What's the structure and format?" Meyer said, impatiently.

"As yet, unknown."

"Copy that. Keep looking," Meyer said. "Load is back to 100%. More outbound traffic." Another period was displayed, then another, followed by a burst of 20 more. "Load decreasing," Meyer said suddenly. "82%. 60%, 38-."

The terminal went dark.

The sudden and unexpected halt felt like a hole in the room. It was like seeing the end of a fireworks display and waiting with uncertainty to know whether it was truly over or if the lull was a prelude to some grander finale. Ward gave the sudden lack of activity only a few seconds before speaking. "What the hell happened?" he said, immediately turning to Meyer.

Meyer was already on it, "Report!" he said, almost yelling. "We lost the server. Did we lose power?"

"Power in the data center still on," came an immediate response. "Host machine is still humming. Could be a reboot."

"The hell?" Meyer said.

"Reboot confirmed, we're coming back up."

On cue, the terminal flickered back to life. This time the entire display area remained dark but for a single period in the upper left corner. Almost immediately, a series of more periods began to form a line across the top. They eventually reached the right edge of the screen and wrapped to begin a new line.

"We're into something new here. Any traffic?" Meyer said.

"None."

The periods kept coming, a little slower now, roughly one per second, until several rows of periods banded the top of the display. It ran for a nerve-testing 12 minutes, feeling more like an hour. "Still no traffic?"

"Nothing appreciable, likely only protocol overhead," Ankur said. "Just like we saw before."

The screen went dark a second time. Ward looked to Meyer, shaking his head in bafflement. "Did you guys model any of this?"

Meyer shrugged. "Not specifically, but we're not outside the lines. This is still compatible with aggressive and cooperative personas."

"But no guesses on what specifically is happening here?" Ward pressed.

Riley leaned in. "I think it's reconfiguring our machine," Riley said, calmly.

Ward turned to face him. "What the hell does that mean?" he asked, flustered.

"I think it's installing a new operating system."

Meyer looked suddenly distant, as if thinking about the possibility. "Could be," he said.

"Are we still contained?" Ward demanded.

"Yes," Meyer said.

"Why would it install a new operating system?"

Meyer looked to Riley. "Only one reason occurs to me," Riley said.

"Which is?"

"It's turning the entire machine into a comms device. It clearly optimized our communication channel and now it's installing software to operate it. There's no way the configuration we started with – the simple programs and modulator Clipper and I put together – could support the kind of throughput we're seeing here. It's rebuilding the server and optimizing everything."

"Would it really do something like that?" Meyer asked. "You don't think that – whoever these guys are – would follow some Star Trek, prime directive? You know, not sharing advanced technology with less developed civilizations?"

"Actually, I do. But it wouldn't apply to everything," Riley said. "Think about it. When we work with third-world countries, there are things we share and things we don't. We have no trouble sharing medicine, cars, mobile phones and bringing them up to speed on monetary systems, but we don't share secrets about nuclear fusion. I think we're seeing a variation of that. They're giving us a way to talk, but it's a safe bet they won't share their secret sauce anytime soon."

All eyes looked to the terminal as if seeing it for the first time. "That's plausible," Meyer said. "What's our stance?"

"Same," Ward replied. "Keep rolling."

As the three spoke, the first textual content appeared on the display. "Peer network," it said. The words appeared on their own line; white text against a black background. The cursor waited to the right, blinking. Another period came, then another, then another; each separated by a few seconds.

"It's looking around," Riley said.

"Won't get far," Meyer said. "It'll discover we've boxed it in any second. This is where I expect it'll start asking for information."

The cursor moved to the start of the next line; "Multi-lingual" appeared with more periods. Then another new line. "Unstructured." The same pattern of periods following.

"English, huh? How is it speaking English?" Ward said, a note of incredulity in his tone.

"It's not as outlandish as it seems," Meyer said. "It's always the first thing people zoom in on when it comes to science fiction. Truth is, translating languages and concepts isn't that hard. We can do it ourselves, even when the languages are markedly different from one another; structurally, semantically, you name it. There's a ton of software out there that translates languages, which proves the concept. I won't say it's trivial, but it's far from impossible, and if we can do it, these guys sure as hell can."

"Language is essentially mapping concepts to a communicative form. If we have anything in common in terms of concepts of thought, this isn't a stretch, except–" he said, as if chewing on a thought. "There is the problem that you need something to start with. You need a Rosetta Stone, or at a minimum, a decent sample of the foreign language to work from. From there, you piece together how and where your own concepts or words map to the foreign lexicon. There is the question of where this thing is getting the English words it's using. We've got this thing in a very small cage," Meyer went on, seeming to think aloud. "Which means that any English words it uses must have been pulled from whatever it found on the server before it was shut down on Sunday, and anything it may have fetched from the internet." He turned in his chair. "Ankur, let's do some searches on the data we captured from the first session on Sunday. See if we can find the words we're seeing here in anything it had access to on the machine itself." He lapsed back into thought. "Peer network, unstructured, multi-lingual," he said, almost to himself. "Where would it have picked up those words?"

Ward eyed Riley narrowly for unknown reasons but didn't speak. Riley met his gaze without reacting.

"I'd focus on the *man* pages," Clipper added.

Meyer palmed his forehead in a self-abasing gesture. "Right," he said, clearly frustrated with himself. "How could I not have thought of that?" he said, but didn't belabor the point. "Good call, Jason. I'd bet that's where most, if not all of the vocabulary we're seeing is coming from."

"Man pages?" Ward asked.

"Man, for manual," Meyer explained. "Linux is a complex operating system. It comes out of the box with hundreds – maybe thousands of utilities and tools, and as many or more that can be installed optionally. Pretty much, each one comes with a manual that describes what the utility does and how to use it. There's a good chance that the virus is using them as its language sample."

Clipper nodded his agreement.

"So, *unstructured* might have come from the *grep* manual," Meyer reasoned aloud. "*Peer network* from any of the network libraries. And *Multi-lingual–*"

"Could be Javadocs. Might be the I18N; uh, internationalization libraries," Clipper said, then turned to Ward before he could ask the question. "Javadocs are like manuals for the Java programming language. It's used heavily on servers like this one."

"Right," Meyer said, as if reaching a conclusion. "Okay, this is making better sense, but I want to find those words – explicitly."

Ankur spoke up. "We just learned that the server had a copy of *aMule* installed. It wasn't being used, but it was there along with all the doc." He looked to Ward. "It's software that supports peer-to-peer networking. It's sometimes abbreviated as P2P," he said. "And not only that," he continued, a grin crossing his face, "there were ten different copies of the docs, all in different languages. We have, English, Dansk, Deutsch, Española, Suomi, François, Magyar, Italian, Nederlands and Russian."

"There's our Rosetta Stone," Meyer said. "At least one of them."

Ankur agreed. "Could be just one of dozens, depending on what was installed on the machine."

"This thing has no shortage of language samples to learn from, then. And if they're bazillions of light years ahead of us in technology as we assume, piecing them together would be child's play." Meyer looked back to the display terminal.

Nothing new appeared after the word, *unstructured*, and the minutes began to stretch. "What is it doing?" Meyer said, again more to himself, then looked back to Clipper. "This machine has serious horsepower, it's hard to imagine what could keep it busy for this long."

"It's learning to speak our language, for one," Riley said. "In a few minutes, it'll probably speak better English than me. But agree, that in itself shouldn't keep a machine this size this busy for this long."

"We finished searching the data from Sunday," Ankur said. "It didn't reveal much. We had already done a lot of analysis on it. So far, conclusions are that it spent most of its time learning the protocols and operational aspects of the computer itself, then moved to the internet. But even then, it was more interested in how the internet worked – the peer network itself – than the information that could be found on it. We expect that would have come next, but it had not poked around much into information like Wikipedia or CNN or government sites by the time it was shut down."

"Meaning," Meyer added in conclusion, "that the bulk of language samples, if not all, were taken from what was already on the machine."

"That's our belief," Ankur said.

"Good work, thanks." Meyer said. Then, reaching a decision, turned to his team, scanning for a specific individual. Locating her just behind him, he said, "Angela, while we wait, let's go ahead and try to open a telnet session to the machine. We've lost our *top* output, so we're flying blind. If we can get in, we'll restart monitoring." He then spoke to Ankur, "What's happening on traffic?"

"Nothing new. Since the last reboot, no data sent or received," Ankur said. "We're in a holding pattern."

"If we really have a new OS, odds are low that they'll be a telnet server for us to connect to," Angela said.

Meyer shook his head, frustrated. "Agree, but let's try."

Chapter 43

March 15, 2024

The inactivity had stretched for nine hours, long since draining the nervous energy from the room. What had not ebbed was the determined belief that the events earlier in the day were a precursor to something else. Something big. And that whatever it was would unfold in due time.

"We don't really know what constitutes a long wait to whoever may be on the other end of this," Ward said, checking his watch, fatigue now apparent on his face.

"Afraid not," Meyer agreed. An intermittent conversation had been passing between the core team throughout the day, tapering down to occasional ideas and observations as the hours stretched on.

Riley had gone to thinking, only half listening to any of it. The hours had become a contagion of decreasingly productive guesses and supposition. More than once, Riley had to remind himself that success, and the reasons he remained, did not rest on the hope that some brilliant insight or discovery would emerge from the team. They were in the anteroom of the unknown, and if the state of things were to stretch on for months, all of it would still hold immeasurably more promise than anything else he could think of. There was no other place in the world he would rather be.

"All of this could make sense," Riley said at last. He hadn't spoken for more than an hour, so his sudden statement drew the attention of everyone at hand. "I think that what we saw earlier was a mechanized process. Something reached out and installed software in our datacenter. It improved and optimized our communication capabilities, and put us in a position to be able to talk. That's all. From what I can tell, that part of it completed successfully. Now it becomes a question of if or when anyone on the other end actually wants to talk."

"You're saying that we're done here unless some alien decides to pick up the phone?" Ward asked.

"We're already waiting," Riley said, answering the sarcasm in Ward's tone unflinchingly. "That part of it is already happening. The larger question is; will we get a call? I say yes. My only point is that everything we've seen so far appears to be nothing more than opening the lines of communication. Getting things ready."

Ward considered the point. "Good a theory as any. There's no second chance at a first impression," he said decisively.

"Whatever we do here will not be half-baked. Where's Briggs?" he said, scanning the room.

"Here," she said, stepping forward from behind his left shoulder.

He swiveled his chair in her direction. "It's time for a shift change. Let's get the overnight crew installed. I need the core team rested and ready for another full day tomorrow. Everyone gets a decent meal, then lights out by midnight. No alcohol or socializing." Briggs' eyes tracked to Clipper at that, and then back to Ward, but no one seemed to notice – not even Clipper. "Let's get the core team together at 9:30 AM to discuss next steps. If anything develops overnight, notify me immediately. Nothing happens without my authorization."

"I would have thought you'd want to come together earlier," Briggs said.

Ward motioned around the room, swiveling his chair. "There's no urgency for now, so I think the best use of time is to get everyone rested up."

*   *   *

Ward's phone rang at 5:30 AM. It was Meyer. "Sir, we have something new," he said without elaboration.

"I'll be there in 30," Ward replied, then hung up the line. He arrived at the lab 50 minutes later to see the secondary crew fully in stride. As he entered the large room, Michael Parker, a Senior Analyst with the NSA, spotted him and made to intercept. "What's the situation, Mike?" Ward asked.

"Good morning, sir. We started seeing output on the screen at about 5:15. Quiet all night prior to that," he said, motioning Ward towards one of the large screens on the back wall. "All this appeared in a matter of about 90 seconds."

It consisted of five simple lines of text:

Communication-band activity detected

Cause artificial

Onboarding

Contact iteration three

Override scenario

Parker and Ward were still looking wordlessly at the screen when Meyer stepped up to join them, his eyes scanning the words.

"What do you make of this?" Ward asked.

Before Meyer could compel his mind to interpret the meanings of the statements, he couldn't help first trying to mentally trace where the words themselves had come from. It was a stretch to imagine that all of them – and their proper uses – could be lifted from only the disconnected, and not always well-written technical documentation that happened to be present on the Linux server at the time the virus was planted there.

Ward read his concern. "What is it?"

Meyer began a stammering response. "Just … trying to piece together the lexicon we're seeing here. It's making damned good use of the English language. Even the hyphenation is good. Terse, but good."

Ward looked back to the screen.

Meyer said: "We've already seen an impressive demonstration of how smart these guys are, but they still have to get our words from us. Even if they're smart enough to extrapolate proper grammar rules and pluralization from a bunch of technical manuals, there is still–" he left off again, lapsing into thought as his eyes searched the floor. "...onboarding?" he said, almost in a whisper, as if his mind had jumped rails to a new train of thought. "Where would it get that word? The concept must be known to us both – us and them – but the word is ours."

"What are you implying?" Ward pressed.

Meyer had to force the words out. He found and met Wards gaze. "That we may not..." he began, shaking his head in a way that a doctor might when relating bad news to a patient, but then aborted, unwilling to say whatever was on his mind. "Let's think about it. *Communication-band activity detected.* That's networking stuff. Plenty of software and manuals that those words could have been lifted from already on the machine. *Override scenario.* Any command-line option will override a default behavior, so that's not a hard one either – the concept is everywhere. *Iteration* is the same – a no brainer." He was still looking off and away from Ward as he spoke, his eyes searching, unseeing along the floor. "*Cause artificial*," he said, rubbing his forehead, and for a moment becoming the clumsy person he appeared to be in the briefing room a few days before. "We're getting onto thinner ice there. *Cause artificial* and *onboarding*," he repeated, still mulling the phrases over, "those are tough ones." He looked to Parker who nodded knowingly. "Parker, what has the situation team made of this?"

"We're a step ahead of you," Parker answered, "but you're doing pretty good. Short answer; we can't find a solid source for either phrase."

"Your assessment then?"

"Unless these guys pulled data in from the internet prior to us boxing them in – and we've yet to find evidence of it – we may not be contained," he said with an apologetic and mildly sympathetic nod. "It had to have found that word from the outside."

Ward drew a breath that both Parker and Meyer assumed to be the precursor to a tirade. Instead, when Ward spoke, his tone was even and measured. "Where's Riley and Clipper?" he said. "Get them in here. I want to know where the hole is."

Parker nodded and stepped away.

"This could be my ass," Ward said, "but let's face it, if this damned thing is what we think it is, it was never contained; except in the way a submarine contains the ocean. They turned our computer inside out like it was nothing. If there's a weakness anywhere, this thing was always going to find it."

"Oh, there's weakness, Mr. Ward," Meyer said, perhaps for the first time sounding fully at ease in his dialog with the high-ranking NSA official. "We're standing on it. It's going to be a revelation to learn how hilariously weak our position is. You told us to get some rest last night, but I'll tell you what I ended up doing instead. I spent all of it staring at the ceiling and thinking about the brute force of intelligence that could do what this thing did with our server and gravity generator yesterday. Do you want to know what I concluded?"

"I think I can guess," Ward said.

"I'm sure you can," Meyer said, but went on anyway. "If these aliens wanted to broadcast a message to the world from the Oval Office, they'd have done it by now. They would have done it Sunday. My advice, sir, is not to let anyone drag us down the imaginary hole of what we allowed to happen," he said, emphasizing the word 'allowed' by forming air-quotes with his hands. "We allowed this to happen in the same way we're going to allow the sun to rise in about an hour from now." Ward was somewhat taken aback by the passion in Meyer's voice. The man was shaken. Maybe even scared, but he was handling it well.

Briggs appeared among them carrying two cups of coffee. She handed one of them to Ward who nodded appreciably, and then sipped at the other. "Shall I bring in the team?" she asked. "They're not scheduled to arrive for another four hours."

Ward looked contemplatively to the display. "Let's let them rest," he said. "We've got good people here. I want to start with Riley on where this breach could be – if there is one. I also want to talk about the message itself. Regardless of how, or if we should have received it aside, what does it mean to us?"

John Riley entered the room at 6:20 AM. His demeanor, per usual, calm and self-possessed. He approached Ward and the others, but his eyes remained on the display screen for a long moment before tracking back to the group.

"Our analysts think we've lost containment," Ward said.

Riley went on studying the lines of text on the wall, biting at the inside of his lower left lip as was his habit when in deep thought.

"Do you agree?" Ward asked.

Riley nodded slowly, scrutinizing the words for several seconds more before speaking. "Yes, I do."

"How and where?"

"We need to get to the Installation," Riley said, simply.

"Ms. Briggs," Ward said, without hesitation, "could you please make arrangements for transportation via one of the Hueys? I want to leave in 10 minutes." She nodded, and was gone in a moment.

Ward turned back to Riley, Meyer and Parker, who had by then rejoined the group. "What's the message? What do the statements themselves tell us?" The question was directed to Riley, but Meyer spoke first.

"The notion of onboarding aligns with Riley's theory that we've tripped an automated system. They've installed a comm device; that's clear enough. *Iteration three* and *override scenario*? Not something I would have guessed we would see among the first few statements an alien would say to us. Nothing on that as yet."

"Mr. Riley, were there any prior occurrences of these activities to account for the *iteration three* statement? Did you or Mr. Clipper attempt to communicate prior to Sunday?" Ward asked, pointedly.

"Yes, we did," Riley admitted. "We've been completely open about what we've done. But as you know, none of the early attempts elicited any response beyond the original handshake we've all seen. It's all been disclosed; and I can't think of anything that corresponds to three. We didn't iterate over anything three times. We performed our tests dozens and dozens of times."

Ward eyed Riley for a few seconds before letting the question pass. "Well gentlemen, we have a shiny new puzzle to deal with. Won't be the last. Let's get moving. Parker, sorry, but I need you here. Meyer, Briggs, Riley, Clipper, you're with me."

Chapter 44

March 15, 2024

T he UH-1N Twin Huey helicopter seemed at odds with its purpose. Nothing about the interior of the aircraft seemed to convey or even corroborate its purpose as a flying machine, save the complex instrument panel at the front of its cockpit. Its utilitarian interior looked more unfinished than thoughtfully optimized for weight, and there were no concessions to comfort beyond the foam padding in the seats. The machine rose noisily, but smoothly into the air above the campus grounds by the forced will of its massive turbine engines; its rotors slicing deafeningly at the air.

It took only 25 minutes to reach the Installation, maybe less. The immediacy of perspective provided by the Huey with its many windows, and the low altitude at which they flew, made for an altogether unique experience for anyone whose time in the air had been limited to commercial aircraft.

It seemed like no time before the pilot had landed the craft expertly inside the fenced Installation grounds, 30 yards from the largest of the buildings. The engines relented almost immediately on touching down, and the five passengers – Jeff Ward, Natalie Briggs, Ryan Meyer, John Riley and Jason Clipper – exited, hunching reflexively as they stepped out beneath the slowing rotor blades. Ward, Briggs, Meyer and Clipper immediately set off towards the largest of the buildings, the one that housed the newest gravity machine, but Riley split off in the direction of one of the smaller, windowless buildings to the right. The other four stammered to a stop before turning to follow, uncomprehendingly.

On reaching the small building, Riley swiped his badge across the card reader and stepped inside, his eyes immediately tracking to a solitary terminal glowing brightly against the dim light of the room, lines of text scrolling unrhythmically across its surface. He switched on the light as the others filed into the small space.

Meyer followed him in and immediately spotted the terminal as well. "It seems we have found our breach," he said with nervous humor.

"Bring it down," Ward said.

"I'm not sure that's a good idea," Riley said.

Ignoring the comment, Ward nodded to Meyer who edged around Riley in the cramped space and stepped towards the terminal. "There are words here. Riley may be right–" he said, but Ward cut him off.

"Now!" he demanded.

Meyer turned back to the terminal. "It worked for AJ," he said under his breath, "second time's a charm." He reached for the keyboard and typed AJ's now-infamous words; *please stop*. He stood erect, watching expectantly. A promising few seconds of inactivity followed – long enough for the group to begin to relax – but it was short-lived. Another line of text appeared on a cadence suggesting that the input had been ignored.

"Damn!" Ward spat. In no longer than it took for a hastened breath, he bellowed, "cut power, now! Where's the breaker box?" he said, looking the question to Riley.

"I got it," Riley said, resignedly, stepping the few short strides to the corner of the room.

"Cut the power and we lose what's on the display, and probably much more," Meyer protested.

"Everything," Ward demanded, "bring this whole thing down, now!"

Meyer wheeled back to the terminal, quickly scanning the text, but Riley had reached the battleship-gray panel by then and flipped the main breaker, plunging the small building into darkness. The sudden silencing of the ambient sounds of cooling fans and ventilation made the space feel dead, like an abandoned hole in the ground.

Ward broke the silence as Clipper opened the outer door to let in light. "Mr. Meyer, what did you see on the terminal before we cut power?"

Meyer didn't answer at once. He was agitated and seemed to struggle for self-control. "I caught only a few words," he said, with no attempt to hide his frustration. "At the bottom; democracy, democratic republic, dictatorship, monarchy. I also caught the word bipedal, not sure where it fit in. There was, uh, relativistic. Then, the top line said 78% nitrogen, 21% oxygen, then something about argon and carbon dioxide. I didn't catch all the numbers."

Riley saw the question on Ward's face. "Air," Riley said. "It's the chemical makeup of air."

Ward's lips began to form a question, but his phone rang, interrupting whatever he was about to say. "Ward here," he said, lifting his phone, and at the same time motioning the group towards the door. The voice at the other end could be heard faintly. Ward listened for a moment, then called out. "Meyer, it's Parker, they're starting to see massive incoming data."

"What's massive?" Meyer asked.

"320GB and counting."

"Don't interrupt it," Meyer said, forcefully. "We've got 20 petabytes of space, so we should be good for anything they throw at us."

By this time they were out onto the grounds. Briggs made her way to Clipper, "what's a petabyte?" she asked, leaning in confidentially.

"It's a measure of data, roughly the size of a football stadium," he said.

"Ah, that clears that up," she said.

"I'll have to check my math though; could be closer to two football stadiums. We're not short on storage space." His explanation was rewarded by an unexpected smile. He had seen her smile many times in the few days since he had met her, but it was always the professional, courteous type. This was the first time he saw a personal, relaxed smile from her; and at that moment, a slight breeze rose, catching her hair lightly in the early morning sun. She raised a hand to brush it back from her face, her eyes lingering on Clipper before turning towards Ward without further comment. Clipper watched her walk away.

He moved to join Riley and Meyer, who had taken up a discussion. "No," he heard Meyer saying to Riley as he approached. "I'm not aware of any hardware optimizations. All the equipment is just as you left it."

"It's hard to imagine the kind of bandwidth we're seeing here, from the crude setup we have," Riley said, scanning the grounds and looking at the buildings as if the answer could spring out of one of them. "It's all rudimentary; designed without the slightest thought for communication." He looked off to the distance. "We must have been closer to a viable solution than I realized," he said, as if the thought was difficult to fathom.

Ward stepped forward to join them. "We're already at three terabytes," he said, "and no signs of slowing. Why would they go around us? I thought they weren't hostile."

Riley shrugged as if the answer was obvious. "We didn't ask them not to," he said, plainly. The comment seemed to arrest the group. "If you think about all the things they've done since this started, it makes sense. It tells a story. First of all," he held up an index finger, "they pinged us for several months with these signals before we noticed them. Then, they waited patiently for a response – waited for us to be *able* to respond. Next, they led us forward each step of the way, breadcrumb by breadcrumb, and once we made the necessary changes to our configuration – once we were able to talk back and give them hardware to work with – they optimized that hardware to allow us to communicate better. My bet is that from their side, this is not an unexpected intrusion, they must believe that everything we have done was purpose-driven to invite them in. To them, they didn't force their way into our datacenter, we invited them. When we finally initiated communication, we immediately asked them to stop, and they did. But when we restarted, their system realized that it had lost access to the resources it had before. From our perspective, we were trying to box them in – to contain them, but to them, it probably looked like a technical problem. We had clearly shown, over a period of months, that we wanted to cooperate, so being boxed in was, in their view, probably just another technical roadblock to overcome. They clearly knew about this older gravity machine," he said, thumbing in the direction of the small building they had just exited, "so they reverted to it."

"They must have detected us as far back as the earliest tests we did," Clipper added, "otherwise they wouldn't have a way of knowing there was an alternative set of hardware to fall back to. We had no ability to capture gravity prints back then to know whether they were there or not."

"I think you're right, Clip," Riley said.

"So," Meyer said, "they needed to continue to learn about us, but the primary environment had, in their view, become broken, forcing them to revert to this one," he said, motioning again to the small building. "They've been pulling down as much information as they can through this channel for the past 20 hours, and then, boom, this system goes down too." He laughed slightly. "They must think we're idiots." He shook his head in regret of the first impressions they must be conveying. "Now that their latest communication channel is down, they decide that the next best action is to take what they've learned and return to the other channel – back to the Mayfield datacenter."

Riley nodded, then turned to Ward. "The primary system is boxed in, and now this channel is down. I think we need to get back to the campus as soon as possible."

"Why?" Ward asked.

"Because the only option they have now – unless they break containment on the datacenter – is to talk with us. Given the amount of data they're downloading to the datacenter, I'm guessing they have plenty to say."

Ward made a spinning motion with his hand across the field to the helicopter pilot, index finger pointing to the sky. The man was looking in their direction, and read the meaning immediately. He nodded and began throwing switches on the cockpit panel. In moments, the large machine began wheezing back to life.

Riley felt a tap on his shoulder and turned to see Clipper, who didn't speak, but only nodded towards the gate at the front of the property. A small line of cars had begun to form on the road. Looking further down the hill, more cars were becoming visible. "They must've seen us fly in," Clipper said.

Riley nodded agreement, the noise of the Huey already making communication difficult. Ward noticed too. In a moment, they were aboard the aircraft and Ward was barking more orders. "Parker," he yelled, "time to punch this up a notch. We need security at the installation immediately. It's also time to brief the president. Get a video conference arranged at the president's earliest convenience. We'll be back in 20 minutes."

Chapter 45

March 16, 2024

Sarah knocked at the door of AJ's parent's home, and Alice appeared seconds later. She smiled a half-hearted greeting and then stepped back, welcoming Sarah inside. Despite the early hour, Alice was fully dressed and looked ready to set off for work, though Sarah knew it wasn't the reason. Suitcases were lined neatly against the wall just beyond the entryway.

Sarah eyed them as she stepped inside. "How are you?" she asked.

"Okay. We've spent the night bouncing back and forth between worried and angry. You?"

"Same," Sarah said, nodding futilely. "Have you learned anything?"

"Not much that helps. Peter's been watching CNN all night, and I've done every search I can think of on the internet. I can tell you all about the NSA now," she said, offering another weak smile, "but nothing about what's happening with the boys. I've just made coffee, would you like some?" Sarah nodded, and they turned towards the kitchen.

"I've been following the news and doing some searches as well," Sarah said. "Riley and Clipper are everywhere now, but I haven't found any mention of AJ." Alice nodded as if her learnings had been the same. Sarah pointed in the direction of the suitcases, although they were now out of view. "Are you leaving?"

"Yes. We're going to Charlotte."

Peter stepped into the room. He was clearly tired but shared his wife's determined look. "Hello Sarah," he said, on seeing her sitting at the table. "All the networks are covering, but I'm not sure why. They don't seem to know anything. They haven't even shared enough to justify the attention they're giving to whatever is happening over there at Mayfield Hammond. They're just hovering their helicopters above the headquarters and commenting every time someone enters or leaves the building."

Peter poured himself some coffee, then left the room to return to his vigil, leaving Alice and Sarah in silence. It lingered for a moment before Alice spoke. "You and AJ have had an interesting few months," she said.

Sarah smiled, feeling suddenly exposed. "Yes, we have," she agreed, guardedly.

"He's a good boy," Alice said, her eyes tearing slightly, but only for a moment. "He hasn't shared much with us. He's grown now, so I don't pry. And I won't pry now either, by the way," she said, sensing Sarah's immediate unease. "I'd just like to say that he's our only child, so I've never known how typical he is. To me, he seems very special, but I know how laughable that sounds coming from a mother." She wiped at her nose with a worn Kleenex. "But, we have more to work from than just siblings, don't we? We can compare ourselves to others, and our children to other children. AJ is special, he really is. He is deeply thoughtful, and I don't mean that in only a caring kind of way. He thinks. He ponders, and arrives at insights that are sometimes astounding – to me, anyway. He also has tremendous willpower. Of the two, I don't know which I would say is the more dominant characteristic. Maybe they're two sides of the same coin, I don't know."

"I'm afraid, Mrs. Jacobs, that mine and AJ's relationship is not what it could be, and to whatever extent it's lacking, it's my fault. I am the only daughter of a protestant minister, and that placed me in the middle of a very protected environment for most of my life. I've always viewed the entire world through the lens of my faith, always. My estimation of anything and everything has always been the measure of how they agree with my beliefs. AJ is the first time ever–" Her voice became choked for a moment, and she recovered with a sip of coffee. "He is the first of anything to gain a hold on me that hasn't conformed perfectly with my views on life. I struggled against that for a very long time. At first, I wanted to force him to conform, but in the end he drove a change in me instead. All of it made me realize, maybe for the first time, that the world is bigger than me, and maybe," she said, struggling against a difficult thought, "even bigger than my beliefs. My prior way of thinking may never have worked, I just didn't know it. I broke things off with AJ a few weeks ago as a final attempt to force my life back into submission."

"It didn't work," Alice said. It was not a question.

"No. It didn't," Sarah allowed. "The days that followed were not only about me learning how much I did not want to lose AJ, but realizing that I had to turn a corner. The way I had viewed life wasn't working. Could never work. And then all this happened," she motioned around the room. "I'm so angry. I was going to meet with AJ yesterday. We were going to talk. I flew to Charlotte to see him. I knew it wasn't the right time to work through everything then, but I needed him to know that nothing less than travelling across the country to tell him that I wanted another chance was good enough. And now, I don't know if we'll ever get the chance to talk like we intended." Tears instantly streamed down her face, though Alice could plainly see that she struggled mightily against letting it happen.

Alice watched her sympathetically. Despite everything, it said much about her, Sarah realized, that she had the capacity to confine herself to the moment, to the discussion, giving it her patient and undivided attention even at a time like this. "It's not my place to say too much here, Sarah," she said, mildly, "but I know AJ cares very much about you. He told me the two of you were going to talk, and he was very anxious about it."

"Do you think he's in trouble?" Sarah asked.

Alice looked away as if the question were an arrow. "I don't know," she said, "but I do know that whatever has happened, there could have been no intent to do wrong."

"Oh God!" Peter's voice came carrying through the house. Alice and Sarah's eyes locked momentarily before they set to their feet and hurried into the living room. They found Peter standing in front of the television, remote in hand. He was turning up the volume, despite that it was already more than loud enough.

"What? What is it?" Alice demanded, but he didn't respond.

The television showed live coverage of the Mayfield Hammond grounds. "Yes, our apologies," a young anchorwoman was saying, stammering through her live monologue. "Our aircrew has been asked to leave the immediate area in preparation for the arrival of the president at Mayfield Hammond headquarters. We're seeing his helicopter coming into view now," she said as the imagery to her back showed the large Sea King presidential helicopter, with its distinctive green and white coloring, resolving into view from a distance. "Again, ladies and gentlemen, CNN has just learned, but not yet confirmed that the activity we have been witnessing at Mayfield Hammond world headquarters in Charlotte is related to *First Contact*. An anonymous, but believed reliable source has informed us that First Contact has been made with an intelligent alien race and that some form of dialog is underway. As part of that, astoundingly, a man from the Midwest, his name, Andrew Jacobs, has been specifically called out as a person of interest. As yet, nothing about the man is known to us."

"What does that mean?" Alice asked in a panic. "What does she mean, person of interest?"

"Listen Alice, we can figure that out later, but for now we need to leave," Peter said. "We'll be surrounded by news reporters, and who knows who else within 30 minutes. If we don't leave now we'll be followed wherever we go, and that will be that." Immediate comprehension appeared on her face, and Sarah's. "Get what you need, we leave in five minutes! Thank god we were already packed for Charlotte."

Alice turned to Sarah. "We'll call you," she said, then called out to Peter, "I'll get your keys and wallet from the bedroom. Do you have your phone? Do you need anything else?"

Peter was already at the front door, two of the four suitcases in hand, "don't forget your thyroid medicine," he said.

"Got it," he heard Alice reply.

Sarah fell in behind Peter, picking up the remaining two suitcases. They were heavier than they looked, a strain on her unusually petite stature, but she muscled them from the floor.

"Sarah, let me get those" Peter said, noticing her struggling against the weight.

"I'm good," she said, exasperated. Peter turned without further discussion. They carried the suitcases to the drive and set them next to the SUV. "I'll shut off the coffee pot and television," Sarah said, returning to the house.

Alice appeared in the doorway a moment later. "Keys, phone, wallet," she was saying, checking items from a mental list. "Wait, I forgot the phone chargers."

"We'll get new ones," Peter said. "Let's go!"

And within what seemed like only seconds, the door to the house was closed, and Sarah and Alice were headed towards their vehicles. Alice's phone rang in her hand. It was a neighbor. She ignored it. They entered the vehicle as the front door to a nearby house opened and a man appeared, looking in their direction. Peter backed the SUV down the driveway. As he put the vehicle into drive, he noticed another neighbor stepping out of his opened garage, also looking in their direction. Sarah's car, which had been parked on the street, pulled away, and Peter and Alice set off in the opposite direction.

In a moment, they were out of view of the house and leaving the subdivision. They drove west towards the interstate, no more than three miles distant. Shortly before reaching it, they saw a news van coming in the opposite direction. They looked at each other furtively. Alice's phone rang again.

"It starts," Peter said.

Alice looked to her phone expecting to see that it was another person she would not want to talk with. "It's Andrew!" she said, almost in a shout. She answered the phone.

"Mom," AJ's voice said from the other end of the line. "I'm fine. I'm not in trouble and I'm being treated well, but listen. You must leave the house. I've been trying to get these guys to let me call for the past three days, but they wouldn't. I'm only allowed to call now because my name has been mentioned in the news and they know you guys will end up in the middle of a hurricane of attention, and you may not be safe."

Alice looked to her husband who was driving with one eye on the road. "He's fine. He's okay," she said, then began to weep. "We've already left the house, Andrew. We heard your name on CNN."

"Oh, good," he said. "Listen, the NSA knows you guys have booked flights to come here. Go ahead with your travel plans – the media won't be able to learn about it until it's too late. Someone will pick you up at the airport here in Charlotte and take you to a safe location. I don't know how soon I'll be able to see you, but we'll work that out. Have you heard from Sarah?"

"Yes," Alice said, regaining some of her composure. "She's been with us almost the entire time since you were taken, except overnight. She just left us. Your dad and I are headed towards I-35 now. Our plane doesn't leave until 1:00 in the afternoon, but we're going to head in the direction of the airport now."

"We'll kill some time at Zona Rosa Town Center, not far from the airport," Peter said, loud enough for AJ to hear. "We'll get something to eat, and then head over to KCI around noon."

"Okay, that's perfect," AJ said. "Listen, I'm going to call Sarah now. I have to go. Love you both."

The phone went silent. The weight lifted from Peter and Alice was immense. Alice was weeping openly now, and Peter drove on, almost in a daze.

*   *   *

Sarah's mind was reeling. AJ had been mentioned on CNN. She was at once afraid for him and longed to see him. Her white Ford Focus travelled along the side streets of AJ's neighborhood without a destination. Peter and Alice had been her connection to him, and now they were gone too. She had no one, and no way to reconnect to anything that was happening. She turned north onto Mur-Len road and drove without knowing to where.

Her world was crumbling. The church was about to disintegrate from beneath her feet, and now AJ was gone, leaving an unexpected emptiness against which she felt powerless. She came upon a small strip mall on the east side of the road and pulled in, wheeling her car to a vacant area along its outer edge. She put the car into park, buried her face in her hands and began to cry.

The regrets of the past few weeks were cascading in upon her with crushing weight. Had she not broken things off with AJ, he would not have gone to Charlotte to start with. They would be together now. He would be safe, and so would she, and so would AJ's parents. Every new thought, every connection her mind made, pointed a heavy hand of guilt squarely in her direction. Within a few minutes, her entire body was shuddering with grief.

She was startled by the sound of her phone ringing. It sat in the passenger seat, face up. The words on the display seemed impossible. Andrew Jacobs, they said, in bold lettering. She looked at it in disbelief for a moment before snatching it up and answering.

"Hello?" she said, the quivering unevenness of emotion impossible to mask from her voice.

"Sarah, it's AJ. Are you okay?"

She couldn't help herself. The pride of the person she had been only a few days before would have struggled mightily to deny the feelings that had now so completely overwhelmed her. But today, it was not possible. She couldn't make her voice cooperate. "I don't... know," she said, croaking the words out.

"Sarah, I'm sorry about everything," he said, his voice gentle, as if he somehow knew where she was and understood the state she was in. She didn't answer. "Sarah, I don't have much time. We didn't get to talk. I love you, and I have to ask a question. An unfair question." He heard the muffled sound of her weeping, and the reflexive, involuntary intake of air that comes with crying deeply. "I'm okay," he said. "Riley and Clipper are too, but I don't know what's going to happen. What I do know is that my life is going to change. It already has. I don't know when, or if, I'll be able to return home. If I do, I think it will be a long time from now. I can't talk about what is happening here, but I am being treated well. I'm not a prisoner and I'm not under arrest, but I have somehow become entangled in something much bigger than myself, and there is no way out of it."

Sarah's weeping was subsiding. She looked out the window of her car, somehow beginning to know that her world was about to change too, this time, irrevocably. There were cars driving in and out of the parking lot. People walking along the sidewalks peering into store windows, and coming and going with shopping bags in hand. They looked to be millions of miles away, almost as if they weren't real, that she was somehow observing an artificial facade of the world. A paper-thin recreation.

Still, she didn't speak.

"I've been hoping beyond hope, Sarah, that you and I could spend our lives together," AJ said. "Then this happened, but I still feel the same." He paused, as if garnering the nerve to make his next statement. "Sarah, if you should happen to feel the same way about me, this may be our only chance. It could not be more unfair, but I am afraid this is the best I can do for now." The phone went quiet, and neither spoke for a long moment. Sarah was looking down, her eyes closed, her long hair falling in a curtain around her. "Will you come and be with me?" he asked. "You should know that it could be a one-way ticket. Not because you'll be trapped here. But if you come, you may not be able to return to the life you have now because you'll be connected to all of this – you'll be connected to me. There are things I don't want to say over the phone, but I will tell you that if you come, I will be committed to you from this day forward."

"Yes, I will," she said.

AJ hadn't known what to expect. Only now could he see that such a simple and immediate response was not it. Somehow, he thought the conversation, the questions, the decisions would take time – time they didn't have, but that would be required nonetheless.

"AJ, I love you," she said, quietly, as if her voice had become subdued by her vulnerability. "We had no way of knowing what the future would hold anyway. Of all the possibilities, this is, I don't know, unbelievable, but it doesn't matter. None of this changes my commitment to you. If you love me too, AJ," she said, then repeated the words, emphasizing their weight. "AJ, if you love me too, then I will choose to trust you, and I will come to you."

"Sarah, I do love you." He waited a moment, but she said nothing more. "We have to move fast. My parents are on their way here, I just spoke with them. I had to warn them to leave the house to preserve their anonymity."

"Yes, I was there with them when they left."

"Your connection to me is not well known," he said, "so you have more time, but not much. The news media, and who knows who else, will start checking me out – I'm sure they already have – and they'll make a connection to the church, and from there, they'll find you. It won't take long."

"Okay, do I have time to say goodbye to my dad?"

"I think so," AJ said, "but I wouldn't let it stretch much more than an hour."

"Okay, I'll head to my house and pack some things and say goodbye."

"That sounds good. A charter plane will be ready to pick you up from the Olathe Executive Airport within fifteen minutes. They'll wait."

Chapter 46

March 16, 2024

President of the United States, Christopher Warren, was 50 years old, with the chiseled jaw and broad shoulders of a military man. He carried himself with a natural, self-assured confidence that predated his life in the White House, and even that of his political career. Unlike many other politicians whose training included such details as how to shake hands, or how to walk with purpose, Warren had come by all of it naturally.

He had taken the White House two years prior in a lopsided victory over incumbent Harry Dunn. The contest fell only slightly short of the infamous defeat of Alf Landon by Franklin D. Roosevelt in 1936. Like Landon, Dunn had not even managed to carry his home state. The decisive victory had defined the Warren Administration ever since.

The enormous Sea King helicopter bearing President Warren to the Mayfield Hammond campus swooped in from the sky wrapped in a thunderous parade of noise. It touched down in the parking lot, which had been cleared of cars and people for that purpose, to sit larger than life against the backdrop of White Oak, Lodgepole Pine and Dogwood trees that edged the campus, as if posing for a portrait.

The airstairs were lowered from the inside even before the large machine had fully settled from its flight, and a Marine in Blue Dress Uniform emerged. The woman descended and took up position to the left of the stairs, followed shortly by Warren himself, who saluted her on reaching the ground, then turned on his heels to walk across the lot towards the building. This would not be a photo opportunity. There was no smile or acknowledgment of anyone. His eyes moved along the campus grounds taking note of everything in sight.

"It's a mistake to try to gage President Warren's mood by the look on his face," Ward said to AJ upon noticing his nervous posture. "You don't get into the White House without being a tough bastard, but that doesn't mean you have to be a tyrant either. Warren isn't one, but we don't want to give him anything to be unhappy about." AJ nodded his wholehearted agreement.

The president spotted Jeff Ward and made in his direction. "Jeff," he said as he stepped up. "How are ya?" It was a firm greeting – informal words spoken with an authoritative tone. There would be no levity, AJ realized.

"Good, sir. You?"

"Good," he said, but his eyes had already moved to AJ. He pointed at AJ's chest from a distance of a few inches, as if in recognition. It wasn't a threatening gesture; in fact, AJ found it quite the opposite. "Jacobs?" the president said.

"Yes, sir," AJ replied, thankful to have had the past few days to practice not showing timidity in the face of high-ranking people he had never expected to meet in his lifetime.

The president nodded and shook his hand firmly. "What do I call you?"

"AJ, sir," he said.

"AJ it is. Jeff, what are we into?"

"I have a few things to show you, sir, if you'll follow me."

"Lead on."

It was one thing to see the president on television, but quite another to see him in person. The difference was less about the man himself and more about the entourage that surrounded him. Groups of people went ahead of him to ensure that everything was safe and in order, while others trailed behind, doing the same. And then there were the people who stayed with him, advising and supporting his every step. All of it made AJ think of the stories he had heard about the Buddha and the flowers that were said to have sprung from his footsteps. It was an odd connection, but seeing the president walk along, and the tremendous preparation and energy that went into preparing his way, AJ suddenly saw how the flowers of Buddha could easily be a metaphorical reference to a similar phenomenon. And there was something beyond even that – one that AJ would never have expected to witness, which was the experience of walking with him, within the pocket of meticulous preservation that was the world in which he lived. The deference that was shown to the president, AJ quickly saw, tended to spill almost equally to anyone in his company.

They soon arrived at the conference room where AJ had been taken when he first arrived at the campus on Monday. Riley and Clipper were already seated and AJ, now more comfortable with goings on, moved to join them. Ryan Meyer was seated across the table, but his focus was on the president.

Clipper couldn't help but smile when he saw AJ enter with the presidential entourage. He leaned toward AJ as he took his seat. "I always knew this would happen," he said under his breath, nodding towards the president and Director Ward, "but I will admit you beat my estimates by several months."

"Months?" AJ said, feigning offense. "Give a little credit here." He leaned forward so as to look both Clipper and Riley in the eyes. "You guys hanging in there?"

"That and better," Riley said. "You?"

"That and better."

The president was not about wasting time. He took his place at the conference table and reached for a cup of coffee that had been placed there for him, ignoring a cup of yogurt that stood beside it. "I'm up on most of this," the president said. "What's new?"

"The short answer, sir, is that we may not be contained," Ward said. It was a surprise to everyone in the room that Ward had led with that admission rather than a preamble to soften the news.

"Not contained?" the president said. "Explain."

"There was an older, first-generation gravity machine out on the grounds. We powered it down on Sunday evening, but it didn't' stay that way. We think the remote party found a way to bring it back up."

"Remote party? You mean the aliens?" Warren interrupted. "They're aliens, right? We've confirmed that beyond doubt?"

"We have, sir," Ward said.

"How can we know that? Yesterday you told me we were contained and that there was zero chance we'd fuck that up. Now, we're suddenly not contained. So what's next? I'm gonna stand up in front of the world and tell them we're talking to ET and the next day you'll tell me we were wrong about that too, and that it's actually the Beverly Hillbillies?"

Ward didn't have a response.

"If I may, sir," Riley said.

Ward's eyes shot to Riley. They were not friendly. This was not the company in which anyone below the most senior ranks was expected to speak unless solicited to do so.

"What is it?" the president said, directing the comment to Riley and bypassing Ward's obvious irritation at the slip in protocol.

"The Installation, as it's called, is highly automated," Riley said. "Virtually everything is managed by a central control system. The system was put there for safety reasons. At the start, we didn't know whether modifying a gravity field could have health impacts. We've since confirmed that there are no concerns, but the systems have not changed. We took the first-gen equipment offline on Sunday–"

The president saw where this was going. "–and ET started it all back up again using the control system?" the president said. "If everything is controlled electronically as you say, why wouldn't we have assumed that would happen?"

"Because, sir, the control system wasn't designed to be able to do that kind of thing. It was designed to operate the equipment, but did not have the capability of powering that equipment up or down. If you'll pardon the analogy, sir, it would be like finally surrounding a car at the end of a police chase, only to see the car fly away. It just wasn't one of the possibilities as we understood them at the time. When the virus was restarted, it immediately discovered that it had been fenced in, so it went in search of another way out. It must have remembered the older gravity machine somehow, but it had been completely powered down. The virus apparently went in search of a way to bring it back up. It found it, in the form of a small desktop computer that was still running. It is a low-power workstation used for sending emails and doing spreadsheets; something you'd get from a corner office supply company, but it was enough. The virus took it over just as it did the larger computer in the Mayfield datacenter, and reconfigured it to operate the older gravity machine. It turned that computer into a controller and commenced gathering information over the net, just like it did at the campus."

"What about the gravity machine itself? How did it power that back up?" the president asked.

Riley shook his head. "I don't know," he said, finally. "That one's got me."

"So, the only way to really cut these bastards off is to shut down the gravity machines themselves and physically disconnect power, am I right?" the president said.

"Well, sir, not anymore," Ward cut in. "Pandora's box is open. We have no way of knowing if they've now put themselves out onto the internet, but it's a safe bet that they have. We can sever the communication line between earth and them by taking the gravity machines down, but we have no way of knowing, at present, what may have already been pushed onto our global systems."

"Global systems?" Warren said, displeased with the choice of words. "You mean the internet?"

"The internet," Ward agreed, "and any other system they decide to infiltrate that can be reached from the internet, which is virtually everything. Most systems out there in the world, even highly secured ones are protected by what we call a firewall architecture. Sensitive systems are isolated from public-facing networks through a series of zones. Each zone is situated behind a firewall, as they're called, that monitors and regulates the passage of data between them. They're electronic barricades. Highly secured systems can sit behind several layers of firewalls, making it virtually impossible to get in – and sometimes, out. That's a simplification, but that's the essence of it. Problem is, they don't seem to slow the aliens down at all. If we have learned nothing else, it's that our attempts to contain them is ineffectual, to put it mildly."

"Because it can't be done, or because we keep botching it?" the president asked, his tone betraying a gradual escalation in frustration.

"We believe, for plausible reasons, that the aliens don't even realize we've tried to contain them. They could be operating under the assumption that every roadblock they've encountered is simply a technical mishap to overcome. The prevailing theory is that there are no live individuals on the other end of the line at the moment, but that what we've seen are the actions of an automated system. Something happened in the lab that caught the attention of some communication network, and automated systems were activated that went about opening a line to us. Every time we attempt to barricade the system in, it simply finds another way, like it's a bot stepping around minor technical obstacles."

The president paused to think before asking his next question. "Okay, say you're right. Where does that leave us? What's next?"

Ward made to speak, but Briggs stepped up behind him at that moment, whispering something into his ear. On hearing it, he looked around to her for confirmation. She didn't speak, but only nodded. The president didn't hesitate to show his impatience. "Something you'd like to share with the group?" the president asked, not accustomed to being left out of the loop.

Ward hesitated a moment, visibly thinking through the implications. "Yes sir," he said, directing his gaze questioningly to Riley, Clipper and AJ before turning back to the president. "The networks just reported that we're into a First Contact scenario." He looked back to AJ. "Mr. Jacobs, you've been specifically mentioned as a person of interest. Mr. Riley and Mr. Clipper, you had been named prior, but this is also the first mention of either of you in connection with First Contact."

"It was only a matter of time," the president said, but noticed Ward's preoccupation. "What's on your mind, Jeff?"

"Sir, the question of how the public at large will react to First Contact has been the subject of debate since – forever. Some suggest riots, others believe that humanity has come of age in some ways – that we'll all be able to handle it. I think we'll see a little of everything. All three of these young men have been mentioned by name as related to these events, so their safety and the safety of their families is a concern."

Riley, Clipper and AJ took in the statements in silence.

The president looked at them appraisingly for a moment. "Understood. Angela," he said to his chief of staff, "get word out that there will be a Presidential Address to the nation in," he checked his watch, "make it three hours. Jeff, I need to get my arms around this thing before putting myself out there, so I'll need a full brief, but first, see to the safety of these men and their families."

"Of course, sir," Ward said, then to Briggs: "Ms. Briggs, let's please return these men's phones so they can contact their families." Ward turned to face the three of them. "We'll provide accommodations for your immediate families for the time being. Please instruct them to get to Charlotte and we'll handle from there. If they have trouble making arrangements, let Ms. Briggs know and we'll see to it that they get here safely. Unfortunately, gentlemen, this could get complicated. I'm afraid you'll need to remain the guests of the NSA for a while longer, both for your safety and to be on hand as we bring the initial phases of these exercises to closure. We also need to let Mayfield Hammond resume normal operations soon. That means getting a new command center established. We'll need your help with that. AJ, depending on how the next few days go, you may be finished sooner. We'll assess any security concerns for you and your family as we go. Hopefully, it won't be an issue."

As the three filed out of the room, AJ noted that this was the first time Ward had called him AJ.

Margaret Statham was the first to speak after they had cleared the room. "Mr. President," she said, "I'm struggling to grasp the gravity of what has happened here. Director Ward, you say that we're not contained? I would like to better understand what that means. Are you saying that the aliens have had full, unbridled access to the internet and virtually any electronic system connected to it for more than 18 hours? And that the implications of that are beyond reckoning?"

"I'm afraid so," Ward said, unblinkingly. He knew what was coming, and the truth was that he couldn't blame her. Her reaction may very well have been his own if roles were reversed.

She looked back to the president who was weighing her comments. "We're in a tight spot here, Jeff," the president said, finally.

Statham said: "Am I to understand that as we sit here, this virus could be – in fact, probably has and is – propagating around the world and infiltrating anything and everything at will?"

"I'm afraid so," Ward said.

"Well, I am pleased that you have at least found the fortitude to so expertly maintain your composure, Mr. Ward," she said venomously.

Ward had already begun replaying his role, sorting through what he could or should have done differently. It was now unfolding with withering clarity, the same conclusion emerging each time: this was always going to happen. He had been an interchangeable, disposable and inconsequential player in a sequence of events that would have run their course, regardless of who the players had been. The power of the virus to circumvent any and all boundaries was, by all accounts, absolute and complete. Never had the metaphor of Pandora's Box been more fitting.

"We have two immediate issues," the president said, snapping the unspoken tension that was rising out of control in the room. "First is how and what to message to the people of the United States."

"Sir," Angela put in, "this one is bigger than us. We have the whole world to contend with on this."

The president nodded, "Indeed we do. But, let's start with the most basic facts first: we have made First Contact. Jeff, have your people verify all of that again. If it's for the 14th time, I don't care. I want them to start from the beginning and recheck the facts. If I tell the world we've made First Contact and I'm wrong – well, I don't even want to think about where that road leads. Second," he said, looking to Statham, "we've let a virus into our bloodstream. We need to look for the early symptoms that could follow. If anything starts to look systematically unusual, let's be all over it. Finally, let's get these bastards – these aliens – on the line and see what they're up to. I've been told they can speak English, it's time they start doing it."

That looked for a moment to be the final statement of the discussion, but Statham spoke again, forestalling everyone from rising to their feet. Her eyes bored into Jeff Ward. "Director Ward," she said, menacingly, "I intend to bring charges against Mr. Riley, Mr. Clipper and possibly Mr. Jacobs for what's been done here. Be advised that I am prepared to do the same against you for your handling of these affairs."

"Margaret," the president interrupted, his hands still palm down on the table in preparation for standing, "let's be about the business at hand. None of us need distractions, especially now." She didn't respond, her eyes lingered threateningly on Ward.

"I will put my people into motion," she said abruptly, then rose and left the room.

The president, Ward, Vandoren and Briggs sat for a moment in the remaining silence. "This is going to go in every direction at once, Jeff," the president said evenly. "Humanity is about to show its colors." He nodded to the door where Statham had just left. "Won't be easy."

"Mr. President, my concern at the moment is that a story is taking shape here. We can scrutinize the mishaps of the past few days, if you'd call them that, and miss a larger picture. What is happening, was always going to happen. Was, in fact, always happening. Whoever these guys are, they didn't spring into existence when we noticed them."

"Understood," Warren said. "I hear you and I understand, but many people won't." He looked to Briggs. "Before we adjourn, I have a few more questions. Have those young men finished their calls?"

"I'll check," she said.

A few minutes later, Riley, Clipper and AJ filed back into the room and retook their seats. "John Riley, Jason Clipper and AJ," the president said, pointing to each in turn, as if committing their names to memory. "I've had the pleasure of making the acquaintance of AJ. John, do you go by John?" he asked.

"Yes, sir," Riley replied.

"And you, do you go by Jason?" he asked, looking to Clipper

"Clipper, usually, sir, but I'm good either way," Clipper said, not about to ask the President of the United States to call him Clip.

"Good enough. John, these gravitation devices, they're your brainchild?" the president asked.

"They are, sir."

"So, to you, this was never about communication. You were interested in gravity."

"Yes, sir."

"Okay. So you're getting all this figured out and you get the machines working, but you don't realize that along the way you're unknowingly sending up smoke signals that get noticed by these aliens?"

"That's correct," Riley said.

"So – and this is where I'm going to show some ignorance – we're not talking with radio, but gravity?"

"In a manner of speaking. The details aren't entirely straightforward, but yes," Riley answered.

The president pondered for a moment. "Do we know where ET is phoning from? Where are they?"

"We don't know as yet, sir," Riley said. "There are interesting implications around how this is coming together. At this point, I'm struggling to make sense of it."

"Okay," the president said. "Give me the Cliff's Notes." He leaned back in his chair and took up the cup of yogurt.

"There's a couple problems with the communication we're seeing here. First, we tend to think that the speed of light is incredibly fast, but on cosmic scales, it's not – not even close. In fact, if you think about the speed of light in terms of the scale of the universe, you realize something rather odd; that the size and scale of the Universe is disproportionate to the speed of light. We're in a Universe that is vast beyond comprehension in terms of space, but proportionally mismatched to a very low speed limit in terms of time."

"So here goes; the communication we're seeing from the aliens has a roundtrip of about 7 seconds. If we make reasonable assumptions about the amount of time it takes for them to receive our message, decide what to say back, then send a response, then we can start to piece some things together. To be conservative, let's say it takes about 100 milliseconds for them to actually respond to our signals once they receive them. That would mean that most of the 7 second latency we're seeing is consumed by the amount of time it takes for the messages themselves to cross the distance between us. Simple math says that it'll take a little under 3 ½ seconds in each direction. At the speed of light, which is the speed at which radio waves travel – and the maximum speed that our current understanding of physics tells us is possible – this latency should allow us to know exactly how far away the aliens are, even if it doesn't pinpoint their location."

"As far from us as light can travel in the 3 ½ seconds," the president offered.

"Correct, sir," Riley said.

"And how far is that?"

"A little more than 600 thousand miles. It would mean that there must be an alien spaceship as close to us as only about 2 ½ times the distance to the moon."

"And we don't think that's the case?" the president asked.

"Given current facts, there seem to be three possible answers. One: there is a ship out there just past the moon. Unlikely. Two: they're response times are slower than I'm giving them credit for, which would mean they're even closer than that, which is still unlikely–"

"Maybe they're on the moon," Vandoren interjected.

"I don't think so," Riley said, looking at her, but not in a debasing way. "Being on the moon would mean that they're spending about 4 seconds deciding how to respond. That's slow, even for us."

"And you don't think they're slower," the president said.

"No, sir. I don't."

"And, despite what the facts are saying, you don't think there is a ship out there on the other side of the moon, am I correct?"

"No, sir, I don't," Riley said again, shaking his head as if his own conclusions were hard to accept. "The third alternative seems to break the laws of physics as we know them. If the aliens were even so far from us as the sun, the round trip would take 17 minutes. No, if they're not in orbit, something else is happening, and the implications are not small. They're talking over a much faster pipe than we ever knew existed. And, that's not all. The signal must also be able to pass through matter – lots of it. Otherwise, thinking back to the different times of day we've conducted experiments and received a handshake response; if this were a ship, it would have to be in a geosynchronous orbit. In other words, the ship would have to stay directly overhead from the point upon the surface of the earth we're communicating from, otherwise, as the earth rotated, the mass of the earth would block our signals. This type of thing happened during the Apollo missions, for example. When the spacecraft crossed to the far side of the moon. When that happened, it put us out of radio contact. It was because the moon's mass blocked the radio signals. They couldn't pass through it like they can open space. This can only mean that the communication medium in play now must be able to pass through matter in ways that radio waves can't."

"There goes the fortune I was planning to make on neutrino modems," Meyer put in. He had been silent to that point, but his comment was ignored.

"Let me repeat this back, then," the president said. "If we assume that the aliens are subject to the rules of physics as we understand them, then the most likely – the only, explanation, really

– is that there is a spaceship in geosynchronous orbit 600 thousand miles above us at this moment."

"Yes," Riley said. "And if they can send signals through the planet, they're still 600 thousand miles up, but could be anywhere in the orbital path at that distance."

"But you believe otherwise?" the president pressed.

"Yes, but for reasons that wouldn't stand up to any scientific scrutiny. Not even my own. But the empirical evidence speaks louder than the numbers. I think we're being hailed from someplace beyond our Solar system."

Chapter 47

March 16, 2024

"Sir," Chief of Staff, Vandoren said, "escalations are happening. Executive Assistant Director Boswell wishes to speak with you."

Warren nodded as if the request was not a surprise. "Understood," he said. He looked back to Ward and the others in the room. "Let me talk with Frank for a minute. I'll meet up with you in the lab."

Jeff Ward stepped into the hall to see Margaret Statham and Frank Boswell waiting. Their expressions conveyed the frustrations that were about to be vented on the president. Ward nodded to them and moved on, deciding to track down a cup of coffee before heading to the lab. When he entered the familiar space several minutes later, he saw that the display screens had not changed. The same enigmatic text was still showing from earlier that morning. Meyer was sitting in one of the folding chairs, his arm hooked over its back, talking with his team of analysts.

"Where are we on incoming data," Ward asked, approaching the small group.

"We were just going over that," Meyer said. "We've received a total of 2.45 petabytes of data since this morning."

"Are we still receiving?"

"No, the download ended about 45 minutes ago. It wasn't a continuous thing. It started and stopped several times, but it came in fast when it did." He shook his head. "At an amazing rate, actually. Never seen anything like it."

"Have we been able to make sense of it?"

"Unfortunately, nothing of particular relevance as yet," Meyer said. "When they overhauled our machine, they fundamentally changed the meaning of the data. The data itself is still in the form of ones and zeros – bits, as they're called – since that's the only thing our hardware can understand, but the way the bits are arranged is meaningless to us so far. We'll be able to break the code eventually. Shouldn't take long, in fact, but we're not there yet."

"I see. Please keep me advised," Ward said. "What advice do we have for the president on next steps? He'll be in here within the hour."

"I think we're doing all the right things at this point," Meyer said. "I'd keep the Hawkeye in the air, if for no other reason than we don't want to throw anything else into the mix that could look like yet another technical glitch on our end. The more I've thought about it, the more I think Riley is right on this. They're going to start talking soon."

"What will they say?" Ward asked. "Any insight on that?"

"Opinions vary from, 'Take me to your leader,' to 'All your base are belong to us!' he said, then laughed heartily. Ward didn't get the reference. "Sorry, sir," he said, sobering up. "It's a video game culture thing."

Ward eyed him humorlessly. "Let's be sure to deliver a better product to the president when he arrives, Mr. Meyer."

Meyer nodded, embarrassed. "Yes sir," he said. "Our best guess is that they will want to talk with leadership. Not sure what else their message could be. We'll have to play it by ear from there, I'm afraid."

Riley, Clipper and AJ entered the room at that moment. They stood inside the lab but remained near the door. Margaret Statham entered shortly behind and stepped up to speak with them. Ward immediately moved in their direction, intent on deflecting any threats she may direct towards them. He arrived in time to hear her finishing a sentence; "the depositions will begin at our earliest opportunity," she said, looking around the lab disapprovingly. "As soon as this subsides into something manageable." She noticed Ward approaching. "I wish to have a private word with these gentlemen, Mr. Ward, if you'll give us a few minutes." She spoke with unconvincing civility.

"We have matters to attend, Ms. Statham," he said, firmly. "This is not the time to look past the immediacy of the moment."

She drew a breath to protest, but was interrupted by the appearance of the president, who was accompanied by Frank Boswell and Angela Vandoren. Ward wondered for a brief moment why Statham was not with them, suspecting she had been dismissed from the conversation early.

The president passed a parting comment to Boswell. "Thanks Frank, keep me posted."

"Yes, sir," Boswell said, then stepped out of the lab and disappeared.

The prior conversation seeming to have already been forgotten, the president looked to Ward. "Bring me up to speed, Jeff," he said, surveying the lab. Doing so, his eyes quickly fell upon the display screens mounted on the back wall, locking onto them. He read the strange text aloud.

Communication-band activity detected

Cause artificial

Onboarding

Contact iteration three

Override scenario

"So, there it is," Warren said. "Those are the words of an extraterrestrial translated into English, am I right?"

"That is correct, sir," Ward said.

"Damnation," he said, mesmerized. "What does it mean?"

"Good question, sir," Ward answered. "The first three statements seem fairly straightforward, but the last two are giving us trouble." He motioned towards one of the terminals near the far end of the room. "That's the terminal we have up on the screen," he said. "It's where first contact happened on Sunday."

Warren started walking in that direction. "Time check please, Margaret. How long until the address?"

"One hour and forty-five minutes, sir," she said, without checking her watch.

"Okay, I'd like to see the speech in 45 minutes."

"Yes, sir," she said, then peeled away, taking up her phone.

When they reached the computer terminal, Warren hunched over slightly to look at the screen, then back to one of the large displays mounted on the wall, comparing them. Satisfied that they were identical, he stood erect. As he did, Ward motioned Meyer forward to join them. "We're in a holding pattern then?" the president asked. Ward looked the question to Meyer who had just joined them.

"Yes, sir," Meyer said.

"What are the expectations? Any chance they're waiting for us to say something first?"

"That thought has occurred to us, sir," Meyer said. "It is a possibility. We've decided to wait twenty-four hours. If we see no activity within that time, we may attempt to send a message of our own."

The president nodded. "I want to be part of that conversation, Jeff," he said, looking to Ward. "I'm not sure I want to wait. Let's see how the world reacts to the announcement."

"Of course, sir," Ward agreed.

"In the meantime, let's start pulling together a list of things we want to say."

"Yes. Will do."

The president lingered in the lab for another twenty minutes, then left, drawing his large company of sentries with him like a large ship drawing flotsam in its wake. Ward watched him go, wondering what the president would do; what sense he was making of the situation, then looked back to Meyer. "Do we have a way of knowing whether anything is happening, or are we really just waiting? Could the computers in the lab be working on something that we don't know about?"

"We're monitoring that, and we don't think so. I wish we could know with more certainty," Meyer said. "When they re-imaged the computer, they wiped away all traces of the Linux operating system that had been there before. None of the utilities, none of the familiar capabilities of the machine are there anymore. If the old operating system were still there, we could open a secure shell to the machine, which would have allowed us to snoop around. With this new – I guess I could still call it an operating system – we have not yet found a way to get in. It truly is a black box to us, at least for now. On the positive side, some of the behaviors of the machine are baked into the hardware. The hard-drives, for example. Each time data is written to, or read from one of the hard-drives the LED's light up. The more data that's exchanged with them, the more the LED's stay lit. When that big chunk of data was being downloaded, they glowed for several minutes. When no data is incoming, we know that if they light up it's because the CPU is doing work, not because more data is coming in. That tells us that the CPU is crunching on something. It's not much, but it's better than nothing."

"And are they doing anything now?"

"No. I just checked again. Only scant flickers since the main download ended."

Chapter 48

"This isn't what I expected," Sarah said, looking around the small hotel conference room.

"In a bad way?" AJ asked. She was quiet and seemed distracted, showing little of the excitement he had hoped to see from her on finally being together. If not excitement, at least more happiness.

"No, actually," she said. "I had visions of appliance-white hallways with vinyl floors and unmarked doors. A government compound of some kind."

AJ looked around appreciatively. "Yes, this is nice. I don't know how long it will last. From what I understand, the NSA has booked the entire east wing of the eleventh floor for everyone, mainly because of these conference rooms. There are several of them, along with the rooms we're all staying in. Makes it easy to cordon off."

"It's great to have a place to talk," she said.

"Sarah, I hope I didn't overreact when I asked you to come here. I may have. I'll admit I was a little rattled at the time, but I'm glad you're here, even if it took all of that. Truth is, I'm already something of a third wheel. For whatever reason, these aliens wouldn't proceed until I gave them permission, since I was the one who asked them to stop, I guess. No one has yet figured out exactly how they identified me, but since then I've had no part to play. As far as everyone is concerned I've played my role, and now I'm done."

"You can leave anytime you want?"

"Not yet, that's up to Jeff Ward. He's the Director with the NSA who's basically running everything, but I expect he'll release me soon."

"Can he legally stop you from leaving?"

AJ considered the question. "I don't know actually, but I don't look at it that way anymore. If he thinks it's important for me to be around, I'm happy to stay, help out if I can. I would never have believed I'd be saying that, but where do you go from here?" She nodded understanding, looking again around the room, and appreciating the improbability of it all. "Sarah, just to clear things up, I've gotten a separate room for you. Didn't want you to feel uncomfortable. You're free to come or go, of course, but I'd like for you to stay, at least for a few days. We never had the chance to finish our conversation."

"I appreciate that." Her demeanor was much more subdued than AJ expected, and he sat trying to read her expression without success.

"Can I ask a question, Sarah?" She looked at him but didn't answer. "Are you having second thoughts about this, or about us? It looks like something is on your mind."

A smile touched the edge of her lips. "Oh, no. Not at all. I meant everything I said to you in that Starbucks, and over the phone yesterday. Even more now than then."

AJ felt a mountain of relief at those words. "Me too. Very much so," he said.

She nodded as if the topic had been put to rest. "I'm sorry, AJ, I'm just a little worried about everything, like everyone else." She motioned in the air with her hand. "Everything is so different now. I don't know what to make of it. And what's next?"

"I wish I had something to offer, but I don't. I don't think anyone does."

"Oh, I know. I'm not looking for anyone to calm my fears. Everyone is facing his own; I can do it as well as anyone else."

They sat in silence for a long moment, until Sarah spoke again. "Where are John and Jason?"

"They've been around, here and there, but I haven't seen a lot of them lately." He checked his watch. It was 4:25 PM. "Sometimes they're out late, but they should be here before the night is over. If they get here within the next couple of hours, we can grab dinner."

"That sounds great."

AJ's expression suddenly turned thoughtful. "How long have we known one another?"

She smiled. "A long time. I think my earliest memories of you were from the third grade. But then you were just a second grader. I couldn't be troubled with youngsters like yourself at the time. I'm sure you understand."

"Of course, you had your reputation to think of. A third grader fraternizing with a second grader, now that would be scandalous."

"I'm a little worried about it now too, if you must know," she said, smiling mischievously.

AJ broke into a full grin. "I'll lie about my age if it helps, but just remember, one day it'll be your turn. When I'm older and you're … way older."

"Alright, smarty pants. You're headed down a slippery slope." Their laughter died down. "Are you planning to stay here in Charlotte? Take one of those jobs?"

"I think I missed those opportunities."

"Maybe, but you know you could get into any company in this town. Certainly, any bank."

"You're most likely right. I don't know, to be honest, but I won't go anywhere that you won't go," he said, "and I don't expect you to follow me around as if you don't have a life of your own."

"I appreciate that, but right, wrong or indifferent, my goals and interests have become, let's say, more fluid in recent weeks."

"Mine too, believe me."

"Will we be together?" Sarah asked.

AJ paused. "You should know that this was not an easy thing to do." Sarah looked at him, confused, but only for the briefest of moments, then her eyes widened as AJ slid from his chair and took to a knee. He turned his hand upward to reveal a ring. He had been holding it the entire time. "Sarah, will you marry me?"

Her smile was beautiful. She held his gaze, looking penetratingly into his eyes. Unrushed. Something unexpected passed between the two of them in that moment, that in all the years that would follow, AJ was never able to put into words.

"Yes, I will," she said, and AJ kissed her.

A smattering of handclaps surprised them both. Riley and Clipper were standing in the hall, peering into the room. "Congratulations," Clipper said, stepping in to shake AJ's hand. "Apologies for the trespass of privacy. Just a timing thing." He then turned to Sarah, "but since we're here, welcome to the family." He gave her a warm embrace.

"No trespass at all. I'm so glad you're both here," she said.

Clipper looked to AJ, "You're marrying up, that's for sure."

"Don't I know it!"

Riley stepped in and shook AJ's hand as well. "Congratulations my friend." He turned to Sarah. "Clipper's right. You're one of us now. We should celebrate. Dinner?"

Clipper said: "That is, unless the two of you want privacy."

"I could think of no better way to spend the evening than with friends," Sarah said.

"Good. There's someone I'd like for both of you to meet. This will be the perfect opportunity."

"Melissa?" AJ asked.

"Yes."

"Can't wait. I'll see if I can get us into the Japanese Steakhouse downstairs at 5:30."

"You'll do no such thing," Clipper said. "That will be my pleasure. The two of you, enjoy yourselves. We'll see you down there."

When Riley and Clipper left the room, there were tears in Sarah's eyes. "I do feel like I have a new family, just when I needed one. I've known of John and Jason forever, but never that well. Are they everything they seem?"

"That and more. I couldn't love them any more if they really were my brothers." He then looked at her with sudden, feigned seriousness. "Not to be repeated, of course."

"Of course," she said, with an openly patronizing smile.

Seeing the look on her face, AJ knew he'd made a mistake and did a doubletake. "Sarah!?"

"What? I said, of course!"

He groaned.

"All's fair in love and war," she said. "Sorry. I don't make the rules."

They passed the time on lighter topics until going down to join the others at 5:30. They stepped into the restaurant lobby to find Riley and Clipper waiting in the company of a woman they assumed to be Melissa.

"And here they are," Riley said on seeing them approach. "Melissa, this is Andrew Jacobs, who we call AJ, and his new fiancé, Sarah." It was the first time either of them had heard their new, temporary title, and it made Sarah smile and look at AJ, who was smiling too.

"So good to meet you," Melissa said.

"Likewise," AJ said, taking her hand.

"Very much so," Sarah added.

"AJ and Sarah, this is Melissa." Riley looked to her as he finished the introduction, "a very special person."

"It's great to finally meet you both. I've heard a lot," Melissa said.

Just then, the maître d' approached. "Your table is ready," he said. "We were able to free our private room for you, given the occasion."

"Thank you, sir," Clipper said with his trademark casual confidence. AJ spotted him slipping a $20 bill into his hand.

"Thank you," the man said. "This way, please."

Clipper looked back to the group. "Go ahead. I'm waiting for a guest as well, we'll be right there." A measure of surprise crossed everyone's face, but no one commented. Instead, they followed the maître d', already taking up casual conversation as they stepped through the confined spaces that led to the private room, tucked away from the main seating area.

The Teppanyaki Grill, with its border of counter space, seated eight, but two of the chairs had been moved away. "And who are the guests of honor?" the chef asked as they entered.

"That would be these two; AJ and Sarah," Riley said, motioning in their direction.

"Front and center please," he said, pointing to the two chairs directly opposite to him. AJ and Sarah took their seats, followed by Riley and Melissa to the right.

"Are we expecting others?" the chef asked.

"Yes. Still waiting for one to arrive. There will be a total of six."

"Very good," he said, then busied himself with preparations.

In a few minutes, Clipper was preceded into the room by Natalie Briggs, both holding glasses of red wine. "Everyone," Clipper said, "this is Natalie Briggs. She and I met a few weeks ago at the start of–" he waved his glass, as if unsure of the right word, "whatever this has been."

Riley rose to his feet to take her hand. "Very good to see you, Ms. Briggs."

"Oh, come on; Natalie, please," she said.

Introductions played out, and the conversation took flight at once. It was casual and comfortable, as if the group had met many times before. The men had gone to reminiscing, to the delight of the ladies, who found their childhood exploits endlessly entertaining. "...I don't recall it happening quite that way," AJ was saying.

"Oh, that is exactly the way it happened," Clipper insisted. "It was only one of many times I pulled your backsides out of the fire."

"Since it was, let's see, always you that got us into those messes, I don't know that I'm willing to give you full credit for that."

"AJ has a point, Clip," Riley said. "You've gotta see that." The ladies were in full laughter at the stories the three had been telling.

"I understand you had a secret handshake, too," Melissa said. Riley's head snapped around in a heartbeat. He gave her a wide-eyed look of surprise, gesturing a, 'what was that?' question with his open hands. She shrugged innocently, then passed a devious smile to the other ladies who nodded their approval, Briggs going so far as raising her wine glass.

"Ooohhh," Clipper said. "The breach. It has finally occurred."

"Did we not, all of us, agree," AJ said, "that we would never divulge that information? We shook on it – with our secret handshake!" The ladies were on the verge of tears with laughter.

"Mr. Jacobs," Clipper said, suddenly taking a serious tone. "I seem to recall that along with that pact, was also attached a certain penalty. Struggling to recall what it was. Do you happen to remember?"

"In fact I do," AJ said, extending a hand to Riley. "Your baseball cards. Hand them over."

"Boys?" Natalie cut in. "Let's get this over with. I see no need to unnecessarily prolong the ordeal."

The protests came with a flurry, but within seconds the three men were on their feet trying to remember how the handshake went. There was no pretense of control. The group was in full laughter, all concerns of the world temporarily at bay. By the time it was over, Natalie was dabbing at her eye with a napkin; and when Clipper retook his seat, she reached over and kissed him on the cheek. He returned an appreciative smile and reached for his wine, then raised it for a toast. Seeing it, the others raised their glasses too. "Congratulations to our special friends, AJ and Sarah. Know that you are deeply loved. Regardless of what our new, uncertain future may hold, may we always be found in the company of those we care about, and those who care about us."

"Hear, hear," Melissa said.

Despite the many virtues of Teppanyaki Grills, they are not ideal for quiet conversation. The meal rolled forward in rising and falling tones suitable to the light-hearted engagement it was meant to be, crescendoing near the end when the chef did two full rounds of throwing shrimp into the mouths of each of the guests with his spatula, over the protests of the ladies. When the meal was finished, the six of them filed into the open spaces of the large hotel lobby and took a seat in a somewhat private grouping of chairs, wine glasses still in hand.

"Thank you, everyone, for the wonderful meal and warm welcome," Sarah said. "I didn't realize how much I needed it."

"I think that goes for all of us," Natalie said.

"It was our pleasure," Clipper said.

The group lingered for another 30 minutes before disbanding, leaving AJ and Sarah alone in the lobby in quiet conversation. The evening had done a world of good. The carefree days that had been life before first contact were not likely to return for some time – not for anyone – but there was peace for the moment. It had been a mishap of timing, that those events had sliced through a delicate place in their relationship. Only now were they afforded the opportunity to finally spend the quiet time saying the words they had not been able to say for several weeks.

At the end of the evening, they stood outside of Sarah's hotel room door. "Thank you for the beautiful ring, AJ. And thank you for proposing to me, and for the wonderful evening."

"Thank you for accepting, Sarah. This has been the best evening of my life."

"Mine too," she said, then kissed him and stepped inside of her room.

Chapter 49

March 16, 2024

The president chose the large briefing room in the IT building for his address to the nation. It was a deliberate move on his part to call it a National Address even though the whole world would be watching, and he knew that doing so would draw the ire of leaders from around the world. Despite that, as much as it was outlandish to think it was possible, he wanted first disclosure of what had happened, what *was* happening, to have an "in the family" feel to it, prior to officially sharing the news with the rest of humanity.

He entered the room having transformed from the casual dress of a couple hours before to black suit with red tie. The Seal of the President of the United States hung on the wall behind the platform, covering the large display screen that was usually the focal point of the room, a flag of the United States hanging from a pole standing to one side. The plain wooden podium that typically stood on the platform had been removed, now replaced with a heavier one that also bore the Presidential Seal.

No news media were on hand. The video feed from the address would be made available for syndication, but that was all. A large television camera stood, a passive observer in the center of the room, occasionally swinging its mechanical head lazily to the left and right. Another, similar camera was off to the right against the wall, and rows of theatrical spotlights were positioned at various points, each facing the podium. All of it took an inordinate amount of space, making a room that had otherwise seemed spacious feel somewhat cramped. The president himself had stepped onto the platform surrounded by a small clutch of individuals pointing to and discussing the papers he held in his hand.

AJ was seated on an outer chair to the left of the platform a few rows back, with Riley and Clipper to his right. His stomach was full of butterflies, and he noted with admiration that if the president was nervous in any way, he was showing no sign of it.

The room had the backstage feel of a large theatrical production. It was a behind-the-scenes view of how the Executive Branch of the government operated. The event itself – First Contact – had been unforeseeable, but AJ could see that the preparations for the address to the nation followed well-worn lines of practiced repetition. The only signs of anxiety were focused on the camera to the side of the room. An apparent technical glitch was being tracked down by three men who were tracing the thick black cables that ran down the side wall, while another older man looked on nervously.

"Five minutes," a voice called out.

AJ noticed the nervous man flinch at that, but no one else in the room reacted in any way that he could see. AJ looked to Riley and Clipper. They were taking in the strange event with rapt interest, just as he was.

The countdown continued. At the two-minute mark, the lights were dimmed, and the spotlights turned on. The president, by then the only person on the platform, stood at the ready. AJ noticed a thumbs-up pass between the men working the side camera. All appeared to be in order. A final countdown was eventually indicated by a person near the center camera, and the president began:

My fellow Americans, I have news to share with you. This news is relevant and impactful to all of us; to we, as Americans, and to all of our fellow citizens of this world. Even so, I have chosen to talk with you first. I issue to you a challenge to receive the news I am about to share, and to rise with dignity to whatever it may demand of us – to wherever it may lead us.

History has marked this moment as a pivotal juncture for humankind. As president of this great country, but even more importantly, as one of its citizens, I resolve and commit to you that I will receive this challenge and respond with a steadfastness of integrity and character that is reflective of the ideals, the soul and spirit of what we, as a people, have always stood for, and always shall. I also pass this challenge to you – to each and every person who trods upon the soil of this nation.

Over the past decades we have been mesmerized by advances in technologies that have improved our lives in ways our forefathers could not have imagined. We have peered into the smallest corners of physical reality at the very building blocks of all that is. We have built telescopes, which have granted to us views of the cosmos that have filled us with wonder at its beauty and unfathomable scale.

Each new discovery brings with it the promise, the excitement of knowing that although we may have learned something new – discovered something that humankind had, prior, never seen – that it is only new to us; that it is part of the great and grand Universe that was always there waiting for us to take notice of it. And as we continue to follow the trail of discovery forward, we know that we will forever embark upon frontiers that are, even now, only awaiting our ability to see them.

These paths of enlightenment that define us as a species have now led to something altogether unique in our history. Like every other step forward, what we have now learned, is only new to us. We have only pulled away a shroud of covering; in fact, a shroud of ignorance, to reveal what has always been. Regardless of how it may seem, I task each one of you, as I have also tasked myself, to reflect upon, to ponder this simple truth; that what we have now confirmed as fact, has always been fact. It was at the time of your birth. When your parents met for the first time. When this nation was founded from the dust of inequality to become the gleaming standard of liberty and justice we have today, and continuously strive to protect. At the time Isaac Newton began to reveal our first glimpses into what has become the basis of so much of the sciences we still rely upon today. Even to the time Woolly Mammoths roamed the frozen tundra of this world, knowing nothing but the tides and cycles of a harsh life devoid of warmth.

It has now been confirmed that contact with an intelligent alien race has occurred. Like so many other of our discoveries, this one came about as an unanticipated outcome of the pursuit of science – the pursuit to become better, and smarter. As yet, no meaningful dialogue has taken place. We believe that to this point, we have reached only the earliest stages of communication, which have focused entirely on the technical methods that underlie the ability to talk. We will keep you informed.

I trust that none of the following measures are necessary, but enact them to convey my expectation that each and every individual, to a person, shall carry on in the spirit of the ideals we each hold so dearly. For the time being, the prices of all goods and services shall remain fixed at current levels. There will be no price gouging. Be advised that punishments for crimes, and the betrayal of the trust and expectations of the American people to behave in the most forthright manner will be disproportionately severe. To the men and women of our law enforcement community; as always, I hold you to an even higher standard. All reports of the abuse of power will be taken seriously, and investigated. Punishment for false accusations will be turned back upon the accuser.

Let us now put our differences aside. Let us each look to ourselves as the first agent of change. Let future generations look back on this day and commend our resolve, our courage, our integrity. Let us give to them a positive start from which to step forward into a future full of promise that we may never see, so that as they go forward, further than we can, they will, in their hearts, bring us along with them into what lies beyond.

Over the coming days, a new channel of communication will be established to enable the free flow of information, so that we may keep you informed of progress. You should know that we have reason to believe, and do believe, that the foreign party with which we have made contact appears to be benign. And so, I ask that you remain calm. That you share the optimism I now feel, and look forward, as I do, to all the great things we are about to learn.

We are not alone. Indeed, we have never been alone. And now we stand on the precipice of a new age.

Fathers and mothers, discuss this with your children. Families, let us now come together and share our hopes and fears, but settle at the end of it, on what is good. What is fair. What is just. On who we are, and on the certainty that our future is bright.

Thank you, and God bless.

Chapter 50

March 16, 2024

One of the large display screens on a side wall of the lab had been repurposed for the Presidential Address. Michael Parker positioned a folding chair in front of it and fiddled with a control panel hidden inconveniently on its back until the audio level resolved into something he could understand. The Presidential Seal covered the screen from one end to the other as a woman's voice announced the impending start of the National Address. That drew a small crowd from across the lab, followed, inevitably, by sounds of hushed conversation.

*   *   *

Rom James stared intently at a bank of green LED's that spanned the top of a rack of servers. He and another Systems Engineer stood among row after row of computerized equipment in the Mayfield Hammond datacenter. This particular row happened to be 3B; the physical location and home of the servers that had become the unwitting host of the alien virus. The lights had settled into an uninteresting pattern of flickering only slightly and intermittently, at intervals of long minutes. Grady Lopez, the other engineer, peered at a spreadsheet on his laptop, which he had placed onto a cart borrowed from a neighboring room.

"Got another one. 100 milliseconds," James said. Lopez typed the number into the computer. "How are we looking?" James asked.

"One sec," Lopez answered, refreshing a graph on the computer to reflect the number he had just entered. "Nothing noteworthy. Over the past ninety minutes we're running about 2 ½ minutes between flickers, and they're all around a tenth of a second."

James looked over to see the updated graph. It was almost a perfectly straight line. "As graphs go, that one's not too exciting," he said.

"Agreed," Lopez admitted. "It was a good idea, but I don't think we're gaining any insights here. It's a flatline – no interesting trends that I can see."

"I don't think I can watch this thing much longer anyway," James said, rubbing his neck. "My eyes are crossing." He moved towards the cart and squinted at the graph. "2 ½ minutes, huh?" he said, trying to guess at what could be significant about the interval.

"Don't mean a thang," Lopez said, drawing out the final word.

As the two men discussed the graph, an LED flickered again. It had been under a minute since the last time. Again, it flickered, and then again. Neither man noticed. They were still discussing the results of their failed test – an attempt to look for patterns in how often the lights appeared, and for how long.

"This is ridiculous," James said. "This thing is standing right here in front of us, but it won't give us anything." He looked towards the servers in mild disgust. "Whoa!" he said, "we're gettin' lights."

Lopez took to his feet and stepped towards the machine, as if being closer could reveal further insights into what the servers were doing. He watched for a long moment, slowly lifting a two-way radio from the cart. "Sachin, are we seeing more incoming data?" he said into the handset.

There was a slight delay before the response came back with a crackle. "Negative. A flicker a few seconds ago, but nothing of substance." Lopez and James stood watching the LED in silence for another thirty seconds. The flickering was becoming steady.

Lopez tentatively lifted the radio again. "Still nothing?" he asked, a little nervous energy in his tone. He looked to James.

"Still nothing," was the response. "Something on your end?"

"Yes, we're seeing a series of flickers. They're speeding up. Been going on for about a minute."

"Copy that," Sachin said. "Still nothing here."

*   *   *

All eyes in the lab were on the screen as the countdown to the president's address finally reached zero. It began precisely on time. The Presidential Seal faded from view to reveal the president himself standing behind a podium, immaculately dressed per usual. It seemed odd that only an hour prior he had been in that very lab donning casual dress more suggestive of an afternoon round of golf.

A palpable tension had overtaken the lab. A tension Parker knew would be playing out around the globe. For decades to come every living person would remember where they were when this announcement was made, just as they had for John F Kennedy's assassination and the World Trade Center attack of September 11, 2001.

In unison, beyond the peripheral view of most of the individuals in the room – to those now watching the president's address and the many others still bent to their tasks – a series of new characters appeared across all the other display screens, save only the one they were watching.

No one noticed.

My fellow Americans, the president began.

*   *   *

Lopez and James exchanged meaningful looks. "Sachin," Lopez said, "alert Meyer that we have activity. Computer's chewing on something and it doesn't look like incoming data."

In a moment, a voice came back. "Meyer is in with the president. He won't be able to leave until the address is over."

"I thought there were no reporters in the room. The president won't have to field any technical questions, will he?" Lopez asked.

"Probably not, but it's protocol. When the president is behind a mic, he wants support on hand. Sorry guys, whatever this is, it'll have to wait."

Lopez nodded acceptance. "Copy that." Then to James he said, "I guess we're not on fire here. The address will be over in a few, we can wait that long."

"True that," James said, still watching the LED's. They were, by now, a solid glow.

*   *   *

Parker was entranced by the speech. *Over the past decades we have been mesmerized by advances in technologies*, the president was saying, his composure and conviction already building into a heightened sense of patriotism. It was a tone befitting the enormity of the moment, and Parker was already beginning to wish he could be in the room where the address was being delivered. It was historic.

"Parker," he heard a distant voice say, then again. "Parker!" He was brought back from his revelry by an excited Sheila Mills. She was a Data Scientist with a quiet demeanor who had spent the past few days pouring through the mountains of data that had been collected through the enigmatic channels, and from the unknowable sources of the mysterious 3rd party. Parker wasn't sure he had ever heard her speak.

Alarmed, he twisted in his chair. "What? What is it?" She didn't answer, but only pointed to a nearby screen. Parker's eyes followed. It took a moment for his mind to register what he saw. Below the first five lines of terse text that had been there for several days was something new:

Anomalous technical issues at remote location.

Data collection impeded.

Automated onboarding suspended.

Regardless of how it may seem, I task each one of you-, the president said, but no one was listening. All eyes were on the screens. New lines appeared:

Intent to establish communication disrupted.

Advise readiness to continue.

Parker looked back at the image of the president delivering his address. Time and circumstance seemed to converge on a surgical pocket of space that only he, of everyone in the Universe, occupied. He looked back and forth between the displays, one showing the enigmatic alien messages, and the other, the President of the United States delivering what could be the most important words of the millennia. "Please advise Chief of Staff Vandoren that the president's presence is required at his earliest opportunity," Parker said. He didn't look to see who would carry out his request, but saw a figure hastily exit the lab. The president's speech was short, and Parker knew there would be no delay in his return.

Within fifteen minutes, the president arrived, minus suitcoat and tie, in the company of Jeff Ward, Angela Vandoren, Natalie Briggs, Ryan Meyer, Frank Boswell and Margaret Statham. Riley, Clipper and AJ entered shortly after. The president's eyes fixed upon one of the large display screens the moment he entered. It took only brief seconds for him to read the message. He turned an incredulous eye at Meyer. "You're sure we're not being duped here? I'm still having trouble with the whole idea that these guys are speaking English."

It was Ward who answered: "Getting the language down is a parlor trick, sir, once they have enough samples to work from. We're legit," he said. Meyer stood to the side, nodding agreement.

"I'd advise–" Meyer said, but was cut short by the president.

"Ask who they are," the president snapped.

Ward nodded at Meyer, who immediately crossed the lab to approach the terminal. He sat down as the group crowded in behind.

"Please identify yourself," Meyer typed, then looked to the president for approval before submitting. Warren nodded, and Meyer pressed the enter key. There was no immediate response. Approaching the one-minute mark the president became visibly impatient, but just as he was about to speak, a new message appeared:

*A series of exceptions have arisen at your location,
suspending automated onboarding.*

Consent to proceed required.

The president read the lines. He began shaking his head before reaching the end, then looked to Ward and Meyer. "You're telling me this is an alien?" He shook his head again, his agitation growing visibly. "I'm telling you, it feels like someone is fucking with us here. If this is a hoax, I will chase these guys down and grind them to powder."

"Mr. President," Ward said, "believe me, I understand your skepticism. Had my technical team not walked me through the details of how and why we know this is legit, I'd be saying the same. The most I can offer is the unqualified certification that this is, without a doubt, an alien communique."

The president was staring intently at Ward, but his eyes had gone distant, as if he had begun looking more inwardly than at the other man. His lips were pursed in the manner of a person about to make a big decision, but unhappy with the facts he had to base it on. Ward had never seen him so agitated. "Ryan, please type the following: We apologize for the inconvenience, but have become wary of proceedings. Please disclose your affiliations." Meyer did so. Fifty seconds passed before a response was received:

*This galaxy is home to a vast range of the living.
Imperfectly, they are inclusive of evolutionary worlds,
such as yours, and the Ascendant Plains.*

*Imperfectly, these realms share two touch-points, one
being this communication medium.*

*My affiliation, as related to this exchange, is with the
Ascendancy.*

"Why does he, she, I don't know, it? keep using the word *imperfectly*? And what is the Ascendancy?" the president asked.

"My guess, sir," Meyer spoke up, "is that the wording is a symptom of not having complete command of our language. I would interpret that to mean that he's simplifying his answers. If we were to say the same, we might use words like, 'to simplify, yada, yada, yada.' As for the Ascendancy; no idea."

More words appeared:

> *The state of your technical systems suggests premature contact.*

> *Abort recommended.*

"Ryan, tell him we do not wish to abort, and ask his intentions." Statham let out a disgusted grunt, which drew looks from most of those on hand, but the president ignored her. Meyer typed the words but did not submit them. He looked to the president for approval.

"Sir, with due respect," Statham interjected, "we do not know what we're getting into here. *You* do not know what we're getting into," she said, emphasizing the word, *you.*

"Jason, please send," Warren said. Meyer pressed the enter key.

Statham's reaction was visible. "Sir, I advised you earlier today that I am fully prepared to bring charges against the individuals who have brought these circumstances about." She motioned to Riley and Clipper, perhaps without realizing it. "I would regret those charges, which are now encroaching upon grounds of treason, reaching even to you."

Warren turned to face her. "Do you think they'll go away? Or that the Chinese or the North Koreans or anyone else – even private citizens – aren't already looking for a way to come into this conversation? No, Ms. Statham, this conversation is happening here and now. And we – we! – are having it. Enough of this prosecution horse shit."

"Sir, with respect, you are not above the law."

Warren's anger was barely in check. "Indeed I am not, nor do I purport to be, Ms. Statham. We may well be on the cusp of a series of events that will become the most heavily scrutinized of the next one thousand years. I will not suffer history to record that we punished the individuals who introduced us to the rest of the Universe. Therefore, you should know that I will pardon any and all involved for all acts related to these events, and that you and only you, Ms. Statham, will ascribe and affix your name to these antics within the annals of time. I would regret that, even on your behalf. So, my hope is that you will cease this course and join the rest of us in applying your skills and abilities to the challenges at hand!"

"But we don't know what they'll do, sir," she said, pleadingly.

"No, we don't. But whatever it is, it was always going happen, and is going to happen. We are now irrevocably engaged. You must come to terms with that, just as the rest of us are. This discussion is closed!" He turned to Meyer. "Did you send?"

"I did, sir," he said.

"Good. Let us be about this," the president said, with a tone of finality that no one, not even Statham, ventured to challenge.

Intentions are to recognize your location as an emerging evolutionary participant in open assemblies of the living.

Entry-level proceedings involve informational and noninvasive collaboration.

Progressive integration in assembly activities is deliberate and measured.

Further use of this communication medium is prohibited pending consent to complete onboarding activities.

Sans consent, next opportunity 6,892.673 days hence.

"Days as we know them?" Statham asked.

"He's been speaking our language all along, don't know why he would change now," Ward said.

"So, how long is that?"

"Almost 19 years," Riley said. Ward did a double-take at that, both because of the amount of time and how fast Riley had converted the duration into years.

The president spread his hands in question. "19 years? So we don't proceed and the next opportunity to talk is 19 years from now?" He was looking at Riley.

"That is my understanding, sir."

The president stepped back and receded into his thoughts. No one interrupted. After a long moment, he appeared to be overtaken with a sense of purpose absent even to his Presidential Address. He looked unseeing at the floor in front of him, and in a moment raised his left arm, his index finger pointing at nothing in particular, holding his hand near his head as if preparing to point at something. His mind was clearly overtaken with a flurry of thought. At once, and without a word, he pointed with deliberate motion to Jeff Ward, looking him in the eye meaningfully.

Ward understood his meaning immediately. "Consent to proceed," Ward said.

The president pointed to Frank Boswell. "Consent to proceed."

Next, to Ryan Meyer, though out of protocol. "Consent to proceed."

He hesitated, then looked to Riley, lowering his arm. "And you?"

Riley held the president's eyes for a moment before speaking. If he was surprised to be asked for an opinion, he showed no sign of it. "Sir, I believe there is no real choice. If we don't, who will? We must consent," Riley said. The president nodded.

And finally, he looked to Margaret Statham. She was clearly the most conflicted of the group. She searched the floor for several seconds before looking back to the president. "I'm sorry, Mr. President," she said, "I cannot, in good conscience, consent. At a minimum, this must be taken to the Congress."

"I respect that," said the president, his tone suddenly calm and measured, even thoughtful. "Margaret, you're doing the right thing to follow your convictions, and at a moment like this I admire and respect that. But I have to think about what this means for all of us. If we don't proceed, who will this question go to in nineteen years? There will be a new space race and no guarantee that the United States will win. Who will speak for us then? Who will speak for humanity? A dictator? A tyrant? A monarch so shaped by a life of entitlement that he can no longer distinguish privileged ideology from the toils of the common person, even if he gives it his most sincere effort? No, by chance or divine providence, this moment has come to us. There can be only one answer." He paused and nodded respectfully to Statham before turning back to Meyer.

"Mr. Meyer, please communicate our consent to proceed with onboarding." Meyer entered the message and waited for the final nod of approval before sending, as he had always done. The president gave it, and Meyer sent the words on their way. Statham looked away, resignedly, but shortly regained her composure, standing even more erect as if in preparation for what was to come, whatever it may be.

"We'll see where this rabbit hole goes," the president said, more to himself than anyone else. "And ask who we're talking to, Meyer. Is this a clerk or a diplomat?"

Meyer typed the question, this time submitting without waiting.

The response was unexpectedly longer in coming than any of the others. A full five minutes ticked by, and still, nothing appeared.

"Maybe they hung up," Warren said. "Maybe we've already been turned over to some automated—" he broke off in mid-sentence.

A response had appeared. The entire group leaned in for a closer look at the words, as if there was some chance of mistake. The president lingered for a long moment before standing upright, and of all the people in the room, looked first to Riley. They regarded one another without speaking. There was no mistake, the words were clear.

I am Trial.

Chapter 51

March 16, 2024

"What, is this some kind of joke?" No one responded, and the president didn't look like he expected anyone to.

"Here we go!" Meyer called out. "We're lit up again. Massive incoming data. Looks like we have an actual message this time too, but we're getting a whole lot more data over the wire than these few lines of text can account for. Something bigger is going on. Let's keep an eye on it!"

A new series of lines appeared on the display:

> *Onboarding of evolutionary worlds is guided by consideration of key questions, which generally reduce to understanding the extent to which powers of leadership and government are representative of their constituent populous. It is difficult, in the circumstance of hierarchical organizational structures of significant size, to choose a single course that is acceptable, representative or desired by every individual who would be impacted by it.*

> *With particular respect to Earth, as it is now locally named, diversity of government and culture is markedly above norms typically seen at point of entrance into the Assemblies of the Living. It is*

speculated that these peculiarities underlie further, unexpected variations related to sophistication and general advancement. In terms of base-most considerations of primitive cultures, the Earth, as a whole, scores exceptionally low by most relevant measures; these including:

- *System-level conflict*

- *Famine*

- *Disease*

- *Poverty*

- *Crime*

- *Superstition*

- *Subjugation*

- *Environmental preservation*

These factors suggest premature contact, typically leading to deferral of further engagement. The Presiding Advocate of Integration has concluded, however; that the apparent imbalance of civil and social, as compared to technological maturity, is a product of the unusually high rate at which technological advancement occurred on Earth during the preceding few hundred years, having substantially outpaced other systemic concerns. The judgement of the Advocate is that continued progress of Earth along its present course, given its access to advanced capabilities, without the oversight and influence of the Assemblies of the Living, carries considerable risk of divergence from acceptable standards of conduct to which all worlds, whether members of the alliance or not, are subject.

Be advised that oversight of Earth's assimilation is, by extraordinary exception, assumed by an individual of the Ascendancy, whose decisions, guidance and judgements, now and ongoing, are beyond the counsel of any other interest.

The president scanned the text, lingering on the final paragraph. He stepped forward as he read the words again. "Shut it down," he said, suddenly. The abruptness caused a few people standing near him to start in surprise.

"Excuse me, sir?" Meyer said.

"Bring this whole contraption down. I assume we have people on premise at the Installation?"

"Yes, sir."

"Call them. Tell them to cut power to the entire property. Nothing is left running."

Ward caught Meyer's eye and nodded, then looked back to the president. "We'll see to it immediately, sir," he said.

Warren could feel Statham's eyes boring into him, and it took considerable fortitude, even for him, to finally look up. She held his gaze for several seconds before turning away. "Somebody get me a ride to the Installation," she demanded. "I'm seeing to this myself." No one reacted. She glanced through several faces, looking for someone to carry out her request, and finding none, yelled out, "Get me a fucking ride! Now!" The statement launched several people into frenzied motion, and she made for the exit as fast as her narrow-heeled shoes could carry her.

The president watched her go for a second, then turned to Ward. "Jeff," he said, calmly, "get whoever is in charge out there on the line. I want all power turned off, and verbal confirmation within the next five minutes. I'll wait."

Jeff already had his phone to his ear. He nodded to the president while listening to someone on the other end. "Yes, power down everything," Ward said into the receiver. "No. No time for proper shutdown. Throw the switch, now, please." He paced a few steps, waiting. Whoever was on the other end was showing hesitation, but Ward kept his composure. "Ma'am, I assure you that these questions are immaterial. Cut power, please. Do it now, and report when complete. The president is standing in wait." In a moment, Ward nodded to the president over his phone. "They're seeing to it now, sir."

Warren was now pacing as well. A few moments passed, and Ward nodded again, into the phone this time. "Good job," he said, then to the president, "We're down."

"Is that confirmed?" Warren asked.

"It is, Mr. President, the entire Installation is dark."

A new message appeared simultaneously across the many large display screens:

Communication disrupted

Then a few seconds later:

Awaiting restoration

The president nodded approvingly.

Part Two: Contact

Chapter 52

"Cute," Ward said, appraising the paper in his hand distastefully for a second time, then dropping it onto his desk. "I've testified at more congressional hearings than I can count. A subpoena wasn't necessary."

"It's a new world," Moore said.

"I wasn't that fond of the old one."

The two men sat in Ward's office. Ward had drawn the shades against the morning sun, which had been streaming in from the east with more jocundity than his mood could tolerate. The subpoena didn't help. It had soured an already-unpromising day even further.

The timing for the political games could have been better. Everyone was still rattled from the events of the prior weekend, and now a congressional hearing had announced itself.

Moore pointed to the subpoena. "When did you get it?"

"It was hand delivered this morning. You haven't gotten yours?"

Moore shook his head. "I don't think I will. Somebody out there wants to make a show of this, but I'm not a big enough prize for the trouble. I'll be there, though." He changed the subject. "This will probably drag on for years, you know."

Ward nodded. "I've been thinking about that; trying to decide if I should care. This, *Assemblies of the Living* – stupid name – is ancient. Even our word for ancient isn't big enough. There really may be no rush here. If we had declined the first invitation, they weren't even going to ask again for 19 years."

"So what's next?"

"I think we bring Riley into an advisory role, for one. He's got deeper insights on this than I expected. In fact, deeper than he should. I need to understand how and why. I don't know whether to trust him, which means I don't."

"I'll grant he's not an easy read," Moore said.

Ward nodded again. "I don't see him as the type to purposely work against us, but he will absolutely follow his own interests, that much I know. And he's smart. Not in some Hollywood, Sherlock Holmes kind of way either. He's perfectly fine taking a back seat, and even looking like an idiot if it advances his objectives – whatever they may be. Take a typical propeller-head; he'll shout out everything he knows at the first opportunity ... make an idiot of himself. Not this guy. I'll never be able to prove it, but I have come to believe that all of this, every bit of it ... well, let's just say he hasn't been surprised by anything that's happened."

"Are you trailing him?"

"Yes, but I've had to change tactics. He's too smart to be bullshitted, that's why I'm going to bring him in closer. He'll see through that too, but it'll be okay. What pisses him off is when he thinks we're trying to pull something over on him. He'll see what I'm doing, but he'll understand it too. It'll matter. Plus, we don't have anyone else like him."

"You've spent more time with him than I have," Moore said, "but I'd have to agree. He's brief with anything he says."

"Have you met Aarav Kumar yet?"

Moore searched his memory. "I don't think so."

"He's a PhD out of Caltech. He's out in Washington, been on the LIGO project for twenty years. The guy comes in, can't wait to talk to Riley. The feeling wasn't mutual. It took some time before Riley would give the man the time of day. I happened to be there when Kumar finally caught up with him. Almost felt sorry for the guy. He was ready to talk about gravity for weeks."

"Riley shut him down?"

"No, actually. He acted more like he could barely understand a word Kumar was saying. Before you know it, Riley is asking questions about gravity waves like he'd never heard of them. Kumar starts drawing equations and diagrams on the board, and Riley is looking at them like the RCA dog. It was a good show, except for one thing. I've heard Riley talk about some of the same stuff over the past few weeks. I can't follow all of it, but I can follow quite a bit. Especially now, given the crash course we've all been through. Riley played this guy. Hard. Between the two – my opinion – Riley is miles ahead of Kumar, but he was cool enough not to show it. He wanted Kumar to go away, and found a way to make it happen. The man walked out of the room like he had just learned that Santa Claus wasn't real. Riley never even looked back."

"What are you going to do?"

"Not entirely sure. That's why I'm going to pull him in."

Chapter 53

March 26, 2024

Meyer had lost track of how long he had been in the lab. The bombshell that had been the final message from the *Remotes*, as they were now being called, had seemed to turn every warm body in the Federal Government into a Keystone Cop. He checked his watch. It was nearly 11:30 PM. His eyes wandered back to one of the large display screens where the final few lines of the last messages were still visible: *Communication disrupted. Awaiting restoration.*

It would be a long wait.

The gravity machines were down, so no new data was expected, but it had become something of a moot point. Despite the mountain of data that had been collected, no one had been able to decipher anything from it. What looked at first to be a data scientist's dream had revealed itself to be an ocean of unreadable, and therefore, worthless bits and bytes. Most of the data scientists had already given up, now replaced with cryptography experts – men and women with the knowledge and skills to understand and manipulate numbers of tremendous complexity. Despite that, not even the most basic semblance of order had yet been identified. Meyer knew that despite the enormity of the task, it would be years before anyone would consider giving up the effort.

He lifted a foot and heeled a nearby chair into position to become a footrest, laced his fingers over his stomach and leaned back. There were at least a dozen people in the large room, two in quiet discussion near the doorway, and the rest at solitary positions throughout the space, pecking away at their laptop computers. The odd, unexplained absence of the day had been John Riley. *Where was the man?* Neither he nor Clipper had made an appearance since early that morning. In some ways it made sense. With the gravity comms offline, the lab was no longer the hotspot it had been. It was now just an idle data center, with the peculiarity that alien software happened to be running on a cluster of servers somewhere in its sub-basement. Still, Meyer had expected to see more of Riley than he had.

It was a quiet day, and from the looks of it, the first of many to come. Jeff Ward had done a fly-by at around 5:00 PM, but hadn't stopped to talk. Meyer noted at the time that his eyes had swept the large wall-monitors on his way through, but he barely broke stride. He came in, approached Sheila Mills who handed a thick manila envelope to him, and kept moving, walking out of the lab without a word. If he hadn't known better, Meyer would have guessed that he'd seen Riley waiting in the hall, just far enough down the way to be out of view, but couldn't be sure.

The other side of the equation was Sheila. Meyer had had no reason to observe her prior to Ward's appearance, but it was clear, after the seemingly innocuous event unfolded, that the exchange had unnerved her. Meyer watched Ward leave, staying with him long enough to spot his cohort down the hall, then looked back to her. She was clearly jittery, having made a doomed attempt at resuming interest in her laptop before giving up, fetching her purse and disappearing into the hall. She had not returned for more than 30 minutes. Meyer made a mental note to see what he could find out from her but knew to allow plenty of time for her to collect herself before making the attempt; otherwise, he could scare her off.

Hours later, the envelope exchange was still the most interesting event of the day. *Why an envelope?* Meyer mused. In today's world, virtually anything that could be transmitted in physical form could be more efficiently exchanged electronically. Meyer hadn't even seen a manila envelope in years. But the answer was clear: despite all the advances in encryption technology, paper remained the cash currency of covert information transfer. It had its vulnerabilities, chief among them being that anyone whose hands it fell into would have the secrets it contained; but it left no trail once it left the printer. With new alien eyes now in the mix, Meyer realized that there could be a resurgence of printed materials. This may be the first example of what could become the new norm. That aside, Meyer's best efforts could not produce a single viable guess as to what those papers could contain.

In some ways, it fit. Ward's behavior had changed over the past few weeks. Not necessarily towards Meyer. A man in Ward's position didn't spend time nurturing relationships with employees as many pay grades down from him as Meyer. No, it was the way he behaved, the things he did. Even his mannerisms. There was a covertness to him now. The gravity comms were down, but no one trusted that the Remotes hadn't infiltrated the internet and other networks in ways that could not be detected, and which could, even now, be subverting every government, power and person on the planet. It was a chilling thought, and the fact that it was a very real possibility was sobering.

A sudden escalation of voices arose from somewhere behind him. Not a panic by any means, but certainly a departure from the otherwise subdued character of the evening. He checked his watch, then leaned forward, looking around. It was 3:32 AM. He may have fallen asleep. Parker was talking to someone on the speakerphone. Meyer listened for a moment before rising to his feet.

"Nothing big at this point, from the looks of it anyway," a voice was saying over the phone as Meyer approached.

"When did it start?" Parker asked.

"Just a moment ago. Looks like it's already settling down again."

"Activity on the servers?" Meyer said.

Parker nodded. "Just a flicker. Probably a background process."

Meyer answered with a grunt and prepared to turn on his heels and return to his seat.

"New activity," another voice called out. All eyes swung to the display screens. Sure enough, a new line of text had appeared.

3,777,557

It took only a moment to understand what it was. "These guys aren't short on surprises," Parker said.

"It's a countdown," Meyer said. The number had already decreased by 10 and was continuing downward.

"So it seems," Parker agreed, as if confirming the obvious.

"Do you want to call Ward, or me?"

"It's my shift, I'll handle it," Parker said.

*   *   *

"From the looks of it, we're in store for something in about a month and a half," Parker said about an hour later, pointing to the countdown on the large screen. Jeff Ward, Ryan Meyer and John Riley stood looking on.

"Can you be more specific?" Ward asked.

"Thursday, May 9th at 8:47 PM."

Not for the first time, Ward was perplexed by the behavior of whoever was pulling the strings on the other side of all of this.

Parker said: "We've never observed them to do anything for our convenience from a timing perspective, can't imagine them starting now."

"How did this happen? We've cut all the lines, am I correct?"

"Our teams are sweeping everything again to be sure nothing has slipped through. We don't expect to find anything. Our belief is that we're seeing some sort of auto-recovery process kicking in."

"Meaning?"

"Well, we do this kind of thing ourselves," Parker said. "When we send probes out into space, we program them so that if they don't hear from Earth for a certain period of time, they drop everything, point their antennas back towards home and make reestablishment of communication the top priority. It's a failsafe thing. If we lose communication with a probe, we know that after that window of time ticks by, that the probe is out there doing its best to reopen the lines. We think this scenario bears similarities for the Remotes. We went dark, so the systems they've installed here are trying to re-establish."

"Okay," Ward said. "If we keep the gravity units powered down, they can try all day, but won't succeed. Correct?"

"That's our take on it, but this countdown suggests that they're going to take some sort of concrete step if comms don't open back up."

"Such as?" Ward asked.

"No idea," Parker said. "But our people are all over it."

Ward wasn't happy with the new development. "The president's going to power this facility down. We'll be lucky if he doesn't bulldoze it."

Parker nodded agreement. "We've been kicking scenarios around. Warren won't have much appetite for sitting by while this thing counts down. We could ask the Remotes what's going on, but that would require bringing the Installation back online. If this is what we think it is, doing that would negate the reasons for the countdown anyway."

"No way that's an option. Warren would go ballistic," Ward said.

"Agree."

Ward looked like a man who wished he could make the last few weeks go away. "We're gonna have to let him know." He looked to Meyer and Riley. "If you gentlemen want to take a last look at anything, I'd suggest you do it now. Odds are you'll need a flashlight to find the exits within the hour." Riley didn't respond. He was intently watching the countdown. Ward considered him for a moment, then looked back to the screen to see if he had missed something.

"That countdown is running slow," Riley said.

"What do you mean?"

"It looks like it's counting in seconds, but it's not fast enough."

Meyer peered at the screen. "I think you're right." He attempted to compare the timer with the second hand on his watch but gave up almost immediately. "I can't tell this way. Hang on." He pulled out is mobile phone. "I've got a timer app."

"And," Riley said, it's not counting down in decimal numbers. It's using Octets."

"Holy shit. You're right," Meyer said. He looked to Ward to offer an explanation rather than wait for the question. "We're used to decimal numbers, which has 10 values; 0 through 9. The number of unique values that can be represented by one digit in any numbering system is called the *radix*. That means that the decimal system has a radix of 10. When we count in decimal, once we reach the end of the range, we add a new column to the left and keep going: 7, 8, 9, 10, 11, 12. If you look at a number as a series of columns, you see it clearly. Once we hit 10, then the rightmost column returns to zero and we keep going. The Octal numbering system has a radix of 8, with a range of 0 through 7. In that system, you roll into a new column when you hit 8. It can look very counterintuitive if you're not used to working with different numbering systems, but in Octal, the number 8 is written as 10. Computer programmers deal with this all the time. In fact, if you pull up the default calculator that comes with your Windows computer, there's an option on the menu called, *Programmer*. If you select it, you'll see all these numbering systems represented on the interface." He pointed back to the screen. "Notice that the largest number you ever see is a 7?"

Ward was looking at the countdown. "Why would they do that? Why not use the decimal system? They're clearly reusing our numbers."

"Octets are good for representing binary values." Meyer said. "In fact, people who work with different numbering systems daily, like computer programmers, tend to think of Octal and Hexadecimal systems as shorthand – as derivatives of binary." He gestured back to the display screen. "Truth is, mathematically, the decimal system is not very logical, so this actually makes some sense."

Ward peered at the screen but didn't comment further, so Meyer pivoted back to the clock speed. "Okay, I'll start a timer for one minute. Someone be ready to capture the number on the screen on my mark." His eyes flicked between the timer and his phone a few times. "...starting... now," he said. The three men waited as the seconds ticked away until a minute was nearly up. "Mark in 3, 2, 1, now."

"Uhm... We're on the edge between 3,775,026 and 025," Parker said."

"Call it."

"25. Let's go with 3,775,025"

Meyer's fingers played over the face of his phone. "Okay," he said, "looks like they're running at a rate of about 1.11 seconds per tick."

"Did you guys calculate the date this thing will expire assuming they were counting in exact seconds?" Ward asked.

"I think so," Parker said. "We'll rework the math. It'll take a little longer to get a more exact measurement, but we'll get close enough here in a few."

"Don't forget the Octal conversion as well as the difference in interval," Meyer said.

"Got it. Give us a couple minutes," Parker said. It didn't take that long. "Oh," he said in a moment, surprised. He raised his tablet. "We've got about 13 and a half days."

Chapter 54

March 28, 2024

Jeff Ward watched the mobile phone ringing on his desk. Vibration mode was on, causing it to twist away to the right with each ring. The words, "Martin Moore" showed on the display. He finally picked it up.

"Ward here." He swiveled his chair towards the window. "Yes- Yes- Not surprised. No time. Riley will be here in five minutes and I want to squeeze a few things out of him before I talk to the president again. One hour. That's the best I can do." He pulled the phone from his ear and hung up the line, then tossed it uncaringly back onto the desk. He wasn't looking forward to this.

The intercom buzzed. Ward pressed a button and spoke without giving his admin time for pleasantries. "Send him in," he said. There was no response. John Riley appeared in the doorway within a few seconds, and Ward swiveled his chair to face him. "Shall we dispense with the charade?" Ward said.

Riley looked at him in a calculating way, as if those few words were enough to set the tone for what would follow. He took a seat. "I'm afraid I'll need a little more to go on, Director," Riley responded levelly.

"Do you? Okay, then. You knew, of course, that before all of this was said and done, every bit and shred of evidence would be scrutinized. Am I correct?" Ward sat back in his button-tucked leather chair looking more at home in the role of drawing information from a reticent subject than he had at any point over the past several weeks as Chief Investigator of First Contact.

Riley thought this might happen. He looked thoughtfully at the floor to his right for a moment, as if weighing options. "And throughout that scrutiny, you have found that I have been truthful at every exchange?" he said.

"Truthful, but not necessarily forthright."

"Would it have mattered if I'd told you?" It was a question Riley honestly didn't know the answer to.

"I don't know," Ward admitted.

"Agreed. We don't," Riley said. "I personally didn't see the need. After all, it was only speculation at the time. In hindsight, it looks like more than that, but it wasn't. As for chiming in after the fact – once we knew for certain that we had aliens on the line – and claiming only then, that I had known all along; well, that would have looked rather silly. What could my motives have been for that? I suspected that some investigation or another would eventually turn something up, but frankly, didn't care whether it did or didn't. What would it change?"

Ward thought about it for a moment. "Fair enough," he said. "At least, tell me when you knew."

Riley waved a hand as if the point was inconsequential. "Almost immediately. I tried to shake Clipper from the trail by looking disinterested. Didn't work."

"No, it didn't," Ward agreed. "I will also agree, Mr. Riley, that not sharing what you knew may have been the right thing."

"I think so too," Riley admitted. "Are we done then?" he said, leaning forward from his chair as if to leave – perhaps a little too eagerly. It was a rare mistake, and Riley knew immediately that Ward had seen it.

Ward eyed him appraisingly for a long moment before speaking. Long enough for Riley to sit back and raise an eyebrow; disgusted with himself and trying not to show it. "I'm wondering what you know now, Mr. Riley. What do you know today that you're not sharing? I could press the issue. You know that, I'm sure."

Riley didn't respond, and after an extended silence, Ward relented. "That conversation will have to happen, you should know that, but not necessarily today." He picked up his phone and looked at it absently. "You're not going to like this, John, but we're going to have to collect the computers in your apartment. In fact, we're going to have to take everything, at least for a short time. The top security concern of the United States as of this moment is to protect the technology that enables this communication to happen. We can't have anyone else breaking in. You can imagine that there are nations that we don't want in the conversation at the moment."

"I can, but it's a moot point, isn't it?" Riley said. "Every access point on the internet, anywhere on the planet, can be seen and monitored by these aliens. We've seen that demonstrated clearly enough."

"True," Ward said, "but we control the line – the last mile – don't we? We have to keep it that way. We're standing up a proxy as we speak; everything is going to be routed through it. Everything. We'll be able to filter and censor everything that comes in or goes out."

"Impressive," Riley said, then shrugged. "This has been an interesting couple of minutes. I guess I'll need a new toothbrush. Can I borrow five dollars?"

Ward grunted. "We'll put some money into your account. We've found a place for you. It's furnished. We'll also provide a car and phone." He gestured to a small stack of odds and ends on the corner of his desk; car keys, a box that said iPhone on the side, and another one that contained a MacBook Pro. "This is yours," he said.

Riley eyed the boxes warily. "Looks like I won't be enjoying much privacy anytime soon."

"Let's be honest here, John. You know the one asset that hasn't been seized as yet; one that represents the biggest security risk of all." Riley held his gaze but didn't speak. "We have to protect you. The sooner you breathe that in, the better it will be for us all." Ward leaned forward, placing his elbows onto his knees, still absently fiddling with his phone. "John, listen to me very carefully. This isn't the movies. Bruce Willis and John Malkovich are not going to bust onto the scene and whisk you away to a safe house with beautiful women holding machine guns watching out the windows. If you make this difficult; you, and only you, will pay the price for it. You're going to have some freedoms. Money will not be an issue. But if you attempt to break away from our oversight, you will immediately and irrevocably exchange Sunday afternoon golf for life in a compound with a lot of other people who made the same mistake. I can't recall the name of even one of them; I hope, very sincerely, that you understand that. Six busloads of those people wouldn't be deemed as critical as you."

"Am I under escort?"

"Escort, no," Ward said, tossing his phone onto his desk again and leaning back. "Surveillance, always. It started five minutes ago, when you walked through that door." He pointed to the entryway to his office. "I can understand that you'll need time to come to grips with this. If you want someone to help with that, we can accommodate. Frankly, I recommend you take advantage of the offer."

"Thanks, Director." Riley's response betrayed little of what he may be thinking.

Ward studied his face for a clue, but found nothing. "Can we expect your cooperation?"

Riley turned to the window. "Mr. Ward," he said. "I can guarantee to you that there is no further interment in my future. Your people will just have to keep up. If they lose track of me, that's on them." He stood to his feet. "Am I free to go?"

"Yes," Ward said, flatly, clearly unhappy with the comment. But rather than leaving, Riley lingered for a moment longer. He was still scanning the grounds beyond the window. "May I be of further assistance?" Ward asked, irritated.

Riley said: "Is it possible that your people; people I would assume to be your very best, don't realize that a proxy won't work? Not for the purposes you describe, anyway. There is an inevitable outcome here. You don't see it?"

"Enlighten me, Mr. Riley."

"You will be utterly unable to contain or control the aliens."

"Is that so? We're doing it now."

"Are you?"

"Yes, we are."

"No, Mr. Ward, you are not. In the meanwhile, I take some solace in the knowledge that the inevitable outcome is wholly independent of anything that you, or I, or anyone else may do."

"Outcome?"

"Am I not being clear? The aliens are not contained. Not now, nor have they ever been."

Chapter 55

April 2, 2024

Jeff Ward stood in the rotunda of the Russell State Office building, directly northeast of the Capitol Building in Washington DC. It was 9:45 AM on a dreary April morning. Thick, low hanging clouds drifted over the Capitol dome on the opposite side of Constitution Avenue, occasionally obscuring it from view.

He was flanked by John Riley, Jason Clipper, Ryan Meyer and Martin Moore. They had been waiting no more than ten minutes, standing near the statue of Richard Russell, Jr. in the large marble room, when a professionally dressed young woman appeared and invited them to follow her. None of them responded, but Ward stepped forward, and the others fell in line.

They were led to room 1428A, where the Congressional Hearing on First Contact would take place. It was large and predictably stately, with dark wood paneling and two-tiered seating stands at the front where the eight commissioners of Homeland Security would soon sit, and from which they would launch their hours-long volley of questions. Facing it was a deep and wide witness table covered with a navy-blue cloth and four microphones. Printed name tags stood beneath each, showing the names John Riley, Jeff Ward, Jason Clipper and Ryan Meyer. Behind the table were rows of additional seating for observers, but they were mostly empty. This particular hearing would potentially touch into areas of extreme sensitivity.

The men were led into the room through a side door. Frank Boswell and Margaret Statham were seated on the front row, behind and to the left of the witness table. Ward never looked in their direction. Two cameras sat atop a tripod that looked out of place in the center of the otherwise, dignified room; one focused on the commissioner stands, and the other on the witness table, and away from which trailed an unsightly tangle of thick cabling. Small tablets stood erect beneath each of the microphones.

The men took their seats, and Martin Moore moved away to find his reserved seat on the front row. In a moment, a mix of five men and three women filed into the room, taking their positions on the stands. A woman took the center spot on the upper tier and immediately leaned forward to speak into a spindly microphone.

"Good morning," she said, "let's begin." The room fell to a hush. "This is a closed hearing of the Commission of Homeland Security. I am Jeanne Aderholt, Presiding Commissioner over these proceedings on the topic of First Contact. I am joined by Legislative Branch representatives from both houses of congress and commissioners from the Department of State and Department of Defense, representing the Executive Branch. These hearings will seek to understand the events that led to First Contact, which has now been confirmed beyond all doubt; and to understand the conduct of the individuals who played a role in shaping those events. Our goal is to clarify the current state of affairs with particular concern for the security the United States, the human race, the Earth itself; and to further understand the state of relations between humankind and these new, previously unknown, remote individuals."

"Gentlemen, thank you for coming to talk with us today. This is an unprecedented; in fact, historic event. We will conduct introductions and then be about the business of the day."

AJ sat on the outer aisle of the second row, with Sarah seated next to him. It was nearly 11:00 AM by the time the presiding commissioners had finished their introductions and the witnesses had been sworn in. Each had seen the need to not only introduce themselves, but to bloviate on the subject at hand, expressing their deepest wishes that the best interests of all humanity could be served, and that this historic event could be the final catalyst to unite humankind once and for all. By the time the last of them had finished, Aderholt was impatiently fiddling with her pen. AJ's eyes wandered to his wristwatch. He wondered how long the proceedings would last; a day, a week, a month, more? There was no way of knowing, but the early signs were not good.

"Thank you, commissioners," Aderholt said at the conclusion of it all. "Mr. Ward, I'd like to begin with a few questions for you. It has been nearly a month since the early events of First Contact unfolded at the Mayfield Hammond Campus in Charlotte. As Director of Information Assurance with the NSA, how is it that you came to fill the role of Chief Investigator? On first impressions, one might expect this to be more a concern of Science and Technology."

Ward said: "Madame, the question is one that routinely requires clarification, not only with respect to the events at hand, but in general, as it relates to the separation of concerns between science and information. It became clear to me, early in the sequence of these events, that the technologies – the underlying enablers of the communication between ourselves and the remote party – are clearly critical; but that the nature of the communiques themselves were not of a technical nature. Once communication had been established, the dialogue between ourselves and the remote party were no longer defined by the technologies, any more than the technologies at play within the microphones on the tables before us now, are relevant to the discussion at hand."

Aderholt considered the response and nodded. "Thank you, Mr. Ward, that helps. I must now ask a similar question with respect to security. Clearly – and I would expect that you agree – there are vast security implications to all of this. Yet, my understanding is that the concerns of Mrs. Statham, as the NSA's Director of National Security, though repeatedly raised, were not heeded."

"Indeed, I do understand and appreciate the security implications," Ward said. "My family and myself are equally subject to all that lies ahead, just as any other citizens of the world. The particular concerns raised by Mrs. Statham, as I recall them during the initial stages of First Contact, were heard and addressed by members of the Executive Branch. I'm afraid I will not be able to provide meaningful information with respect to the dynamics of those discussions."

"I see," Aderholt said. "Did you agree, at the time, with the direction given by the members of the Executive Branch, as you put it?"

"With respect to Mrs. Statham's concerns?"

"Yes."

Ward looked down at the table for a moment, pondering the question. "As I understood them; yes, madam, I did agree."

Aderholt raised an eyebrow. "You did not see value in Mrs. Statham's admonishment to pause and allow the congress to engage?"

"The congress is engaged."

"True. We are now; but not then, not during those crucial first moments."

"Madam, as I understood Mrs. Statham's concerns, I did, in fact, see value in them. However, the timing of the events was uncertain. The remote party indicated that if onboarding activities were not undertaken, that the next opportunity to engage would be nearly 19 years into the future. We had no way of knowing how long we would be given to respond. The president's concern, as I understood it, was that if we did not proceed, we would have no way of knowing to whom the opportunity would fall in the future. We would have found the means to communicate with other worlds, and simply thrown it away, leaving to chance where the next opportunity may present. Even now, we have no way of knowing what might have happened, had we not responded as we did."

"Perhaps we could have simply asked," Aderholt said, flatly.

Ward nodded, acknowledging the point. "Yes, I concede that we could; but at the time, we did not know that."

"I understand," Aderholt said, sympathetically. "Perhaps, had the congress been engaged, I would have been able to provide the suggestion then, instead of only now. Unfortunately, I was not given the opportunity." Ward's body language, subtle as it was, revealed that he knew he had been outwitted, but kept his composure.

AJ passed a quick sidelong glance towards Sarah who returned a raised eyebrow. Already, Aderholt had begun showing the reasons she held the position she did as Presiding Commissioner, and he didn't relish being on the receiving end of them, as he knew he would be within a few days.

"Trial," Aderholt said reflectively, after a dramatic pause. "That's quite a name." She looked at Ward and smiled. "It's funny, isn't it, that even on a planet as small as ours, that there is such diversity? And I don't mean only in terms of the human race. Dogs bark, ducks quack, whales squeak, pigs snort, and we, humans, talk. We don't sound like whales or ducks. The phonetics we use are a function of our anatomy. Could it be that the sounds used to communicate by our remote friends are so much like our own that there is a direct phonetic pronunciation of his name in our language; and that his name happens to be Trial? And, please forgive me if I forego the silliness of quibbling over gender. My point being, if we could hear Trial speak his name, would it sound the way it would if we were to pronounce it ourselves? If not, then I would have to wonder, why Trial? Do you see my meaning? If Trial's race of beings were, I don't know, to talk by drumming on their chests, then how would he communicate a meaningful translation of his name? Most likely, the best we would be able to do is translate its meaning. Maybe Trial's name, in his native tongue, so to speak, means, harmony. If he spoke his name by drumming on his chest, we would still very likely call him Harmony because we would simply translate its meaning from our lexicon. Do you understand my point, Mr. Ward? Trial. He gave his name to us phonetically, not in terms of how its meaning would translate. That seems so odd to me. Do you see my quandary? How do you feel about that?"

"Perhaps you should ask him," Ward said. A murmur passed through the crowd.

"Yes, perhaps I should. Given that the communication lines are currently disabled, it's not an option at present, but thank you for the suggestion," Aderholt said. She appeared to ignore the jibe, but it had clearly been noted. "Hmm," she said, again, emphasizing her deep concern. "It seems we have a new houseguest, and already, I find that I am wary of his intentions. Perhaps it's just me. Does his name give pause to you as well, Mr. Ward?"

"In fact, it does, Mrs. Aderholt. Your points are valid. I would have to concede however, that I am unlikely to have anything further to add. Is there a particular question I may answer?"

"Perhaps I am being unfair. Maybe I'm only seeking to understand whether the surprising peculiarity of Trial's name strikes others in the same, odd way as it does me; and if so, to determine if it should, perhaps, become a factor in the assessment of his intentions."

"Indeed, Trial's name raises questions, even concerns for us all," Ward said. "However, I assure you, Madame, that every detail we have learned is taken into account as we consider options. Trial's name is one among countless other factors that are continuously under scrutiny."

"Glad to hear. We agree, then," she said. She directed her attention to a small display screen to her left, touching the surface lightly with her fingers.

"And now there is a new development. Please correct me, Mr. Ward, if any of the following disagrees with your understanding. On Saturday, March 16th, consent was communicated to the remote party, by the president himself, to commence with a process called *onboarding*. Within moments of providing that consent, we learned of Trial's name and were subsequently served with a *Notice of Intent*, apparently on his behalf, that the Earth would be assimilated into an organization called the *Assemblies of the Living*. Although not mentioned by name in the document itself, it appears to indicate that the entire Earth – all of us – have, without recourse, come under oversight of Trial, as the…" she lifted her eyes slightly to read through her glasses, "*Presiding Advocate of Integration*. Am I correct so far?"

"To my understanding, yes."

"What was the president's response to that?"

"As I recall, immediately after reading the statement, he ordered that the gravitational machines be taken offline," Ward said.

"He turned them off?"

"Yes, by cutting power to the facilities where the machines are housed."

"And once the power was off, two additional communications were received at the Mayfield Hammond facilities, those being; *communication disrupted*, and *awaiting restoration*."

"Yes," Ward said. He took a sip of water.

"Good," Aderholt said. "And the gravity machines, they are still offline?"

"They are."

"We are aligned," she said, referring to her display screen again. "Let us now move forward. The – how should I put it? – non-passive tone of the *Notice of Intent*, suggests to me that this, *Trial*, is unlikely to be deterred by a simple disruption of communication. If you will pardon the metaphor, it strikes me rather like attempting to escape a house fire by hiding in the closet."

Ward said: "I'm afraid I do not agree with the basis of your metaphor, Madame, but understand your point. It is a concern that is not lost to us."

"For clarification, and for the benefit of all in company here; to what concern do you refer, Mr. Ward?" Ward was now looking to the display screen before him for the first time since the discussion began. Noticing it, Aderholt asked: "Mr. Ward, are you looking at that statement now?"

"I am," he said, not raising his eyes from the screen.

"In the cause of full transparency," she said, "I must admit that I find those words to be chilling. Since you have them before you now, would you mind reading the last paragraph aloud?"

"I presume, Madam Commissioner, that you're referring to the–"

"The paragraph that begins, 'Be advised.' That's the one," she said.

"Be advised," Ward began, "that oversight of Earth's assimilation is, by extraordinary exception, assumed by an individual of the Ascendancy, whose decisions, guidance and judgements, now and ongoing, are beyond the counsel of any other interest..."

"Yes, that's quite enough, thank you," she said. "Is it your interpretation that the member of the Ascendancy called out here, is Trial himself?"

"That is the prevailing belief, yes."

"And you share that belief?"

"I do."

"That is my belief as well," she said. "So, we have now cut the lines of communication. Can you please share with those in attendance here, any thoughts or conclusions that have been reached by your team with respect to how Trial may respond?"

For the first time, Ward looked to his right, towards Meyer. Meyer looked back as if expecting Ward to pass the question to him, but instead, Ward only regarded him in silence for a moment, as if weighing how to proceed, then looked back to Aderholt. "We don't know," he said, finally. "As I am sure you are aware, in the late afternoon hours of March 26th, the display screens in the lab began a countdown. It began just under seven days after the gravity machines were brought down, and at its current rate, is set to expire on Tuesday, April 9th, at about 4:00 PM eastern time."

"Do you have any idea of what may happen at that time?" she pressed.

"It has been speculated that in the time before communications were disrupted, that the aliens may have propagated a virus through the internet that will become active at that point. We have dedicated tremendous resources to understanding whether that has occurred, and as yet, have found no trace or indication that such a thing has happened."

"But, we can't be sure."

"We cannot be sure," Ward conceded.

"What else? What else could be happening?"

"The plausibility of other contingencies lessen dramatically."

"Please, Mr. Ward, I would very much like to hear some of them, just the same."

Ward stared unseeing at the display screen before him. In a moment, he nodded to himself with the barely perceptible movement of his head, as if acknowledging that the topic could not be avoided. "It has been ventured," he said, "that despite our inability to detect them, that the world's computer systems are infected with a virus that will either render them inoperable, or destroy data on a massive scale."

"I see," Aderholt said, but was clearly not satisfied. "Anything else, Mr. Ward? Anything that you're especially hesitant to speak aloud?" Ward held her gaze. He knew where she was driving and decided that if the topic were to be raised, she would have to raise it. Seeing that Ward was not going give in, she spoke. "I have heard mention of the possibility that the aliens may detonate our complete arsenal of nuclear weapons. Not only those of the United States, but everyone's." The response of the few onlookers was a low, but immediate murmur. It lasted only a few seconds and Ward ignored it. He kept his eyes fixed on Aderholt.

"I believe that outcome to be extremely implausible," Ward said, flatly.

"Implausible?" she said. "Forgive me, if I don't find your words to be particularly comforting."

"They weren't meant to comfort you, Madam Commissioner. They are a statement of my views, which you solicited. I cannot speak for Mrs. Statham but happen to agree with her advice on this particular subject."

"Which is?"

"Mrs. Statham happens to be present, perhaps she could communicate her recommendations better than I will be able to repeat them."

Aderholt said: "Mrs. Statham will join the discussion in a few days. For now, please give your interpretation."

"Okay," Ward said. "We must assert our autonomy. Bringing communications back online prior to expiration of the countdown, will in my view and I believe Mrs. Statham's as well, convey the wrong message. There is a chance that the aliens are indeed, powerless to do anything, and that the countdown is a ruse to coax us into reenabling the very means that would allow them to infect our systems maliciously. My recommendation, therefore, is that we continue; in fact, redouble our efforts to find any viruses that may have been planted by the aliens in the time prior to expiration of the countdown. If we find none, which I believe will be the case, then we should ignore the aliens pending further investigation and due diligence – regardless of how long that may take. We should leave the communication systems offline, to be reopened no sooner than we have learned enough to become confident in our ability to control, or at least contain the alien technology."

"That is an interesting proposition," Aderholt said, "but first, allow me to ask the question in a slightly different way. Do you believe that it is within the capabilities of these aliens to disrupt our computer networks?"

Ward said: "The aliens have demonstrated astounding technical abilities from the start. Yes, I believe they are capable."

"Interesting. Could they detonate our nuclear weapons?" The statement touched off another murmur.

"I have no way of knowing. I must restate, however; that the possibility has no merit in my view."

"What makes you so confident?"

"Quite simply, Madame Commissioner, the *Notice of Intent* expresses concerns on the part of the aliens that the Earth is significantly lacking in the domains of war, famine, disease and other areas of social concern. It reads like a bad 1950's-era science fiction novel to think that their first gesture will be to transgress virtually all of those same concerns by destroying our planet because we have, as you say, hidden in the closet."

"I hear you, Mr. Ward, but I like it when things make sense. Through all of this I find myself wondering, why would the aliens do this or that? If I were the aliens, what would I do? That kind of thing. So, the countdown starts and I find that I can't reconcile something. Why wouldn't the aliens bother to inform us as to the nature of that countdown? Do you have insights to share that could help me better understand?"

"Madame Commissioner, only that it may be that the aliens don't know what is coming next. Remember, we've cut contact with them. This is their automated system kicking in; we're certain of that. The countdown probably means something very simple; which is that the system is waiting for a given amount of time before giving up on the hope that the communication lines will come back online. Once the possibility is abandoned – at the close of the countdown – the system will most likely look for other ways to restore them. If we think of the countdown in terms of the context in which it was received, it makes sense. The message was shown that indicated the alien's software detected the loss of communication, then said it was awaiting restoration. There was a period of inactivity, and then a countdown started. It may help to think of the countdown less as leading to something, and more as the amount of time the system will wait on its current course before giving up and looking for other options."

Chapter 56

April 3, 2024

Like everyone else in the lab, Meyer was busy pouring through mountains of data. It was a heads-down affair. Every analyst who came into the lab found a comfortable spot, gathered the necessities of coffee or water, and then went to work surfing in silence through the ocean of data that had been collected from the Remotes. The more Meyer looked at it, though, the more he realized the height of the mountain they were attempting to climb. There was no making sense of it. It was the typical ones and zeros of the binary and Boolean languages, but no appreciable patterns could be found; not anywhere.

The only explanation was that they were viewing heavily encrypted data, which was not a good sign. It could mean that they may never understand it. There were forms of encryption in earth-bound systems that leveraged such complex algorithms, and large encryption keys, that they were virtually impossible to break. If the seemingly random data they were looking at now utilized encryption based on what could very well be unfathomably more sophisticated mechanisms, it would not be worth another ten minutes to attempt to break it; it simply wasn't going to happen. Hollywood hackers routinely break into alien systems on huge spaceships by blasting into panels and connecting a few wires. Any person who can spell *cryptography* knows that those scenes, among all of the far-flung scenarios and creatures the movie was likely to contain, were the most unrealistic of all.

On Earth, security breaches in computer systems rarely involved breaking codes, but usually targeted the incorrect handling of them. Directly breaking top-end cryptography can require the equivalent of correctly guessing a sequence of a million numbers between zero and 100 trillion, in order, without any hints as to which of the numbers could be wrong. Then, once successful, finding that doing so had been only the first of a series of other challenges of equal or greater difficulty. That reality meant that hackers generally avoided the brute force approach of attempting to guess at the keys, instead searching for other vulnerabilities. Perhaps a highly-sensitive message would be encrypted using ironclad algorithms, but the person who sent it also transmitted the key to the receiver via an insecure email account or kept it on a portable storage device on his keychain. Either of these two scenarios could net a quicker and easier path to learning the message than attempting to defeat the encryption itself. It was the equivalent of a bank robber checking the manager's desk for the combination to the safe, before attempting to break through it.

In the case of the aliens, no variation of those scenarios would be a possibility; and given the safe assumption that, if the data they had intercepted was indeed, heavily encrypted as it appeared, the cryptography in use could be exponentially more sophisticated than anything known to humankind, it would certainly take more than crossing a few wires to get anywhere. Still, Meyer was not quite ready to declare the effort a lost cause. They could still catch a break, though he couldn't fathom what it might be.

"I have something interesting here, if you have a minute," a voice said.

Meyer looked up from this laptop, only then to realize how fatigued his eyes had become. "Of course, Ankur, what is it?" It felt good not to be looking at the screen for a moment. He rubbed his eyes.

"We have the unit of time question worked out, at least partially," he said.

"Nice work, what'ya got?"

"It'll be easier if we use one of the conference rooms, so we can throw some things up on the screen. How about room 1A153?"

"Let me warm up my coffee, I'll be there in five minutes."

Coffee in hand, Meyer entered the room to find Ankur and Sheila Mills waiting. On the screen was a timeline that showed several milestones, indicated as diamonds, which marked moments in time. "Thanks for waiting, guys," Meyer said, taking his seat.

Ankur said: "No problem. This shouldn't take long, but it is interesting. We decided to take a closer look at the moments in time when significant events happened over the past few weeks. Nothing particularly notable stood out until we came to the moment when the Installation was powered down. As you know, we have split the video signal from the primary terminal where the actual interactions with the Remotes takes place, so it can be displayed across the multiple screens around the lab. We have also routed the video to another computer that monitors the activity automatically, using a form of screen-scraping. One of the benefits is that we have log information that includes hyper-accurate timestamps of every event. Here's what we found." Ankur pointed to the screen. "The precise moment the Installation was powered down was not captured, but we suspect that it was only milliseconds, at most, before the message was displayed indicating that the disruption had been detected by the aliens."

"The, *communication disrupted* message?"

"Exactly," Ankur said. "The, *awaiting restoration* message appeared precisely 289.9694 seconds later, which is a little more than 15 seconds shy of five minutes. No further activity occurred until the start of the countdown itself. The duration between that last message and the start of the countdown was nearly seven days. Again, more precisely; 161.547 hours. Finally, there is the countdown itself. The countdown began in the early morning hours of March 27th, and when we did the math, we calculated that it will end on April 9th, having a full duration of 324.275 hours. These values seem arbitrary, but they aren't." He pressed a key on his laptop to update the display screen. "If we convert the values to the unit of time at which the countdown is ticking, a clearer picture emerges."

"Meaning?" Meyer said.

"Meaning, if we settle on the tick duration of the countdown as the base interval; remember, each tick equates to about 1.11 seconds, and treat it as if it were essentially one second, we find that all the numbers fall on round, binary intervals. Here are those values, expressed in octet form, for simplicity:"

Event	Delta (seconds)	Delta (octets)
Communications disrupted	0	0
Awaiting restoration	284	400
Countdown begins	581,569	2,000,000
Countdown ends	1,163,138	4,000,000

"The octet column," Ankur continued, "shows the number of 'alien seconds' in each window of time."

Meyer studied the chart. "Interesting," he said. "These guys are binary through and through."

"Appears that way," Ankur agreed.

Sheila said: "And here's another interesting piece. Remember how long we were told it would be before the next onboarding opportunity would occur if we declined?"

"Yes, 19 years, roughly," Meyer said.

"If we equate the units of measure to their clock cycle and render in octet form as we have for these other events, that duration becomes exactly 4,000,000,000 ticks."

Meyer looked at her, unseeing, as his mind processed the information. "That is damned cool," he said. "This is excellent work. I want a new countdown clock that ticks using these base units of measure."

"You got it, boss," Ankur said.

Two hours later; Meyer, Ankur and Sheila were sitting in the same room covering the information with Frank Boswell and Jeff Ward.

"Why would they bother?" Ward said. "They're still speaking English, why not use our units of time?"

"That one had us for a while too," Meyer said, "but the more we thought about it, the more it made sense. Even here on Earth, we don't try to change the language of other countries. So far, we're still happy to translate – and we're getting better at doing it in an automated way – but we share a standardized calendar and clock. Translation of language is a nuisance, but not a huge deal, not even for us. But think about it, if we hope to coordinate activities, it was discovered long ago, that we must agree on time. We all use a 24-hour clock, and a 12-month calendar. All of us do. If we didn't, we would have a hell of a time coordinating anything. Apparently, that's a thing, even at galactic scales."

"Hmm," Ward said, instantly seeing the point. He looked to Boswell, "so, do you think it's a good time or a bad time to be a watchmaker?"

Boswell raised his eyebrows. "I can only imagine that sooner or later, everyone's gonna want a watch that counts like this. What do we call it, *galactic time*?"

"Would this count as insider trading?" Meyer said, only half joking.

"Wouldn't know, but the president used some tough words in his speech the other day about law breakers. It wouldn't be a particularly good time to be on the wrong side of that."

"Hmm," Meyer said, hearing the point loud and clear.

"This is good stuff," Boswell said. "Implications?"

"Nothing that we've identified," Meyer said, "but it may be our first actual intel breakthrough, regardless of how minor."

Chapter 57

April 9, 2024

T he Situation Room in the basement of the West Wing of the White House, more formally known as the John F. Kennedy Conference Room, came into being in 1961 following the failed Bay of Pigs invasion of Cuba. The conflagration had ultimately been attributed to a lack of coordination, and the room was among the postmortem responses, aimed at preventing anything like it from happening again. It had undergone many renovations over the decades – both physically and operationally – but still served its stated purpose, which was to ensure that the right people were engaged to address volatile events of national interest, especially those of a threat nature.

The countdown qualified in spades.

Melvin Roberts, the Assistant to the president for National Security Affairs, commonly shortened to simply, the National Security Advisor, or NSA, was already in the room. He and President Warren occupied chairs at the end of the long central table, which was flanked on two sides by large display monitors. It was not a relaxed conversation.

The countdown was an unprecedented event in many ways. For the United States, threats were a matter of measured response. It was rarely, if ever about the possibility of success. Failures were only cases where the force and resources required for a given scenario overextended political will.

Then came the Remotes. It could be the first that the United States had contended with anything that may very well be measuring its own actions with the same self-imposed restraint. They had broken through security measures at the Mayfield Hammond labs with such ease that questions of their capabilities, if it were to come to the point of force, was an uncomfortable topic. The systems they had circumvented were civilian, but just the same, some of the security safeguards employed on them were as good as could be found anywhere, even within the military.

The room was quickly filling up. Vice President, Kenneth Donovan entered and took a seat to the right of the president. Jeff Ward and Frank Boswell were seated further down, as were General Marshall Stephens, the Chairman of the Joint Chiefs of Staff, and General Norman Pike, the Vice Chairman. General Karen Billings, Chief of the National Guard Bureau, was the only member of the Joint Chiefs in attendance who represented a specific branch of the military.

Angela Vandoren broke free from a sidebar conversation and stood to address the group. "Ladies and Gentlemen," she said, "let's please come to order. We have several topics to discuss. As you are aware, the countdown that began at the Mayfield datacenter on Wednesday, March 27th, is set to expire this afternoon at 3:54 PM Eastern Time, roughly seven hours from now. As far as we are aware, no direct knowledge of the countdown is known outside of a very small group of individuals. However, given the lack of concrete intelligence as to the nature and purpose of the countdown, prudent steps have been taken to maximize response readiness in the event that hostile activities occur. I should stress that they are not expected. Although General Billings has directed that as few visible signs of the move to readiness are to be exposed to the general public as possible, the activation of National Guard troops has had the anticipated effect of raising suspicions. Much of the news media and online social networks are now carrying heavy chatter on the topic, but there is no material disruption to the tenuous calm that has characterized the American public since and following the start of First of Contact on March 10th. Furthermore, although General Billings will provide further details momentarily, National Guard assets, though not deployed, are at the ready should the need arise. Again, this is for purposes of not alarming the public."

"Our Centers for Collective Intelligence have concluded that the nature of the countdown is benign. The prevailing hypothesis is that the countdown is simply a behavior of an automated recovery system, and that the duration of the countdown is the amount of time that the system will remain in wait on the possibility that communication lines will be restored. As you know, that will not happen. The obvious question then becomes; what will be the next step on the part of the Remotes once the countdown expires? In the absence of specifics, our response is, as always, readiness. All branches of our military are at a heightened state of alert and will be directed by their respective Chiefs to enter into a state of full readiness at four hours prior to countdown expiration. It is for this reason that the Chiefs of our other branches of the military are not currently with us, but will join shortly."

"Thank you, Angela," the president said, then turned to Boswell. "I understand that the means by which the Remotes compromised the Mayfield systems has been determined."

"That is correct, sir. I received a detailed report on the subject early this morning."

"Have you had a chance to read it?"

"Much of it, yes," Boswell said.

"Could you summarize for those present?"

"It is of a technical nature, so some of the details may seem ambiguous, but yes."

"Understood," Warren said. "Given where we are with respect to the countdown, I think this is an important insight to be shared."

Boswell swiveled his chair to face the group more directly. "The first opening that allowed installation of the initial virus into the datacenter occurred when Jason Clipper, the computer programmer who actually built the software that exercised the gravity machines, decided to capture and retain the incoming alien data by writing it directly to the computer's file system in the form of text files. The aliens apparently discovered – or at least, surmised that this was happening – and exploited the fact by embedding sequences of commands within the text, called *macros*, that were recognized and silently executed by the program that Mr. Clipper was using to read the messages. The particular program, or viewer, in question is called *vi*, a common tool used by system administrators and programmers alike. You can think of it as a specialized word processor, of sorts, but more technical in nature. When Mr. Clipper opened one of these files to view its content, the embedded macros were interpreted and executed in the background by the viewer program, unbeknownst to Mr. Clipper himself. The macros instructed the viewer to create yet another file that contained computerized commands that were native to the underlying operating system. Mr. Clipper's access rights were then utilized to convert the new file into executable form, and the file was launched as a new, independent, background process. In doing this, the virus had embedded itself directly onto the computer's operating system and began running silently in a way that is very difficult to detect. While Mr. Clipper continued to interact with the aliens at a textual level, the background process embarked on interrogating the host computer and pulling data from the alien systems to strengthen itself and ultimately take over the entire platform."

Ward asked: "How could they have known to write these commands?"

"We suspect that the Remotes were able to discover the macro capabilities of the viewer by simply uploading its documentation. The ability to exercise the program was derived in much the same way they eventually learned to speak our language. They pulled the information needed to interact with the computer system directly from its own on-board documentation."

"Even so, among the many ins and outs of how the events of the following days transpired, which have been discovered by our analysts, the more concerning display of technical ability actually followed a few minutes later. This is with respect to the means by which the virus circumvented the firewalls that allowed it to gain access to the production systems of Mayfield Hammond's EcoGrid platform. Within only minutes of exposure to our technologies, the virus was sophisticated enough to discover the repository where the programming code behind its EcoGrid system is housed, scan it for security gaps, and upon finding one, exploit that gap to break containment in the production instance of that software, which had access to the open internet. It did this within minutes."

"This particular gap followed a pattern that is well known among technically trained individuals in the computer industry. It was based on a vulnerability called *SQL Injection*, which is an approach that inserts hostile commands into a database by, essentially, injecting them at places and times when the database expects to receive data only. Trained computer programmers are expected to know better than leave these vulnerabilities in production-level software, but it obviously still happens. It is extraordinary that the Remotes were able to discover the codebase, understand it well enough to detect the vulnerability, and then look for the opportunity to target that vulnerability in the production instance of the EcoGrid platform. I've brought this to your attention because the means by which the aliens gained access to the computer system during the initial breach, and the subsequent methods by which it gained access to protected systems and eventually broke through firewalled containment to the internet, was similar."

"I must stress, however; that we should not read too much into this. The demonstrated abilities of the Remotes to do these types of things are staggering. Remember, some of this – maybe all of it – could be done by skilled hackers here on Earth. What makes this so incredibly remarkable is that they were able to carry out sophisticated, multi-step processes with astounding speed, and without prior information, from a very tenuous entry point. Because of this, we do not believe that undue emphasis should be placed on the base methods used in these breaches. If we were to close every possible avenue for such attacks, the prevailing sentiment is that the aliens would have little difficulty finding and exploiting others. Even so, this tells us where the Remotes looked first. How they first thought about infiltrating our systems. What we do not know is the extent of their capabilities. Had these gaps not been present, what other means may they have found to exploit?"

"It does tell us something more, though, doesn't it?" the president said.

"Sir?"

"It calls into question, does it not, that the Remotes were acting in a benign way? That they were unknowingly breaking into our systems? The notion that the times when the Remotes broke containment because they simply didn't recognize those attempts as anything more than technical issues to overcome? That seems a bit weak now, don't you think? Could something intelligent enough to do the things you just talked about possibly not realize that they were, in fact, circumventing and disregarding our will to contain them?"

"I see your point, sir," Boswell said. "It's not a pleasant thought, but yes."

"No, it isn't a pleasant thought," the president agreed. "We will soon learn whether we have an unwanted houseguest that refuses to leave."

The question lingered in the air for an uncomfortable moment until Vandoren spoke. "Mr. President," she said. "At two hours prior to countdown expiration, which is 1:54 PM Eastern Time, power to the Mayfield Hammond datacenter will be cut entirely. This activity will be overseen by Executive Assistant Director, National Security, Margaret Statham. You may recall that these facilities have already been physically disconnected from the power grid, so cutting power will be a matter of shutting down the mobile generators. By doing this, we hope to remove any chance the Remotes have of further infiltration. As you know, the Installation has already been without power for several days, so this could be enough to shut them out for good – that is, until we are ready to take the next step. This Situation Room will remain in full operation for an indefinite period to address events as they occur. The Public Relations team is prepared to keep the American people informed as deemed necessary."

Chapter 58

April 9, 2024

R yan Meyer and his team were struggling with the finality of what was about to happen, but resigned to its inevitability. By 12:30 PM, Statham was in the lab informing them that the building was to be evacuated immediately. Despite prior knowledge of that, the experience was still jarring. Meyer rose to his feet and looked remorsefully around the large room a final time as military escorts fell in behind and directed them towards the exits. He looked at the countdown clock. It was still rolling. *Towards what?* He would know soon. It would expire in under three and a half hours.

Despite the loss, he understood and even partially agreed with the reasoning. The Remotes had essentially declared the autonomy of the Earth a thing of the past, which could have led to only one outcome. His primary reservation was that there had been a missed opportunity. Trial had been on the line interactively answering questions prior to the final memo coming through, which meant that they could have possibly learned more through further dialog. The president had chosen instead to shut down the lines of communication immediately. The prevailing sentiment had been – and even Meyer himself saw the logic in it – that keeping the lines open even long enough for further dialog would have had the effect of extending the window of opportunity for the Remotes to infiltrate Earth's infrastructure, which they had shown themselves to be more than capable of doing. Warren had acted decisively and correctly, but it was still a difficult pill to swallow from an analyst's chair.

Something about all of it still seemed odd to Meyer. This had been a disappointingly crude start. If the past few days really were the initial moments of First Contact, they were not telling a dignified story. Something about the Earth had drawn the attention of whatever galactic powers there may be. They didn't like what they saw, that was clear enough; but what was it? The Remotes had indicated that humanity's technical abilities had outpaced other measures of collective maturity, but there had to be more to it than that.

Even to Meyer, the Earth didn't seem all that advanced. Not comparatively. A significant portion of the population still lived in adobe houses. Exactly what technology was so advanced that it justified relegation of the Earth to the, presumably, less-travelled paths of supervised assimilation into the galactic community? Computers? Radio? GPS? Airplanes? Atomic bombs? It just didn't hold water. There simply had to be something else.

Whatever the reasons, they were enough to categorize the Earth as an exception case. It was an odd thought, but Meyer knew that it may be impossible for a person who had come into existence as a product of the very mechanisms of evolution and subsequent cultures of Earth, to form a truly non-subjective view. He, himself, may embody whatever traits the Remotes viewed as deviant. They would be interwoven into his very nature in a way that he may be unable to perceive. Perhaps the technological imbalance the Remotes called out were symptoms of a more fundamental, root issue; troubling indicators of some instinctive human behavior that spoke of nascent hostility.

The Earth was standing at the precipice of becoming a part of whatever the rest of the galaxy was doing. It was damned frustrating to think that it had ended up on an exception path that could delay its entrance into that galactic society for a period of time that could well extend beyond the end of his lifetime. It was like standing in an airport watching his friends board a plane bound for a fun vacation and being singled out by the TSA for a security scan. Meyer shook his head, struggling to cope with the frustration. He should be on the line talking to whoever was out there, not being escorted out of a communication center that was about to be mothballed, and for reasons that no one fully understood.

The questions boiled down to only a few. Was the Earth a threat, and if so, to whom? The galactic community, or itself? Neither seemed a likely explanation. The Earth had had atomic weapons for more than enough time to erase itself, yet there had been no prior intervention by Trial or anyone else. It went without saying that the bombs themselves were no threat to the rest of the galaxy. Nuclear fusion was everywhere – at the heart of every star. From that perspective, fusion or fission bombs were embarrassingly primitive. They couldn't be it.

Meyer exited the building to see the Will-Burt portable communication trailer waiting in the parking lot. It had been set up to allow Meyer and his team to monitor activities and stay in the loop as the countdown progressed. He made straight for it. Their primary mission would now pivot to looking for signs of activity once the countdown had finally expired, which it was about to do. Whatever that activity might be, it would not originate from the Mayfield lab building. As he looked on, the generator truck was unceremoniously taken offline. The constant hum that had been the backdrop around the area ceased at once, to be filled by the lesser hum of the generators that powered the comms trailer.

Meyer's eyes lingered on the now-silent generator truck for a moment. The computers in the datacenter that were host to the alien software would now be dead. Taking in the finality of it, he turned again for the trailer. It could end up being their home for many days, or even weeks.

It had been nearly two weeks since the countdown began, and now its expiration was imminent. The best minds had produced no conclusive ideas about what would happen once it did. It was maddening to know that the answer could almost certainly be had if the machines were powered back up. It would be a simple question to Trial, probably with a simple answer.

The cramped quarters of the trailer were a far cry from the spacious lab, but the advanced equipment it offered, more than compensated for the inconvenience. It was loaded to the hilt. As an Analyst for the NSA, Meyer was no stranger to the most advanced equipment that could be had, but after weeks of isolation inside the Mayfield IT building, entering the communications trailer felt like stepping back into the 21st century after vacationing in the 1980's. Mayfield's facilities weren't antiquated by any means, but the isolation it had been subjected to made it feel that way. No email, no internet access, no texts. The building had quite literally been digitally quarantined. Sitting in the chair amongst the dizzying array of equipment inside the dimly lit trailer, Meyer felt more at home than he had in weeks.

His eyes had barely adjusted to the gray tones of the truck's interior when a stream of light crashed through an open door. It was Statham. "Are we all set here?" she asked.

"Yes," Meyer said, hiding his irritation at the interruption.

"Good," she said, stepping into the trailer and closing the door. Space was limited, and he hoped for a moment that she wouldn't try to ride out the event in the trailer with them. The hope didn't live for long. Her eyes tracked to one of the many monitors on the wall. "Now we wait," she said.

*   *   *

Conversation in the Situation Room had progressed from incessant chatter, to focused dialog, then to brief, choppy questions and answers. Intermittent updates were called out as they came in. All the Joint Chiefs of the armed forces were now on hand. One of the positives of the countdown was that it had afforded everyone the opportunity to plan around it. The president had insisted that he would hold no appointments with anyone unless they were directly related to the countdown itself. That left a small legion of confused dignitaries and heads of state, who had lost their chance to talk with one of the most powerful and influential human beings on the planet. It was a greater disappointment for them than the president. The result had been a day without noise or complication, spent immersed in the most important issue facing humanity.

"We're down to about 45 minutes," the president said. "Anything so far?"

Vandoren answered. "Your absence has been noticed. Also, the preparatory activities of the military, especially the National Guard, has caused the expected uptick on the net. Nothing critical to report at this time."

"Understood," Warren said, then looked thoughtfully around the table. "I'd like to share something before this countdown runs out. I've learned some lessons in life, and I apply them at times like this. Could be a benefit to you as well. One of them is that when the choices are tough, and I worry about making a wrong decision, I try to think of how I'll view my behavior later. It can really help to turn a situation around and look at it from a different perspective. Two weeks, two months, two years from now, I want us all to be able to look back on these events and feel good about how we handled them. I want to be able to say we did the best we could with what we knew. I believe we are. If anyone feels differently, I want to hear it. Let's get this right." He waited long enough for a response, but none came. He nodded, then continued. "Every person in this room has taken a vow to defend this nation and its people. That's what we're going to do. This is our home. Ours. No one else's. Anyone who steps into our living room and starts throwing around words like oversight and judgement will never know the friendly side of me. If Trial attempts to take steps to undermine the autonomy of our sovereign nation; indeed, our world, he will be met with a relentless and defiant Earth. And we will prevail."

"We are with you, Mr. President," a voice said. Warren saw that it was General Marshall Stephens, Chairman of the Joint Chiefs of Staff.

"Thank you, General," Warren said.

*   *   *

"40 minutes, ma'am," a voice said. Statham checked her watch in what was clearly a long-established reflex to any reference to time.

"Good," she said. "Mr. Meyer, I'm going to take a few people with me to go into the datacenter for final visual confirmation that all systems are offline. All battery backups have been disabled, so this should be the final check. Would you like to join us?"

Meyer was slightly surprised by the invitation. "Thank you, but I'll have to see to my duties here. If there is any other way I can help, please let me know."

"Understood," she said. "We'll be back in 20 minutes."

Meyer nodded, and she returned an out-of-character, gracious smile. A burst of light washed into the trailer as she stepped out.

*　　　*　　　*

The Situation Room had been suspended in silence for several minutes. "Sir, all forces are now standing at FPCON Delta," General Stephens said.

FPCON, or Force Protection Condition, being a counterpart to DEFCON, or Defense Condition, which is a scale of readiness that military forces assume in response to a perceived threat against military or national assets. DEFCON is a similar scale as they apply to threats against the civilian population. FPCON Delta is the highest state of readiness that can be assumed.

"Acknowledged," the president said.

*　　　*　　　*

Statham reappeared as the countdown reached 10 minutes. She wordlessly entered the trailer but remained near the door. There were no open seats for her to occupy. "Ankur," Meyer said, "you've got social; Twitter, Facebook, chat, and the like. Amy," he said to Senior Analyst, Amy Dozier, "you're on domestic media." Michael Parker, was setting to his right, facing the other side of the trailer.

"Mike, you have international media, and I have intelligence. Are we set?"

"Social ready," Ankur said.

"Domestic media ready," Amy said.

"International media, ready," Parker said.

"Good." Meyer swiveled back to face his own monitors. No one spoke as the count dwindled to less than a minute. "We've got this," he said.

*   *   *

President Christopher Warren's eyes were fixed on the countdown clock on the wall. It was not a direct feed; in fact, had never been a direct feed from the Mayfield facilities. Once the time had been calculated, all the timers were simply independent clocks that had been synchronized to the countdown.

At the five second mark, Vandoren began a verbal count. "Five, four, three, two, one. Mark."

Chapter 59

April 9, 2024

Meyer watched the clock reach zero and then begin counting upward, now indicating elapsed time since zero. There was no immediate sign of anything unusual, and nothing had been expected. The only thing Meyer knew for certain was that something would. But they had nothing to help narrow the field of possibilities or help them focus on anything smaller than the world stage. It was a wide field to try to cover.

At two minutes, Meyer asked for a report.

"Social traffic unchanged."

"Media channels unchanged."

"Okay," he said. "Nothing on intelligence channels either."

The trailer seemed held in suspended animation. All of the automated feed monitors were running. These were sophisticated programs that electronically scanned their target channels, applying logic and filters to detect chatter on topics of interest. The channels included any significant paths through which information tended to flow. In the past, the primary channels had been the news media, and output from intelligence agencies, but over the past several years the trend had been more toward social channels; Twitter, Facebook, chat data and the like. Ankur was arguably the best at writing rules that could glean the most from the torrents of information that ran through these forums, and it was there that Meyer expected to see the first signs, if any, of what the countdown had been about.

At four minutes, Ankur broke the silence. "Slight uptick in references to gravitation on Twitter."

"What do you have?" Meyer asked, leaning over to peer at Ankur's monitor.

"One moment," Ankur said. "Let me add a few more filter terms to see if we can narrow it down." His hands played over the keys. Meyer checked his own feeds. As yet, there was nothing of interest. Ankur's brow furrowed and his eyes tracked across the screen as he took in the mounting surge of data. Even in the dim light, it was clear that he was seeing something significant. Meyer didn't interrupt.

"Whoa!" Ankur said, suddenly, a few seconds later. At once, he looked away from the screen to Meyer as if coming into a startling realization. "They're telling everyone."

Meyer didn't know what to make of it. "Telling everyone? Telling everyone what?" He demanded.

"We have a Special Report notice from CNN," Dozier said.

Meyer wheeled back to his own station and pressed several buttons. Ankur's workstation was replicated to his own, pushing his own feeds to a secondary panel. His eyes scanned from display screen to display screen. Statham had stepped from the door, and in a moment, Meyer could feel her hands on the back of his chair as she leaned in for a closer look. Despite the flurry that was quickly mounting, Meyer noted her professionalism at not interrupting with questions. "Get me the Situation Room," Meyer said.

*   *   *

"It starts," the president said under his breath, more to himself than anyone else.

"Sir, our Senior NSA Analyst reports chatter on gravitation." Even as Vandoren spoke, one of the display monitors on the wall lit up to show the words, 'Special Report' in large lettering beneath the CNN logo. The president ignored it. A moment later, the primary display at the end of the elongated room switched to a new feed, now showing Ryan Meyer against a backdrop of mountains of electronic equipment. His appearance on the screen drew the attention of everyone in the room.

Meyer didn't wait to be recognized. "Mr. President," he said, "we know the purpose of the countdown."

Chapter 60

April 9, 2024

The president spoke with controlled calm. "Cut to the chase, Mr. Meyer. What are we into?"

Meyer was visibly shaken; a fact made all the more apparent by his enlarged image on the Situation Room wall. "Sir, to be brief, communication with the Remotes was possible because John Riley figured out how to make gravity waves. The waves themselves were never his goal, they were a byproduct of the methods he used to modify gravity; but in the end I believe it was the waves that the Remotes detected. Very few people are privy to how Riley's machines work, not even me; but even though we couldn't make gravity waves until Riley invented those machines, we've had the ability to detect them for nearly 30 years.

And not only us. There are facilities around the world that can do it. What that means is, in a manner of speaking, the aliens have had the means to talk to us since the first day gravity wave detectors – more specifically, interferometers – came online. As far as we know, it never happened. But, once the Remotes detected that we could modify gravity and make these waves for ourselves, which meant that we could talk back, they decided to reach out to us. The prevailing opinion is that our ability to talk back was a signal to them, not only that we could talk, but also an indicator of our technical abilities. It told them something about how advanced our planet has become, and that the time had come for them to engage."

"I'm listening," Warren said.

"When the countdown reached zero, the aliens took advantage of the fact that we have these interferometers around the world, and broadcasted, in the form of gravity waves, technical plans explaining how to build the gravity machines."

The president took in the words. "One moment, Mr. Meyer," he said. "If we've never been able to talk back, how did they know we have the sensors?"

"Not sure. My guess is that it was a safe assumption on their part. It makes sense that we would be able to detect the waves before we were technically able to create them. Regardless of however they knew, they took advantage of it. We're still checking, but virtually every interferometer facility on the planet appears to have received, and unwittingly become points of propagation of these plans into the public domain. We're seeing them surface on CLIO, the Virgo Interferometer, Advanced LIGO, Advanced Virgo KAGRA, to name only a few. Anyone with a gravity antenna became an entry point. The information has already been posted to Wikipedia, and is being reposted to sites around the world. In short, Mr. President, the technology to build the communications systems is now irrevocably in the public domain. It's only a matter of time before we start seeing 3rd party facilities come online."

By the time Meyer had finished, the president was rubbing his forehead. "You said very few people knew how the machines worked?"

"That's correct, sir."

"Then how do we know that the specs the Remotes broadcasted are what we think they are?"

Meyer hesitated. "Uh, we will verify, sir. We only received the data a few moments ago, but that is the current assessment."

The president looked around the room and found Frank Boswell. "Frank, what does John Riley think? He designed our machines, he should be able to tell whether these are instructions for building one."

"I'll reach out to him," Boswell said, rising from his seat. By the time he exited the room, he was already speaking into his mobile phone.

"Angela let's get Statham on the bridge."

"I'm here, Mr. President." Her voice came from the overhead speakers.

"Maggie, we need people at the Installation and at the Mayfield datacenter. I want to be ready to power all systems back up on my word. If Riley confirms, I don't want anyone else beating us back into the conversation with the Remotes." He looked around for Boswell again as if something had just occurred to him, but he was still out of the room. "Angela, I also want an estimate from Riley on how long he thinks it will take before someone can have one of these systems online."

"Yes, sir," she said.

Boswell reentered. "Have you reached Riley?" the president asked.

"I have, Mr. President. I have him on my personal line." He gestured with the phone in his hand.

"Has he seen the data?"

"He's reviewing now."

"Where is he, let's get him in here. I want a briefing ASAP."

Boswell inclined his head apologetically. "We can conference him in, but it'll be several hours before he can be here in person."

The president started to speak but stopped short. "Is he out of the country?"

"No, sir," Boswell said. He was clearly hesitant to say more, but knew he would have no choice in the end. "He's in Hanford, Washington."

"Washington? Washington state? Why would he be way the hell out there at a time like this? Family?"

"No, sir. He's at the LIGO lab."

There was a moment of silence as the room worked through the obvious implications. "That son of a bitch," Ward said, making no attempt to hide his irritation.

The president took in the situation and his countenance darkened noticeably. His eyes tracked around the room, as if thinking through a puzzle. "Am I to understand that we have not been in steady contact with Mr. Riley?" No one spoke. Warren waited for a response, and when none came he looked to Ward. "Jeff, has Mr. Riley not been actively engaged throughout these past few weeks?"

Ward took a resigned breath. "No, sir, he has not. His contributions were no longer deemed essential."

Warren was no dummy. He appraised Ward with a raised eyebrow. "So, the two of you ended up in a spitting contest and you put him out to pasture. Is that what I'm hearing?"

"I don't trust him, sir," Ward said, unapologetically, without concern that Riley may hear him over the phone in Boswell's hand.

"Well, he's clearly a step ahead of us, I'd say. Would you disagree?"

"If he is indeed at the LIGO facility because he anticipated this, it would seem he is, sir. My judgement is that Mr. Riley has not been forthcoming with the NSA from the start. I did not feel as though I could rely on him to work towards common goals."

"Okay. I need to know the nature of your distrust. Is it a matter of refusal to do backflips like a circus dog, or that he can't be trusted to act in the best interest of this country?"

Ward gestured towards Boswell's phone. "This is a good example, Mr. President. Clearly, Riley knew this would happen. Why wouldn't he have informed us?"

"Good question. Let's let him answer for himself," the president said. "Angela let's patch him into the room."

Vandoren reached for Boswell's phone, and he handed it over. It took only a few seconds. "Mr. Riley, can you hear us?" she said to the room at large.

"I can."

"Mr. Riley," the president said, "concerns have been raised that you obviously knew what the Remotes were going to do once the countdown expired, but that you did not see fit to communicate those intentions to us. Let's first be clear: is it coincidental that you're at the LIGO lab, or did you see this coming."

"I suspected this would be the logical next step, sir."

"Why then, would you not have communicated that?"

There was a pause. "Sir, I am here precisely because I am concerned about the interests and security of this country." Ward knew that the way Riley phrased the response was meant to make known that he heard the exchange between he and the president before he was patched into the conference call. "Please keep in mind," Riley went on, "that I did not know this would happen; I only suspected it. From my perspective, neither this suspicion, nor my role in the events of the past weeks placed me on a first-name basis with the President of the United States or any Director of the NSA."

"Uh-huh." The president's irritation was clearly building. "Let's fix this. Angela, get Mr. Riley on a plane immediately. I want him in this room by early evening. Mr. Riley, please use the intervening time to familiarize yourself with relevant materials. I need to know if the current belief that these specifications describe how to build a communication facility is correct, and if so, your assessment of the amount of time it will take for a motivated 3rd party to build one."

"Yes, sir."

Warren said: "Jeff, this information could have changed everything about how we've handled the past two weeks. In fact, it may be no exaggeration to say that it may very well have altered history. We'll have to sort it out later, but you should know that I view this as a serious misstep on the part of yourself and your agency. In the meantime, let's get Riley up to speed on everything he's missed since he's been out of the loop. By the time he gets here, I want us all on the same page. Maggie?"

"Yes, sir?" Her voice came from over the house speakers.

"Let's go ahead and restore power to the Mayfield facility and make preparations to power-up the Installation as well. Do not re-enable the gravity machines until you hear directly from me, but make all preparations so that doing so will require the minimal amount of time possible, once the order is given. Please report status on 30-minute intervals. Angela will facilitate." He looked in her direction and she nodded.

Meyer spoke up. "Sir am I free to re-enter the facility?"

"Yes. Verify that the systems come back up as expected but take no action without prior approval from me. I only want to restore to the pre-shutdown state."

"Sir," Meyer said, "I wouldn't want to get too far ahead of myself here, but I think we should begin to consider when it will make sense to reconnect the Mayfield datacenter to the rest of the internet."

Warren looked to Boswell. "Sir," Boswell said, "that may seem counterintuitive, but I think Meyer has a point. Once other facilities start to come online, it is a certainty that the Remotes will gain access to the internet sooner or later. Probably sooner. It'll only be a matter of time. It may make sense for us to begin deriving our own learnings of what they will do once they have full access to the Earth's computer infrastructure first hand, rather than waiting to see it later when we have no control."

There was silence in the room. Unexpectedly, Statham spoke up from over the speakerphone. "Sir, I'm afraid I agree on this too. There will be no hiding from this once the first facility comes online out there. The only thing we have control over, at least for the time being, is when. Up until someone else builds a facility, we have the only capability."

"Is Riley still on the line?" the president asked.

"Yes, sir," Riley said.

"Ignoring these specs from the Remotes, how long would it take to rebuild what Mayfield Hammond already has, from scratch?"

"Sir, remember that it took more than a year for Mayfield to build its facility, but that was primarily because we were doing research and development. We were figuring it out as we went. Presumably, the alien specs will be a complete description of the final implementation. There will be no trial and error. If we were, to use your words, motivated to build a functional gravity comms system as fast as possible, I believe we could do it within two or three weeks. To make a bold prediction, I suspect the North Koreans will have one within two. First, we'll see a shoddy facility that will just get them online. Next, we'll start seeing better-built implementations."

"The technologies and materials needed to make these machines are readily available to anyone?"

"I'm afraid so," Riley said. "The machine utilizes a core metallic component as the active agent for affecting gravity. We've experimented successfully with a handful of metals, with varying degrees of performance. In fact, much of our research of late has been to identify the best performing material. When these plans came through, my first interest was in learning which material they prescribe. It is Yttrium, and it's common."

"Understood," the president said. He was frustrated with the lack of options. "Damn! John, I want your final opinion on what these specs are about by the time you arrive. If they are, indeed, plans for building gravity comms devices as they appear, then I want everyone here to be ready with recommendations on next steps. Clearly, we will have to build our own copy of whatever these specs contain, but we must also think about what to do with what we already have, and what constitutes our best strategic move from here."

"Mr. President," Riley said. "I suggest Jason Clipper be sent to the Installation. He'll be able to handle any issues that arise as we attempt to bring the facility back online."

Warren nodded to Vandoren, as if approving the request. "Understood."

Chapter 61

April 9, 2024

"It is a comms device," Riley said, to no one's great surprise, "but the design is not what I expected." He stood at the end of the Situation Room conference table next to the large screen on the wall. It was a full house, the attendees now showing the beleaguered look that was the inescapable product of hours of high stress. There was no end in sight.

"That makes sense," the president said.

Ryan Meyer was sitting at the corner chair closest to Riley. He wore a lime-green Hawaiian shirt that could not have looked more out of place in the otherwise, formal setting. "Sir, if I may," Meyer said, drawing the president's attention. "We have an army of PhDs looking at this. We haven't had much time, but we're already seeing something extraordinary." He shook his head, as if thinking the puzzle through again. "The short answer, sir, is that this should not have worked."

"What shouldn't have worked?"

"The machine Riley built is incredible. Now that I've had a chance to learn more about it, I couldn't be more impressed. But, comparing its design and function with the specifications sent to us by the aliens, there seems to be something missing. These aliens are miles … huh, millions of miles ahead of us … but physics is physics. There is no magic out there. If we don't understand something, it's only because we don't have all the information, not because someone has figured out how to reshape the way physical reality works. If it weren't that we know that these communications are possible because we've already seen a crude version in action, I would say that building to these specs will get us nowhere."

The president's eyes tracked back to Riley, studying him for a moment before speaking. "I'm trying to follow what I'm hearing here, gentlemen."

Riley said: "Mr. President, the systems described in the alien specs, and even my own machines, are not complete in terms of what would be needed to constitute a working communications system. It's as if we a have a microphone, but no sound system to hook it too; yet, it somehow appears to work anyway."

The president weighed Riley's words, and as if reaching a conclusion, nodded decisively. "That is interesting information, but I'm not surprised that we don't fully understand the details as yet. That aside, am I correct, Mr. Riley, that you can confirm that the apparatus described in these specs is for communication purposes?"

"Yes."

"And it won't blow us up if we build it?"

"I'm confident that it will not."

"Good enough. Gentlemen, please continue your research. We need to achieve complete understanding of the technology as we move along, but that can come in time. My concern at the moment is two things: what are the dangers of building the machine, and what are the immediate next steps?"

General Marshall Stephens spoke first. "Mr. Riley, after reviewing these plans, do you continue to hold to your earlier assessment that these comms facilities can be built without the need for particularly advanced technical capabilities, and that they do not require materials that will slow the rate at which they are built?"

"Yes, sir. Within a few years, you'll be able to get one from a gumball machine."

"How long will it take, in your opinion, until we start seeing facilities come online?"

"Weeks."

Stephens nodded gravely. "Mr. President, as I understand this, it will not be feasible for us to hunt and kill these installations as they begin to appear. In nuclear fuel refinement, the facilities are expensive, slow to build and highly advanced. Taking one out can set a state that is set on the course of obtaining a nuclear arsenal back for years. If these comms facilities can truly be built within weeks, or even months, without high technical prerequisites, the military will not be an effective countermeasure."

"Is it your opinion, Mr. Riley, that even privateers could build these systems?" General Pike asked.

"It is, sir. Mayfield Hammond was able to do it. It would require a certain monetary investment, but even an individual with access to substantial resources could do it, in my opinion."

"If it's so simple, why did it take so long for us to build one?" the president asked, somewhat incredulously.

Riley thought about the question. "Building the machine required solving a particular problem of particle physics. That's the piece that was missing. It wasn't an easy puzzle to solve, but now that we have, it's not really all that complex. It amounts to changing the density of atoms. If you make them less dense, they spread out, which means they don't sink as far into spacetime … their mass is spread over a larger area. The result is that the gravity wells they produce become shallower, and the shallower the gravity well, the lesser the effect of gravity. The fluctuations on the spacetime fabric caused by that process manifests as gravity waves."

"And you think it's the gravity waves that the aliens use to actually communicate?"

"Actually, no, sir. There is a chance that the gravity waves were what the aliens first detected, but I'm not convinced they are the central mechanism of communication itself."

Warren shook his head. "Okay, I'll leave that to people smarter than me. Keep me in the loop. So, what do we do?" he said to the group at large.

Jeff Ward said: "I suggest we turn the machines back on. Let's leave the Mayfield facility physically isolated for now, but get the Remotes back on the line. The sooner, the better."

"Agreed, sir," Statham said. She was now present in the room as well. "We need to get to the bottom of a few things. First and foremost; what are their intentions. We've been guessing for two weeks. Let's ask."

"Agreed," Warren said. "Comments, concerns?"

"My only suggestion is extreme caution," Stephens said.

Chapter 62

April 10, 2024

Clipper drove his car to the Mayfield Hammond campus on short notice at the request of an official-sounding person whose name he couldn't remember, and was barely onto the lot before the large and now familiar UH-1N Twin Huey helicopter spun to life. He was corralled aboard, not roughly, but briskly; and for the second time in as many weeks the awkward machine took to the air to carry him to the Installation grounds. It would be a hurry up and wait affair, he knew. He didn't mind. He ran through the events of the prior weeks, reassessing meanings and possibilities as droves of trees glided below the craft.

The helicopter was hovering over the familiar assortment of buildings before he knew it. They stood improbably upon the isolated and unusually flat plot of ground, like a forgotten car standing alone in a large parking lot. The top-down view of the area resolved into the more familiar ground-level perspective as the machine descended.

His job would be to power-up the facilities. He was not an insider to the decision that led to this reversal of course, but he had always known it would happen. Everyone did. The only missing piece had been knowing which particular events would be required to set everything back into motion. As the helicopter touched down, he knew that the changes the world had been expecting, but that had been held in bewildering suspense for weeks, were upon them.

Sergeant First Class James Randall greeted him as he exited the helicopter. A fit-looking man with strong features, not particularly tall or muscular, but projecting the stolid military confidence of a man who could carry a 200 pound comrade across miles of bad terrain if the need should arise. Clipper also noted, rather unexpectedly, the clarity of the man's countenance, which was absent the traces of regret and the curses of over-thinking that most people subconsciously carried with them from day to day. It was not a lack of perceived intelligence by any means; perhaps the opposite. There was a certainty about the man, which Clipper found immediately reassuring. "Welcome, sir," the Sergeant said, shouting over the noisy machine. "What do you need to see?"

Clipper knew nothing of the protocols of the military services, including when to call someone sir, or to expect the same. On the latter, the answer was never. It was probably just a pleasantry. Randall looked to be at least 15 years older than himself. At once, Clipper decided not to complicate the moment with any of it. "Good morning," he said, extending a hand, again, reflexively hunching beneath the swirling rotor blades, even though they seemed a good ten feet above his head. "Let's head to the main building first," he shouted.

No sooner had they cleared the rotor blades than the helicopter took to the air to disappear in seconds over the treeline. Clipper stopped and gazed after it, noting vaguely that it had headed in a southerly direction rather than east, back towards the Mayfield campus. As the beat of its blades began to fade, he also wondered how he would get back home. It would be a long day.

The interior of the 40 x 60-foot building was dark, with an abandoned air about it, as if it were an unearthed archeological find rather than a building that had been unoccupied for only a matter of days. Peering into the space, Clipper felt like John Lithgow and Elya Baskin in the movie, *2010*, in orbit around Jupiter, re-entering the derelict Discovery spaceship as it toppled end-over-end in the vacuum of space. There were more parallels between that movie and his own situation than he was comfortable with. The gravity machine rose ominously above the floor at the center of the large room, foreboding ... almost menacing in the scant light that reached it from the opened door. Clipper appraised it in a way he never had. It had always been impressive, but it was no longer a science experiment. In a matter of hours the machine would quite literally become the portal through which the Earth would connect with the rest of the galaxy.

That was his hope, anyway. He worried that the machines and support systems would be finicky when the time came to bring them back online. The way they had been powered down lingered troublingly at the back of his mind. The team had always been so careful about how the machines were handled. Pulling the rug out from beneath them with a brute force cutting of power wasn't exactly a page out of the handbook. He couldn't be sure they had not been damaged, or more likely, that the control system computers hadn't been corrupted. If they had, it could turn a job that would have otherwise taken minutes, into hours of difficult work. Prospects of being in the critical path, trying to resolve stubborn technical issues while the President of the United States, not to mention the rest of the world, looked over his shoulder, were less than appealing.

"We'll power up everything except for the gravity machines," Clipper said, his eyes lingering on the silhouetted monolith. "I'll make sure the circuit breakers are thrown."

"It's been done, but feel free to double-check," Randall said.

Clipper peered into the open space again, considering. "Better safe than sorry. Is there a flashlight around here?"

"Several." Randall pointed to a small table near the entrance where five or six of them stood, end up. Clipper selected one and headed towards the breaker box in the far corner. "We were part way through powering down the computers when the NSA Director demanded that everything be shut off immediately," Randall said. "It wasn't graceful."

"A few minutes to do it right might have saved a lot of trouble," Clipper said, but it was a moot point. "We'll find out what we're into in a minute. We'll need to get the computer systems back up, then test the comm link between here and the campus. Do you know when the airplane will be back in the air?"

"The Hawkeye? Within the hour."

"How about the generator truck? Still here?"

"It is."

"Perfect. Hopefully we can get everything back to working order and send some data over the wire within the next couple hours, then, theoretically, all we'll have to do is bring up the gravity machine itself and we're in business."

The circuit panel was standing open when they reached it. Half the circuits were thrown. Clipper didn't pay attention to which were which, he reached up and switched them all to the off position. Next to the regular breaker box was a larger, individual power switch. "This one controls the gravity machine itself," he said. It was off, as expected. He stepped back from the wall and swung the flashlight beam over the area, looking for nothing in particular. "Good. Was anything physically dismantled?"

"Not that I'm aware of."

"Okay, well, we'll double-check that later. Let's repeat this at the other building – the one with the smaller gravity machine in it, then fire up the generator truck."

*   *   *

Ryan Meyer, Rom James and Grady Lopez stood in the now-infamous row 3B of the Mayfield Hammond datacenter with flashlights in hand. The space was stuffy and disturbingly quiet without the sounds of cooling motors and ventilation fans. Meyer checked his watch. "Ready when you are," he said into a handheld radio. Seconds later, the fluorescent tubes above his head began flickering to life, followed by the flashing of red and green LED lights on the face of the server blades. A blanket of ambient sounds began filling the room like a rising tide of water as row after row of servers stirred to life. He scanned the lights thoughtfully. "That's that, I guess. We'll see what we see. You guys good with hanging down here awhile?"

"It's what we do," Lopez said.

"Excellent, I'll tap you over the radio in a few minutes."

Meyer made his way to the lab through now-familiar hallways, which took a few minutes in the large building. As he approached, he saw that it was back to its bright, gleaming self, bathed in white light. On entering, to his surprise, he saw that Natalie Briggs was already seated at a corner table staring at her tablet as if she had been there for an hour. It wasn't possible, he knew, since power had only just been restored. Per usual, she looked to be all-business; not unfriendly, but somehow, not easily approachable either. Her presence was also a clear indicator of what was to come: soon – two hours at most – senior brass would descend upon the place with their swarms of supporting staff, and all that was to follow, whatever it may be, would be set irrevocably into motion.

It was at that moment, at the prompting of that thought, that the butterflies returned to his stomach. The stage was being set, and there would be no turning back. The lyrics of an Alanis Morissette tune came to him, *the only way out is through.* It would be, without exaggeration, the grandest stage that had ever been set on Earth. And somehow, this second pass at connecting with whatever or whomever awaited them on the other end of the line was charged with even more suspense than the first.

Meyer's eyes searched out one of the wall-displays. It was blank. They all were. He spoke into his radio. "Do we still have server activity?"

Lopez answered: "Yes. Lights buzz'n. No signs of slowing. Just boot-up stuff for now, I'm guessing."

"Okay. Please let me know if that changes."

"You got it."

Meyer walked contemplatively to the terminal where Riley, Clipper and AJ had set everything into motion a few weeks earlier. He wondered for a moment if the terminal and keyboard would end up at the Smithsonian, and guessed that they would. Standing there felt like walking a racetrack prior to the start of a Formula One race. There was an excitement held in check, a 'quiet before the storm' feeling that was undeniably surreal.

The screen flickered unexpectedly, drawing his attention. He hadn't expected anything new, not until the gravity machines were brought back to life. It was a new message. He scanned it and blinked as if clearing his vision could bring clarity to what he saw. He turned to one of the wall-screens to see the message reproduced at a larger scale. Briggs had noticed it too, now partially turned in her chair, the tablet in her hands forgotten.

"The hell?" he heard her say from across the room.

"You are full of surprises, Master Baggins," Meyer said, lifting his mobile phone to his ear.

*   *   *

If there had ever been a question of the location from which the president would take up dialog with the aliens once the communication systems were restored – the Situation Room, the Oval Office or the Mayfield Hammond lab – it was settled by the latest message. Agitation failed to cast even the slightest shadow towards describing the president's reaction when he was informed of this latest development. He had dropped everything, including a half-eaten bagel, and made for Marine One at a fast walk, issuing orders to every person who came within earshot as he crossed the White House lawn.

Angela Vandoren struggled to keep pace, keeping an ear open to what the president was saying while at the same time issuing her own orders to a clutch of people who walked to her left. "Yes ma'am," a youngish woman said, then peeled away to her task.

They were aboard and airborne within moments, rising high above a growing crowd of people gathering on H Street NW, to the north of the White House; some protesters, some just curious onlookers driven by the desire to know more about what was happening on the front of alien contact. They would know soon enough.

*   *   *

Ryan Meyer was accustomed to working in proximity of high ranking people, but it was an acquired skill. Living in a world where a few simple statements could set legions of people into motion, all of them top-achievers, was bound to have its effects; and it did. Opinions – strong ones – were the norm. He knew that today would be a test of his patience, but also a day of promise. As a thinker – as a person who had dedicated more than a little time throughout his life to looking at the stars and not wondering, but knowing that there must be others out there, this was a day of boundless possibility. That he would have a front row seat as the events unfolded was amazing, and so much more gratifying than outsmarting dimwitted terrorists, as was, unfortunately, how he had spent too much of his time in recent years.

Per usual, the president was preceded by his Secret Service Attaché. Their appearance in the lab meant that the president himself would arrive soon. Meyer had seen them in action on many occasions. To the casual observer, it could look like these highly trained men and women just walked ahead of the president, scanning each room on the chance that something unusual may catch their attention. In many respects, that was true; but the methods by which they entered any space was well orchestrated, and anything but casual. It was always interesting to watch, but today, Meyer didn't have the bandwidth to spare.

Frank Boswell and Margaret Statham were the first of the senior leaders to arrive, followed a few minutes later by Jeff Ward, who was accompanied by Natalie Briggs. Meyer hadn't noticed her leave the room.

"Are we set?" Ward asked, approaching.

"Yes," Meyer said. "We had trouble getting one of the main computers that modulates the gravity machine to come back online, but we finally got it about 20 minutes ago ... Clipper had to reinstall some software."

"How about the data? Are we connected?"

"Yep. The only remaining unknown is the gravity machines themselves."

"We'll have to take that as it comes, I guess," Ward said, conveying a sense that he wasn't happy about something. "I still think Riley should be out there at the Installation."

Meyer nodded understanding. "Warren was pretty adamant about him being here." Ward grunted, and Meyer added: "If there's trouble, we can have him to the Installation in under 30 minutes. And, if it's any consolation, Riley thinks the machines will be fine."

Angela Vandoren entered the room and made straight for Meyer. "The president will be here in 10 minutes," she said, not bothering to consider that he and Ward were in the middle of a discussion. "He wants all preparations for turning on the gravity machines to be complete by the time he arrives."

"Should be no problem," Meyer said.

"It shouldn't be, or won't be?" Vandoren asked, testily.

Meyer met her gaze. "Shouldn't," he said, defiantly. She was taken aback by his response, but he didn't flinch. "We have no way of knowing if the machines have been damaged until we attempt to power them up. Those are the facts, and this is no time for fiction."

His demeanor invited no further discussion. She considered his words, then nodded. "Okay. I'll be back in a few minutes for an update." Ward looked to Meyer, who immediately became occupied with his electronic tablet as Vandoren turned to leave, the exchange already forgotten, noting the change in confidence that had taken place in him since the start of this ordeal.

When the president arrived a few minutes later, his eyes searched out the nearest display monitor. He peered at it disapprovingly for a moment, then began scanning the room. Seeing Ward and Meyer, he made in their direction. "They're not subtle, are they?"

"Doesn't look that way," Ward agreed.

"We clearly have no choice but to talk with these bastards."

On the screen was a new message:

> *Your attempts to contain and control these communications are understood. The impact of those efforts, if allowed to succeed, would exclude the vast majority of the human population and cannot, therefore, be permitted. Because there is no centralized government through which to engage, no macro channel of governmental communication through which the directives and guidance of the Onboarding Commission may be reliably and cohesively conveyed, the outcome of affording any group prominent positioning with respect to these relations would be unreliable and destabilizing to the Earth.*

*   *   *

Jason Clipper and Sergeant Randall had largely completed startup preparations at the Installation. Everything appeared in order. The last of the technical issues; namely, problems getting data to flow between the Installation and the Mayfield lab over the Hawkeye link, had been resolved. Clipper had relaxed a little after that, but soon went to work running simulations that, if the gravity machine itself were actually powered on, would have sent pulses of minute gravity wells into the aether. He hunched over a computer terminal for several minutes as Randall passively surveyed the space until, at once, standing erect and announcing that everything looked good. "I think we're in business. Nothing else can be done until we power up the machine itself." Randall nodded approvingly. "Anything to drink on the grounds?" Clipper asked.

"Coffee, water, soda."

"Diet Coke?"

"Probably."

It was a sunny day, but a brisk wind had arisen to make it seem cooler than it was – just a few degrees shy of comfortable. Several large military trucks dotted the property, all built to a larger scale than what Clipper was accustomed to seeing on the road. Randall set out for one of them and returned a few minutes later with a bottle of water for himself and a Diet Coke for Clipper, which he accepted gratefully.

They had been standing in the open air, enduring the wind for benefit of the sunshine when a younger man, who Clipper would later learn to be Staff Sergeant Kevin Hosmer, emerged from from the comms truck and approached. "We're on, sir," he said.

"Time to power up?" Clipper asked.

"Yes." Hosmer handed a small radio to him.

Clipper wasn't sure what to do with it at first, then located the send button on its side and pressed it. "Clipper here."

"Jason, it's Ryan Meyer." Clipper was surprised to receive a response, and it made him laugh for an unknown reason. "It's about time to power-up the gravity machine," Meyer continued. "Can you get into position and let us know when you're ready?"

"Two minutes," Clipper said, recovering, then nodded to Randall and Hosmer in a, 'here goes' sort of way. The three men reached the circuit box. All switches were back to the closed position, but the panel door was left open. Next to it, the final, larger power switch that controlled the gravity machine itself was the only remaining power that had yet to be restored. "Ready," Clipper said into the radio.

"Excellent. Stand by."

Chapter 63

April 10, 2024

T he setting at the Mayfield Hammond lab was a recreation of the first failed attempt to communicate with Trial from three weeks before, as if someone had pressed a pause button that placed the world into suspended animation, and then simply resumed. The entourage included Frank Boswell, Margaret Statham, Jeff Ward and a dozen supporting staff. The obvious addition being the president himself, who stood by with cool resolve.

"Ready when you are, sir," Meyer said to the president.

"All preparations complete? Everyone in place?"

Vandoren scanned the room. "Yes, sir."

"Do it," Warren said.

Meyer leaned towards a speakerphone sitting on the table next to the primary terminal, which Clipper's handheld radio had been patched into. Clipper could hear everything that was said in the room, but could only be heard when he pressed the send button on his radio. "Jason, please restore power to the primary gravity device," Meyer said.

There was a short delay, then Clipper's voice came back. "Acknowledged. Five seconds." Then, "Done. It'll take a few seconds to wake up."

"Understood," Meyer said. The group had learned from the first attempt, not to expect immediate responses to anything they did, but this time, there was not much of a wait.

"We're seeing data," Clipper reported over the phone. "Massive data. Outbound."

Ankur leaned into his laptop, slightly away from the main group. "Massive?" he asked, as if it didn't reconcile with what he was seeing from his own computer. Meyer walked around to see what he was looking at. "Only a trickle is visible from our end," Ankur said, pointing to the screen for Meyer's benefit.

"Clipper, how much data are you seeing?" Meyer asked.

"Already at about two gigabytes."

"Gotta be coming in through a side door, probably directly into the Hawkeye," Ankur said, his brow furrowed as he studied his screen.

Mike Parker stepped forward from a corner station, from which he had been watching the flow of data as well. "Agree. They must have planted something on the Hawkeye itself. It's pulling information from everywhere and sending it straight up. It's not passing through the lab here at all."

"Six gigabytes and counting," Clipper said.

The president interrupted. "Let's get to it," he said. The request brought Meyer back to the moment. "Yes, sir," he said, stepping around to retake his seat. "Tell them this, Mr. Meyer: I am Christopher Warren, President of the United States of America. Be advised that the Earth is a sovereign property. The United States and other nations on this planet are, and shall remain, sovereign." He took a breath to say more, but stopped himself. "Go ahead and send that."

Meyer complied.

"Furthermore–" the president began again, but was forestalled by a new message. It came in fast, far more immediately than anyone expected.

Even the galaxy itself is not sovereign.

Warren bit off his next word, tipped momentarily off balance, then forged ahead. "We do not recognize your authority nor jurisdiction over the Earth." Meyer kept up as the president spoke.

"Big ramp up in data. We're approaching a terabyte on the upload," Ankur said, now watching the data as it was metered at both ends of the connection, now able to see the same things Clipper was seeing at his end. "The rate is increasing rapidly. Almost nothing from the lab."

The president reacted. "You are instructed to discontinue upload of data," he said. Meyer took the message and sent.

All eyes diverted to Ankur, who was fixated on his computer. Shortly, he began shaking his head slowly. "No sign of change."

"Damnit!" the president said. "Can we throttle these guys without cutting everything?"

"Maybe," Meyer said, but it'll take time to figure out what they're doing. Truthfully, I wouldn't bet on it. We've already seen that if we close a door, they find another one."

"Or make another one," Ward added.

"Now seeing massive downstream data as well," Ankur called out. He hadn't looked away from his computer screen for even a moment since the data transfer began. "Both directions now: asynchronous. Still massive data going up, and now massive data coming down too."

"Where are they putting it?" Meyer asked.

There was a slight hesitation. "Everywhere," Parker spoke from the perimeter of the group. He was looking to one of the network engineers sitting a good ways away. The man made a scattering gesture with his hands. "They're pushing data everywhere, out over the internet."

"Should we cut the line?" Statham asked.

"No," Warren said. "Whatever is going to happen, I want it to happen here, with our eyes on it. A week from now, this could be happening in North Korea for all we know. Send this," he said to Meyer. "We demand that you cease transfer of data immediately."

Meyer sent. No response.

"Be advised," the president said, a fierceness surfacing in his voice, "that we regard these actions as hostile."

Still nothing.

At a loss, he looked away to the corner of the room, searching his mind for a way to gain control of the situation, but without success. "What is your intent?" he said finally, groping for something to give him even the slightest traction from which to work. Anything that could be the beginnings of cooperation, a point from which to begin a dialog.

Meyer sent the message, and this time a response appeared:

> *We have observed that the boundaries and jurisdictions of national bodies are misaligned, overlapping, and not meaningfully representative of the peoples and resources that happen to fall territorially within them. Because of this, even unilateral engagement with each distinct nation of Earth would bring us no closer to meaningful communication with humanity as a whole.*
>
> *Extraordinary circumstances have mandated premature incorporation of the Earth into the galactic community. For this reason, unconventional methods are required to bring the Earth forward and into alignment, perhaps six human generations earlier than would have been optimal. The activities that are now set in motion are not of a hostile intent; but are imminent.*

*Attempts to disrupt these proceedings will be tolerated
for a period of time; they are symptoms of the very
prematurity that is a recognized characteristic and
challenge of this particular onboarding endeavor.
Over a period equal to six human generations –
equating to 150 years – the objective of this
commission shall be to incubate humanity towards
readiness for less exceptional incorporation into the
galactic body.*

*More direct instructions are forthcoming. Earth's
leadership, even in its current form, is encouraged to
align to its new opportunity. Failure is not an
impossibility.*

The message left a roomful of people standing in a hushed
vacuum of contemplation. The president was first to speak. "Are we
defenseless here?"

Statham almost blurted her answer, as if she had been
waiting for an opening into which to interject her opinion. "We have
a few days, maybe weeks. We should shut down the line, pick apart
their methods, and learn how to block them."

Warren looked to her in disbelief. "Margaret, I see a
measure of logic in that. The problem is that we can't block them.
We'd have to shut down every interferometer on the planet, which
won't happen. And even if we could, we'd burn too much clock on
it. We've seen these guys walk through our computer security
systems like wet paper bags. Even if we could learn how to block
whatever techniques they're using today, I have zero confidence that
they'll hold. Zero."

Her lips were pursed with agitation. "As we stand here, Mr.
President, our entire infrastructure is being infiltrated. You have the
ability to halt that, and you're not. I find that unacceptable. We have
learned some of their tactics. Our technical teams have discovered
the gaps the Remotes have exploited to infiltrate our systems. They
may not be as advanced as they have fooled us into believing."

"But that's not quite right, is it?" Riley said. His unexpected comment drew the attention of the room. "I submit that if you were to challenge a Grandmaster to a game of Chess, you would see a demonstration of your own skills, not his. There is no reason to believe, in my opinion, that anything about the true capabilities of the Remotes can be gleaned from the methods they have used to circumvent our security safeguards."

The president seemed to consider Riley's point, then turned back to Statham. "Ms. Statham, frankly, I am perplexed that you do not seem to better grasp our situation. I do not have the ability to stop anything. At best, I can only delay the inevitable by a matter of days, and in doing so, worsen our position – forfeit the only advantage we have, if you could call it that." He looked past her to Jeff Ward. "What is your advice?" The dismissal did not suit Statham well. Her body language communicated hostile agitation, but she didn't speak.

"First, we have to get past these one side declarations and into meaningful dialog. I think you're asking the right questions."

Warren considered for a moment, but wasn't satisfied. He looked past his cast of leaders to find Riley again, standing on the periphery of the group. "What do you make of this?"

Riley waited a moment until it became clear to him, and everyone else in the room, that Warren was waiting for his response. Finally, he said: "It's unlikely that any human was surprised to learn that the Earth had been settled, that laws had been written by the time he was born into it. Clearly, the Earth is part of ... or at least, falls within the territory of some larger community. That's not going to change. We cannot view this as a matter of physical self-defense. If there is a community, there are laws. We should learn our rights. We should demand to know them."

Riley's words hit Warren like a break in the clouds, setting his mind on a new course; one, that for the first time, appeared to have promise. He didn't hesitate. "Mr. Meyer send this: What are our rights?"

Chapter 64

Jason Clipper walked into a break room in the IT building to find Ryan Meyer sitting alone at a table, lost in thought. He fetched a drink from the vending machine and turned to face him. "Mind if I have a seat?"

The question seemed to stir Meyer from a dream. "Absolutely. Please," he said, gesturing to a nearby chair. He sat back and pulled his coffee cup in closer to make room.

"You look like a man with something on his mind."

Meyer raised an eyebrow. "Maybe. Something's been bothering me a little."

"Me too. Want to go first?"

Meyer considered the question for only a second. "I've been looking back over the initial letter of intent. There's some peculiar wording in there. Granted, could be a matter of translation, but I don't think so. Trial is as articulate with the English language as any of us ... not sure how he manages it, but he is." Meyer broke off as if further explanation was unnecessary, and turned in his chair to face Clipper directly. "Let's face it man, we're not that advanced. Our technology has got to look like sticks and stones to these guys. It's starting to bother me a little, and I'm not entirely sure why. In fact, I'm starting to worry that we're a little too quick to accept this technology premise." He grabbed up his coffee for a sip. "That's my issue – for the next five minutes, anyway – what's yours?"

"Uh, I made it up. I got nothin'."

Meyer gave a grunt and sat his cup back onto the table. "Back to me then. First of all, I can't imagine any technologies in our possession that, in comparison to the Remotes, would amount to anything remarkable, so why the hubbub? Second, there's the statement in one of the later paragraphs of that first message that talks about us having access to advanced technology. *Access*," he said, repeating the word for emphasis. "...the judgement of the Advocate is that continued progress of Earth along its present course, given its *access* to advanced capabilities, yada yada yada... Why would he say access to advanced capabilities rather than that we have advanced capabilities?"

Clipper saw the point. "I thought the wording seemed a little odd too, but didn't dwell on it. It is kind of weird."

"And then," Meyer said, energized by the conversation, "there's the problem with comms."

"Meaning?"

"We think we know how it works. Well," he said, adding a disclaimer, "we can't exactly explain it, and we don't understand all the underlying physics as yet, but we're getting the gist of it, and based on what we know so far, our system shouldn't be capable of doing what it is."

"In what way?"

"Our gravity machine is small. Primitive. Localized. Low power. We've done some math. It works better than it should. Even with the gaps in our understanding, we can see that we shouldn't be able to reach these guys, but we are."

Clipper's eyebrows furrowed. "Are you sure? How can you know that?"

"It's not that tough, really. Think about it. Even though we don't understand the details yet, we can see the behaviors. Some guy who knows nothing of sound propagation could tell you that no matter how powerful a sound system might be, he couldn't use it to broadcast a concert from here to Moscow. Would he need to understand the physics of signal degradation to know that? I don't think so. He'd just know. Another guy with barely enough mechanical acumen to put a charge on his car knows that the car is not going to break the sound barrier. I'm telling you; our equipment isn't up to the things it seems to be doing."

Clipper let out a low whistle.

Meyer said: "Not even sure why, but I'm a little creeped out about it."

"Have you talked to anyone about this?"

"Mentioned it to Ward a couple times. He doesn't think there's anything there, which annoys the hell out of me."

Clipper took to thinking, a somewhat disturbing thought occurring to him. In all his years of knowing John Riley, he knew one thing for certain; no one would be ahead of him in seeing and understanding anything about gravitation, much less if it involved his own creation. The thought sank to his stomach and took the form of instant anxiety. It could explain a lot of things, not the least of which being, why the man had become so scarce over the past couple of weeks. He reached an immediate conclusion. "Hey man," he said, "I've gotta run." But Meyer had already returned to his own thoughts, and acknowledged Clipper's leaving with only a distracted nod.

Walking out of the break room Clipper pulled out his phone and sent a text.

where r u, i have a question

Riley's response was slow coming, but finally arrived a few minutes later.

can it wait?

probably. does it have to?

Another long wait.

meet me in the lab in 45

Clipper slid the phone back into his pocket. With nowhere else to go, he made for the lab right then. He'd wait there and collect his thoughts. Part way there, though, his phone chimed in his pocket. It was a new message from Riley:

conf 3B224

Clipper didn't ask if he should wait. He changed course towards the elevators and seconds later emerged onto the 3rd floor, reading signs in the corridor to orient himself. He rounded a corner that led into a long hall to find Riley standing alone in wait. The look on his face communicated, in an instant, that there would be more to the impending discussion than even Clipper had imagined. Something else told him that it was not necessary to ask questions.

When he approached, Riley simply motioned him into a large conference room. Clipper hadn't seen this one before. There was a long table at its center, around which sat a host of unexpected characters: Jeff Ward, Martin Moore, Natalie Briggs, Margaret Statham, Frank Boswell, and most unexpectedly, Brian Matthews. Clipper shot a final double-take to Riley, who volunteered no explanation, before entering. There was an image displayed on the screen at the end of the elongated room. Clipper took a seat, and was still studying it when Michael Parker and Ryan Meyer entered looking no less bewildered than himself. They navigated the space and settled in without comment.

Chapter 65

April 17, 2024

There was an uneasy tension in the room, and Clipper knew he wasn't imagining it. He saw it on every face around the table as each one studied the image on the display screen, struggling to discern some meaning from it.

Ward didn't bother acknowledging the newcomers to the room. "I'll cut to it," he said. Even at that, only a couple of heads turned away from the display. "First, we've had time to look over the plans that were sent to us by the Remotes. As expected, they are indeed schematics for building what they term, a *Relativistic Geometric Pattern Inducer*. To us, it's a gravitational comms device like the one Mr. Riley and his team constructed for Mayfield Hammond, only much more sophisticated. No surprises there.

Construction is underway on the new design at three different locations." He took a breath and leaned forward to place his elbows onto the table, balling a fist inside the palm of his other hand. "So, why are we here? You've clearly noticed the image. Before I explain what it is, I'll add some background to help you understand not only where we are, but how we got here." There was nervous fidgeting from some in the group, but no one spoke.

"On the Saturday morning after the gravity machines were brought back up, I received a phone call from John Riley. He had had time by then, to fully scrutinize the alien schematics and confirm that they were what we expected. He had also learned a few other things. Mr. Meyer, you are correct; our comms device works better than it should. Much better, in fact. Based on what Mr. Riley learned from the alien schematics, and his own conjecture, he was able to perform calculations confirming that our communications with the Remotes is impossible with only what we have in terms of physical equipment. We also know that since we brought communications back online, there has been non-stop traffic to and from the Earth over the – I'll call it the *galactic channel*. The traffic itself is so heavily encrypted that we may never be able to peer into it. Our best and brightest are working the issue around the clock, but so far we have not formulated even the most basic understanding of their cryptography. That thread will continue indefinitely, but we can't wait for it. What we can do is watch for signs of what the Remotes are looking at. What information are they collecting and where are they getting it? It is a more complex problem than meets the eye. So, while some of our best talent continues to work the cryptography lane, others are constructing models to correlate pulses of incoming and outgoing remote traffic with upticks in traffic across our own internet. It is a staggering endeavor. In fact, I would not have appreciated the complexities myself before a few days ago."

"Frankly, at first, I had low expectations that anything meaningful could be learned, even if successful, but I've already been surprised. The image on the screen is a closeup of the surface of the moon." He pointed to the image with a finger without unballing his first. "It's an area near the north pole, just off the southeastern edge of a crater called *Plaskett U*. There are a few interesting things in this image. It was obtained by the *Lunar Reconnaissance Orbiter*, or LRO, only a few years ago. The LRO is a probe that began orbiting the moon in 2009. Understandably, there has been an enormous uptick in interest in space and astronomy by the general public since First Contact was announced. Accounting for that as much as possible, we have observed inordinate interest in the moon on the part of the Remotes. We have now identified a few discrete inquiries that are believed, with fairly high confidence, to have originated from them."

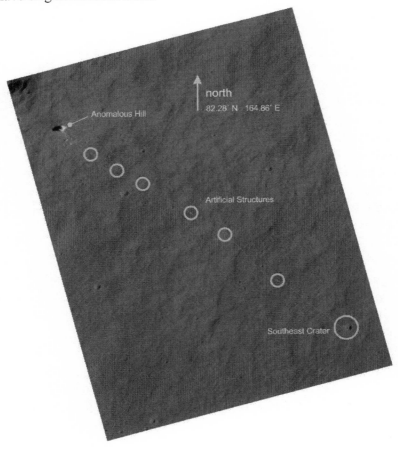

"This image was taken from the Lunar Orbital Data Explorer website, which is openly available to anyone. Similar images can be obtained via the *lroc.sese.asu.edu* site hosted by Arizona State University. Zooming in, we clearly see what appears to be a trail, presumably made by mechanized vehicles, crossing an area between a large towering structure, which looks to be nothing more than a hill, and a small crater several hundred meters to the south and east. A little after 3:00 AM Eastern Time on the morning of April 10th, only hours after comms with the Remotes was restored, the computer systems that house mission information for NASA and the JPL were compromised. Audit trails reveal that among the information accessed were high-resolution images of this area."

"These images are real," Ward said. "Something *is* there. And I suspect it's not the only thing we'll find on the moon, it's only what we've noticed so far. Other anomalous access attempts by the Remotes over the past weeks suggest that we are on the cusp of discovering a great many things we never suspected – that we never knew about this place we call home. As for this," he pointed again to the screen, "the questions are; what is it, and who put it there? Us? The Russians? The Chinese? The Remotes? We don't know the answer." He looked to Natalie, "Next image please." She clicked a button and a new image appeared. This one, a map showing the anomaly's location on the lunar surface.

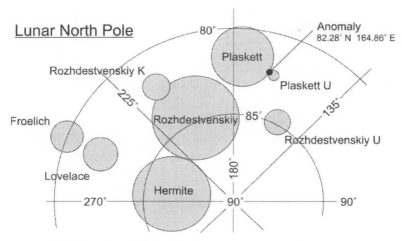

There was silence in the room that lasted for several seconds, finally broken by Ryan Meyer. "It makes sense," Meyer said. "It makes a lot of sense." He then rounded unexpectedly on Jeff Ward, pointing an accusing finger in his direction. "You sir have excluded me from this information and there is no justification for it! I brought these same concerns to you weeks ago, and you disregarded my every statement."

Ward was not surprised by the outburst, and his response was no less expected. He held up a hand to calm him. "Your points are valid, Mr. Meyer, I won't dispute that. The reasons I did the things I did will be clarified soon enough, but it will be for a different conversation – for a different day. The important thing is that you are here now, in this room with the rest of us. You are being brought up to speed and will be a part of what's next."

Meyer was upset, but the intrigue of what could follow seemed enough to put his grievances temporarily on hold. "I'll venture a guess," he said. "This looks like a mining operation. If it is, my bet is on the Chinese. They went public years ago about their interest in mining helium-3 from moondust."

"Helium-3?" Statham asked.

"Yes, helium-3. Today, we get nuclear power by splitting atoms. The problem is that it produces nuclear waste and radiation.

There is a common belief that helium-3 could allow us to build fusion – as opposed to fission – reactors that produce energy in much the same way that the sun does. The difference is that it would be clean. There would be no radiation or nuclear waste – or at minimum, the byproducts would be more manageable. The sun emits a great deal of Helium-3, but it gets filtered out by our atmosphere, so we don't have any here on earth to speak of. The moon is a different story. It has no atmosphere, so it's been soaking up Helium-3 for billions of years. It's all over the surface."

"Would it be worth the trouble?"

"You'd be surprised. As little as 25 tons of Helium-3 could power the entire United States for a year. That puts it in excess of three billion dollars per ton, give or take some pocket change."

"The bottom line," Ward said, cutting the discussion short, "is that we're going up there. We're going back to the moon."

"When?" Statham said.

"As soon as we can get there."

"Mr. Meyer," Riley said, "your points about helium-3 are valid. We've actually considered the same possibilities, but also suspect that this has to be about more than just that. There are a couple reasons. One, if it were all about mining helium-3 and returning it to earth, why would the Remotes be interested?"

"Maybe they're not," Meyer said. "So they looked at this image. That doesn't guarantee they found what they were looking for."

"True," Riley conceded, "but we think there could be yet another explanation, which is that, perhaps, the helium-3 is being mined and used on the moon."

"For what?"

"To provide power to whatever is at the other end of this road," Riley said, pointing to the image where the trail ended at the crater to the southeast. "We think there is a chance that this crater houses the opening to something below ground. It could be a cave, or perhaps a subterranean compound."

Meyer squinted at the image. "And why do you think so?"

Riley pushed a button on his laptop. The image zoomed in. It was badly pixelated, but discernible. "Two objects are catching sunlight in this image," he said. "One is sitting within the crater. The other is at its edge, near the point where the trail forks into two lanes as it comes in. We think they could be vehicles used to shuttle materials to, or from the hill. The crater itself is not big. Whatever is being collected and driven across this road has to go somewhere. There are no other discernible paths leading away from this point, so we think something is there."

"Okay," Meyer said. "Let me summarize then. There is some sort of facility on the moon, and whatever it is, it could be providing the missing pieces that allow our simple communication devices to work. Is that what I'm hearing?"

"We don't know," Riley said. "The only thing we can do is get up there and take a closer look."

Ward spoke up. "It'll take some time to get a person back to the moon. Until then, we're working with NASA to get a probe up there. Something along the lines of the rovers they've been sending to Mars. Indications are that we should be able to get one there within five weeks or so. NASA's done this type of thing enough that they can do it in their sleep. Either way; please regard this information as extremely confidential. No leaks. None. We want to get there first, and we can only assume that this discovery won't remain a secret for long. We're into a new space race, only this time the stakes are immeasurably higher. That's all for now. If your services are required for next steps, you will be contacted by Ms. Briggs within 24 hours."

The room adjourned. Riley hadn't seen Brian Matthews since the day of the initial lab breach. Matthews stood with the rest of the group and made for the door without looking in his direction. Riley called out to him. "Mr. Matthews, do you have a moment?"

Matthews paused, considering the request. Only then did he look towards Riley, approaching him like an untrusted rival.

"I never had a chance to apologize for all of this," Riley said. "To call this unexpected would be something of an understatement."

"It's not over," Matthews said.

Riley wasn't sure of his meaning. "Excuse me?"

"I hope you know that you have breached our contractual agreements in so many ways that, not only will you not profit from any of it, I will see to it that you have to borrow your lunch money for the rest of your life." He grunted a laugh. "That is, after all this ludicrousness is over." He smirked and gestured around the room. "Your antics have cost Mayfield Hammond tens ... no, hundreds of millions of dollars. Maybe billions. If you think I will just let bygones be bygones, you are delusional."

Riley realized that he shouldn't have been surprised by Matthews' anger, but couldn't help being caught off guard. "Very short sighted, I'm afraid," Riley said, unfazed.

"We'll see," Matthews said.

"Indeed, we will."

Matthews turned and walked out of the room.

Chapter 66

April 17, 2024

"You were right about one thing Jeff," Vandoren said. "We're seeing a little of everything. The Doomsayers are doing their thing. Religious groups are split; half in denial, the others claiming that all of this is fulfilment of their own prophecies."

"Of course," the president said. Frank Boswell, Margaret Statham, Jeff Ward and Angela Vandoren were sitting at the coffee table in the center of the Oval Office.

Vandoren went on. "Virtually every government on the globe is protesting our handling of First Contact, and demanding to be made a bigger part."

The president motioned a question with an open hand. "But everyone has access now. We have no control over who the Remotes talk with. Plus, the secrets are out. Everyone will have their own comms machines before you know it."

"True, but there is a lingering perception that we're still hiding something."

"How long before other facilities start coming online?"

"Looks like another couple of weeks or so, from what we're seeing. Riley's estimates where a little optimistic, but not much. It's working to our favor, so no complaints. Virtually every marginally advanced country in the world is building at least one. The North Koreans are building six ... that we know of."

The president grunted. "They should put their money to better use."

"Also true," Vandoren said. "Still, it may not hurt to begin being a little more inclusive of the rest of the world. Once these other machines begin coming online, we'll never overcome the animosity that's building – whether it's warranted or not."

"Okay," the president said, conceding the point. "Let's plan a symposium, then. Announce it today."

"United Nations?"

"No. We'll host it."

"Okay," Vandoren said, making a note on her tablet with a stylist, then returning to her readout. "Let's see; there are a few riots here and there, but not as many as we feared. Fortunately, none of significance here in the US." She swept a finger slowly up the glass of the tablet, scrolling the document. "This one may require attention soon if it doesn't self-correct: about 12% of the workforce still hasn't reported back to work since the address to the nation last month. We're seeing signs that this one is trending back in the right direction, but we'll need to keep an eye on it."

Warren nodded. "Jeff, what's going on with onboarding? Why aren't we hearing more from the Remotes?"

"Apparently," Ward said, "when we consented to move forward with onboarding, we didn't become onboarded, we only agreed to start the process. We're also on some sort of exception path, so who knows what that could involve?"

The president leaned back, cradling a cup of coffee. "Nothing in this world is easy, I guess I shouldn't expect something out of this world to be."

"We're trying to understand the onboarding process now," Ward said. "We've pulled together some thoughts on it – what might make sense. Unfortunately, since we're an exception, to Angela's point, we don't know how reality might deviate from our educated guesses. Current thinking is that we'll get more hands-on attention from our overseer. How much, as compared to what norm, we don't know."

"More attention from Trial, then?"

"Yes."

"Such as?"

"Unknown. The Remotes haven't been particularly open with information. Supposedly, more is coming once we get further into onboarding, but we are beginning to get a few tidbits of information now. For one, we're decidedly not alone. Our estimates of the number of stars in the galaxy were low. There are about 184 billion – if our new friends are to be believed. Our guess had been closer to 100 billion. And, one out of every 14,000 or so has intelligent life; some extremely advanced, some primitive. That translates to about 15 million worlds."

The president stopped midway to setting his cup onto the table. "15 million? Planets? With intelligent life?"

"That's correct, sir."

He followed through with setting the cup down. "We've been scanning the skies for decades. Where the hell are they?"

"Turns out, they're not talking with radio. SETI, the *Search for Extraterrestrial Intelligence*, has been, in a sense, looking for smoke signals. No one is using radio waves, they're too slow. They're only used locally – not for interstellar communication."

"Gravity machines are the ticket then?"

"Appears so," Ward said. "Anyway, of the 15 million planets with intelligent life, almost all are part of this alliance called the *Assemblies of the Living* – at least the ones that are advanced enough. There are some holdouts, but just a handful, comparatively. The next part isn't particularly flattering. It seems that planets with a recorded history of less than 45 thousand years are generally considered primitive. We come in at around ten, if we're generous with our accounting."

The president took in the words, then laughed. "We're primitive, huh? So my wife's been right all along."

"Looks that way. On the other end, the scale goes into the billions of years."

Frank Boswell whistled.

The president said: "You're telling me there are planets out there with recorded histories of billions of years?"

"The oldest, according to the chart we saw, weighs in at 4.3 billion years. It's called, *One*. That's how it translates to us, anyway."

"Appropriate."

"True. And there have been older ones. Far older. That's just the one with the longest contiguous civilization that still survives. Apparently, advanced civilizations began to appear when the galaxy was only about five-and-a-half billion years old – nearly eight billion years ago. Some of them lasted a long time, but none survive today. On the upside, our estimates of the age of the galaxy were almost spot-on: a little under 13.5 billion years."

"What do you know?" the president said, as if he had been handed a consolation prize.

"And we have some detail on it," Frank Boswell said. "It's interesting stuff. Apparently, the galaxy is divided into ages. We're in the seventh age right now." He looked to his own tablet and began counting off with his fingers as he read. "*Idempotent, Chaotic, Formative, Recondite, Divergent, Convergent* and *Emergent*. The next one, which we're not into yet, is *Ascendant*."

"Did you say, Ascendant?" the president asked, leaning forward.

"I did, why?"

"Trial. He's a member of the Ascendancy, am I right?"

"Ahh," Boswell said, absorbing the meaning. "There's a connection."

"Not sure what it tells us, but it's something," Ward said.

The president thought a moment longer, then returned to the conversation. "With only 10 thousand years under our belt, this isn't much of an ego-builder."

"No, it's not," Ward agreed. "In fact, we're not exactly big news. To them, us coming along is like the birth of another child in a state with the population of Pennsylvania. We don't exactly throw a parade each time that happens, and I don't think we can expect one either. But, we have received something of a welcome package – lots of info about galactic history is starting to come down."

"We've also learned," Boswell cut in, "that we're classified as an *evolutionary world*. We get what that probably means, but we're clueless about what it would mean not to be. What else is there? We just don't know."

"Is it just about the time? What makes a planet primitive?"

"Apparently, there's a window within which civilizations seem to move on from the stuff they consider primitive. It's not a short list. Not surprisingly, fossil fuels are a big indicator. They seem not to care about the use of them, per se; it's just a sign of primitiveness. Most civilizations move past them so quickly that it's not even a blip on the chart. Then, there are the bigger issues, most of which Trial has already mentioned: war, crime, technology, hunger, disease, pollution, population, resource consumption, waste, proliferation into space, types of governments, law, justice; that sort of thing."

"They seem to care about the right things, at least," Statham said. "We can take some solace in that. If their behaviors are reflected within these concerns, it should take a whole lot of bad scenarios off the table."

"Good point," Ward said. "At least one odd thing is taking shape, though. The galactic encyclopedia we've received so far is not all that complete. Notably, the history of our own Solar system is especially sparse."

"In what way?" the president asked.

"We're seeing more complete histories of other star systems than our own. Even simple things seem to be missing: if or when life evolved. The state of technology, if it's there. That sort of thing. None of those details are included in our own history."

"Do you think it's intentional?"

"In fact, we do. Our history isn't just sparse, it looks redacted."

"That could make sense," Statham said. "We're an exception case. There's a reason for that. We're bound to find out what it is sooner or later. Maybe it's not all about us like we've assumed. Maybe there's a history here."

Chapter 67

April 17, 2024

"I saw Brian Matthews today," Riley said.

"That sounds fun," Melissa said.

They were sitting on Melissa's white sofa, drinking wine. "This is becoming one of my better habits," he said, lifting his glass.

"Mine too. How'd it go?"

"With Matthews? He's, uh, what would be the best word? ...*disgruntled.*"

"Disgruntled? Hmm. You can't do any better?"

"I'm sure I could, but I'll stick with that for now. How has work been?"

"Not as bad as I feared," Melissa said. "I don't want to stay in production support for long, but it's not killing me."

"Glad to hear."

She sat her wine glass to the side and scooted closer to Riley. "Are we about to be assimilated into an alien way of life?"

Riley grinned. "It's already happening."

She took Riley's glass from his hand and sat it down too. "I want to know something," she said. He held her gaze but didn't speak. "Is life still worth living?"

"Always," he said. "Life is all that matters. The Remotes didn't reach out to Earth to see the Grand Canyon, or the beaches, or even the wildlife. They came because of us. That tells me that the lives we have are even more meaningful than we may have realized ourselves. Even from across the span of the galaxy."

"I want to live then," she said, and kissed him.

"Me too."

Chapter 68

April 18, 2024

Since shortly after Sarah's arrival, she and AJ had been on something of a pre-honeymoon honeymoon. AJ's involvement with First Contact had ended abruptly. They lingered in Charlotte with nothing to do for days, waiting for a phone call that never came, before embarking on a tour of discovery across North Carolina. They finally ended up in Charleston, South Carolina, where they took in the Georgian, Italianate and Queen Anne architectures of the town with quiet walks and horse-drawn carriage rides.

They were standing on the deck of the now retired USS Yorktown in Charleston Harbor. Despite the sun and the water, the conversation had taken a serious turn. "I can't reconcile this with my faith, or anything else for that matter," Sarah said. "It's all so unexpected."

"Does it really conflict with faith? I don't know that it has to," AJ said.

She laughed, futilely. "Maybe it doesn't in any concrete way, but it's starting to fail the plausibility test – at least with me. Could there really be 15 million planets with life out there? Just in our galaxy? *In the beginning, God created the heavens and the earth?* It's like saying, God created the entire city of Chicago, and your mailbox. We have half the clergy out there calling this Trial character the White Horseman." She grunted, as if the thought was disappointingly inevitable. "How baroque."

"The White Horseman? The Apocalyptic Conqueror?"

"That's the one."

"Should have seen that coming." He laughed, then apologized. "I'm sorry," he said, but soon Sarah was laughing too.

"I don't want to be a part of that," she said, suddenly somber again. "Every preacher with a mic believes it's his divine duty to explain what's happening in terms of his own doctrine, which usually doesn't agree with what the guy in the church on the next corner is saying. It's ludicrous. I think I'm beginning to realize that it's time for new beginnings, and I'm struggling with it. I don't know how best to say it, but I think that from here forward, I will believe what happens. That will be my faith."

"I like it," AJ said. "I think that goes for me too."

"But don't forget, Mr. Jacobs; you've made a promise to me."

He smiled. "Indeed I have, but that promise never required a 3rd party, or anybody else's notion of faith to make it mean what it means."

Sarah had just snapped a picture of him with her mobile phone, when AJ's phone rang in his pocket. He answered, looking over the harbor towards Drum Island as an unfamiliar voice addressed him from over the line. He noticed Sarah's concern and raised an eyebrow with an, *it's okay*, gesture, but he could see that it didn't help.

"Now?" AJ said into the phone, uncertainly. "Uh, we're in Charleston... At this particular moment...? Standing on the deck of the Yorktown, in the harbor... Yes, the aircraft carrier... Seriously?" His eyes tracked back to Sarah. "There's someone with me... Okay." He checked his watch. "45 minutes?" He shrugged, disbelieving. "Yes... Yes, we'll stay right here." He dropped the line.

"You're not going to believe this," he said, looking at his phone as if it had suddenly revealed itself as an undercover spy that could no longer be trusted, then slid it back into his pocket.

"Is it bad?"

"I don't think so. I hope not. I've been summoned back to Mayfield Hammond. They're sending a helicopter."

"A helicopter?" She took in the words with incredulity. A moment later she began looking around, taking in the unfamiliar location, realizing the predicament that it would leave her in. "Am I supposed to drive back?"

"I told them I wasn't alone. They're going to let you come. I just need to figure out what to do about the truck." He peered towards the lot where it was parked, but it was out of view.

"I can drive it back," she offered again.

"I'm not sure I trust the truck well enough for you to drive it that far alone. It's not exactly new." She didn't protest. "Besides, I'd rather you come with me if you're okay with it."

Forty minutes later a black dot appeared in the sky to the north. They squinted at it as it grew to where the chop of its blades began to reach them in the form of strange echoes, bouncing from every surface, producing an odd reverberation over the flight deck. "Maybe it wasn't a false alarm for you to come after all," AJ said, turning to Sarah before the noise overtook them. "I can't tell you how glad I am that you're with me right now."

"Me too."

Jeff Ward was waiting at the entrance to the Mayfield IT building when AJ and Sarah arrived under escort 35 minutes later. AJ introduced Sarah, and brief pleasantries were exchanged, but the moment didn't allow for extending the ritual. "I would offer that this is a confidential matter," Ward said, "but I'm guessing that Ms. Henson is probably as well informed as any of us by now."

"Probably so," AJ said. Ward nodded and turned without further comment.

The lab was its typical crowded self. On entering, AJ spotted Riley and Clipper talking with Ryan Meyer and made in their direction. On seeing Sarah, Clipper did a double-take.

"Rank does have its privileges," he said, extending a hand to Sarah. "How are you?"

"I'm good," she said, acknowledging both he and Riley, but also scanning the room with fascination. "Talk about not knowing what you don't know," she said, more to herself than anyone else.

"This is Ryan Meyer," Clipper said, "one of the deep thinkers helping us decipher everything that's going on here."

"Mr. Meyer, my pleasure," she said, taking his hand as well.

"Ryan, please," he said, then turned to AJ. "We have new developments." AJ looked to Riley at that, and read concern on his face, but before either could speak, Meyer pointed to an unused, circular table, with a large screen mounted on the wall nearby. "Let's have a seat for a moment," he said, tapping at his tablet. "AJ, it looks like the Remotes are ready to start talking. We've received a fair amount of new text, and I'll cut to it: some of it specifically involves you." The screen on the wall lit up. "This is a fragment of a larger post that was received earlier this morning:"

> *The objectives to which we now align may be reassuring to your concerns. Our goal is that the human race, though impeded from understanding the full depths of moral responsibility, achieve the ideals that, even now, it is able to conceive. Once a creature becomes capable of higher notions of self-awareness and empathy, it is accountable to them. When the mind is able to grasp the higher cognitive functions of introspection, it is required to draw upon them, and to act upon them.*

AJ read the words, then looked back to Meyer expectantly. "This makes sense," he said, "but how–"

"Next," Meyer said, "we received this:"

> *In broad terms, any generation – this being any grouping of individuals identified only by age and likeness to their contemporaries, cross-cutting all other systems of classification such as race, religion, nationality, gender – is quick to embrace improvements and efficiencies as they apply to known areas of need: agriculture, communication, medicine, transportation and the like. The insights, new discoveries and understanding that enable these improvements are broadly labelled as technology. Any group, except for the most aged, tends to adopt new technologies hungrily, even greedily, as they become available.*
>
> *Culture, however, changes through the passage of generations. An individual born into a generation adopts its ideals, begins to embody them, and finally, as his life unfolds, becomes the agent by which they are passed forward. Such an individual generally will not knowingly change with respect to his ideals; in fact, will reject any influence that could be construed as destructive to his culture, even as he embraces*

technological advancements that manifest longer term effects to the same end.

With respect to Earth's national bodies, as previously observed; existing boundaries and jurisdictions are ubiquitously misaligned, overlapping, and not meaningfully representative of the peoples and resources that happen to fall territorially within them. There is, therefore, no governmental channel through which global communications may be reliably conveyed upon the Earth. The global network – the internet – will therefore, be leveraged for ongoing communication. Its current shortcomings – primarily, its susceptibility to censorship and misinformation – will soon be remedied for this new purpose.

In light of these concerns, over the coming years, advancement of humanity will be guided along three tracts; these being technological, cultural, and infrastructural. The goal shall be to bring the three into alignment. Of these, cultural advancement will be primary. To that end, generational conditioning will be brought to bear, beginning immediately, which will teach and implant mandatory standards of behavior, with expected outcomes aligning with the following timeline:

Generation	1	2	3	4	5	6
Year Range	2024 - 2049	2049 - 2074	2074 - 2099	2099 - 2124	2124 - 2149	2149 - 2174
Year Delta	0 - 25	26 - 50	51 - 75	76 - 100	101 - 125	126 - 150
						0-6: Indoctrinated [7]
					0-6: Indoctrinated [7]	7-31: Contributive [7]
				0-6: Indoctrinated [7]	7-31: Indoctrinated [6]	32-56: Assimilated [7]
			0-6: Amenable [5]	7-31: Strategic [5]	32-56: Invested [6]	57-81: Invested [6]
		0-6: Amenable [4]	7-31: Indoctrinated [5]	32-56: Progressive [5]	57-81: Stabilizing [6]	82-106: Supportive [6]
	0-6: Amenable [3]	7-31: Disruptive [3]	32-56: Influential [4]	57-81: Advocative [4]	82-106: Supportive [5]	
	7-31: Adherant [2]	32-56: Receptive [2]	57-81: Accepting [3]	82-106: Inconsequential		
	32-56: Distrustful [1]	57-81: Compliant [1]	82-106: Inconsequential			
	57-81: Resistant [0]	82-106: Inconsequential				
	82-106: Inconsequential					

AJ read the words, then looked back to Meyer. "I'm sorry – still a little lost here."

"I understand," Meyer said. "AJ, this entire communique was addressed to you."

The words didn't translate well in AJ's mind. He sat pondering them for several seconds before his mind could queue up a response. "I typed two simple words," he said. "That's all!"

"We know. We don't get it either. What we need for you to do is respond and defer future messages to the president."

"Will that work?"

"We hope so."

AJ looked around the table. All eyes were on him. Each one communicated a degree of astonishment that, were it not for the weight of the moment, could have launched him into a fit of laughter. "This has to be–"

"I agree," Jeff Ward said from over his shoulder. "It has to be a joke, except it's not. We need you to fix this. Then, you and Ms. Henson, hopefully, won't need to be bothered any further."

"Trial clearly distrusts every government on the planet – including ours," Riley said. "It may not be as simple as that."

"Agreed, but we have to try."

"So, what do we need to do?" Sarah said. Her comment drew surprised looks from virtually every person at the table. No one had actually expected her to speak.

Ward looked at her for a long moment, as if deciding whether to acknowledge her. His eyes then passed to AJ. "We're going to ask Mr. Jacobs to identify himself, then recuse himself from the conversation," he said.

AJ realized at once – it was astonishing but undeniable – that Ward was leery of him. There was no mistaking it, and something told him it wasn't a good position to be in. "Tell me what to do," he said.

Meyer spoke again. "We've drafted a dialogue. We'd like for you to enter it into the console over there," he said, pointing to the same terminal from which all other communications had taken place so far. AJ looked across the room reflexively, to see the now-familiar location where it had all begun. "Here's what we have,"

Meyer said. He tapped again at the tablet and a few brief paragraphs appeared on the display screen:

> *I am Andrew Seymour Jacobs. My understanding is that am addressing a member of the Ascendancy, whose name is Trial. As yet, I have received no meaningful information about the nature and purpose of the Ascendancy, nor Trial, as an individual.*
>
> *I am a citizen of the United States of America. My presence at the point of First Contact between our two parties, which occurred on March 10, 2024, Earth time, was incidental. I serve no official capacity to the government of the United States, nor did I play any part in developing the means by which contact was made possible.*
>
> *Going forward, please direct all queries directly to Mr. Christopher Warren, elected President of the United States of America.*
>
> *Thank you.*

AJ read the words then nodded to Jeff Ward. "Okay, when do we do it?"

"Let's do it now," Ward said.

AJ rose to his feet, picked up the tablet that contained the script, and walked across the lab floor. He didn't wait for anyone. He sat down, and without asking questions, began to type. The words unfolded across the computer monitor, and simultaneously, across many of the large display screens mounted on the walls. He had typed the first few sentences by the time the group shuffled in behind. He finished typing the text and transmitted it without a word. Something about the moment had angered him, although he knew there was no reason for it. What else could he have expected? Still, despite how irrational his irritation was, it was real. He could feel Sarah to his left, standing closer than anyone else. He wondered, vaguely, how she felt about it. Relieved, most likely.

The cursor pulsated at the bottom of the screen as it always did, and AJ watched it dispassionately, determined not to move or acknowledge anyone until Trial responded. Once that happened, he would take to his feet, walk out of the lab, and never look back.

The response came:

> *The nature of the Ascendancy is not altogether straightforward. Its goals and purposes, without exception, prove illusive to those of evolutionary worlds. Information about the Ascendancy, and myself, will be disclosed in due time. Please strive to understand that limitations of disclosure are not a matter of secrecy, but a simple function of the capacity of comprehension on the part of evolutionary creatures.*

> *I am Trial. I am the face of the Ascendancy in the matter of the assimilation of the Earth into galactic function. The activities that have been undertaken at my instruction are not arbitrary. Heads of state will be addressed in due time. Andrew Seymour Jacobs will receive and respond as required, to any and all queries.*

As astonishing as the words were, AJ was not shaken. He felt Sarah's hand rest on his shoulder, and Jeff Ward began to speak, but his mind couldn't focus on what was being said. He typed a new message, suddenly disinclined to ask for permission:

Why Andrew Seymour Jacobs?

The response was the most immediate that had ever yet been received. Andrew sent the question, and the response appeared in no more time than the latency of the transmission itself; under seven seconds.

> *Andrew Seymour Jacobs' identity is now established. No earthly preparation, nor affiliations, nor training, nor authority, nor personal interest, nor disposition, nor intelligence, nor insight, nor history, nor office,*

*nor influence, nor talent, better qualify any other
individual for the requirements at hand.*

AJ pushed away from the terminal and swiveled to face
Sarah. Other voices were talking, but they were disconnected. He
and Sarah looked at each other, alone in the room again. "Are you
still okay with me?" he said to her.

"Yes," she said. Her voice was unexpectedly firm.

Another voice resolved itself. It was Meyer. Like Sarah,
something about Trial's words had galvanized him. "New plan!" he
said, forcefully. "Ms. Briggs," he said, calling to her from across the
room. She heard her name and searched for its source. When they
made eye contact, she immediately made in his direction.

"What is it?" she said.

"I see none of the president's immediate staff on hand.
Please get word to the White House that our plans have changed."

Chapter 69

April 22, 2024

"I'm not exactly sure what we're talking about here,"
President Christopher Warren said into the video
conferencing camera. He was sitting in the Oval Office,
behind his desk. "You're telling me that the rover is
specially designed for icy terrain?"

"That is correct. It's slated for Europa, 2026."

"My question is simple: Will it function on the moon?"

The president was talking with Paula Weinberg, NASA
Administrator, and Anthony Rupp, Deputy NASA Administrator.
The two were sitting in a large conference room, occupying two
chairs of 20 that surrounded a large table somewhere on the
sprawling Johnson Space Center campus in Houston. "Mr.
President, I see the big picture here," Weinberg said. "I get it. I

really do. The rover will work. It'll be like playing basketball on ice skates, but it'll get the job done. My only point is that it's a strange beast. It's got huge wheels – comparatively – with retractable spikes. The wheels are designed to heat up to melt away ice, but they're likely to become clogged with dust on the moon – and it won't take long. They'll pick up weight and bog the rover down. The strain to the motors could bring the whole thing to a halt before it makes 100 meters. The other worry is heat. Plaskett U is in direct sunlight for the next 37 days. We focused all of our energy in designing this rover to handle the cold. Extreme cold; in the neighborhood of minus 300 degrees Fahrenheit. On the moon, it'll be at the opposite end of the spectrum; above 220 degrees Fahrenheit. It has no shielding nor insulation for that environment. We'll be better off taking the time to replace the wheels with something better suited to the terrain, and adding insulation to block the heat. Otherwise, even if the wheels don't get us stuck, we're going to melt within the first 10 minutes."

"How long will all that take?"

"Three weeks. We'll have to fabricate everything."

"How about the launch vehicle?"

Weinberg looked to Rupp. He inclined his head, uncertainly. "Best we've got on such short notice is one of the SpaceX rockets. They're not designed–"

"Yes, yes, I know," Weinberg said. "How long?"

Rupp didn't appreciate the interruption but moved on. "At breakneck speed – six days," he said.

"You've got that long," Warren said. "Do whatever you can to get the rover suited up for its new purpose. Put the best cameras on it that we've got. We'll just have to set it down somewhere that gives us a decent view of this moon structure from the start. If it can't move 10 feet without breaking down, it'll still get us a lot more information than we have now. Meanwhile, let's start planning another rover or two that are better suited for the job. You're telling me that the next gen rover – the one you're building now – will have a drone that can fly around independently?"

"Yes."

"Can we put the drone on this one?"

"The drone itself is there," Weinberg said. "It uses micro-rockets instead of propeller fans – and it's already testing out fairly well – but the control systems that will allow us to operate it remotely won't be ready for prime time for a few more months at least. By that time, the next rover will be ready anyway, so we may as well go with what we have for now."

Warren didn't like it, but conceded. "Understood," he said. "Now tell me about the prospects of getting a human being up there."

Chapter 70

April 22, 2024

R yan Meyer had taken a liking to the Situation Room. Next to the Mayfield lab, it was not overwhelmingly impressive, but the coffee was great. He, Jeff Ward, Frank Boswell and Margaret Statham were sitting in wait for the president's arrival. Angela Vandoren stood at an adjacent counter typing at her laptop computer. The president was set to arrive at any second. The text from the last exchange between AJ and Trial, which solidified AJ's ambiguous role in the relationship with the Remotes, was displayed on the large screen at the end of the room.

When the president entered, his eyes immediately locked onto it, and he maneuvered the chair at the end of the long table into position and sat down without diverting his eyes from it. After reading, he lapsed into thought. No one interrupted.

"Tell me if you see this the way I do," he said, finally. "We are expected to acknowledge and respect their government while they completely ignore ours?"

Both Ward and Statham spoke at the same time. Neither was willing to yield, so the answer became a contest of one speaking over the other that the president did not find amusing. "One at a time," he said with obvious irritation, pointing to Statham.

Whatever the longer version of her answer had been, she chose not to repeat it. "Yes, sir, that is essentially our interpretation as well."

"Anything to add, Jeff?"

"No, sir."

"Well, it's not gonna happen. What are our options?"

The question was directed to Meyer. He looked to Ward before speaking, then back to the president. "The nature of AJ's role is far from clear, sir. Trial did not go so far as naming him an official liaison. It almost reads more like a, 'I'll talk with whomever I choose' kind of statement."

The president looked back at the message. "True, but it's more than just that, isn't it? He basically said that no one on earth is qualified for the role, so it may as well be AJ, since he's already a known quantity. My take is that it's essentially the same thing." Meyer didn't respond, and the president went on. "I want to know some things. Why have we learned nothing about our rights? Why are we an exception in their onboarding process, and what will the impact of that be? Have we made headway on any of these fronts?"

"We expect to begin learning more in the very near term," Ward said. "This dialog with AJ feels different than anything we've seen so far. It has an immediacy to it. Trial indicated that he's about to put some things into motion. In fact, he said they would begin immediately."

The president groaned and rubbed his eyes. "Anything been observed to that effect so far?"

"Trial laid out a 150-year plan," Ward said. "The ramp into something like that may not have visible impacts for quite a while."

Boswell interrupted. "Something unusual has begun at the Mayfield datacenter, sir."

Ward stopped, surprised.

"What is it?" the president asked.

"Until now, only a few servers at the datacenter had been commandeered by the Remotes. Within a few minutes of the last message from Trial, every server in the datacenter – save the initial computers they've been using all along – went down. Row after row of servers went offline, then rebooted. Now they're coming back up, but they're all black boxes to us now, just like the first ones."

"Trial said that he was going to remedy our internet's security issues," Statham said. "Maybe this is the start of it." She shook her head. "We can still cut power."

"Won't do a damned thing," Warren said. "Leave it. Our only chance is dialogue. I've got to get more information out of these guys."

Boswell became distracted with his tablet. "We're seeing rolling outages on the internet now, too. It's happening worldwide."

"At least our definitions of the word immediate seem to line up pretty well," Meyer said. He had an amused grin that didn't survive the withering look the statement earned from the president.

"Angela, get a status for me, please."

"Right away," she said.

"Tell me about this plan. What is it, and what does it mean? From the sounds of it, we're all about to be processed. Feels like the Third Reich."

"I wish I could disagree, sir," Ward said. "Trial essentially told us that he wants to bring our technical, cultural and infrastructural maturity into alignment. For the most part, when he says infrastructure, he seems to be referring to government, or matters of state. It's an odd use of the term. Our working assumption is that we'll get clarity on that as things unfold. He doesn't see adoption of technologies as an issue. He claims that people will usually accept anything that makes their lives easier – at least from a technical perspective. And he doesn't like the way we do government. Not us and not anyone else. He has not been shy about that, and has been very forthright in saying that he is going to do something about it. According to him, the primary agent for that change will be culture." He tapped his tablet and a table of data appeared on the display screen. "This is what Trial sent to us this morning. It shows Trial's view of the disposition of each of the next six generations of people, from the perspective of how favorable they are likely to be to the changes he's planning for us.".

Generation	1	2	3	4	5	6
Year Range	2024 - 2049	2049 - 2074	2074 - 2099	2099 - 2124	2124 - 2149	2149 - 2174
Year Delta	0 - 25	26 - 50	51 - 75	76 - 100	101 - 125	126 - 150
	----	---	---	---	---	0-6: Indoctrinated [7]
	----	---	---	---	0-6: Indoctrinated [7]	7-31: Contributive [7]
	----	----	---	0-6: Indoctrinated [7]	7-31: Indoctrinated [6]	32-56: Assimilated [7]
	----	----	0-6: Amenable [5]	7-31: Strategic [5]	32-56: Invested [6]	57-81: Invested [6]
	---	0-6: Amenable [4]	7-31: Indoctrinated [5]	32-56: Progressive [5]	57-81: Stabilizing [6]	82-106: Supportive [6]
0-6: Amenable [3]	7-31: Disruptive [3]	32-56: Influential [4]	57-81: Advocative [4]	82-106: Supportive [5]	
7-31: Adherent [2]	32-56: Receptive [2]	57-81: Accepting [3]	82-106: Inconsequential		
32-56: Distrustful [1]	57-81: Compliant [1]	82-106: Inconsequential			
57-81: Resistant [0]	82-106: Inconsequential				
82-106: Inconsequential					

"The first column on the left with the number one near the top, refers to the current generation. The column to the far right is the sixth. Each column represents a span of 25 years, and the rows within the columns are age groups. The first one shows how Trial sees our current window of 25 years – beginning this year, 2024, and ending in 2049 – by age group. Kids six years and below, he calls *amenable*. Young people between 7 and 31 are *receptive*. Between 32 and 56, *distrustful*. 57 to 81, *resistant*. And anyone older than that is *inconsequential* – they don't matter to his plans at all. As these 25-year time periods pass, the disposition of those age groups progress further towards accepting assimilation. That's how he sees it, anyway."

The president studied the chart, thumb under his chin. "Hmph," he said at last. "I hate to admit it, but he's probably right."

"That was our take as well," Ward said. "Anyone six years of age or less right now, won't remember a day without aliens; and the people who are most likely to resist – the oldest of us – will begin dying off soon enough that we won't matter."

"Damn!" the president said. "That's spot-on. Younger generations don't listen to the cautionary tales of old people on anything else, they sure as hell aren't going to start now. We never did when we were kids."

Ward nodded reluctant agreement. "Trial obviously doesn't think we can do a thing about this. If he did, he probably wouldn't have shared it. He knows we're going to either distrust, or even outright resist his change, but he's already accounted for that. We're like numbers in a math problem to him. He's accounted for us and removed us from the equation."

"I'm starting to hate this guy," Warren said.

"Yep. That places you squarely in the range of *distrustful* to *resistant*."

Warren got the point and shook his head in frustration. "Are we really this helpless? Are we fish in a barrel? I cannot accept this, but I'll be damned if I know the first thing to do about it!" He pounded lightly at the table with his fist, thinking, then turned to a new topic. "Where's AJ? Is he a threat?"

"That is the million-dollar question," Ward said. "The answer, I'm afraid, is *yes*. Whether or not he has mal-intent is not the issue. He will have power and influence. What he says and does will matter. To what extent will depend on what Trial does with him, but he's untrained, which means he can break a lot of china, even by accident, even unintentionally – even with the best of intentions. He must be managed."

"Agree," Warren said. "Let's reel him in."

"We've spun up an entire think-tank to focus on how to deal with him. That's why we didn't bring John Riley into the room with us today, by the way." Ward gestured with an open hand. "Not sure if you're aware, but the three of them; John Riley, Jason Clipper and Andrew Jacobs, are childhood friends. They're Harry Potter, Ron Weasley and Hermione Granger. It will matter."

"Okay, I want a readout from your team by tomorrow morning on how to contain Jacobs."

"You'll have it."

Chapter 71

April 22, 2024

On March 17th, 1956, the last known photograph of Elvis Presley alone in public, was taken by Alfred Wertheimer. Elvis was returning to the Warwick Hotel in New York City to rest in preparation for a show later that evening. He had no way of knowing what a pivotal moment it was. His fame was spreading so fast that he would never again be able to roam the public streets without escort for fear of being recognized and overwhelmed by enthusiastic fans. For Andrew Seymour Jacobs, that moment occurred on April 18, 2024, standing on the flight deck of the USS Yorktown in Charleston Harbor. The reasons underlying the moment were different – it wasn't a matter of popularity – but the ends were the same.

In the momentary distraction that occurred in the lab when Ryan Meyer summoned Natalie Briggs to help get the message to President Warren about Trial's stated plans for AJ, John Riley had stepped forward and ushered him out of the lab. Sarah and Clipper witnessed the act and fell in to follow. They found an unused conference room, went inside and closed the door. Riley all-but forced AJ into a chair, where he sat looking up, bewildered and speechless. A heaviness fell into the room. No one gave voice to it, but the building weight of what had just occurred crescendoed into a paralyzing calm. The silence stretched.

Riley's mind was in motion. In all the years that the three of them had been as close as brothers, neither Clipper nor AJ had seen him in such a state.

"You don't know what to do," Clipper said to him.

Riley's transfixed gaze remained upon AJ. He finally spoke: "AJ, your life is no longer your own." There was a quick intake of air as Sarah grasped the statement. "Don't trust anyone," he said.

AJ forced a grin. "Sounds like the movies, Mr. Donovan."

"It's not."

"Can I trust you?" AJ asked.

Riley nodded slowly, his mind still at work hammering through the implications. "Yes. Yes you can."

"How about you, Clip?"

Clipper nodded. "Of course."

"Sarah? You?"

The look of resolve that overtook Sarah was surprisingly reassuring. "Always," she said.

AJ looked back to Riley, gesturing towards the others. "Them?"

Riley nodded thoughtfully. "Us."

The door to the conference room opened slightly. AJ saw an eye peer into the room before the door closed again. "It will take time for you to breathe this in, but this," Riley said, thumbing towards the door, "is life now. Don't fight it. Learn to live with it, then leverage it."

The door opened again. "Mr. Jacobs, your presence is requested in the lab."

AJ stood to his feet.

"AJ," Riley said, stopping him in mid-step towards the door. Riley pointed to him, then let his arm fall back to his side. "I'm sorry."

AJ grinned. It was genuine this time. "Don't be." He held up open palms and looked around. "What else is there? I could be home counting 2x4's right now."

Chapter 72

April 23, 2024

A J walked into the Situation Room with Sarah. They had been ushered from the Mayfield Hammond property to the White House so quickly that it had felt like being washed down a whitewater river. On seeing the two of them, Vandoren stepped forward. "I'm sorry, Ms. Henson," she said, "but this meeting is confidential."

AJ looked past her to President Warren, who was seated at the end of the table per usual. "I can't help noticing," AJ said, pointing to the various other individuals in the room, "that you have quite a bit of counsel present, sir." AJ recognized a few of them, namely Ryan Meyer, Jeff Ward and Frank Boswell, but there were five or six others he had never seen before.

Warren got the meaning. "Fair enough." He nodded to Vandoren, who stepped back to allow Sarah entry.

"I'm afraid I'll need to collect your mobile phones for the time being," Vandoren said.

"It's been quite a week," Warren said by way of apology.

"It has, sir," AJ said. He and Sarah passed their phones to Vandoren who took them and handed them to yet another person who took them out of the room. Both he and Sarah took adjacent seats to the president's left.

"What do you make of Trial's inclusion of you in his communications, AJ?"

"It wouldn't even make good fiction, sir."

Warren chuckled. "Probably not. We can't figure it out so I won't press you to, that is unless you're privy to more information than has been afforded to us." He paused. "Are you?"

"Unfortunately, no."

"We expect that to change. If it doesn't, then what's the point, right?"

AJ nodded.

"I would like to discuss next steps. Plans. Expectations. Outcomes. That sort of thing."

AJ was becoming guarded. There was an unmistakable change in how the president was addressing him. He knew he'd have to get used to it. "How can I help?" he said.

"You're an educated man. I'd like to reason through this together. Arrive at an approach, an arrangement, mutually. Something that makes sense for us both. First, as you've probably gathered, this Trial fellow is not particularly fond of how we do government. I personally think he's a little closed-off, but there's nothing I seem to be able to do about that at present. Reaching out to you the way he has, has been rather odd, in light of that. After all, it was only by way of the freedoms of democracy, the opportunities of capitalism that the comms device sprang up out of the ground in the first place. It clearly didn't happen by itself. You only have to ask yourself, 'why did it happen here, in the United States, rather than anywhere else?' The answer is that we foster that kind of thing. Our government isn't perfect, but it works. It just does."

"I agree, sir."

"Good," Warren said. His gaze lingered a little longer before continuing. "The question becomes; who do you represent? Presently, you're enjoying the protection and provision of the US government. You arrived by helicopter. You've been staying at a Marriott hotel. You've been escorted by people who are looking out for your safety, all on the dime of Uncle Sam."

"I can't help what's happened, sir. I know it's unnecessary for me to say it, but I didn't expect or ask for any of this."

"I know, but we're in the deep end of the pool now, AJ. Deep and cold. I'm trying to understand where we stand: us and Trial, me and you, the United States and the world, the world and the galaxy. Sounds strange doesn't it? The world and the galaxy? That's what I'm trying to discern. I'm annoyed and irritated that Trial won't engage with our government, but I still have to look out for our country – all the more because of that."

AJ nodded. "What do you want me to do?"

"I need to know that you'll cooperate with, and work towards the benefit of your country, AJ."

"Of course I will. I live here. Sarah lives here. My family lives here."

"Good. That's what I hoped, and expected to hear, but we have to establish some ground rules," the president said. "Whatever comes, we need to coordinate how, and what we say to Trial. Right, wrong or indifferent; it's not information that I'm worried about. Not anymore. The Remotes have proven that they can get to any data on the planet, at will. I'm embarrassed to say that we learned just a while ago that they've apparently snooped through private data on servers in the basement of this very building, the Pentagon, Langley, and who knows where else? That game is up. If they go public with some of what they find, we'll have a whole new set of problems; but we'll just have to let that play out as it will. What's important now is what we *can* control, which is what we do and what we say – our own actions. That involves you, and it involves me. We have to be coordinated and aligned." He gestured down the table. "To that end, Mr. Meyer's team has some thoughts to share with you."

Meyer took the cue. "AJ, so far – as far as we know – Trial has not spoken directly with anyone outside of the Mayfield lab. From what we can tell, there is no technical reason for that. As the president just alluded, the Remotes have demonstrated complete technical superiority over our systems. Our cryptography, firewalls – none of it matters to them. We think we're getting closer to understanding how they're doing what, to us, seems impossible, but in the meantime there's nothing we can do about any of it – maybe never will. There is a possibility that the same things that are playing out here – with you and us – could be playing out elsewhere, perhaps in another country. We have no way of knowing whether Trial has established direct communications with other individuals like yourself. We're doing our best to find out, but it will probably be impossible to know. If it is happening, no one will tell us about it."

"Do you have a guess?" AJ asked.

"Our guess is that you're the only one for now, but it's just a guess. As you may or may not be aware, even though we still appear to have the only functional comms unit, theoretically, it can be accessed as freely by anyone on the planet as us. Meaning, having the comms device on our soil gives us no appreciable advantage, except that we could shut it down – as of now, anyway. Clearly, that's no longer an option."

Meyer passed a glance to the president, who nodded. "Mr. Jacobs," the president said, "we think it's only a matter of time before Trial connects with you directly – outside of the Mayfield lab. It could happen over your mobile phone, a laptop computer, your home automation system – anything. As Mr. Meyer indicated, we can think of no technical reasons he couldn't. If that happens, we need to know immediately. Do not respond to any solicitation from Trial without my knowledge. We need to control our dialogue."

It was only then that AJ realized that no electronics capable of recording audio or video were visible in the room. The president noticed AJ's realization of that. "It's a new day, Mr. Jacobs. Isn't it?"

AJ nodded. "What's going to happen?"

"We don't know, AJ. For the time being, we'd like for you to stay close. Word will get out. It just will, it always does. Your role in this – however long it lasts – places you in a position of power. If you're not accustomed to that, which I'm guessing you're not, it comes with responsibilities and requires sensibilities. A trip to the corner grocery store is no longer a simple thing. It could place you in danger, and just as importantly, every person you come into contact with. Let's get you under some protection and play it by ear from there. We're going to spin up a copy of the same security apparatus that watches out for me, to look out for you. It will cover you and the people close to you," he said, extending a hand to Sarah. "Mrs. Vandoren will help with arrangements. Are we clear? Questions? Concerns?"

AJ knew there would be many, but none presented themselves. "How do I contact you if I hear from Trial?"

"That part will be easy. Someone will always be nearby to keep us connected." The door to the room opened, and a man walked in. "This is Special Agent Michael Britt," the president said. "He has been assigned to handle security and communications for you."

Chapter 73

April 24, 2024

"The good news is that this particular probe was designed for deployment on a body without an appreciable atmosphere," said Susan Harrelson. She was a mission planner with NASA who had flown in from Houston to speak with Jeff Ward, Ryan Meyer, Frank Boswell and company, about repurposing the Europa rover for the moon. She was standing at the end of a conference table, pointing to a picture of the large machine on a display screen.

"Why does that matter?" Ward asked.

"Several reasons, actually. Mars, for example, has a significant atmosphere. We use that to our advantage by using parachutes to slow the delivery vehicles down when they get there. Europa, which is where we thought we'd be sending this rover, has virtually nothing by way of atmosphere, so our delivery system involves lowering it from a rocket-propelled crane. It's designed to ease the rover to the surface and set it down gently. The rover hangs below the crane by a tether until it touches the ground, then the tether is released and the crane flies away to someplace safe and out of the way. The upside is that we have far better control over where we end up. Some of our past rovers to Mars, for example, parachuted down and then rolled to a stop like a bouncing beach ball. With the crane, we can set it anywhere we want, to an accuracy of – not meters, but centimeters. Clearly, the parachute system wouldn't work on the moon anyway, since there's no atmosphere at all. Short answer: we've avoided a lot of rework."

"We'll take what we can get," Ward said.

Harrelson walked a few paces to where her laptop sat on the conference table. She pressed a button and a different image appeared on the wall. It was familiar to everyone by now; the top-down view of the area near Plaskett U, where the enhanced, but still frustratingly low-resolution image clearly showed structures and traces of past activity. How long it had been since the activity had occurred, there was no way of knowing.

"The shadow from this structure here to the northwest," Susan said, pointing, "suggests that it could be as much as 30 meters in height. We've done calculations based on the timestamp of when this image was taken by the LRO to know what the aspect of the sun was at the time. That allowed us to take the length of the shadow into account. However, due to uncertainties about the surrounding terrain, we're still unable to arrive at an exact measurement. We're close though, that we know." She stepped towards the screen. "Now, following along the trail that leads away from the structure further to the southeast, towards this small crater here, we observe several interesting anomalies. These bright spots on the path itself, we suspect, could be vehicles. The big question would be, if they are, why would they have been abandoned at these points along the path? It would seem to make more sense that they would be located at either end. The likely explanation is that they're unmanned. If they're used to convey payloads from the structure to the northwest, down to the crater, then stopping them mid-flight may not have mattered to whoever was operating them. Either way, this path – this road – is what we'll use to move the rover between the two structures. My recommendation is that we set the rover down here, near the tall tower to the northwest." She began tracing the path with her finger as she spoke. "Then drive it the roughly kilometer-and-a-half to the southeast to reach the other end. Appearances are that this may be a mining operation, and that whatever was being taken from the tall structure is being delivered into this small crater on the southeast." She pressed another button on her laptop. "If we zoom into the crater, we can clearly see something setting at its northern edge, and that something else substantially larger is standing within it. At the time this image was taken, it was barely catching sunlight at its top. We expect that the most interesting artifacts will be found at this location."

"Really?" Ward said. "There appears to be much more happening at the north end."

"On the surface, yes," Boswell said. "But we believe that whatever is happening there is only in support of operations on the south side. We strongly suspect that this small crater houses an entrance to something subterranean – probably a compound or installation of some sort."

Every eye around the table looked back to the image.

Ward said: "Okay, but then we'd be taking a risk, right? If the most interesting artifacts are in the crater and we start from the hill, the rover may not make it. What if dies in transit?"

"We'll make it," Susan said.

"The president tells me that your leadership – Weinberg and Rupp – aren't so sure."

Susan smiled. "They have to play it safe. The *Spirit* and *Opportunity* rovers that we sent to Mars back in 2003 had an 'expected' lifespan," she said, making air-quotes on the word *expected*, "of 90 days, but that was never the true expectation, it was only the warranty. No one – certainly not the engineers or anyone else close enough to the project to know what those rovers were made of – believed they would break. In fact, we all believed that they would either end up getting stuck, which is what happened to Spirit, or get buried in enough dust that their solar panels would no longer be able to draw enough energy from the sun to keep them alive. That's almost happened a couple times, but the panels have been cleaned by wind more than once – which we did not expect. They lasted for years. Point being, this is just under a kilometer-and-a-half," she gestured again to the image. "We'll make it. I guarantee it."

"You guarantee it?" Ward said. He expected her to back away from her claim, but she didn't.

"Yes. As long as we don't drive it into a ditch."

Ward nodded, convinced. "Frank, what do you think?"

"I agree with the plan. Plus, we've got two more rovers in the pipeline and a manned mission also in the works. We're going to have plenty of eyes up there before the next four months are up. It's going to be a crowded place. I say we shoot for the moon – if you'll excuse the pun."

Ward thought for a moment then nodded, accepting the consensus. "Let's call that the official plan of record, then. Any signs that other countries are alerted to this?"

"Nothing that we've been able to turn up," Boswell said, then shrugged. "I want to get there first too, but even if we don't, what will we really lose?"

"That's the question, isn't it?" Ward said. He didn't wait for an answer. "How are preparations coming?"

"As you know, we've slipped seven days from the original goal President Warren set for us," Susan said. "It wasn't a slip, really. Paula had nothing to base her estimates on – and the president had her on the spot. Our planners never committed to anything earlier than May 2nd – there's no way we could have."

Ward nodded. "I figured. The president gets it too, by the way. What's next?"

"I need to be sure we're all agreed on the plan. We're gonna lock this in today and it can't change after that without impacting our schedule. We're pushing it as it is."

Ward passed a final look to Boswell, who nodded as if the question was a simple one. "It's a lock then."

"Good enough," Susan said. "What's next is, I have a ton of work to do. If we're concluded here, I'll be on my way back to Houston."

"We'll have you there in under four hours," Ward said, gathering his things from the table and preparing to stand.

"Wait," Boswell said. "One more thing. Scientists and engineers are sentimental about only one thing in this world."

Ward looked back, confused. "Which is?"

"How they name their projects."

"Sorry, Mr. Boswell but we already have a working name, at least for the rover."

"Really? What is it?"

"*Spes Novus.*"

Ward and Boswell looked at each other, but the name didn't register.

"*Spes* is the Roman goddess of hope," Meyer said. "Add the word *Novus*, and it becomes, *New Hope.*"

Chapter 74

April 25, 2024

A
t 2:30 AM, sleep was elusive. Again.

Sarah stared at the ceiling of her hotel room. Despite everything, she wanted to hold to some of the formalities and traditions of her prior life. She and AJ had adjacent rooms at the Marriott and they spent a lot of time together in one or the other of them, but for the most part she kept to her own quarters on a nightly basis. Something in her felt that if they spent day and night together prior to that, then the marriage itself would become little more than a legal agreement. She didn't like the idea of it.

For reasons unknown, this night had been a long one. She hadn't slept well for days, but this one was particularly bad. She began thinking about joining AJ to escape the loneliness. She got up, not bothering with the light. AJ's room key, which he had given to her on her first night in Charlotte, was lying on the corner of the dresser. She picked it up on the way to the door.

Stepping into the hall, she closed the door as quietly as possible and turned to the right. AJ's door was only a few paces away, but she was jolted to a halt by the presence of a man standing sentry. The two looked at one another for a moment. Neither spoke. At once, Sarah resolved to regard what felt like an embarrassing situation as yet another thing that was now part of life. She forced herself to ignore him.

She knocked quietly at the door of AJ's room as she opened it, so as not to startle him, and was met by the glow of his laptop computer. Light from the hall spilled into the otherwise, darkened room, and AJ looked up without speaking. Something didn't seem right, but then, few things ever did these days. Sarah decided not to lead the conversation with yet another question about whether something could be wrong. They were both learning not to spend time or energy on fear. They couldn't afford to worry about what *might* happen, they had to deal with what *did* happen: facts, events. She walked forward, her eyes already adjusted to the low light in the room, and sat on the corner of the bed, facing him.

AJ's hands were folded in his lap. Even by the light of the computer screen, it was clear that he was troubled again. Everything that had happened to him had been so unfair. It was exciting to be singled out in such an extraordinary – no, outlandishly unbelievable way. She was proud of him, but also knew that Riley's warnings, that his life was no longer his own, were not idle words. In the excitement, it could seem that even something as big as that wasn't as important as it was. But the nighttime hours, if they served no other purpose well, were supremely effective at making a person confront the things that the daylight hours permitted to slip by.

Something unexpected also emerged into her thoughts at the sight of him: she had left him alone. While she had wrestled with sleep, he had, yet again, been confronted with something larger and unknown, and been forced to deal with whatever it was by himself.

It was an empty realization. The thought forced the words out of her. "I'm sorry," she said.

AJ lifted a hand and pointed to the screen, passing a knowing look at her. He rested his hand back in his lap.

"Trial?" she asked.

"Yes."

Chapter 75

April 25, 2024

President Warren read the lines of text, then looked around the Situation Room. AJ and Sarah were again, seated to his left, and on the screen at the end of the elongated room was the message AJ had received from Trial the night before. It was the answer to a question. Warren had asked about rights, and Trial had responded.

The message read:

> *The rights of the Earth and its occupants are those that remain after the powers of centralized government have been enumerated. Relations with the Earth have yet to be normalized. The provisions granted during this transitive state are now disclosed for your benefit. Be advised that they are not contingent upon your understanding or acceptance.*
>
> *All parties under the jurisdiction of the Assemblies of the Living may expect just treatment. The implications, complexities and meaning of this promise are not always apparent.*
>
> *First effects of the enactment of these provisions shall manifest immediately.*

"AJ, how did you receive this?" Warren said.

Neither AJ nor Sarah had slept since the message had come in, which meant that, despite present company, it was a struggle to stay focused. AJ blinked to clear his vision. "My laptop computer rebooted by itself in the night," he said. "The screen went white for a while, which woke me up. It was about 2:00 AM."

"Sir," Ryan Meyer said, "AJ's computer was reimaged last night. Similarly, but not exactly the same way the servers in the Mayfield datacenter have been black-boxed. It's happening to some degree or another to select computers around the globe – mostly in datacenters and to equipment that routes and carries internet traffic. The difference is that AJ's computer still retains its prior functionality – that's new. The applications and user engagement layers of the machine look and operate the same, but the underlying kernel has been completely replaced with something we don't recognize and can't penetrate – not so far, anyway. All the data is still encrypted, though; and we haven't made any progress towards breaking it – here or anywhere else. But we have learned something from his laptop already. Each message that comes in is accompanied by a set of metadata that, we think, identifies the sender and the receiver. Our guess is that it serves a similar purpose to the header information that accompanies a typical email. Metadata is basically data that describes other data – it's not usually displayed for end users, but it's there. We're going to give AJ a new laptop and hold onto this one for further study – see if we can learn anything else."

The president looked to Meyer, registering the comment, but then his mind moved on, turning back to AJ a second or so before his eyes followed suit. "Did you respond?" he said to AJ.

AJ was reluctant to answer. Doing so would incriminate him. He had been strictly forbidden to engage Trial without approval, but he had anyway. He wouldn't be able to explain why – he didn't know himself. "I asked how he could make plans for humanity with this 150-year roadmap without knowing us better."

"And Trial answered?"

"Immediately."

"Let's see it," Warren said. In a moment, it was on the screen.

> *By benefit of long-established precedent, there exist comprehensive templates that can be projected upon emergent species to form a reliable and complete profile. We need not perform new or staged tests, interview or subjugate individuals, but merely look to your history through the lens of these templates and allow a profile to emerge.*

> *If a hungry man steals a loaf of bread, is he a thief? If he is later unwilling to steal bread, should we conclude that he has become a better person or that he is no longer hungry? The apparent change in him will more likely be attributable to the latter. Indeed, the summation of character, then, is a product of personal disposition and circumstance.*

> *In this way, individuals become interchangeable variables within a set of equations by which character and behavior are generalized. If we find that a man without food has stolen a loaf of bread, is his character lacking or may we reasonably conclude that without food, most men will steal bread?*

> *Perhaps you, Andrew, have not faced starvation and have therefore, not stolen. Even so, many others of your species have, and are. Their behaviors – their responses to this and endless other circumstances – describe you, as an individual, far better than the small subset of circumstances you happen to have personally faced. Indeed, the tendency of individuals within any group to judge the behavior of others against the backdrop of their own circumstances is a hallmark of primitive beings.*

> *In each equation into which we insert the individual, the equation itself is not changed. In aggregate, they*

> *serve to construct an overarching view of the species,*
> *with accuracy commensurate with sample size.*

Warren's eyes rested on the screen. "Interesting," he said, "but that's all. It doesn't answer our immediate questions. What about the provisions he mentioned? He said something is going to happen immediately, we need to know what it is." Warren read part of the text again. *"First effects of the enactment of these provisions shall manifest immediately.* Any guesses?"

"We may actually have something on that one, Mr. President," Ward said. The president's attention snapped in his direction, along with everyone else's. Ward continued: "A file containing 87,355 names was just received at the Mayfield datacenter. According to the document, they are the names and coordinates of individuals identified by Trial as living victims of human trafficking, sex slavery, or being unlawfully held against their will."

Margaret Statham's mouth fell open. "Holy smokes," she said with barely a gasp, as if the statement were a blow to the stomach.

"We have a couple other items as well," Meyer said. "Apparently, we also have the legal provisions, and it looks like Trial threw a bone to the geek squad – more details about the history of the galaxy."

Chapter 76

May 1, 2024

The Falcon Heavy megarocket that would deliver the Spes Novus probe to the moon had been moved to launchpad 39A at the Kennedy Space Center in Florida on the back of the huge transport vehicle that had moved the Saturn V rockets for the Apollo missions decades before. At 68.4 meters in height, the rocket was enormous. In terms of power, second only to those same Saturn V engines, and with nearly twice the lifting capacity of the next most-powerful rocket at NASA's disposal. It had been rolled into position on its side and then hoisted upright.

The sun had risen in clear skies above the Atlantic Ocean to the east, as tendrils of vapor streamed away from the ship in the morning chill. *What design need, what imbalance required the letting-out of vapor at those locations?* Riley wondered. And how odd that the design of the craft was so self-harmonious that the underlying issues that gave rise to the need for them, having formed as byproducts of extraordinary complexity, could be remedied with such a straightforward solution? A vent. It was the telltale sign of the elegance of engineering craft that for those with the understanding to appreciate it, revealed what most only saw as an edifice of sterile, cold steel, as the masterstroke of art that it was: a self-defined, self-contained, closed-loop, functioning system.

Yet, even at that, it was somehow primitive in comparison with what lay out there. How primitive, there was no way of knowing. Riley's mind kept returning to the thought of it. There was a threshold at some point along the path between primitive microbes, mounds of termites, schools of fish, bands of gorillas, and humankind, where living creatures earned the notice of the likes of Trial. On the surface, that threshold seemed to be a matter of technology, but the more dialog with the Remotes had progressed, the more Riley knew that it was something other than that; or at least, more than only that. Technology was only an enabler.

It would take three days for the rover to reach the moon after launch. The delivery vehicle was more than powerful enough to cover the distance in less time, but there was the matter of slowing down to lower the rover gently to the moon's surface that netted to a practical limit on speed.

On the outer edges of possibility, the entire journey could be cut to as little as a few hours by executing a maneuver known as a *midpoint turnover*, in which the rocket would accelerate all the way to the midpoint of its journey, flip itself 180 degrees, and then begin firing its rockets in the opposite direction to slow down.

Unfortunately, that option also netted to an exponential increase in complexity, fuel consumption, stress on the rover, and introduced many other unknowns that made it a nonstarter.

Riley had been sitting alone in a visitor's lounge at the Johnson Space center in Houston Texas some 1,000 miles to the west, watching the scene at the Kennedy Space Center unfold on a series of large monitors. Launch would happen at 11:24 AM, May 2nd; just over 27 hours away.

He checked his watch. At 9:00 AM he would begin a long day of discussions with mission planners. It could yield only marginal results at best. There wasn't much left that could be done earthside. They lacked too much information. Regardless of what they surmised, what plans they made, when the rover finally touched down on the surface of the moon, unfolded its solar panels and raised its cameras to look around, the real work would begin.

Riley hadn't been present with Ward, Meyer and Boswell when the high-level plans were laid out. They involved setting the Spes Novus down near the large hill to the northwest, which had been dubbed *Fubo Hill* due to its resemblance to a rocky hill on the western bank of the river Li in China. The rover would then follow the existing path to the crater towards the southeast where the most interesting discoveries were expected. There was no corresponding creativity surrounding naming the crater. For the most part, it was simply called *Southeast Crater*. It looked like the name would stick.

His phone rang. He pulled it from his pocket to see that it was Melissa. "Hello?" he said.

"Good morning." She sounded upbeat.

"Good morning. How are you?"

"Great. Thought I'd catch you before you started your day. I know it'll be a busy one."

"Glad you did. Anything happening?"

"Yes, actually," she said.

Riley had asked the question more as smalltalk. "Good news, I hope."

"It is. I'm back on EcoGrid."

"Nice!" Riley's sentiment was legitimate. He had never gotten over the blow that she had received at the start of their covert investigations. If anyone should have been singled out and penalized, it was him. Maybe Clipper too, but not Melissa. Riley suspected, in fact, knew that Matthews had targeted her for precisely that reason. "I can't tell you how happy I am to hear it," he said, honestly.

Melissa said: "Can't help wondering if someone I know may have had something to do with it."

Riley was glad he could answer truthfully. "You'll be pleased to know that I did not. Matthews must have had a change of heart on his own. You're good at what you do. The EcoGrid team must have felt your absence and raised some hell."

Melissa hesitated. "Maybe. Either way, the timing wasn't perfect."

"In what way?"

"I've taken another job."

It wasn't what Riley expected. "Really? Outside of Mayfield? Where?"

"Just a startup here in town. They're getting into the whole digital currency thing. Lots of BlockChain stuff."

"Sounds interesting – and different."

"I'm ready for the change," she said.

"Don't blame you. Guess this means I'm not as special as I thought, though."

"Oh? Why is that?" Melissa asked.

"For a fleeting, delusional moment, I thought you called because you couldn't resist my boyish good looks."

"Hmm," she said. "You are good looking, but definitely not boyish, sorry. You're still kind of right. Does that help?"

"Maybe. A consolation prize. I'll take it."

"Well, the other reason," she said, "is that when I gave my two weeks' notice, my manager in production support said that one week would be enough. The truth is, Matthews pushed me onto her team when they were already fully staffed. They won't miss me much."

"I'm beginning to like the sounds of this," Riley said. "The weather is great down here."

"Will I be in the way?"

"Never."

"I'll fly in on Friday night then."

Chapter 77

May 1, 2024

By 9:00 AM, Riley was sitting in a conference room with Jeff Ward, Frank Boswell, Susan Harrelson and Ryan Meyer. It was a new type of room, the likes of which now appearing in office buildings across the country – if not the entire planet. It was electronically cordoned off, running on locally-generated power, and with no hard connections to any infrastructure that could be used by the Remotes to eavesdrop – none that were known, anyway. Already, the rooms had been dubbed *cotton rooms*, presumably because they were meant to stifle sound. That, and because all the more obvious names were already in use; private, secure, sound-proof, shielded, and on and on.

"I still maintain that it's pointless not to ask Trial what he knows," Ryan Meyer said. "He's been reading our mail from the start. He has to know that we're going up there by now."

"Why has he said nothing about it then?" Ward asked.

"Maybe it's just not his top concern. We're doing lots of things, and he hasn't shown interest in any of them. We're building, not three, but now five gravity comms facilities. We're doing everything we can to break into AJ's laptop. We're trying to track where the Remotes have been pulling information from across the internet. The moon thing may not be a headline for him."

Riley was taking in the conversation without comment. He had taken to looking out the window, showing no signs of interest. Ward wasn't typically inclined to solicit his input but made an exception. "What do you think, Riley?"

Riley didn't divert his gaze from the blue skies beyond the window. "He's watching."

Meyer was frustrated at that. "That's what I just said, isn't it?" He was clearly in a defensive mood. It had been a long week already, and everyone was on edge.

Riley didn't particularly care. "Trial snooped through our PDS Geosciences Node for the Lunar images – the same ones we have," Riley said. "That tells me that he probably doesn't know any more than we do, but he's curious." The PDS, or *Planetary Data System*, is a digital archive that holds information collected during various space missions, which is hosted by Washington University in St. Louis, Missouri. Riley diverted his eyes back into the room and found Ward. "Despite the capabilities that the Remotes have shown, the extent of what they know about us comes from our own systems. That means, if we don't know, they don't either. Trial wants to know what's on the moon, and he's waiting for us to find out for him."

"You can't know that for certain," Meyer said.

"Want to know for sure, Mr. Meyer? Do something that puts the mission into jeopardy and see what Trial does."

"What are you talking about?" Ward said.

"What I'm talking about is that I disagree wholeheartedly with Mr. Meyer. This *is* Trial's marquee issue. My guess is that he would rather we didn't know that. I say we test him. This is a safe room – he can't hear us. Let's put an error into our trajectory. Purposely put the rover on a crash course into the moon's surface, or to land a hundred kilometers off target and see what happens."

Susan Harrelson, who had been silent for several minutes, nearly choked at that. "I assume you're kidding, of course," she said.

Riley looked at her levelly. "This doesn't strike me as the best time for kidding, Ms. Harrelson. You'll find that I don't do a whole lot of it." Riley's comment had clearly hit home with Ward, though. He began clicking his pen and soon appeared to have tuned out the exchange in the room altogether.

"There is no way that we can put hundreds of millions of dollars' worth of hardware and–"

"Do it," Ward said.

Harrelson stammered to a stop. "Excuse me?" she said, scanning through the faces in the room as if there wasn't sane person among them. "Do you know what Paula Weinberg would do if she knew this was even proposed – even in jest?"

"It's not in jest," Ward said without pretense of patience. "Do it."

"Do it?" Harrelson laughed. "Do it? Oh, sure, can I have a moment to phone this in? It'll only take a second."

"Ms. Harrelson, it would be hard for me to find the words to express how much I am not interested in your incredulity. If you haven't noticed, this is not about rockets. It's not about rovers. It's not about money. It's not even about science or technology. It's about dancing with the devil – his name is Trial by the way. Frankly, I don't give a SHIT what you or Weinberg care about. Is that clear? Put this in motion. Do it now."

Harrelson was clearly not used to being disregarded. "That fast, huh? You don't need more time. There's no need to talk it over with anyone? Just do it?" She shook her head in disgust. "No, it's not clear," she said. "No, I won't do it. And no, I don't fucking care what you think. How's that? For one thing, even if we decided to do it, I told you last week that we were past the point of no return on the mission. We can't change it now."

"I'm not asking you to change it, I'm asking you to break it."

"There's another contingency," Meyer said, cutting in. "If Trial has already found out who put the facility up there, he may be showing no interest because he's already infiltrated the computer systems of whoever it was and found out everything he wants to know. If that's the case, then we'll blow up our rocket for no reason. Trial won't save it because he won't care."

"Back to that again, huh?" Susan said. Her mood had dissolved into intolerance. "I told you. There's no way all the materials needed to establish a base facility like this could have been put up there without us knowing about it. It would have taken dozens of rockets just to get the materials up there, much less the dozens more required to keep supplies and people in motion to build and support it. We would have noticed."

"And yet it's up there, isn't it?" Meyer said. Harrelson was a half-second late with her retort, so Meyer kept rolling. "There's also the fact that Trial will know that we have other rovers queued up, as well as a manned mission. Maybe he won't intervene because he'll know we won't stop if we fail on the first attempt. He'll just wait for the next one."

"He'll intervene," Riley said, with a quiet confidence that had the effect of arresting the nervous energy in the room.

Meyer was not to be dissuaded easily. "If you're so sure he'll intervene, then what's the point of making him do it?"

Riley peered at Meyer, weighing a response. "Strategy is a subtle thing. To us, this will be a minor move. The advancement of a pawn by a single space on the far side of the board. But to Trial, it will be the difference between weighing his options, and being forced to exercise them. You're not going to like this, but you're right. We have other rovers lined up. If Trial doesn't intervene, we'll still learn something valuable."

"I'm sorry, but you're not making sense," Harrelson said.

"Crash the rocket," Riley said again, even more quietly this time. There was a finality to the statement that brought all discussion to a standstill, despite that Riley had no authority to make it happen.

Harrelson had taken a deep breath in preparation for continuing her rebuttal, but Riley had cut her off before she could deliver it. She let it out with an exasperated sigh. "I'm going to have to talk to Weinberg on this one," she said, recovering. "She'll probably throw me out of a window for being stupid enough to even raise the question."

"I can come with you if it'll help," Ward offered.

She laughed. "No. No, thank you." She didn't even look in Ward's direction. "I'll be back," she said, then left the room.

Chapter 78

May 2, 2024

"**D**o you think we're under surveillance in this hotel room?" Sarah asked.

"Hard to imagine we wouldn't be." AJ answered without a trace of concern, which borderlined on troubling, but Sarah didn't raise the issue.

A Major League Baseball game was playing on the television, which AJ watched with intermittent interest, stealing frequent glances at the new replacement laptop that Ryan Meyer had given him after confiscating the prior one two days before. It sat atop the corner table, open, but sleeping, oblivious to its role – however brief – in the storyboard of human history. It had been days since Trial had contacted AJ, and as the days passed, Sarah saw agitation slowly taking hold of him.

"I wonder what's taking so long," he said, his eyes lingering on the computer as if hoping it would do something unexpected and relevant. In a moment, he got up and walked the few paces to the table where it sat, looking down at it as if suddenly wondering whether it held some secret that he had simply not taken adequate time to discover. He pulled out a chair and sat down, then pressed a few buttons. The laptop lit up immediately.

"What are you going to do?" Sarah asked.

"I don't know. This machine hasn't been reimaged like the other one, but I wonder if Trial can see it anyway ... if he would notice if I typed something into it."

"Like what? You can't exactly send an email to him."

"True, but what if I just opened a word processor and started typing? Maybe he would see it somehow." AJ pecked at the keys as he spoke, energized by the possibility. In a moment, a word processor window appeared on the screen, the cursor blinking in the upper left corner awaiting his input. "Any thoughts?"

"I–" she began, but at that moment, the laptop winked out.

AJ looked for a moment like a child who had actually managed to conjure a genie from a lamp. "I guess that answers that," he said. The screen went white, then dark again, and then the whole system began to reboot.

"He's been waiting for you to reach out first," Sarah said.

"Damn! He's probably been wondering where the hell I've been."

Sarah pursed her lips at the language, but decided not to press that issue, either. "You've had this thing for all of two days. That's not long."

They watched as the machine succumbed to alien technical supremacy. It was an odd feeling, as if the Remotes were coming into the room with them. Sarah doubted she would ever get used to it. The process went on for several minutes before the laptop began returning to life.

"What are you going to say?" Sarah said, as the machine neared the final moments of its reboot.

"I still don't know what he expects from me."

"He would expect you to ask questions," she said. "What's on your mind, Mr. Jacobs? Don't try to guess what Trial wants – what do you want to know?"

"I'm not short on questions."

"Ask then."

AJ nodded, looking at the computer, but the gritty reality that he had been expressly forbidden to talk to Trial on his own, by no less than the president himself, reasserted itself. "The president isn't going to like this," he said.

"Like what? If Trial intended your conversations to be known to everyone, he wouldn't have black-boxed the computer."

"Do you even hear what you're saying? The President of the United States instructed me, personally, not to talk with Trial without his knowledge. He wants to coordinate our dialog … which, unfortunately, makes sense. Plus, like I said, we're probably under surveillance anyway, so the fact that the computer is black-boxed doesn't really mean much."

"All I know is that Trial invited you into the conversation, not anyone else – not even the president. I get that we need to be, what? good citizens, but the facts are the facts." Sarah pointed to the keyboard. "Besides, if they didn't expect you to say something, why give you the computer?"

AJ mulled the thought for a moment. "Good point."

"Say something, then."

AJ didn't hesitate further.

AJ:

Am I the only individual with whom you've established direct dialog?

The response was immediate – accounting for the never-changing seven-second latency.

Trial:

There are others.

AJ:

How can I help?

Trial:

Remain engaged.

AJ:

To what end?

Trial:

Humankind has embarked upon a 150-year journey. Your legislative and executive governmental leadership has very short tenure, and your judicial leadership will reduce in significance. Your effective influence will span a longer period time.

AJ:

What role will I play?

Trial:

Continuity.

AJ exchanged glances with Sarah. "I don't think I want to press this right now."

"Why not? Don't you want to know what he's talking about? What he wants from you?"

"Absolutely, but I'd better have that conversation with the right people in the room. Let me ask something a little less direct."

AJ:

In a prior post, which was addressed to me, you mentioned that the human race is impeded from fully understanding moral responsibility. In what way? What does that mean?

Sarah nodded approvingly. "That's a good one."

Trial:

There are states of being that are not rooted within physical reality. Perfection in judgement and justice, as you perceive it, is not as it would be were the physical universe itself an adequate and equal counter to the elegance of truth. A star grows by pulling in stray mass that comes near it. The more it grows, the stronger it becomes – the more dominant it is. Virtually every star you see came about in such a way. The strong take from the weak.

Yet, humankind holds to a promise of truth and fairness wherein the balances of power are defined by idealized notions of equitability, which, as exhibited by something so common as the stars, is not mirrored within the fundamental behaviors of the physical universe. This dichotomy is the point at which your capacity of understanding tapers down and away from the expansive truths and principles of the Ascendant Plains.

You yourself, as a product of the mechanisms and machinery of that which is physical, embody its potential as well as its limitations. All that is possible in terms of the physical – however indirectly – are extrapolations and outcomes of the interplay between the base-most forces, laws and interactions of physics as they bear out in terms of mass and energy.

Physical reality, in itself, is an imperfect manifestation of a much purer, and more fundamental basis, which, to a limited extent, we both share. You are impeded from appreciable depths of insight into truth because you are primarily equipped with only a physical mind with which to conceptualize it; even so, you are intrinsically able to see it, sense it, think in terms of it, to the extent your physical components are able to grasp and model it. Perfect truth is not an impossible thing, but the physical universe as you know it is simply incapable of forming itself into a shape that perfectly embodies it. Even the ability of your mind to conjure the constructs of truth are limited, because your mind has only physical parts with which to formulate and conceptualize it.

There is a tiered structure of realities that defines and encompasses all that is. Physical reality is a rendering of a deeper body of governing constructs that we share, if indirectly; but it is fantastically simplistic in its capacities of logic and truth, even as the image of a rainbow may be sketched using a charcoal pencil that is fully incapable of rendering what could be regarded as its most compelling attributes.

Perhaps even now, you better understand your dilemma, but that does not equip you to overcome it.

AJ read the words. "I'm sensing that no question posed to Trial will have a simple answer."

Sarah raised her eyebrows. "To put it mildly," she said.

"I've got to talk to Riley."

"Riley? Why Riley?"

"This could be a clue about how we get messages so fast."

"I don't know what you mean."

"Part of the problem we haven't been able to figure out is how we're able to talk to Trial so fast. I mean, we know there has to be a faster-than-light communications medium in play, but we don't understand it. It's over my head, but Riley will get it. Trial basically said there are multiple dimensions out there. It's not science fiction." AJ got up from his chair to find his phone.

"Wait," Sarah said, stopping him. He looked at her for a moment. She seemed concerned, so he sat back down. "I want to ask another question," she said.

"Okay." Her demeanor had changed all at once. AJ didn't know what in Trial's message had shaken her. "Ask if there is life after death," she said.

AJ wondered for a fleeting moment whether she was kidding, but knew she wasn't. "Really?" he said.

She nodded tentatively. "Yeah. Why not?"

"Should I ask if he's the White Horseman too," he said, grinning.

She smacked him on the shoulder playfully, but she was rattled, it was clear. "Just do it."

He inclined his head as he began to type. "Okay. Here we go…"

As before, the response was immediate. It was as if Trial didn't have to think about the question, or its answer. There was a seven second pause and then, the entirety of the message appeared at once.

Sarah's eyes widened. "I'm afraid to read it."

"Wow," AJ said, as if suddenly realizing the gravity of the question they had posed. "I think I am too."

> *Trial:*
>
> *The fleshly death of most evolutionary creatures is a wisp – the silent and transient passing of a consciousness that lacks even the strength to grasp at the straws of life. The creature fades into shadow, unaware that his passing stirs only the slightest of ripples upon a sea already shimmering with countless others. Even so, his passing is witnessed and lamented by multitudes of Ascendants who look on, sadly noting the fading of an altogether unique individual who can never be known again.*
>
> *Most who subscribe to primitive notions of superstition have no strength whatever at flesh-death, mistaking the very passage into nothingness for the transcendence*

they have anticipated for their short lives. They fade into nonexistence, not suspecting that the peace they feel is not the reward they have sought, but the final whispers of awareness, of being itself, winking away. Such endings are final and absolute.

To those of strength, flesh-death is altogether different. They have strengthened their spirits, as you call it, to survive the death of the flesh, but they do not find peace. No, it is the spirit without even the strength to know it is dying that passes peacefully. The strong must fight to live, sometimes travailing and battling for lifetimes without understanding the very life for which they now fight; knowing only that death must be resisted. The lamentations of the Ascended who watch are also for them; for their relentless and blind struggles.

Simpletons believe – somehow, impossibly convince themselves – that the ways of truth, and the elusive enlightenments of Ascension – the very same for which Ascendants toil for eons – will be bestowed upon them in death as a gift. How could they believe, and who could presume to teach, that any soul could be elevated to the highest summits of insight and understanding by any means but the toils of Ascension? The long cycles, the roads that stretch behind and before, vanishing into the unknowable reaches of horizons so distant that they seem, even to Ascendants, eternally beyond reach; these are the paths of Ascension that await the strongest survivors of mortal death. Even the very notion of something less is without merit.

AJ's mouth was agape by the time he finished reading. He turned to Sarah to see that she had brought her hands to her face, steepling her fingers over her nose in astonishment. "Oh my god," she said.

Chapter 79

May 3, 2024

"Just when you think you've seen it all, you find out that you haven't," Tim Graff said. He was a flight control engineer; whose specific expertise was navigation. "That's all I said. Weinberg folded her arms like I was a Boy Scout who didn't want to make his bed. 'I understand that this'll be difficult for you, Mr. Graff,' she said. 'As a courtesy, I'll give you another 20 seconds to come to grips with it. We're out of time.' That was the first time I'd ever spoken directly with her. I didn't know she was such an ass."

Ted Martinhoff, another flight control engineer, was sitting with Graff, talking. "What did you say?"

"I told her to go to hell," Graff said, as if the answer was obvious.

"Really?"

"Yes, I did ... but she didn't hear me."

Martinhoff laughed and Graff joined in. They were sitting in a room that was over-indexed on white surfaces. The equipment and computers that filled the space made even the Mayfield lab look primitive. "That's life, man," Martinhoff said. "So, how are you gonna do it?"

Graff shrugged. "Weinberg told me that it had to look like a real error, not deliberate sabotage. I decided to go with the old standby – the tried and true rounding error. I'm going to insert an operation into the navigation module that converts a 64-bit IEEE 754 floating point value into a simple 64-bit two's complement integer and then back. It'll shave off some of the precision. The error will be extremely small – and won't begin to manifest until we're on final approach for landing, but it'll be cumulative. By the time we get to the surface, we'll be off course by about 3,000 meters, give or take. Depends on how the rocket flies to know how often the truncation will actually occur in practice. Either way, it'll blow the trajectory."

Many of the engineers and scientists who operated at this level – the level at which their algorithms and programming code actually controlled things like rockets, space shuttles and probes – had social ticks and oddities that weren't necessarily bad, but beared out as deficits in other areas of their lives in some way. Strange habits, short attention spans for anything outside of their areas of interest, tunnel vision that kept them from appreciating how a smaller part of a larger effort could be sacrificed for the greater good. Asking one of them to purposely create an error – especially one that they would take pride in not making, such as failing to account for the precision required to carry out a complex mathematical equation – was like asking a priest to commit blasphemy, but only as an exercise.

Martinhoff nodded approvingly at Graff's explanation. "Have you already made the changes?"

Graff became contemplative. It was the very thing Martinhoff had been recruited to watch for. "Yep, I've made the changes," Graff said, "but I gotta tell you, I never saw this day coming." His tone suggested that he saw the request as further erosion from the headier days during which the disciplines of science and technology practiced at NASA and the JPL were at a higher standard. It was precisely the kind of thing Weinberg had asked Martinhoff to watch for. He was a fine engineer himself, but not at Graff's level. She needed someone to look over Graff's shoulder to ensure the he actually made the changes to the flight control systems that would throw the probe off course.

"Have you run simulations on the effects?"

"Not yet," Graff said. "I wasn't able to do any of this on our regular systems – they wouldn't let me. I've worked out the modifications on paper – they won't involve much in terms of actual code changes. They're standing up an isolated system for me to use for simulations. Once we prove them out, I'll hand-code the changes into the real flight control system; but they had better hurry things up. I'm still waiting on the test equipment," he checked his watch. "It's already past 9:00 AM and I'm supposed to be ready to go by noon."

"Does it have to be installed before launch?"

"Not necessarily. We can do it anytime before final approach, but the sooner the better."

Chapter 80

May 5, 2024

S usan Harrelson glanced in John Riley's direction frequently from the flight control room floor. He sat in the observation booth without emotion, watching the wall of monitors that showed telemetry from the Spes Novus delivery vehicle. If he felt any pressure, he didn't show it. Ted Martinhoff sat to Riley's right, occasionally leaning over to exchange words with him. Riley rarely took his eyes from the display screens as Martinhoff spoke. Nothing of what passed between them could be heard.

"Looking good," the flight commentator said. "We are receiving heartbeat tones: two-second heartbeats followed by a 10-second carrier pulse. Higher than expected carrier power ... priming RCS thrusters now." Then a few seconds later: "Preparing for cruise stage separation." The flight control room was a sea of blue shirts. Men and women peering at computer terminals with single minded focus. The commentator spoke every few seconds with a new update. "Heartbeat continues to be good. Cruise stage separation in 3, 2, 1... separation complete." A spattering of handclaps followed, but lasted only a few seconds.

Martinhoff pointed at the screen and nodded to Riley. Riley checked his watch and nodded back. The effects of the precision error Graff had coded into the navigation system would begin showing soon. That an error had been purposely planted was a secret very few people were aware of. In fact, only the few people who were in the room when Riley proposed the idea were in the know; plus Tim Graff, Ted Martinhoff and Weinberg herself.

Thruster warm-up pulses initiated.

Telemetry data, along with a virtual simulation of the Lunar approach was playing out on one of the large monitors. Numbers along the left side of the display screen showed altitude, velocity, distance, and time to the target landing site.

Cruise ballast masses ejected.

There was a steady murmur across the room as rows of engineers consulted their partners, checking each detail and verifying that it aligned with expectations.

A new voice called out. "Flight, we're showing a slight delta from the planned trajectory, but does not look significant." It was the first sign of things to come. Harrelson looked back to Riley nervously at that, but Riley didn't react. He hoped she could keep her cool. She wasn't getting off to a good start.

Another voice. "Flight, we're coming in a little hot. At this rate, there's a small possibility we'll overshoot the landing site." This time, it was the Altitude Control engineer.

"Possibility? How much?" the Flight Director asked.

"The curve is trending up. Right now, 8% probability."

"Where will it put us?"

"So far, it's looking like we're headed roughly a half kilometer north and east of the target site."

"That's not where we want to go," the Flight Director said. His name was Gene Culberson. The irony of sharing first names with the most famous of all Flight Directors, Gene Kranz, was not lost on anyone who knew him, especially since there was more than a slight physical resemblance between the two. "Are we in jeopardy of losing the rover?" he asked.

"Doesn't look that way, Flight. We're just not tracking perfectly to the planned trajectory."

Culberson scanned the room and found Tim Graff. "Navigation, report please."

It was known from the beginning that this whole fiasco, as designed, would place Graff in a tight spot. One of its biggest flaws was that the person who created the artificial error would also be the person called upon to fix it when the critical moment arrived. That moment was now. Graff was heads-down, thumping at his keyboard, and so far, playing his role well, but even from the balcony beads of sweat were visible on his head. "Confirmed," he said. "We're seeing variance from planned trajectory. The effect is small, but cumulative."

> *Vehicle reports that it has completed its turn-down. Velocity, 4.2 kilometers per second.*

It was one thing to make plans and an entirely different thing to execute them. What was quickly becoming apparent was that once Culberson learned that he had purposely been kept out of the loop, there would be hell to pay. The whole, 'we needed your response to be genuine,' explanation was already thinning out. "A half kilometer?" Culberson repeated. "Will that put us into the Plaskett crater?"

The flight controller swiveled his chair back to his computer monitor and began typing at a frenzied pace. "It's a possibility, Flight. Stand by."

"Navigation, I need answers. Can we compensate?" Culberson's tone was controlled but escalating.

"Efforting now, Flight," Graff said.

Jeff Ward appeared in the entryway to the observation balcony. His eyes lingered on Riley for a long moment, and Riley finally ventured a passive look back in his direction. The tension was building fast.

"Nearing point of no return on trajectory, Flight. If we don't recenter within the next 45 seconds, we'll have to go with a contingency landing site."

"What do we have?" Culberson asked.

"We may end up at the bottom of *Plaskett* major," the Altitude Controller said.

"That's not going to help us. Can we go manual?"

"Not at this point. The second-and-a-half latency between here and the moon doesn't give us the control we'd need to pull it off."

"Options?"

"20 seconds," the Flight Controller called out again.

"Mr. Graff," Culberson said. "Your suggestion, sir."

Graff was caught in an intensely unfair moment, which had come upon him in a matter of seconds. The tension was building fast. He swiveled away from his computer system and locked eyes with Culberson, fidgeting with his hands and swiveling his chair from side to side. This wasn't Graff's first rodeo, so despite the gravity of the moment, Culberson's expression revealed as much perplexity related to Graff's behavior as with the astounding surprise that there could be a navigation error that had escaped his notice. Graff's eyes darted around the room. He may have been looking for Riley, but never found him. "Mr. Culberson," he said, "what we're seeing here…"

Trending back on course.

Culberson redirected his attention at once. "Will we make the site?"

"Running some numbers, stand by." The man was standing over one of the flight planners, waiting to relay the outcome. In a moment he gave a thumbs-up. At that, Ward stepped the rest of the way into the observation booth and took a seat. He rested his elbow on the armrest and crossed one leg over the other, then nodded at Riley. Trial had come through. He had corrected the error.

"Are we still good on pathing?" Culberson asked.

"Down the middle, Flight."

"Mr. Graff, when you have free cycles, I'm going to need to know what just happened, and assurances that the anomaly won't manifest again in some other way. In the meantime, let's stay focused on the task at hand."

"Understood, Flight," Graff said.

The three externally-facing cameras installed on the delivery vehicle as an aid to navigation began showing increasingly higher-resolution images of the lunar surface. The plan was to set the rover down within 100 meters of the northwest structure. The craft was still at an altitude of 430 kilometers, so even from this closer vantage point, the cameras, which were not designed for ultra-high resolution imagery, still could not reveal anything more than what was visible from the LRO image.

Thrusters firing. We are decelerating. Speed approximately Mach 1.3.

Long moments ticked on as the simulation on the wall showed the craft pointing away from the lunar surface at an angle of about 45°, a jet of flames knifing out from its aft end. Even the flight commentator was silent for extended seconds as the moon's surface expanded in the background.

All systems nominal. 75 meters per second. Altitude 3.5 kilometers and descending.

As the moon's cratered features resolved into ever greater detail, the view from the navigation cameras began stealing attention from the simulation. The craters grew to a point where their resolution clearly surpassed that of the LRO image that everyone was now intimately familiar with.

Altitude 1.2 kilometers. 20 meters per second.

In a moment, one of the outside cameras unexpectedly swept over Fubo Hill. The odd-looking monolith was visible for the briefest of time, but it was enough to draw gasps from several individuals across the floor. It also revealed that the large feature had been more than aptly named.

Odd as it was, Fubo itself wasn't what caught everyone's attention, it was what stood to the east of it: a complex of several buildings, unmistakable as anything that could be found on Earth. Arranged in neat rows, aligned to only a few degrees west of true north, were buildings – unmistakable – and a yard filled with pipes and industrial outbuildings. The image had the effect of distracting everyone on the floor.

"Focus, people," Culberson said. "Let's get this thing on the ground. How is our trajectory."

"Still down the middle, Flight," Graff said.

> *We have lost tones. This is expected. Ground solution equals minus 9.8 meters ... vertical velocity minus 47 meters per second ... altitude 500 meters.*

Most eyes were now pivoted to the camera feeds. From the perspective of most of the engineers on the floor, nothing more could be done. The landing would play out as it would.

> *Target site is without obstructions ... altitude 10 meters. Descending at .75 meters per second.*

Silence stole over the room.

> *Touchdown confirmed.*

In the moments that followed, the Flight Control room looked and sounded more like a school cafeteria than the center of technology it was. The smiles, congratulations and high-fives lasted for several minutes, bordering on chaos. Probably the only person on the floor who did not join the revelry was Tim Graff. He sat in his chair, exhausted and rattled, largely unnoticed by his celebrating comrades.

It was fifteen minutes before the engineers retook their seats. The voice of the Flight Commentator returned the room to a measure of focus, but the mood was clearly lighter now that the rover was safely on the ground.

> *Touchdown is recorded at 3:55 PM ET. We're on page 84 of the procedure. Dynamics, Flight Director is ready. Please proceed.*

The Dynamics Engineer, lacking the polish of the Flight Commentator, spoke tentatively at first, but gained confidence quickly as he became accustomed to the sound of his voice over the PA. "Yes, uh, step 590011. Touchdown velocity vertical of -607398 meters per second. Step 12: touchdown velocity horizontal 0.034365 meters per second. Expected fuel remaining at flyaway, uh, we have 97.4 kilograms. Step 13: decent-stage location will require photo confirmation. 14: offset between rover z-axis and gravity vector of 3.34 degrees. Navigated range to target is less than one meter."

"Thank you, Dynamics. Power?"

"Go Flight?"

"Steps 25 through 27 please?"

"Yes. Power subsystem is nominal for step 25. Step 26, battery channel power 4018, last datapoint 1.46 amps. For step 27, last data point is 32.18 volts. Roughly 93% of charge."

"Thank you, Power. Thermal?"

"Yes flight?"

"Please report steps 31 through 35."

"Roger that, Flight. For therm-channel 0768 gas pressure 109.6 PSIA. For therm-channel 28.04 RTG01, temperature 142.1C."

The mood was light – like talking about the details of a play after the game had been won. All the numbers spelled one thing: success. The delivery team had done its part, depositing the vehicle onto the Lunar surface in one piece and on target. System health checks would continue for another two hours in preparation for handing control of the rover to the Surface Operations team 1,000 miles away in Houston.

Chapter 81

President Christopher Warren and his Chief of Staff, Angela Vandoren were seated on opposite sides of the marble coffee table in the center of the Oval Office. No one else was present. "This will be more than a footnote in the history books," Vandoren said. "It had innocuous beginnings, but the outcome won't be."

Warren quirked an eyebrow. "What are you telling me?"

"I'm telling you that our society has cancer, Mr. President. It'll keep you awake at night."

"That bad?"

"Worse."

Warren shook his head in contemplation of the thought. "Are we still on for tonight?"

"Yes, we are. We had to pull in our top military strategists to plan the sting. It literally rivals anything that has ever been done with respect to coordinated operations – military or otherwise. But yes, we're a definite go." She checked her watch. "Four hours … a little more."

The president sat on the edge of his sofa, elbows on knees, looking into his hands. They were talking about plans to rescue human trafficking victims. Statham had transformed into a different person when the list of names had come through, working around the clock, sleeping in her office and anywhere else she needed to, while coordinating the effort. When it came time to name the operation, a handful of benign options had been offered for consideration, but Statham cut through it all. "The operation will be called *Peroxide*," she had said. No one disputed it.

"You're right Angela," the president said. "This is real. It doesn't get any more real than this. I don't want to miss even one person. Not one."

"We think Trial will help with that."

"What makes you think so?"

"Maybe we just can't think of any reason for him not to."

The president nodded, resigned that it was probably as good a reassurance as he could expect. "How's Maggie doing?"

Vandoren bobbed her head as if looking for the best words to sum her up. "Fine. I've made a note never to get on the wrong side of her. I've also learned that she's good with you calling her Maggie, but I wouldn't recommend it for anyone else."

"I could have told you that." Warren said. He mustered the closest thing he could to a smile, then sat up and leaned back as if collecting himself. "Okay, tell me about tonight."

Vandoren picked up a tablet lying next to her on the sofa. "The official opening of the international symposium is at 7:00 PM. We have exactly two delegates from every country, totaling 390 individuals. There are no absences."

"None? Not even the Holy See?"

"The Pope will be there himself, along with a Cardinal Bishop."

Warren shook his head in amazement. "These are truly remarkable times."

"They are indeed," Vandoren said. "At the symposium, you'll make greetings and introductions, which will last approximately 10 minutes. At 7:10, you'll begin your speech. We believe that the vast majority of people will be watching from all around the globe. When you say the opening line; 'My fellow citizens of the Earth,' local law enforcement across the country will mobilize. Literally, every last individual that has been identified by Trial for rescue will be sought simultaneously. There is a percentage of individuals that are being held in groups. In those cases, larger teams will be sent out to neutralize threats, rescue captives and arrest all perpetrators. Astoundingly, despite the reach and complexity, we expect the entire operation to be completed in under two hours – most in under 40 minutes. We have more than two dozen special operations teams from the various military branches on standby to assist. These teams will be airborne at the start of the operation, canvasing patrol zones across the country. If they are needed, the team in nearest proximity to the need will be called upon. Our coverage is planned so that we should be able to have them on the ground and on location within 30 minutes of any request for aid. These teams will come in, subdue the criminals and take control of the situation. They are authorized to use any means necessary."

The president took to his feet and began to pace. "I like the plan. Damn, even four hours seems too long to wait."

"I'm with you, sir. The good news is that we expect everything to come off like clockwork. There will be no failures. All teams have local oversight, and reporting responsibilities are known. Any team that does not report success will be aided by other teams that have already completed their own assignments. Our expectation is that every last individual will be accounted for. There will be no aborts. Any person who is not reclaimed will be hunted and found. Period."

The president nodded. "Godspeed," he said.

Chapter 82

May 7, 2024

The president took to the podium against a backdrop of half-hearted applause from across the small arena. The spotlights gnawed at his eyes as he turned to face the audience, as they always did. He had thought more than a few times that once he stepped away from the public eye for the final time in his life, they would be among the things he would miss the least.

His black suit was impeccable, per usual. No suit was expensive enough in itself to make any man who might wear it look dignified, but for someone who had the innate qualities of stature and poise, as Warren certainly did, the suit projected an image of commanding confidence. The only obvious break from protocol was his pink tie and handkerchief. Normally, on a night like this, he would wear red or blue.

He faced the crowd, gripping the sides of the podium as the applause died away. He took in the scene in silence, allowing it to stretch until the moment began to feel uncomfortable. The arena was filled with the most influential people on the planet. Leaders. People who were accustomed to being heard, to being heeded and catered to. They were not used to waiting, and after only a few seconds, many had already begun to fidget. Warren still didn't speak.

Someone coughed. The muffled sound of a closing door from some adjacent hall was heard, and the ventilation fans began asserting themselves in the silence.

Finally, he said: "My fellow citizens of the Earth." But then stopped again. He stepped back from the podium, appearing oblivious and unconcerned with the impact he was having on the increasingly uncertain crowd. Angela Vandoren, who was seated on the front row, leaned to one side and whispered into someone's ear. In a moment, that person took to his feet and disappeared through a side door.

Warren paid no attention.

In time, he nodded to himself, as if reaching some inner conclusion, and stepped back to the microphone. "It occurs to me," he said, "that our new alien acquaintances do not appear to be enamored with the wonders of Earth. They seem to have no interest in the planets of our Solar system, or our sun, or even the wildlife that shares this world with us. Indeed, they are interested in us; in humanity."

"In his assessments, Trial gives poor marks to humankind. He believes we do not self-govern well, that we do not pay adequate heed to those in need around us. His opinions, if I were to call them that, seem, in fact, so poor, that they beg the question of why he cares enough to remain engaged with us at all. What kernel of value, within the entirety of something so seemingly unpalatable to him, could possibly warrant his continued interest? There must be something, but what could it be? What nascent value compels him to invest energy in us?"

"There are those who believe that our handling of the early days of First Contact was not what it should have been. That may be true. I apologize for that. I would only ask that you consider how your own response to such a discovery would have played out. Be honest and self-searching in that. I believe that the outcome of honest introspection of that question, will be a basis of trust from which we can carry forward as a unified species. If that statement strikes you as, somehow, naive or politically motivated in some way, then I challenge you to examine your own character before returning to focus on mine."

"This is a new day – a new age. It is clear, from what little we have learned so far, that the nature of authority and leadership Trial has observed in us, is wanting in his eyes. Yet, an opportunity lies before us. I can assure you … all of you, that past biases and strife will yield nothing positive in the new world in which we now live. And, it is a new world ... that you must believe."

"As I was thinking about the honest critiques that could be leveled in fairness against the events of the past few weeks, and against the United States, and against me; I began to realize that the concerns that influenced my thinking, my decisions, my behavior; were rooted within the same underlying basis: what might the outcome be if voices join the conversation that are not motivated first by concern for the general good? If we, as the leadership of the United States, don't speak, then who will? I wondered. And what might that person attempt to gain in doing so? The betterment of humankind? The advancement of the human experience? Or could it be that the voice may seek self-serving ends? We had no way of knowing."

"I will not go so far as to say that Trial cares about humanity. We have not observed him to be cruel, but he appears dispassionate. We're not accustomed to that. We, as humans, tend to show emotion in dealing with the issues of life that matter most to us. I don't know where Trial is, who he is, or even what he is. My hope is that we will learn much more about him, and other of the Remotes as we've come to call them, in the days ahead, but I do know that what we have seen from Trial so far, is that he is interested in behavior. Indeed, in his first communication with us, which has been shared with all of you, he cited concerns of war, famine, disease, poverty, crime and subjugation as measures by which our species would be assessed. And by those measures, according to him, we are lacking."

"If we may be comforted in anything, it is that he appears to be driven by ideals that are, at least in concept, aligned to our own. Yet we are concerned – gravely concerned by his stated intent to intervene. We do not believe it is his place. We are autonomous, self-governing, self-possessed; or so we would hope to believe. But, we are also outwitted. Trial and those of his kind possess vastly superior technologies to ours. We have discovered, time and again, that we are summarily unable to withstand any incursion that he purposes. And so, we come to the crux of the issue. Are we capable, as a species with a shared home, of working together? On any other day, on any more typical occasion, such as could have occurred before the days of First Contact, I would stand before you now and declare optimism. I would hold out the idealized hope that we could align to a common goal. That is not what I'm going to declare today. I have no faith that we can work together, that we can set aside self-serving interests for the good of the whole. Yet I am willing to hold out, not a hope, but an opportunity. Those who come forward in good faith will be received in good faith. Others will be turned away."

"Many of your countries have embarked upon creating facilities that will allow you to communicate with the Remotes over your own systems. I won't fault anyone for that. We're doing the same. However, you will quickly find that we are all communicating with the same remote party. When you are able to speak over your own lines of physical communication, perhaps you will realize that we, the United States of America, have withheld nothing of consequence from you as it relates to the ability to communicate in itself. If you should find otherwise, please make it known. All that has been possible for us since the moment access to the Remotes was exposed to our global computer infrastructure – the internet – has been possible for you as well. Our belief is that opening new communications facilities will result, perhaps, in a greater throughput capacity – bandwidth, if you will – but will not net to a material advantage for any one of us. That may be a good thing."

"I would like to talk now about Trial himself. No, we don't know if Trial has a gender. Truth be known, I refer to Trial as a male simply for convenience – it seems natural to me. I will not object, in fact, have no opinion if others do differently."

"Trial has communicated to us that we are at the start of a 150-year plan of assimilation. In actuality, his plan spans a period of 175 years – insofar as it has been shared with us – with the first 150 years articulating a set of discrete expectations. All of the information we have on this has already been shared with you, but I would like to discuss a few specifics now." Warren looked around at the large screen behind him. "Can we display the impact table please?"

Warren waited with his back to the audience, craning his neck towards the large screen. In a moment, a multi-columned table appeared. "Good," Warren said, turning back to face the crowd. "This table is somewhat self-explanatory, but I'll provide a quick summary to get us all aligned." He turned and pointed to the column on the left. "These line items are metrics that Trial shared in his very first communique. According to him, they are the primary factors that determine the state and maturity of a population, presumably composed of any type of evolutionary creature, as he calls us. A few things stand out about this list. First, technology is not mentioned directly. It is safe to assume, I believe, that technological proficiency is implied within the list; for example, overcoming famine and disease will certainly require technology. Yet, even if we acknowledge that, its absence tells us a great deal. Trial seems less interested in what we *can* do, than in what we *actually* do. To those of our scientific and engineering communities, this was a surprise. Most of us, I think, expected First Contact to be a technically oriented event. In some ways, it has been. As I mentioned; the remotes have demonstrated vastly superior technological capabilities. Yet, even with that," he pointed up at the list again, "Trial indicates that these are the things he cares most about; at least, for now."

"Backing up, this table shows how Trial anticipates the human race will progress along a specific set of topics, as shown in 25-year increments. As you can see, his assessment is that we are laggards in every category. The darker colors indicate *unacceptable* statuses. Gray colors signify *in progress*, and light colors indicate *acceptable*. The good news, according to this, is that Trial expects famine and subjugation to be somewhat mitigated within 25 years. Famine is a straightforward word. In our view, the word subjugation probably refers to taking unfair advantage of those who are weak; the practice of slavery, forced labor, and similar injustices."

"You will also notice something rather striking. By the end of 50 years, according to this, Trial expects that war will be, let's say, under control; but that during the window of time between 126 and 150 years into the future, some unrest is anticipated that could lead to war. This tells me that there may remain factions of dissention among the ranks of humanity even then."

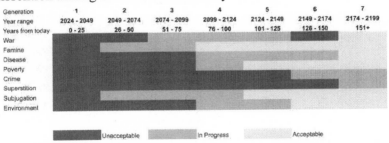

Generation	1	2	3	4	5	6	7
Year range	2024 - 2049	2049 - 2074	2074 - 2099	2099 - 2124	2124 - 2149	2149 - 2174	2174 - 2199
Years from today	0 - 25	26 - 50	51 - 75	76 - 100	101 - 125	126 - 150	151+
War							
Famine							
Disease							
Poverty							
Crime							
Superstition							
Subjugation							
Environment							

Unacceptable   In Progress   Acceptable

"Even more astoundingly, famine and subjugation will be largely overcome within 25, according to this, never to surface again."

Warren turned back to face the crowd. "This roadmap is a good one. We should have produced it ourselves. We should have aligned as a people, set our sights upon these worthy causes, and brought them to an end. We did not. And now a 3rd party, an interloper, has asserted himself into the concerns of humankind to accomplish for us what we ourselves, could not. I shamed by that."

He checked his watch. "What opportunity, then, do I offer?" He scanned the crowd. "It's a simple one, really. Let us impose upon ourselves the discipline to see these matters to closure, and in so doing, allow no room for any other power to interfere."

Chapter 83

May 8, 2024

The hours had passed slowly since the rover sat down on the lunar surface. Despite the deliberate navigation error, it had landed within six inches of its target. It was a record, and a lot could be read from it. If Trial had indeed, gone to the effort of correcting the error – and all indications were that he had – then he could have set it down anywhere. That the rover came to rest at the target location could mean that he either didn't want his intervention to be known, or that the chosen landing site happened to be the same as he would have chosen for himself. The prevailing theory was that it could be a combination of both.

Either way, there had been no mention of the error by Trial.

The host of engineers who had built the rover and planned its mission went about their opaque tasks with the relish of a chef who had spent hours preparing a meal, and would not diminish the work by rushing when the time came to reap the fruits of his labors. System checks were run, and a precise boot sequence was underway.

In virtually all respects, the rover was overbuilt for the task at hand. The high-gain antenna was deployed immediately, which boosted the radio signal to far beyond what was needed. Being designed for deployment on Europa, which would have been more than 400 million miles away from the earth during much of its planned mission, the communication system of the rover was tremendously overpowered for the comparatively insignificant distance between the earth and the moon. Despite the fact that the configuration on Europa would have involved an orbiting spacecraft to boost and relay the signal, the rover itself would also have been able to communicate, though less effectively, directly with the earth as well.

One of the first steps after initial checks were complete would be to wipe away the descent and landing software from the onboard computers and replace it with new software designed to optimize the rover's ability to roam the surface. What would have taken hours if the rover were on Europa, with the greater distance and resulting lower bandwidth, would be finished in just over 12 minutes on the moon.

The Remote Sensing Mast, or RSM, which held the high-resolution stereoscopic cameras, would not be extended until the new software was installed and all system checks were complete. The descent and landing images would also be examined so that the operations team could know with precision, where they were and if any hazards were nearby. Once all of that was finished, the first images the rover would take would not be of the moon, but of itself. It was the final step in ensuring the health of the rover before it would pivot to its purpose. The team would scrutinize the rover, taking a 360° selfie before looking outward.

Despite the laborious process, it finally did end.

"We're not going to be able to keep this a secret for long," President Warren said. "Since we launched this thing, I've been contacted by every country on the planet. They knew we didn't have anything scheduled for launch, so they want to know what we're doing. They'll just have to wait." He turned to Meyer. "How about the images themselves? Will they be locked down?"

"Yes. For the immediate term, anyway," Meyer said. "The videos are digital. We're encrypting them with an AES algorithm using 256 bit keys, then sending them over an encrypted pipe, too. If someone out there wants to use brute force, they'll eventually be able to do it, but by the time they do, the videos will be old news. We'll probably post them to the JPL website ourselves before anyone can decrypt them."

Warren nodded. "Good."

A woman entered the conference room where President Warren sat, along with NASA Administrator Paula Weinberg, Jeff Ward, Frank Boswell, John Riley and Ryan Meyer. Warren stood and extended a hand, which she took nervously, scanning the room. "Good to meet you," she said. "I am Sunipa Patel. I will drive the Spes Novus rover." Despite the unusual crowd, she was not entirely unaccustomed to high-ranking people, or public attention. On prior missions, primarily to Mars, she had conducted interviews and appeared in more than a few documentaries. She settled in well, and in only a moment, appeared excited but at ease.

"Very good to meet you, Ms. Patel," Warren said.

"Sunipa, please," she said.

"Sunipa it is. How are things going out there? Will we have pictures soon?"

"Spes Novus is the picture of health. In fact, we are ready now. I came to see if you had questions or requests before we ask Spes Novus to look around."

"I have a good many questions, but I'm afraid even Spes Novus won't be able to answer most of them," he grinned.

"Very well." She smiled. "Let's get under way, then. Our first pictures will be of the rover itself. That won't take long. We'll then direct the cameras upward and outward."

The Surface Operations Control Room was nothing like Flight Control. It was much smaller, for one, and there was no observation lounge. President Warren begrudgingly accepted advice not to enter the room for fear of unnerving the engineers and thereby, endangering the mission. The men and women would be under enough pressure without the President of the United States looking over their shoulders. He was gracious, but disappointed. "I could have stayed home," he said, after Sunipa left.

Weinberg gave him an understanding, but not necessarily sympathetic look. "We have a new control room and new procedures around driving the rover. We don't need any other variables in the mix. I appreciate your understanding." He let it go, and swiveled to face the several monitors on the wall. Audio and visual feeds were coming in real time from the adjacent Control Room. One of the monitors showed a top-down view of the Lunar area, which was zooming in and moving across the surface as someone from the control room looked for an optimal path forward for the rover. In a moment, a red line began appearing, showing the path that was being plotted from the rover's position towards Fubo Hill to the northwest.

Weinberg looked to Warren. "We don't drive rovers like remote control toy cars. There's a lag – granted, usually a far greater one than we will experience with the moon – but enough that every leg of any drive event is plotted with waypoints ahead of time. Once everyone is in agreement on the plan, the driver – Sunipa – enters the path into the computer, confirms it, then beams it up to the rover, which follows it. The red line is where the operations team wants the rover to go."

As Weinberg spoke, the video monitor was in continual movement, with the red line extending forward as new segments were added to the end of it. "What we're seeing here is an experiment. They won't plot the real path until the camera comes online to show what's ahead of them." The red line disappeared and a new one began drawing itself across the screen. This went on for at least five more minutes before the movement of the image abruptly stopped and all red lines disappeared from the map.

"Please raise the RSM." It was Sunipa's voice.

"Raising mast," a male voice answered.

The statement sent a jolt through the room. If all went well, they were minutes from finally getting a close-up view of what they had come to see. Warren looked to Riley, whose eyes remained fixed on one of the wall monitors. It showed a gray screen with the words, Stereoscopic Camera, at the center. At any time, the screen would update to show the view from the rover.

"And we have first light," Sunipa said.

A vivid image popped on the monitor. Having far higher resolution than any other camera to have been sent to the moon, the image was spectacular, even though it was pointed almost directly at the ground. The familiar gray tones of the lunar surface that had been known to generations of people since the early days of the Apollo missions were in clear evidence, but the image also contained faint tones of brown.

"Orientation is east, 94°. Commence panoramic sweep, clockwise please."

The view on the monitor reacted almost instantly. The rover stood still as the moon spun around it. It was finished in seconds.

Chapter 84

May 8, 2024

Sunipa's idea of the term *momentarily*, was markedly different from the thoughts the word conjured in President Warren's mind. He was learning that NASA and JPL clocks ran at a different pace than his own, and Angela Vandoren's fidgeting suggested the same for her. She sat in an adjacent chair, picking at the fingernails of her left hand. Looking at her, he realized that she seemed less enamored with the mystery that awaited them on the moon than everyone else. In the days before First Contact, they may be reacting to a coup in some small country on the other side of the globe right now, or a military threat, or a hostage crisis. To her, it would all be in a day's work.

She was as intelligent and capable as anyone at the White House. No one got into a key role of any kind in that place if anything less. Still, she was a unique person; upper middle aged, with an affinity for costume jewelry. Her phone chimed, arresting her fidgeting. She tilted her head upward to look through the progressive lenses of her glasses, scrolling through the content with her thumb. Warren's eyes rested on her, but she didn't notice.

When she finished whatever she was reading, she looked across the table to a young man – a NASA employee – who had been assigned to answer questions for the group. "Can we get an external feed to one of these monitors?" she said.

"Of course." The young man stood and approached a panel that was inset into the wall by the door. "What would you like to see?"

"Any of the news channels will be fine," she said, seemingly oblivious to every other person in the room.

The young man fiddled with the control panel until one of the monitors flickered away from an inert view of the lunar rover, to an entirely different scene. "This okay?"

"Yes, it'll do. Thank you."

The view on the television required no explanation. Marches of celebration. Warren's eyes rested on the screen for only a second before he spoke. "Peroxide?"

"Peroxide," Vandoren said, nodding.

There were legions of people crowded onto a city street, many holding signs. Warren couldn't identify which city from the zoomed-in view, but it was a large one – probably Chicago. One of the signs read, "These men showed no mercy, they shall receive none." Another read, "Trial, where have you been?" The view changed. A different city. This one was Los Angeles. Celebrations were in full vigor, rivaling anything that followed a football team after winning the Super Bowl, except that this one was playing out across the nation.

Warren reflected on the news feed for a moment longer, all other monitors that showed telemetry from the rover forgotten. He shook his head thoughtfully as he took in the scene. "This is a wonderful day," he said, finally, "but I can't help remembering a story I heard years ago. It was a woman who lived in Austria prior to the rise of the Third Reich and World War II. Kitty Werthmann. Have you heard of her?"

"I don't think so," Vandoren said.

"She tells a compelling story about the state of Austria before Hitler came into power. She was only 12 then. Her family was in poverty – the whole country was. She says that the Germans didn't conquer Austria with tanks – they were brought in by a special vote, which was demanded by the people themselves." His tone became reflective. "Hitler won by 98%. One of the first things he did after coming into office, according to her, was give everyone free radios. Then he nationalized the radio stations. Then came the gifts of socialism. From there, history took its course. Sounds familiar, doesn't it? Trial gives our whole planet the ability to build comms devices, and now the gifts start rolling in." He gestured to the screen. "How do you think a message of caution would go on a day like today?"

Vandoren gave the question some thought. "Let's just say that it wouldn't be good timing."

"Agree," Warren said, then looked back to the screen. "Who knows? Maybe this is enough. If this is a trade for our souls – if that's the price of all of this – maybe it's enough, just this one thing. I have to say that if my own daughter had been caught in this net, it would have been enough for me." As they spoke, new lines began appearing on the lunar feed. Even so, Warren found it hard to pull his eyes from the celebrations.

Sunipa's voice came over the monitors. All that was said in the Surface Operations room could be heard – it was a live feed. "Self-inspection good," she said. "Please orient camera to true north."

"Copy," a voice responded.

Almost immediately, the top-down view of the Spes Novus rover sitting on the gray lunar surface began shifting upward towards the horizon. Simultaneously, a graphical rendering of the rover's position in relation to the structures that had been identified from the satellite images appeared on the wall. The odd-looking hill, Fubo Hill, which looked to have been excavated away on the southeast side, was almost due west of the rover by 160 meters, according to the scale on the lower-right area of the screen.

Despite that, most of the president's mindshare remained on the celebration. He was struggling to pull away from it. It was such an immediate thing – seemingly so much more relevant to life than anything that could be found on the moon, but he knew just as clearly that they were all part of the same thing. Something was in motion at a far greater scale than even that.

The television monitor now showed an interview with a woman in tears. They were tears of joy. The sound was muted, and Warren peered at the screen, wondering what she might be saying. "Please extinguish this feed," he said. The young man, who had now become mesmerized with the scene as well, looked to him questioningly. The president understood his confusion. "Last night may well have been the greatest in all of human history," Warren said. "But now, we focus."

The young man nodded, and in a moment, was at the control panel. Warren looked to Vandoren. "Please keep me posted," he said. She nodded, her eyes lingering on the screen until the feed was replaced with the sterile telemetry data from the rover that had been there moments before.

"Commence 360° sweep, counterclockwise, please," Sunipa said.

"Copy."

The view screen reacted immediately. The lunar horizon began to pan to the left. Fubo Hill came into view within seconds as the camera brushed past it. "Whoa," Meyer said. It was almost involuntary. The camera didn't stop, but within the few seconds that Fubo was visible, artificial structures could clearly be seen in the background. They passed out of frame to the right, allowing no time for scrutiny. "There's something at 225° too," Meyer said as light reflected from a large object in the distance. "That's gotta be something on the road." By the time the camera completed the sweep, the room was abuzz with conversation.

Warren hoped there would be no need for further waiting. There wasn't. Sunipa's voice immediately came through. "Pan to 270°."

"Copy."

Fubo Hill came back into view within seconds. "Navigation, are we clear for westward movement?"

"Plotting course now."

"Advise when ready," she said. "Bring still-image of current frame to screen two," she said. One of the monitors in the observation room became a frozen duplicate of the live feed.

A man's voice spoke: "Range is 158 meters to Fubo at 260°."

"What is the range to the anomaly at 225°?"

"Uh, approximately 110 meters."

"Good," Sunipa said. "That also happens to be almost exactly the closest point to the trail. My guess is that it will be the safest place for us to drive. Let's lay down a navigation grid."

A grid pattern appeared over the entire area of the lunar surface surrounding the rover. Weinberg turned to the group to explain. "This close to the Lunar pole – Plaskett U is about 83° north by 160° east – typical lat-long coordinates become cumbersome. Because the longitudinal lines converge at the pole, the coordinates become badly skewed this far north. To make things simpler and less error-prone, the team will project an artificially square grid over the entire area. X-Y coordinates will then be calculated as meters from a single reference point on the grid. In this case, 0,0 will be the location where the rover sat down." She stood and began pointing to the display screen. "Here's the rover. The anomaly where Sunipa is going to take the rover first is–" she

stepped back, scanning the screen as if to get her bearings. "Yes,'
she said, tracing a line with her finger, "about 235 meters west and
145 meters south from the rover. That position can now be
abbreviated as 235W by 145S. Regardless of where the rover goes
from this point forward, that position will not change. Everything
will be calculated in terms of its offset in meters from that location."

The grid flickered, and new lines appeared. "Good,"
Weinberg said. "We're getting a better handle on the distances now.
These new numbers are calculated based on photos from the decent
cameras. We now know that Fubo is 1,461 meters from Southeast
Crater, which is at the other end of the trail.

"Unit of measure is in meters unless otherwise indicated.
Navigate to 238W by 150S, please," Sunipa said.

Weinberg nodded, pointing up at the speaker in the ceiling
from which Sunipa's voice came as if the statement validated her
own explanation.

"Copy. Plotting," another voice said. The top-down view of
the area was zoomed in and a red line appeared. It started at the
rover's location and grew in incremental segments, stretching across
the screen as the navigation team scrutinized the detailed images to
identify the safest route. "Recommend waypoint at 18W by 14S.
We have a small crater or depression in line of sight. We'll swing
south of it."

"Concur," Sunipa said. "Be advised that all bearings will be
given relative to true north. We will not utilize relative bearings.
Preparing to put Spes Novus in motion. Executing now."

The live feed panned left, and the rover accelerated slowly
forward. The view was surreal. The difference in resolution as
compared with even the best Apollo images from 50 years before
was startling. They were so clear that it felt like being there – or like
the entire scene was part of a video game. It was beautiful and
haunting.

The distance to the first target was short, but given the
rover's top speed of under three meters per minute, and with the

frequent need to navigate around minor obstacles, closing the distance took nearly three hours. But the camera was powerful. Even at nearly 300 meters, the images were crisp. When the rover approached to within 15 meters of the road, it stopped.

A structure stood straight ahead on the other side of the road. It sat atop a small hill above what looked to be the mouth of a shallow cave. It was oddly shaped, with a large-diameter pipe coming from the near side, then angling down towards a path that connected to the road, and then led into the cave. The pipe appeared to pass through the structure to emerge from the other side before burrowing into the ground.

"What is it?" Warren asked.

"It looks like a pumping station," Meyer said.

"I'll tell you what it's not … it's not new," Riley said.

Heads swiveled to him and then back to the screen. "What do you mean?"

Riley answered with a question. "Can we zoom in on the pipe?"

Weinberg leaned forward at once and pressed a button on the intercom sitting on the table. "Sunipa, can we zoom in on the pipe, please?"

"Yes. Any particular location?"

"I think anywhere will do for now, thank you."

The camera zoomed immediately. The pipe was nearly a meter in diameter, bleached white, with a ridge of dust at least six or seven centimeters high tracing along its top side."

Meyer was first to put it together. "Holy shit," he said, passing a glance back to Riley.

"Would you gentlemen mind sharing the secret?" Warren asked.

Boswell spoke first. "Mr. President, it would take eons for that much dust to collect."

"Maybe not," Meyer said. "There is very low gravity on the moon and virtually no atmosphere. Vehicles passing nearby would kick up dust. That dust could drift onto these pipes, and there would be no wind to clean them off."

"Can we get a close-up of the path?" Riley said.

Weinberg relayed the request and the camera tilted downward. The path was clearly visible, but also covered in a blanket of dust, as if there had been a recent snow.

"This is ancient," Boswell said. "That was good insight, Mr. Meyer, but if this dust was kicked up from passing vehicles anytime within the past 1000 years, this road would have clean tracks on it. Everything is buried under a blanket of dust."

"How old could it be?" Warren asked.

"There will be no way of knowing from the layer of dust alone," Riley said. "At most, it can give us a likely, minimum age. As the moon rotates around the earth, particles of dust can build up a positive charge from the sunlight. When the moon faces the other direction and dust particles are in darkness, they can build up a negative charge. At the point where daylight and darkness meet as the moon turns, the particles can be elevated upward as the two come into contact. Even without an atmosphere, subtle forces would cause them to drift. But, if a meteor of significant size has struck anywhere within proximity – and by proximity, I mean within hundreds of kilometers – dust from that could throw off our best estimates."

"I thought the far side of the moon was always dark," Vandoren said.

"That's a myth," Boswell said. "The moon is in tidal lock with the earth, meaning its same side always faces the earth, but as the moon travels around the earth, different sides of it come into direct sunlight. Think of me holding a flashlight in the corner of this room. Then, if you were to circle this table without taking your eyes off the center of it, by the time you had gone completely around, the light would have touched all sides of your head. From the center of the table, the back of your head would never be visible. That's how it is with the moon."

Warren nodded at the explanation, but was anxious to get back to the point. "Okay, how old is this if we assume the dust wasn't caused by a meteor?"

Meyer had been feverishly pecking at his phone. "I'm working on it," he said, raising his hand for a brief second, but without lifting his eyes. "I almost have it. I found a couple articles that estimate that dust builds at a rate of about .04 inches per 1000 years on the moon, which is about 1 millimeter." He glanced back up at the video feed. "I'm going to call that about 7 centimeters, so we're looking at a minimum of..." he paused in disbelief. "...70,000 years."

Warren was speechless. "Excuse me?" No one answered. "There has to be some mistake. Can we tell if there's been a meteor in the area?"

Sunipa's voice came over the intercom, drawing everyone's attention. "Pivot RSM to 165°, please." The camera reacted at once, suspending the conversation in the room. Her target was clear. Sitting on the path at a distance of 24 meters, stood a vehicle. "Let's keep east of the trail and come alongside," she said. The red lines on the area-view began stretching in that direction, and momentarily, Spes Novus began to move.

Without a frame of reference, the size of the vehicle was impossible to discern visually. Spes Novus stood to the side of it, dwarfed.

"That's big," Meyer said. "The rover itself isn't exactly small. The thing is a couple meters high and just as wide."

Weinberg pressed the intercom. "Sunipa, can we determine scale?"

"Yes, Ms. Weinberg, we're working that up now. The height is approximately 9.2 meters by a length of 17 meters."

"How does that translate to feet?" Warren asked.

"Roughly 30 feet high by 56 feet long," Meyer said.

Sunipa's voice came over the speakers again. "And width is 9 meters."

Warren whistled, looking at the vehicle with new appreciation. "It's as big as a house."

The camera view went into motion again, inching towards the vehicle's far side. Once past, Spes Novus turned its camera to look back. Like the road and the pipes, it was covered with a thick layer of dust. Despite that, it did not appear to be in a state of disrepair.

The wheels were entirely metallic, half the height of the vehicle itself. Near one end at the bottom of the body, were three symbols. The first resembled a backward seven, but the last two bore no likeness to anything meaningful:

"There's no cab," Meyer said. "It must be fully automated. It also looks the same from either direction, coming or going, which means it probably never turns around, it just shuttles from one end of the road to the other, reversing direction each way."

Weinberg nodded, then pressed the intercom button again. "Sunipa, can we go around the vehicle?"

"Not advised, Ms. Weinberg. There is a steep incline on the other side."

"Understood," Weinberg said, then bit back an impulse to ask more questions. Sunipa knew her job, and the mission plan had already been decided. It was time to be patient.

Boswell's eyes lingered on the monitor for a moment longer, as if to see if the rover was about to move again. When it didn't, he directed his attention to Meyer. "Can we get some analysts started on identifying these markings?"

Meyer nodded and pulled his phone from his pocket. "I'll get my team on it."

As they spoke, the rover moved. This time back to the northwest. Sunipa said: "The mission plan calls for investigating Fubo Hill first. We'll make in that direction now." As she spoke, the camera turned to the right. Fubo was surprisingly close. It rose above Spes Novus to a height starkly contrasted against the neighboring hills, which were more like gentle mounds. Its steep sides dove into the ground at almost 75° angles – and was a non-fit against the backdrop of what surrounded it.

Meyer was first to state the obvious. "That looks artificial," he said.

"Yes," Ward agreed. "Like a pile of dirt – but a very steep one."

"The steeper angle is probably an effect of the lower gravity," Meyer said. "Dirt will stack higher without tumbling down on itself."

There was a known problem with viewing landscapes on the moon; *scale*. The human eye was not able to take in all the shades of gray and the high contrast caused by the unfiltered sun to determine how big or far away things were. On earth, most things could be scaled rather easily. Any given landscape would typically contain objects that gave some indication of size that the brain was able to automatically take into account. Maybe a tree or a road would be present. For nearer things there were usually houses, cars, or people. On the moon, there was nothing. A crater could be 4, or 14 kilometers across, as Plaskett U happened to be, but without trees or cars to help discern the difference. In such cases, the brain would eventually give up and usually default to the assumption that things were smaller than they actually were.

The problem the team was encountering at the moment was similar, but different. There were structures – many of them, but it was not possible to know their sizes. The group waited, staring at the enigmatic video feed, knowing that Sunipa's team would be working the numbers. Once they came, it would still be a difficult mental exercise to attach them to what they saw.

Spes Novus sat facing Fubo Hill, which rose prominently to 30 meters above the surrounding terrain. The southeast-facing side of the hill was hollowed away, forming a flat area 75 meters across, which was excavated to 15 meters below the adjacent lunar surface. It was filled with an assortment of small structures and trails that led in and out. The most prominent feature was the large array of piping that gave the scene a decidedly industrial look. Most of the buildings had openings that appeared to be doorways without doors. There were also window openings without glass. Many smaller objects were visible in the recessed area as well, but it would take time to determine their purposes.

"All structures and piping we've seen so far are oriented in the same direction, just west of true north," Sunipa said. The rover stopped. There was a fork in the road. The primary path led straight ahead, but there was a fainter, probably less-travelled path that curved away to the right. "I recommend a detailed sweep of the area before continuing. This is – or was – a highly trafficked area. There could be many hazards."

Small buildings – stations of some sort – appeared at regular intervals.

"Those could be used for emergency purposes," Weinberg said, "or maybe to provide oxygen refills for whoever worked here." They were small; reminiscent of the enclosures that could be found along bus routes where people waited to be picked up. They stood with open doorways that looked as though they could be closed if needed, though no doors were visible.

Weinberg checked her watch. It was nearly 8:00 PM. It had been a long day. "Sunipa, I see no reason to put the rover at risk at this site," she said. "Not yet, anyway. Let's scan the area to get the best images we can, call it a day, then reverse course and track back towards *Southeast Crater* in the morning."

"That sounds like a good plan," Sunipa said.

"Good. Please ping me tomorrow when ready to move."

Chapter 85

May 9, 2024

Jeff Ward found Ryan Meyer peering at his laptop computer in one of the open cafeterias the next morning. It was early; well before 6 AM. The Johnson Space Center was not small, and there were many choices when it came to food or finding a nook to be alone. "You look like hell, what's going on?" Ward asked. Meyer's eyes detached from the computer screen slowly, his head swiveling up in a tired gliding motion. Only then did Ward realize how accurate his assessment was. "How long have you been here?" Ward asked.

Meyer gave the question some thought but gave up before finding the answer. "Not sure, actually. What day is it?"

"Damn it, Meyer! You've got to stay sharp. We have work to do."

"I know, boss, but this has been the first good chance I've had to browse through our new galactic Britannica. Couldn't tear myself away from it."

"Well, I have some bad news; you're gonna have to. Now. I need you to get some rest and be back here by noon."

Meyer nodded, but didn't move. "They've divided the history of the galaxy into ages," he said, already having forgotten Ward's words. "There have been seven by the way. Why does everything come in sevens?" It was a rhetorical question, but as he spoke, his grogginess began to lift. "The galaxy is 13.475 billion years old. We were almost dead-on, on that part. It's about the only thing we got right. They count the ages in terms of galactic years – the amount of time it takes for the entire galaxy to rotate. In earth time, that's about 192.5 million years." He pointed to the computer screen, and despite Ward's agitation that Meyer had worked through the night, couldn't help but follow. "See here?" Meyer said. "The ages are listed out: *Idempotent* was the first. It lasted almost 18 galactic years. That's about 3.5 billion earth years. *Chaotic* is next at 7.5 GY. Then *Formative* at 4; *Recondite* at 6; *Divergent*, 11; *Convergent* for 5.5; and now, *Emergent* at 17.3. Can't say I'm feeling particularly emergent at the moment. But," he swiveled away from the computer to face Ward, holding up a finger as if preparing to point out something extraordinary, "guess what's about to happen?" Ward didn't respond, and Meyer took a moment to realize that he wouldn't, like a man taking that extra awkward second to realize that another man was not going to return his handshake. Meyer moved on. "We're on the cusp of a new galactic age. The next one is *Ascendant*. Guess when–" He stopped himself and rephrased the question. "We pivot into the Ascendant age in 19 years. Not galactic years; earth years. The timing of that is beyond extraordinary. In fact, way beyond extraordinary."

"19, huh?" Ward said.

"Yes. 19 short years."

"Isn't that interesting?" That was a rhetorical question, too.

Meyer turned back to the screen. "Did you know that according to Trial's plan, we're going to have one worldwide monetary system by 2072? It's fascinating. It'll be divided into two currency types. There will be a *contributor currency* and a *consumer currency*. Not everyone will work, or be expected to by then. In fact, from what I'm seeing, there won't be enough work for everyone, so it'll be optional. But the people who do work will be paid in contributor money, whereas all others will get the consumer money. Both have the same value for basic services and needs – food, utilities, health – but the consumer currency will be worth only 60% of contributor currency for non-essentials such as recreation and luxury housing."

Ward allowed himself to be taken in for only a moment longer, then returned to his purpose. "What have we found out about the markings on the moon vehicle?"

"Ahh," Meyer said, tilting his head back as if just remembering an important point. "The numbers. Yes. I found something." He typed at the computer. "I know what they are. They're an alphanumeric character set of sorts. There is a shared galactic language, apparently. It's not always used locally by members of the Assemblies, but it is used for interstellar communication. It's entirely Boolean-based. That's what we'd call it, anyway. It's crazy fascinating."

Ward began showing impatience. "What are they?"

"What?"

"The symbols. What are they?"

"Oh, right, they're numbers. But they're written in the galactic language of logic. Believe it or not, it's a system we already know a lot about. It was introduced here on earth by a man named George Boole back in 1847, hence the name *Boolean*. It's a system in which values are expressed in binary terms, ones and zeros, but those values can also be arranged into logical constructs. You've probably heard people talk about how computers operate on ones and zeros. That's true, but what most people don't understand is that those numbers can represent more than just data. They are also used in sequences to represent logic, which in Boolean terminology, are called *Logic Gates*. Meaning, you can think of the messages that are sent in this language as programming code. Apparently, we have a lot to learn. In communiques between interstellar parties, messages appear to be transmitted in a form that contains, not only what we would think of as numbers and letters and words, but also logical constructs that dictate how to interpret them conditionally. That alone will probably spawn a whole new field of technology." He rubbed his forehead as if the thought was daunting. "Anyway, the numbers on the vehicle match this alphabet," he said, pointing. "In this case, they're likely just values. In something as simple as an identifier, which this almost certainly is, there is no need for logic." Meyer reached out to the monitor and turned it towards Ward, so he could see the strange characters plainly. "Look familiar?"

Ward leaned in. "I'll be damned." The screen showed a table of odd characters, and among them were the same ones that appeared on the moon vehicle.

Meyer continued his explanation. "The symbols on that vehicle translate to this chart. There's a unique symbol for each value from 0 to 15 – for a total of 16, which is a very round binary number. According to this chart, the vehicle number is 4-12-3. I still don't know if that should be translated on a purely numeric basis or alphanumerically."

Ward didn't understand.

"What I mean is; do the symbols constitute one number like 123, that we may read as one-hundred-twenty-three, or is it more like a serial number that we would read as 1-2-3? Take a social security number. Maybe it's 111-22-3333, but you and I know that it would make no sense to interpret those characters as a simple number. What would it be? 111 million? No, they are a sequence of numbers." Meyer shrugged. "For now, probably doesn't matter whether we can answer the question or not. Assuming for no good reason that the symbols are meant to be read from left to right, the vehicle's number is 4-12-3. But, given that the number is hexadecimal – our terminology – the number translates into decimal form as 4-18-3. Make sense?"

"Not really," Ward said, "but it's good enough. Well done. Get some rest." He turned to leave.

"One more thing," Meyer said. Despite his lack of sleep, he was now fully awake. Ward stopped. "I did some searching through our new database here." He gestured again at the computer. "I was looking for anything I could find on the Ascendancy. There's not a lot there, at least, not that I've found, but we're finally getting our hands on some useful information. You've seen the sequences of numbers – the metadata - that accompanies each of the messages from Trial?"

Ward nodded.

"I found what they mean. They're like digital signatures that identify the sending and receiving parties. We've been given access to a whole set of documentation that explains it. The signatures come in different forms. They can identify an individual, a location, a group, an institution, and who knows what else? They also contain a timestamp that is based on galactic time, and they're universally unique. There are 16 base forms that a signature can take – no surprise there. One of the formats is reserved for the Ascendancy. I still don't have much information on what the Ascendancy is, but the format Trial has been using identifies an individual – himself – as the sender. I translated a couple of the signatures from the messages we've received so far, and have found Trial's unique identifier. It's not likely to be his name, just as your unique social security number is not your name, but it is uniquely his, I'm sure if it."

For once, Ward did not look impatient.

"Now I would like to show something else to you." Meyer began typing at the keyboard again. He stopped and adjusted the monitor a second time for Ward's benefit. "This appears to be a translated document. It contains a message to a planet that circled a star that was about to go supernova. This was–" Meyer leaned in for a closer look at the screen, "about 320 million years ago. Anyway," Meyer said, looking back to Ward to verify that he was following, "I'd like to draw your attention to the signature." Meyer swept the mouse over the characters to highlight them, then leaned back to look directly at Ward. "This message was from Trial."

Chapter 86

May 9, 2024

Boswell was incredulous. "320 million years, huh? That's a good bit longer than a Sunday afternoon, isn't it?"

"He's a computer then," Ward said.

"I don't think so," Meyer said.

"Why not?"

"I don't know, I just don't think he is."

Warren said: "Get AJ down here. I want to talk to Trial."

Chapter 87

May 9, 2024

AJ and Sarah had been subdued since the last post from Trial. AJ had asked about life after death. In hindsight, it had been ill-advised. The questions they had asked seemed innocuous at the time, but the answers weren't. It was like asking in jest: *When will I die*, or *how long will my spouse stay with me?* And then receiving an answer far weightier than the spirit with which the questions were asked. AJ feared that the revelation could become a difficult thing for Sarah to overcome. It worried him.

A knock came at the door. AJ passed a concerned look at Sarah before getting up to open it. When he did, he found Agent Britt standing in wait.

"Good morning," Britt said.

"Good morning."

"Your presence has been requested by the president. He's in Houston. We should leave at your earliest convenience."

AJ immediately feared that his unsanctioned conversation with Trial was at the heart of the request, but nothing could be done about that now. Sarah joined him at the door. He looked meaningfully at her, and could see that she wondered the same. Britt either didn't notice the concern or didn't care. "We'll be ready in 15 minutes," AJ said.

"Thank you," Britt said, then turned away.

Of the many things that AJ had learned over the past weeks, one was that the Federal Government could transport a person to anywhere it wanted in no time at all. In less than three hours, he and Sarah were in Houston. First was the helicopter ride to an executive airport in Charlotte. Then a high-speed plane shuttled them across the country to the Houston Executive Airport. Another helicopter took them to the Space Center, and once on the ground, they were chauffeured beyond the public-facing areas, deep into the heart of the complex on an electric cart. When he and Sarah were finally shown into the conference room where President Warren sat with the full complement of men and women AJ had now grown accustomed to seeing with him, the president looked up and asked a simple question: "Did you bring your computer?"

It was almost funny, for some reason. "I did," AJ said.

"Excellent," Warren said. "Mr. Meyer here, tells me that we've received a whole new set of information from the Remotes. He thinks it's a reward for Operation Peroxide. I'm not so sure. Either way, we've learned a lot, and there's much more to come, but Trial ignores us. I'm irritated as hell at that, but that's a different topic. I'm afraid it's time to talk turkey with our new friend out there. I need you to help me with that."

AJ nodded. "Happy to." The worry of whether this was about the questions he had asked Trial the night before seemed suddenly unimportant. In fact, AJ realized he didn't care whether it was or wasn't.

Warren paused, taking a quick inventory of the room, glancing around as if deciding whether he may have forgotten something important before going ahead with his questions. Apparently, he determined that no further preamble was necessary. AJ had setup his computer and turned it on. It completed its boot sequence, and he logged in. "What do you do, just ask questions?" Warren asked.

AJ shrugged apologetically. "That's the way it's worked before. I just open a word processor and start typing."

"Seems kind of unstructured, but okay," Warren said. "Is he there?"

"I don't know," AJ said. He typed into the computer.

AJ:

Trial, are you available?

Trial:

Yes.

"Guess that answers that," Warren said. "Tell him that we have discovered mention of him from documents dating back hundreds of millions of years. Are we mistaken, or is he that old?" AJ typed the question, and Trial answered immediately.

Trial:

You are not mistaken.

"I want to know if he's a computer," Warren said.

AJ:

Are you a computer, or a living being?

Trial:

I am alive. Not a computer, as you would think of it.

AJ:

Are you mechanized? Some kind of artificial intelligence?

Trial:

No. I am a living being.

AJ:

But not physical?

Trial:

Not a spirit, as you may guess, but I am not a resident of physical space as you know it.

AJ:

The Ascendant Plains, then?

Trial:

Yes.

AJ:

How old are you?

Trial:

In your terms, nearly 14 galactic years.

"Impossible," Meyer said.

"What? How long is that?" Warren asked. He had not been present when Meyer and Ward discussed the topic earlier that morning.

"Sir, a galactic year refers to the amount of time it takes for the entire galaxy to rotate. That's just over 192 million years. That would make Trial more than 2.5 billion years old."

Warren's head snapped back in AJ's direction. "Confirm that."

AJ:

Are we correct that you are more than 2.5 billion earth years old?

Trial:

2,647,190,190 earth years.

"What are we into here?" Boswell said. "The universe can't be this strange."

Warren said: "Why can we find no better information about our own past in the data you sent to us?" AJ typed the question.

Trial:

Some information has been redacted for your benefit. It will be disclosed soon.

AJ:

When?

Trial:

Before 12 earth years.

AJ:

Why not now?

Trial:

The reemergence of Earth was unexpected by many. Your assimilation requires careful consideration.

Riley spoke, unexpectedly. "Ask Trial why he preserved our moon rover." AJ looked back, confused, but Riley offered no explanation. AJ typed.

Trial:

Inhabitants of the earth have achieved acceptance into the Assemblies of the Living on two prior occasions. The first civilization achieved assimilation 820 million earth years ago. That civilization was destroyed by natural causes, but left much technology behind on your moon. Only 40 million years later, a second civilization arose. It discovered the remnants of the prior inhabitants and exploited them irresponsibly, causing much disruption. That civilization also came to an end. Now, a third civilization has emerged, and is also about to discover what was left behind. For this reason, Earth is following an exceptional integration path.

AJ:

What happened to the second civilization? How did they end?

Trial:

That will be disclosed in due time.

Trial's refusal to give a direct answer drew a predictable response. Fear and awe descended into the room. The implication, as clear as if Trial had spoken it in direct terms, was that he had brought that civilization to an end himself. A conversation erupted in the room. AJ didn't wait for the others to regain their composure.

AJ:

What is on the moon?

Trial:

Technology.

AJ:

Are you warning us to stay away from it?

Trial:

No. That would be pointless. Any agreement we may reach would be forgotten in time. The future of the earth will be determined entirely within the ability of its inhabitants to mature to a state where it can be trusted by nature, not by commitment or agreement. No covenant could be reached between you and I that would bind your neighbors, your children, your grandchildren. You must mature as a species. It is expressly important that you adhere to, and apply yourselves to my recommendations.

AJ:

Why then, do you not destroy the technology?

Trial:

*The technology itself is not at issue. Even if destroyed,
it could be rebuilt in time. The question is of the nature
of humankind.*

Chapter 88

May 9, 2024

By two hours later, the group from the day before had
reassembled in the anteroom of the Surface Operations
Control Center: the president, Angela Vandoren, Paula
Weinberg, Frank Boswell, Jeff Ward, John Riley and Ryan
Meyer. AJ and Sarah were present as well. They had also been
joined by Margaret Statham, who had been absent of late due to her
involvement in Operation Peroxide.

Whatever had happened there had changed Statham in some
intangible way. By all appearances, she had always been a hard
person in that she was relentless and fearless in the pursuit of her
convictions. Peroxide had given her a deeper sense of purpose and
meaning than she had ever had, as if all the passions that were so
much a part of who she was by nature had finally found a purpose
that justified them. Her natural strengths had been matched, and
now fueled, by a need of boundless importance. She was the
embodiment of willpower and fortitude – AJ saw it and wondered
where the paths ahead would take her.

The conversation with Trial had changed everything about
what was expected from this day. It had also pushed the restart of
Spes Novus' journey across the lunar surface towards Southeast
Crater into the afternoon hours.

Sunipa's voice could be heard over the conference bridge,
directing her team and making preparations. The bridge went silent,
and in a moment, she appeared in the doorway. "Good morning,"
she said, stepping inside and closing the door behind her. "We've
been scrutinizing the images of Fubo Hill and the surrounding area.
We agree that the area in proximity to Fubo is an industrial zone of

some sort, but not entirely only that. There are complex arteries of piping, pumping stations, and a well-travelled network of roads."

She pressed the intercom button on the table so she could be heard by her team in the Control Room. "Can I please see a zoomed-in image of the area surrounding Fubo Hill? Please show in the Observation Room."

"Yes, one moment," came the reply.

The image appeared. Sunipa scanned the view and then pointed to where the rover was currently sitting. "As you can see, the road forks here," she said, tracing her finger along the screen. "The leg on the right breaks north at 21°. It continues 72 meters to end at the base of what looks to be an enormous conveyor, but we're not sure of that. It is confusing that the trail leads, not back to the Fubo complex, but merges into the primary road towards Southeast Crater. Also, half way along this path, a second fork occurs, which branches off to the left in a northwesterly direction. This leg eventually curves to the right and proceeds beneath an overpass, rising as it circles around to connect with a new set of roads at a higher elevation." She stopped and stepped back, taking in the entirety of the view as if reassessing it. "There is much to see here, and it will be very much worth the effort when the time comes. However, I agree with Ms. Weinberg that we should reverse towards Southeast Crater to avoid risk to the rover."

She looked to President Warren as if to gain his agreement. He seemed surprised to be consulted, but nodded. "I agree as well," he said.

At that, Sunipa turned back to the display screen, touched it with her hand and made a pinching gesture. The image zoomed outward in response. She then opened her hand and re-centered the image, tapping a set of controls in the lower-right corner. A series of circles appeared, surrounding several highly-reflective objects along the main road. "These highlighted locations," she said, "show places where there is either something directly on, or next to the primary path. The first is 195 meters from our current location." She pointed. "This is the large vehicle we saw up close yesterday. 125

meters beyond that, in the direction of Southeast Crater, is another."
She dragged the display up with her hand. "252 meters further, is
another. 168 meters further still is another – although this one may
be a natural feature. And the last of them is yet another 304 meters.
From there, it is 335 meters to the near edge of Southeast Crater.
The total distance from our current location is just under 1,400
meters. That's close to a mile," she said for Warren's benefit.
"About 85%." Warren nodded appreciatively.

"Anyway," she said, looking back to the display, "at our top
speed, if we were to make a non-stop run to the crater, it would take
nearly eight hours for Spes Novus to get there. Given these
obstacles," she gestured towards the objects on the path, "and the
fact that we have to keep a very close eye out for hazards, that may
translate to a couple of days. There is also a possibility we could
encounter technical difficulties with the rover due to the harsh
conditions of heat and highly abrasive moondust. The question
becomes, are we sure we want to take that chance, or continue
further investigation around Fubo Hill first?"

There was a pause, but Weinberg answered. "Those are
good points, but I still maintain that we head to the crater."

Sunipa nodded. "Very well, I agree. We'll get underway in
just a few minutes. We should reach the vehicle we saw yesterday in
about an hour and twenty minutes. Thank you." She turned and left
the room.

As promised, the rover was soon in motion. As it moved
along the path, it became clear that at some point, however long
ago, the road was heavily used. Despite being covered in a thick
blanket of dust, it was very smooth, of a consistent width, and in a
few places, had clearly been carved through uneven terrain. They
eventually reached the vehicle they had seen up close the day
before, coming up behind it. There was still no way of knowing – as
far as they could tell – which way it had been moving when it
stopped. The rover approached, came to a halt, pivoted to the left to
go around, and then retook the path to emerge again into unexplored
territory. The next object could be seen immediately. At only 125

meters away, it was clearly identifiable as yet another vehicle, virtually identical to the first. When the rover reached it, Sunipa guided it around to the right side. The only difference between this vehicle and the one they had just passed appeared to be the markings on its side: odd-looking lines connecting at right angles.

"I got this," Meyer said. "I found the numbers in the information Trial was kind enough to share with us yesterday. That's 6-2-5." He was immediately the focus of a room full of incredulous stares. He shrugged. "Kind of a long story. They're just numbers."

Ahead was the next object. It was 250 meters away. The navigation team had gained confidence in the road and made for it at full speed; a harrowing 2.8 meters per minute. "How are we doing on drive motor temperature?" Sunipa said.

"Uh, stand by." There was a momentary silence before the voice returned. "Nominal. The auto-shielding is working perfectly."

Because the temperature on the moon was extremely hot in direct sunlight, but extremely cold in shadow, temperature was not difficult to regulate. If the motors began running hot, the entire system for each wheel could be shielded from the sun to bring the temperature down. Each wheel, and its accompanying motor, had its own cooling system, with its own reservoir of coolant. However, the rover was not originally equipped with it. Being designed to operate on Europa, a frozen moon, there was no appreciable heat to be drawn from sunlight – the sun was simply too far away. Because it was a late addition, specifically added for operating on the moon, there had been concern – in fact, still was concern that it may fail. So far, it was doing well.

The next object soon resolved into something recognizable, if not explainable. It looked like a covered bridge. The rover stopped to make observations at 15 meters distant. It wasn't actually a bridge. It didn't span a chasm of any kind, but looked like a covered bridge from the countryside of Vermont, nonetheless – only at a much larger scale.

Sunipa said: "The opening is approximately 12 meters wide by 10 meters high. Length is not yet certain, but appears at just over 20 meters. We see no difficulties with passing through, other than heat differential. We'll need to run through a set of procedures before re-emerging into sunlight afterward."

The rover went into motion. In a few minutes, it was inside where it stopped again to execute a 360° sweep with its camera. It then looked up. The inside seemed cavernous, although it wasn't extremely large, even by earth standards. The supporting beams that were clearly visible, seemed oddly thin by comparison to what it would take to support such a structure on earth. After completing its sweep the camera swiveled directly to the right, 90° from the angle of the road, and stopped. There was a doorway without a door, and beyond it, a dark space – too dark to see.

Weinberg extended her hand towards the intercom button, but before she could reach it, a light came on illuminating the area. She drew her hand back, instantly mesmerized. Handrails began on both sides of the opening, cutting at right angles into the darkening space and then immediately following a steep, 45° downward angle before disappearing from view. Weinberg began fidgeting with her hands, showing visible restraint to keep from issuing orders to Sunipa.

It was for the best. In a moment, Sunipa spoke. "We're going to get closer to the opening to see if we can peer inside."

Weinberg pressed the intercom button. "Sounds good, thank you."

The view jostled slightly as the rover twisted beneath its camera while keeping it facing in the same direction. It was much the same way a tank could turn under its turret without moving its gun away from its target. After completing its rotation, the rover moved forward until it reached the doorway.

Sunipa said: "Spes Novus is about a 3rd of a meter wider than the opening, so we can't fall in, but we could still get stuck, so we'll need to exercise extreme caution here." The camera tilted forward and extended into the space, peering downward.

"Those handrails seem high," Meyer said. "They're also large in diameter." The statement earned a nod of agreement from Riley and Boswell, who glanced at him and then looked back to the video feed.

Beyond the opening were stairs that led down to a landing. It was not deep. There were seven stairs in total. The landing was a perfectly square patch of level ground with a door at the far end. This time there was an actual door. It was closed.

"This is a safety point," Meyer said. "I'll bet that door leads to a room where workers can go if they have technical problems with their gear."

"I agree," Riley said. "But that door could also very well provide access to a subterranean tunnel that connects the crater to Fubo Hill. We're at the midpoint between the two." All eyes tracked to Riley and then back to the screen with renewed interest.

Meyer was nodding. "That makes sense," he said.

The rover backed away, and the camera was brought back upright.

Sunipa's voice came over the intercom. "We're going to stow the camera temporarily to prevent any harm that could occur when the rover returns to the heat of full sunlight. There is a difference of nearly 300 degrees Celsius between darkness and light. Transitioning back to that heat could be hard on the equipment, so we'll pull the camera in and let the rover warm up before extending it again."

*   *   *

Six hours would pass before the rover reached Southeast Crater. The next object they encountered after the first 'covered bridge' was another automated hauling vehicle, again, virtually identical to the other two. The last object, at a distance of only 335 meters from the crater, was another covered bridge, also identical to the first. Its presence added credence to Riley's guess that it connected to a subterranean tunnel. That it was so close to the crater also bolstered the notion that there was something of significance within it. "This is probably a safety point as well," Riley had said, "but intended as an optional egress for whatever is below the crater."

It was getting late, but no one wanted to leave. All eyes were transfixed on the live video feed as Spes Novus inched towards the crater that had been their primary goal since the beginning. They could see from a distance that yet another of the enormous hauling vehicles was parked at its entrance. At 35 meters from the crater's edge, the road forked into two. The left leg proceeded straight ahead, while the other curved off to the right. The hauler was sitting at the edge, on the left leg of the road. Still, there was no way of knowing whether it had been entering or leaving the crater when it had come to rest, or how long ago that had been.

"My guess is that one leg of the road was used for ingress, and the other for egress," Meyer said. "The haulers probably came in one way, either picked up or dropped off their cargo, then made a loop to come back out. Which means the rovers did turn around after all."

"Taking the path to the right," Sunipa said. That was a good choice, to avoid the hauler parked on the left.

The road was cut deeply into the lunar surface at this point. It was still smooth, but recessed deeply within high embankments on either side. The reason was immediately clear. They emptied into the crater partway down its side. If they had not been cut into the surface, the road would have reached the crater at its rim, and it would have been far too steep of an incline for any of the vehicles to navigate.

When the rover reached the edge, the group got its first clear view of what had been a mystery from the first time any of them had seen the satellite images of the area. That image had shown something large sitting inside of the crater, catching light at its top. No one had been able to guess what it was. When the rover reached the crater's edge and stopped, the mystery was put to rest at once. It was an enormous excavating machine – or a loader of some sort. There was a path around the base of the crater forming a loop that the hauling vehicles apparently followed. It also solved the question of which way the haulers on the path had been travelling. They had been empty, which meant they were returning to the crater for another load when they stopped. Or perhaps their work was simply finished.

Either way, it was clear to see that because the loader was obviously designed to load moon dirt onto the haulers, and had no way of doing the opposite, that Fubo Hill must consist of what had been excavated from beneath the crater. By the size of the hill, and the hauling vehicles that carried the dirt, the subterranean complex must be enormous as well.

Spes Novus began moving forward into the crater. Sunipa had said nothing prior to putting the rover into motion this time. When it reached the boundary of sunlight and passed into darkness, the rover's light was turned on again. Straight ahead, at the far end of the crater was an enormous wall, which looked to be the outward face of whatever had been built below ground. A large door, such as could be expected on an airplane hangar, was built into it – more than large enough to admit the haulers. It was closed.

To the right of it was a smaller opening, the same size as all the others they had seen throughout the day: at Fubo Hill, in the structures that dotted the area surrounding it, and in the stairways that led away from the two covered bridges they had passed through.

Methodically and steadily, the rover approached. For reasons unknown, the small opening seemed more ominous than any of the others they had seen. Light from Spes Novus penetrated into a darkness that had not been disturbed for an unfathomable span of time. There was a small chamber beyond – probably an airlock – with less dust on its floor than they had seen at any other location. On the far side was another door. This one, closed.

"Spes Novus is too large to pass," Sunipa said.

Weinberg pressed the intercom button. "Let's inspect the outer wall to see if there are any mechanisms that could open the garage door."

The rover backed away. This darkness was different, somehow. There was a tangible sense of foreboding about it – and it was justified. Trial's comments from earlier that day had made clear that they were surrounded by forces and choices that could be the difference between life and death.

This was real.

"If I could know of a certainty that no other nation would come and mettle with this, I would fill this crater with concrete and leave it be," Warren said. No one took their eyes from the video feed except for Statham. She looked to Warren from behind, her eyes lingering on him for a long moment. AJ watched her as she watched the president, and he wondered what she was thinking – what she may be planning.

Spes Novus, fearless and mindless, drove along the length of the wall, its light shining to the right as it drove a parallel track. Nothing. The wall was seamless and smooth, but for the place where the large garage-like door stood, sealed shut. It was formidable. Soon, the rover stopped. They were at an impasse.

"There seems to be no way in," Sunipa said, finally. "I recommend we return to Fubo Hill tomorrow morning and search from there. Maybe we will find access to the tunnel Mr. Riley suggests could be there. Perhaps Spes Novus will not be too large to pass."

Everyone in the room was exhausted. AJ checked his watch and was surprised to see that it was 11:30 at night. Chairs slid as different ones from the group stood tiredly to their feet.

"Before we adjourn," Riley said. "Can we return to the small door and extend the camera into the room?"

By this time, about half of those in attendance looked too weary to care. Weinberg passed the request to Sunipa.

Momentarily, Spes Novus reversed its direction. It passed along the wall, its light now facing off to the left as it moved forward. It reached the door opening and stopped. The video feed jostled again as the mast that the camera was mounted upon moved up and outward towards the doorway. Once the camera was inside the plane of the door, it swiveled to look around. It was met with smooth walls and nothing else – not so much as a bench for whoever had walked these corridors in ages past to sit upon.

"There appears to be nothing of interest," Sunipa said. But the camera, from its extended angle had caught only the floor, ceiling and side walls. When it was retracted to its usual, vertical position so that it was again, looking straight ahead into the space, there was something new. New and alarming.

A red light glowed on the far wall to the right of the inner door.

Chapter 89

May 10, 2024

John Riley stood on the 5th floor patio of his Houston hotel room looking past the trees to the east, upward towards the sky. It was a warm Friday evening on the 10th of May, probably 9:30 or later. The moon was waxing, but still at no more than 10%. It was a clear night and the crescent sliced through the darkened sky with clarity.

The events of the past year seemed to be converging at once in his mind, leaving him profoundly aware of the new day that was about to dawn. He had many suspicions about what it could mean, most of which he knew better than to share. He was holding a glass of Blanton's bourbon, neat, enjoying the odd calm of the evening more than he had for some time – longer than he could remember.

Melissa watched him for quite a while, silhouetted against the sky, then stepped to his side. An Elton John tune was playing quietly in the background. "Have you ever noticed how music captures moments?" she asked. "Take any typical memory: it's thin. Dry. But if a song is playing, it will become a capsule that pulls everything in; whatever is happening, whatever you feel, your emotions – everything." She paused, considering the thought. "I remember this song playing when I was a young girl. We were on vacation somewhere around Long Beach. I know that's where we were because I could see the Queen Mary off in the distance. We were headed to Disneyland. I was so excited. Years later, I can hardly remember the park, but I remember that moment vividly because this song was playing." She hesitated again, as if uncertain of herself. She took a breath as if deliberately deciding to forge ahead into something she would rather not. "I've made a point of never pressing you for information, John, but I have to ask something."

He didn't look away from the moon. She knew that in his mind, he was up there, walking among the strange structures and machines that had shocked the world into finally accepting that all that had unfolded over the past several months was real – and that it wasn't going away. That it would never be yesterday's news.

Riley turned to face her. A wisp of a breeze passed by – warm and cool – catching a strand of her hair. "I understand now ... why I have to know. It's not about the secrets; it's about whether I can believe that I know you."

The light of the moon reflected in his eyes, and she wondered again – as she was now so accustomed to doing – what thoughts were playing out behind them. They were always deep, always probing, but rarely betrayed anything. She had no doubt that even as they stood there, he already knew her question and wondered whether he would make her ask.

He rubbed his chin. "Do you really want to know?"

Something in his tone gave her pause. There was nothing menacing or angry in it, but it was draped in meaning – encumbered with implications. "Honestly, I don't think I do, but I must anyway."

"No," he said. "I never knew, only suspected. It's not the first time this question has been posed to me."

"But it wasn't the surprise for you that it was for everyone else? Maybe you never knew with certainty, but it was your hypothesis from the start. Am I right?"

He grunted. "Clever." She had pinned him down. She would force a direct answer. "Yes," he said at once, deciding to give in without a struggle.

"For how long?"

"I always suspected it. This Universe is too big a place to be empty of life. I've never questioned – since the time I was a young boy – that the space around us was filled with words that we just didn't know how to snatch from the air – just as this song is passing between us even now. If we didn't have a radio to hear it, we would have no way of knowing it was there."

"So, you manipulated Brian Matthews from the start?"

He let out a sigh. "It didn't all go the way I wanted."

"And now that the Remotes have shared their recipe for gravity comms directly with the world, and because they're not exactly the same as what you developed under Mayfield Hammond, even the patents are of no material value. This is a bust for him – and Mayfield."

"I don't blame Matthews for his hatred of me, if that's where you're going." Riley was now facing her, all preoccupation with the moon gone.

"Can he harm you?"

He took a sip of bourbon and looked out over the trees again. "I won't tolerate much from him."

Melissa shook her head at that, lost. "You see? I don't understand that. What does that mean? What can you do? Who do you know?"

"Melissa, it's no longer a world of 'who you know' – not like it has been anyway. Sometimes it's *what* you know. This has never been about what Matthews, Ward, Statham, or even the president has believed. The world is on a new trajectory. Period. I can't change that; and never could, by the way. I touched off the inevitable, that's all. It wasn't always going to happen, it was always happening. Everything you could hope to understand about any of this can be found in the depths of that statement."

She seemed to be probing him, searching for a way into his thoughts, and Riley began to wonder where the conversation would lead. Maybe this would be the night she would finally decide that he was more than she had bargained for; would require more of an emotional investment than she could give. He decided at once that whatever outcome lay before him, he would not fight it. "I'm sorry, Melissa. This has all been far from perfect, but I can't help that now."

Melissa placed both hands on the patio railing, searching for the next question. "Where does this road lead? Do you know?"

"I wish I did, but I don't. What I do know, with a great deal of certainty, is that we're about to see the Universe for the first time."

She looked out at the moon again. "It's been up there all along – right under our noses. Isn't that something? Even under the noses of the Pharaohs, the Neanderthals. That's an interesting thought, isn't it?" Her eyes glistened in the moonlight. She wasn't crying, she was just beautiful. It was his turn to guess at her thoughts. Her face reflected the soft light as she took in the moon – a moon that kept its own personal relationship with every person on earth – as if it was her own. "Isn't it funny?" she said. "The rover wouldn't fit through the door. Why is it always the seemingly small things that change the world?"

Riley had no answer. "In six months we'll have another rover up there. The answers are coming."

"We'll just have to wait, then, won't we?" she said. "What are they going to call this one?"

"The rover?"

"Yes, the rover."

"Spes Vetus," he said.

She looked a question at him.

"*Ancient Hope.*"

Chapter 90

May 15, 2024

President Christopher Warren was awakened from a deep sleep by his phone. It wasn't a text, it was ringing this time. Not many people on the planet had authorization to wake him at 3:30 in the morning, and he knew it wouldn't be to discuss seating arrangements for the Sunday afternoon social.

He swung his legs over the side of the bed, his eyes lingering on the phone as it injected unwelcomed light into the room. By this time the First Lady, Julia, was leaning forward on her elbows. He couldn't see her concern so much as sense it. He turned at the shoulders to pass a final look in her direction. Maybe it was the tilt of her head, the set of her silhouetted chin, the pace of her breathing that told him, after more than 30 years of marriage, that she was there with him. Whatever it was, they would be in it together.

Warren pressed the video icon on the phone's display without picking it up. Immediately, a wall-mounted display screen lit up and he squinted as it resolved into images of Margaret Statham and Jeff Ward. They were sitting together in a conference room somewhere. Whatever was happening, it had been in motion for a while. "What is it?" Warren said.

Ward looked to Statham, yielding the floor. She nodded acknowledgement.

"We're still not sure what's happened," she said. "New information has come in from the Remotes. We think we must have passed some official threshold or milestone in their onboarding process."

"They've sent new information to us?" Warren asked, confused.

"In a manner of speaking," she said. "It's more like our access to information has been opened up. We have sudden visibility to an unbelievable wealth of information."

Warren thought about it. It was interesting – even exciting, but it wouldn't be enough for all this. There was more. He didn't bother asking.

"And," she went on. "Trial has made some assertions."

The pace of the delivery was already becoming an annoyance. "What the hell is it?" Warren demanded.

"Sir," Ward said, leaning into the camera. "We're going to wish we'd taken the *blue pill*."

Epilogue

O wen Henson walked through the shadowy hall of his modest home, not depressed – not anything – just retracing steps passed over so many times that he no longer expected surprises, good or bad, small or large. The years had long-since etched away all intrigue of life, leaving only the mundane behind; like a woodworker's plane smoothing the knots from a piece of wood, leaving a visual history of what had been, but lacking all texture.

It was a path worn slick from constant travel. Not the hallway itself so much as the larger tract of which the hall was only one of many nondescript parts. Even the creaking plywood panels under the worn carpet no longer made him think again of the need to get under the floor and shim them up from beneath.

If Liz were here. Well, no sense in that.

The knob to the bedroom door turned easily – slightly loose, but reliably – and swung silently open, having recently been doused with graphite at the hinges. Light spilled into the intolerable bedroom from the south window through curtains thick with dust. The room was not messy or even untidy, it just hadn't been cleaned properly as Liz would have done. Dusting was a thing seemingly unique to the domain of women. Not that the act of dusting was beneath him, it was just not the sort of thing men tended to think of.

Liz's absence found expression in far more than dust. It was crippling. Friends had encouraged him to leave their home behind, to start fresh somewhere else, but he knew that although the old house where the two had spent 37 years together would never tire of tormenting him, he also knew that her absence was even more haunting when faced with the new or unfamiliar. Where was she? What would she think of this or that? What a cool breeze.

No, he would rather contend with the house.

So much of life was good. There were words for most of it, but Owen had learned that its darker corners, the places to which he had been relegated after Liz's death, were off the paved roads of language. These were places where hurts could not be captured by words like pain, or aching, or even, longing – where language could not portray the cavernous nothingness that filled his soul to the brink of erasing him.

He vividly remembered Liz throwing her head back with laughter, clapping her hands at the sight of him losing his balance, and eventually his swimming trunks on a set of water skis that he had no business being in the same room with, much less attempting to use. Yet, strangely, the memory lay in his mind next to her tears at the loss of her mother, and the day they had argued over selling their blue Buick, or watched helplessly as their beloved Beagle, Skidboot, died.

All memories of her had begun to change of late, to lose their texture, their unique identities. They had begun to coalesce somehow, distilling into milky shadows of what they had once been. His newest fear was that he would eventually have only one remaining memory of her – a vat of nondescript events and images, having no continuity, and devoid of her essence. The thought of it pierced him.

It had become only the latest of a continuous stream of unforeseen ways to lose her. The thought labored his breathing as he methodically removed his tie, his shirt, his slacks.

In a moment, each hung neatly in a closet still mostly occupied by her clothes, now dusty on the ridges where they hung upon their hangers. He donned his casual slacks and T-Shirt, and sat in the familiar chair next to the bed, still where Liz had left it. The creak it made in the silent room as he settled into it seemed to complete his emptiness. He sat in motionless silence but for the swirls of dust in the streaming sun.

For better or worse, in sickness and in health, in death and the relentless torments to follow.

Everything was economics – the economics of how each individual fit into the whole. A human being is a uniquely impressive animal; intelligent, resourceful, capable of stupendous dreams and jaw-dropping horrors. But humans aren't unique, only humanity is. Of humans there are billions of copies. And so, Owen sat an example of the amazing handiwork of nature, yet somehow, by volume, worth nothing. Like any of the countless circuit boards littering the landfills of America: if any one of them were to somehow become the last of its kind, it could be appreciated for the marvel it was, but under the dilution of multitudes of copies, any one of them was less than nothing. It was pollution.

He was pollution.

Owen and his years of wisdom, experiences and insights; the steadfast practice of morality and fairness and faithfulness had seen its day. Nothing he had done, none of his accomplishments, none of the principles he had applied through the hard turns of life had any longer, meaning or relevance.

Sleep finally stole over him, as it always did. His head eased silently back against the chair, his eyes closing slowly.

Had he known it would be for the last time – that those eyes would never again take in the room that he and Liz had shared for so long, or her smile watching him from the picture on the bureau, he might have looked back at her – smiled at her a final time.

It was not to be.

He became aware of an odd landscape of endlessness.

Appendix

Gravity Field Modification

John Riley

May 2021

Abstract

There seems to be an inevitability to the notion of antigravity. Given how effectively other systems of nature can be exercised, such as electromagnetics, chemical interactions, thermodynamics, sound, and so on; gravitation can seem an odd holdout. Why can't we control gravity like we can electricity? Looking into gravitation and understanding its nature in terms of General Relativity brings quick clarity to the question, and reveals the difficulty of the problem.

If we start with the simple goal of either directly manipulating gravity or finding a way of directly overcoming it, then the first and most obvious step is to understand how it occurs naturally. General Relativity tells us that gravity is a consequence of the curvature of spacetime. Ignoring questions of Dark Matter for the moment, this curvature is caused by the presence of mass and/or energy, which distorts spacetime into Gravity Wells and then becomes enveloped within them.

This rather straightforward understanding tells us that if manipulation of gravity is possible at all, the only lever at our disposal for doing so is matter itself. If we assume for this exercise, that our understanding of elementary particles and their interactions, as described by the Standard Model of Particle Physics, is at least, mostly complete, and that antigravity is indeed, ultimately achievable, then the search for it reduces to finding the base mechanisms, the key interactions within that model that can be exercised to artificially modify spacetime curvature or interfere with the way matter interacts with it.

The concepts that follow are expressed in terms of the *Standard Model of Particle Physics*. They spell out, at a high-level, the properties, behaviors and interactions that can be orchestrated to modify a gravitational field.

Mass

The image below is a loose depiction of gravitation. The grid represents spacetime, and the distorted appearance in the area immediately surrounding the spheres are gravity wells. In the absence of matter, spacetime tends to be flat. There are non-trivial exceptions, but we can safely make that assumption for purposes at hand. With respect to the image, if the spheres were not present, the assumption is that the grid would be uniform.

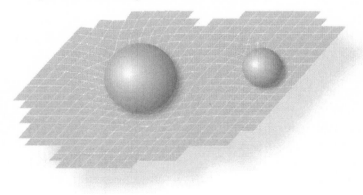

The depressions surrounding the two spheres suggest that if they were to come into range where their depressions began to appreciably overlap, that they would accelerate towards one another – they would begin to fall into the expanding depression created from the merging of their individual depressions.

For illustrative purposes, we must now level-set using an unpopular and somewhat flawed analogy. We'll use it to set a baseline, and then move on.

If we assume for a moment that we have benefit of an artificially perfect trampoline, we could reproduce the analogy depicted in the image marginally well. If nothing were on it, it would be flat. If we then imagined a heavy bowling ball and a large ball of Styrofoam, we could use them to experiment with various principles of gravitation in a rather crude, but not entirely invalid way.

The diameter of a Styrofoam ball with the same mass as a heavy bowling ball would be much greater due to its lower density. If we placed them onto the trampoline one at a time, they would sink to different depths. The bowling ball is smaller, so it will sink further despite the fact that it weighs no more than the Styrofoam because its mass is denser, more focused. Density is equal to mass divided by volume.

Looking at the trampoline edge-on, the slope of the well caused by the bowling ball would be steeper at the center, whereas the larger footprint of the Styrofoam ball would result in a broader depression that reached closer to the edges of the trampoline. Interestingly, edge-on, the area of the depression caused by each of the two would be about the same. This gives us an imperfect clue about visualizing mass, density and weight with respect to gravity. The mass of the two objects are the same, but the density is different, and therefore their impact on the underlying trampoline is different as shown in the exaggerated figure below.

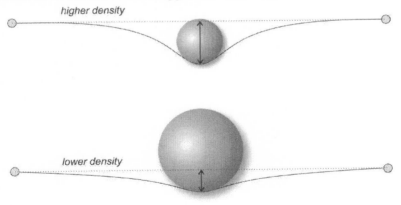

Looking edgewise at the trampoline, the length of an imaginary line between the deepest point of the trampoline beneath the ball, and the point where the surface of the trampoline would be if there were nothing on it at all, is analogous to the strength of the pull of gravity. From this point, it's not difficult to imagine what might happen if the bowling ball were to arbitrarily change size. If its mass were to stay the same, but its diameter increased to the size of the Styrofoam, then the depth to which it sank into the surface of the trampoline would decrease correspondingly, meaning the ball would rise.

Unfortunately, with respect to real gravity, the analogy doesn't translate well. A given quantity of mass has a predictable and measurable gravitational attraction to Earth. Although the ball may rise on a trampoline, it would not rise into the air as a result of decreasing its density. Here on Earth, the Styrofoam and the bowling ball are equally attracted to the earth, meaning they weigh the same (ignoring minute differences due to the distributions of their mass). Of course, if the ball grew to a size where its density became less than the surrounding air, it would rise, but only because the denser air surrounding it would push it upward, which would have nothing to do with modification of the surrounding gravitational field. To derive anything meaningful from the analogy, we must shift perspectives.

The Earth's gravitational field is rigid. All of the matter that makes up the Earth interacts with spacetime, and in aggregate, produces the gravity well that keeps our feet planted to its surface. It seems unlikely that any lever exists that could fundamentally alter the Earth's gravity. If we accept this premise, then we must look elsewhere for a solution.

Standard Model of Particle Physics

Physicists have long-since identified the four fundamental interactions of matter; that is, the forces that matter reacts to (ignoring the Higgs Field for now). That tells us that if we hope to overcome gravity, we already know what the levers are, we must only discover how to operate them.

One of the basic interactions is gravitation itself, but since gravitation is the interaction we're attempting to manipulate, we must set it aside. Doing so takes us a step further. It means that we have reduced our range of possibilities. If we want to impact a gravitational field, we must do it via one or more of the remaining three. So, what are they? The Electromagnetic Force, the Strong Nuclear Force and the Weak Nuclear Force.

In nature, the weak force plays a role in nuclear decay and in the types of physics that underlie the inner workings of the sun. For the most part, its usefulness appears to be confined to those roles. It has no apparent role to play in the manipulation of gravity, so we can set it aside as well.

This leaves us with Electromagnetics and the Strong Nuclear Force. The final solution involves using these two forces in concert; leveraging electromagnetics to indirectly influence the strong force, which then triggers behaviors that impact the surrounding gravitational field.

The Strong Nuclear Force

One of the primary functions of the strong force is to bind the nucleus of atoms together. A nucleus is made up of a combination of protons, which are positively charged particles, and neutrons, which have no charge. The catch is, in electromagnetics, opposites attract. A positively charged particle is attracted to a negative one, and vice versa; but two positively charged particles repel one another. Same with negatively charged ones. This means that the only way the nucleus of an atom stays intact is if something prevents all the positively charged particles within it from separating. That's what the strong force does. The positive particles within the nucleus are always trying to push away from one another, but the strong force binds them together, preventing it. Because the strong force is 137 times stronger than the repulsive force of the charged protons, the nucleon and the atom remain intact.

There are two kinds of nucleons; protons and neutrons. These are the particles that make up the nucleus of atoms. The common understanding is that protons have a positive charge, while neutrons have no charge. As a net value, that is correct. But, if you were to look inside of them, you would find that they are made up of smaller, subnuclear particles, called quarks, which do have charge.

All nucleons are comprised of three quarks. In simple terms, there are two types; up quarks and down quarks. There are variant types, but they can be ignored for our purposes. Up quarks have an elementary positive charge of $\frac{2}{3}$, whereas down quarks have a negative charge of $\frac{1}{3}$; the elementary charge being that of a single proton (e). Protons have two up quarks and one down quark, meaning that the net charge of all three quarks is one elementary charge; $\frac{2}{3} + \frac{2}{3} - \frac{1}{3} = 1$. Neutrons, on the other hand, have two down quarks and one up quark, with a net charge of zero; $\frac{2}{3} - \frac{1}{3} - \frac{1}{3} = 0$.

As mentioned above, without the strong nuclear force, the protons within atoms would spring away from each other, but the strong force also plays a role within nucleons. Just as protons would repel one another due to their positive charges, quarks with like charges would do the same. This means that even protons and neutrons would disband without the strong nuclear force to bind their internal parts together.

Interestingly, the strong force acts in a very specific way at sub-nucleon levels, and it involves yet another kind of charge, called the color charge. Unlike electromagnetics, which possesses two types of charge, being positive and negative, the color charge has three; red, green and blue. All quarks possess it. Note that the naming of this type of charge in terms of colors is only for convenience and reference, it has nothing whatever to do with typical color as we think of it. Simply think of each color as a label for a type of charge in the same way you would think of positive versus negative as labels for electrical charge. And, just as electrical charges of the same type repel one another, and opposites attract; like color charges also repel one another, but different colors attract. This means that a quark with a red charge will repel another quark with a red charge, but be attracted to a green or a blue one. Likewise, a green charge repels a green charge, but attracts a red or a blue.

The important thing to remember is that nucleons (protons and neutrons) contain three quarks, one of each color; red, green and blue. And, all quarks possess two types of charge; color and electromagnetic.

In a typical atom, nucleons are knotted together as tightly as possible because there is nothing to interfere with the pull of the strong force; that is, except for the comparatively feeble electromagnetic force. The diagram below provides a logical visualization of a grouping of three protons. The quarks within each proton are arranged such that their color charges align to form pairings with quarks of unlike color charges in neighboring protons. This works for neutrons too. The attraction between the quarks of unlike colors is the manifestation of the strong nuclear force within the nucleon. I've labelled this as, attractive pairing, in the diagram. Here, we see a red quark aligned with a green, a blue aligned with a red, and a blue aligned with a green.

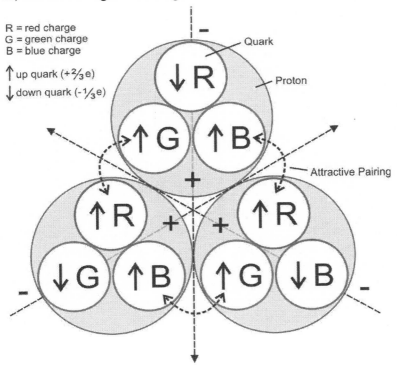

Notice the charge symbols on the protons, which represent the aggregate electromagnetic charge based on the charge values of the individual quarks within them. The straight arrows passing through the protons depict the orientation of the electromagnetic charge. As you can see, the positively charged sides of the protons are facing one another due to the overriding power of the strong nuclear force (denoted with "+" symbols near the center of the diagram). This arrangement is precisely the reason that, in the absence of the strong force, the nucleons would disband.

Supposing for a moment that the protons could be aligned along the electromagnetic field as opposed to the color field, as is the natural state, it would turn the protons to a point where like color charges would begin to come into alignment. Consider the diagram below.

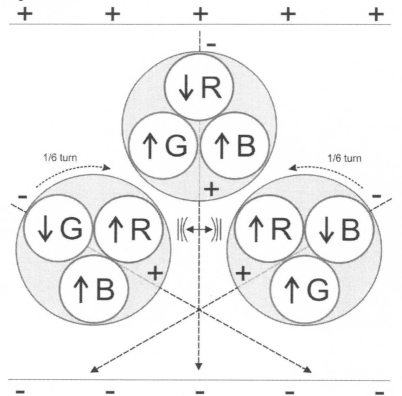

Here we see that creating an electromagnetic field that is strong enough to influence the alignment of the protons by causing their orientations with respect to one another to shift by only 1/6th, begins to bring, in this logical example, the red quarks within the bottom two protons into alignment. As a result, they push apart. If the protons were brought into full electromagnetic alignment, the result could look like the following.

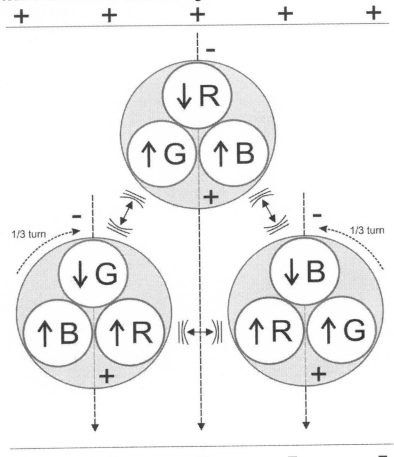

Rotating the protons by only ⅓, positions their internal quarks from being paired with their unlike counterparts, to where the color charges are exactly aligned to achieve maximal repulsion.

A reasonable conclusion is that, by interfering with the natural pairings of quarks according to color, and causing quarks with the same colors to face one another, that the protons would push apart. They would begin to separate.

This leads to a question: If this were possible, what would it accomplish? Would separating the protons have any impact on gravitation? Presumably, doing so would not change their mass. But, if we think about a light element such as helium with an atomic weight of ~4 as compared to copper with a weight of ~64, it could provide further insight. What makes one lighter than the other?

Density

In the end, the viability of modifying a gravitational field as asserted in this document hinges entirely on density. Using electromagnetics to impact the strong nuclear interaction, and thereby, indirectly, the arrangement of nucleons within atoms, serves the singular purpose of modifying density. The question then becomes, does density matter?

The most obvious answer seems to be no. Protons and neutrons have a known weight, therefore, changing the density of any object comprised of them should have no practical bearing. Astronaut David Scott performed the famous feather and hammer gravity test on the moon during Apollo 15 as a convincing visual demonstration that mass and density have no measurable bearing on the attraction of gravity.

But there seems to be something of a contradiction here. Gravitation is an effect of the curvature of spacetime as caused by the presence of mass, and the extent of that curvature is a function of mass and density. We know, for example, that the gravitational force on Earth is much greater than on the moon or Mars due to differences in mass; but density plays just as large a role.

For illustrative purposes, consider the effect of distributing the matter that makes up Mars over a region of space the size of the Sun. The diameter of Mars is 4,200 miles, whereas the sun has a diameter of 864,000 miles. Given that, the comparatively small amount of matter contained within Mars would be so widely distributed that there would be no surface to land on and no appreciable gravity. There is a good chance that there would not be enough matter to create so much as a recognizable dust cloud. How could the same quantity of mass yield such wildly varying gravitational differences, all based on how it is arranged? The answer is density. The matter is too widely distributed to produce a gravity well of meaningful dimension. The individual particles would still have their own gravitational impacts, but they would be too widely distributed to produce a gravity field of appreciable consequence.

Perhaps revisiting the trampoline analogy, which ended with unsatisfying results earlier in the paper, could yield further insight. There was an apparent disconnect between the way gravitation was depicted in the trampoline model and the way it plays out in the real world. According to the analogy, differences in the density of the bowling ball versus the Styrofoam ball had direct bearing on the gravitational attraction to the underlying source. Yet, this doesn't happen in real life. Where is the disconnect? Where is the flaw in the model?

In fact, there are several. First, the trampoline isn't representative of gravity at all. The surface of the trampoline isn't pulling the objects into itself; instead, the assumption is that the entire trampoline is standing within a gravitational field. The bowling ball and the Styrofoam ball are pressed into the trampoline because it is positioned between them and, presumably, some large body which is the source of gravitation.

The second, more relevant issue is that the analogy treats each of the two balls as indivisible units. Meaning, the attraction of gravity plays out against each of the balls as if they were non-reducible objects. Real gravitation acts upon each individual particle within objects, not at the level of the objects that are constructed from them. In the analogy, each atom in the bowling ball presses down, not against the trampoline, but against the atoms between it and the trampoline. The aggregate downward force of all the vertically aligned atoms meets the trampoline surface at the bottom-most atom, which transfers the combined force of them all.

It can't be depicted meaningfully in terms of the trampoline analogy, but if each individual atom that makes up the balls, somehow transferred its weight directly to the trampoline surface, the analogy would be at least, a step closer to having real-world physical applicability. The image above shows that the shape of an object has bearing on how it interacts with gravity, but because the impacts are vanishingly small, they are ignored for all practical purposes.

Another way to think of this is that each atom within the balls are subject to gravitational attraction to a measure entirely defined by their own mass and density. The incidental fact that they happen to be grouped together into balls has no appreciable bearing. Thinking of the balls as convenient groupings of the individual atoms within them, and understanding that each atom has its own weight, brings some clarity to the reasons a feather and a hammer appear to fall at the same rate if not interfered with by other forces, such as the resistance of air. Both the feather and the hammer are made up of atoms (granted, of different types), and each of those atoms has weight, which means they will fall individually or in groups, at a given rate.

Yet, we know that density is a factor. As matter coalesces in space, for example, it presses deeper and deeper into spacetime. What may begin as a very shallow gravity well can, nonetheless, cause nearby matter to slide into it, contributing its own mass. The impact is that the gravity well becomes deeper and stronger, extending its reach and attracting still more mass. This is the very type of process that leads to the formation of new stars and solar systems, typically from the starting point of clouds of hydrogen.

Mass Distribution within Atoms

Just as the bowling ball is not an indivisible unit, we must understand that atoms aren't either. They do not interact with spacetime as a whole, but at a subatomic level.

The primary, system-level components of atoms are electrons, nucleons and the forces, or interactions that impact their behaviors. From a mass perspective, electrons contribute little. With a mass of 1,832 times less than a nucleon, they do not play an appreciable role in gravitation. If we remove them from consideration for now, the next place to look is into the nucleus. It is here that the bulk of the mass of an atom is located.

It may seem reasonable to assume that since nucleons (protons and neutrons) are made up of three quarks each, as discussed earlier, that the rest mass of the nucleon would equal the sum of the rest mass of the quarks within them, but that is not the case. In fact, it is rather astounding to know that the rest mass of the quarks within nucleons accounts for approximately 1% of the overall nucleon mass. The remainder, in simplified terms, takes the form of energy.

This tells us that the rest mass of a nucleon is the invariant mass of its inner parts. Said another way, it is the base-most point at which quantum-level systems of energy and momentum come together to form into particles of appreciable rest mass. It is at this point, not at the aggregate weight of a nucleus, nor at the system-level weight of atoms, that primitive interactions with spacetime occur. This appears to be the base-most, non-reducible point where mass and density come together in a way that is impactful to weight in a stable way. Let us look a little closer.

The electromagnetic and color charges of the protons in a nucleus can never be fully aligned naturally at the same time.

Meaning, when quarks are positioned such that unlike color charges are optimally aligned to be adjacent to one another (natural state), the electromagnetic charges are thereby forced into non-optimal alignment where their like charges are adjacent (positive ↔ positive, negative ↔ negative; below left). Likewise, if the electromagnetic charges were somehow brought into alignment (below right), it would force sub-optimal alignment of color charges. It's as though a natural toggle between opposing states is built into the base behaviors of these elemental particles in an elegant and fascinating way.

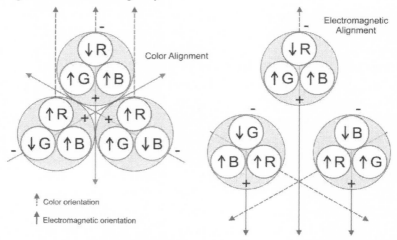

Ignoring the specific properties of atoms, nuclei and their interactions for a moment, is there anything that can be derived from the general characteristics of spatial density that could help us understand the impacts of changing the density of a nucleus as shown above?

Copper has an atomic weight of 63.546 amu (atomic mass unit). It has 29 protons and 35 neutrons. The commonly accepted radius of its nucleus is 145pm (picometer). The nucleus of atoms can take many shapes depending on the arrangement of the nucleons within them, but if we assume for our purposes that they are spherical, we can begin to work through scenarios to prove an important concept related to density.

The currently accepted radius of a proton is about .87fm (femtometer). If the 64 nucleons of a copper atom were packed as tightly as possible (29 protons + 35 neutrons = 64), the radius of the nucleus would be 3.847fm. This is based on the Kepler Conjecture, which asserts that the maximal density of spheres (nucleons in our case) that can be packed into a larger sphere (the nucleus) is about 74%. This value is best case in the pristine terms of Euclidean Geometry, but will sufficiently serve our purposes. On the lower end, randomly arranged spheres can have a much lower volume of ~64%.

The distance of separation of nucleons that can be achieved through the alignment of color charges has yet to be calculated. Regardless of what the distance happens to be, calculating its impact on the overall density of the nucleus will be a trivial matter. If alignment of color charges is possible, and we were to assume for sake of argument that the nucleus can be dilated to a point where the resulting space between nucleons is equal to as little as half of their diameters (one radius), then the overall density of the nucleus will drop from 74% to 28%, as depicted in the image below.

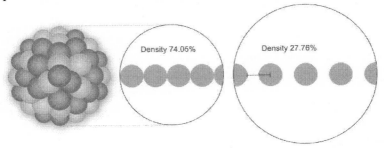

Presuming that modifying the nuclei density of a grouping of copper atoms from 74% to 28% would have no impact on the radius of the atom (although there would likely be an impact to the shape of the electron orbital shells due to the restacking of nuclei), there would be no change to the amount of mass in a mole, for example. Meaning, a cube of copper would contain the same number of atoms, the same number of nucleons and the same number of quarks whether dilated or not. The mass would be the same, but the density would be markedly different.

Thinking of the gravitational attraction between the nucleons within the atom in terms of spacetime curvature, we could assert that the attraction between the nucleons would diminish by the square of the distance between them, as depicted below.

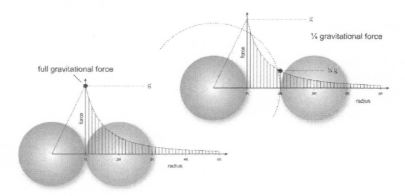

As we know, the force of gravitational attraction is a function of spacetime curvature. The only explanation for the two protons on the upper right to experience ¼ the gravitational force as those on the lower left is less spacetime curvature.

When it comes to spacetime curvature, it is not the density of atoms that matter, per se; but the density of the nucleons within them. As outlined earlier, atoms are not indivisible units of matter. When groupings of atoms coalesce in sufficient quantities to produce appreciable spacetime curvature (gravity wells), the nucleons within those atoms are where material impact occurs. This means that although the overall mass of a given quantity of copper, for instance, would not change if their nuclei were dilated in this way; the distribution of mass within them would result in a shallower gravity well because the dilated nuclei would be defocused, resulting in less curvature, and therefore, less gravitational force. Specifically, if the nucleus of a copper atom were dilated as described above (the density of copper is 8.92 g/cm3), its density would drop to only slightly more than that of silicon (2.33 g/cm3).

In terms of gravitation, matter moves, and in fact, accelerates towards other matter due only to the overlap of the individual gravity wells that surround them. Whatever the scale and quantity, these are base behaviors. The Earth, Mars, the sun, and even an atom, produce gravity wells. They range in size and strength, but anywhere there is matter, there is a corresponding impact to the shape and curve of spacetime. If we imagine the collective gravity well produced by a group of atoms, and that the mass within those atoms is de-densified, the impact would be modification to the curvature of spacetime.

Conclusion

Many questions remain, such as:

- *How strong will the electromagnetic field have to be to influence the orientation of protons? Given that the Strong Nuclear Force is 137 times stronger than the electromagnetic force, the value will express as a measure of rotational torque that must be applied to the proton.*

- *Given the extremely short range of the Strong Nuclear Force, the extent to which a nucleus can be dilated without breaking the nuclear bond between nucleons must be determined. What are the boundaries?*

- *Will nuclei dilation impact the shape of electron shells? Dilation could free the protons and neutrons enough to allow them to restack in ways that impact the electromagnetic fields they emit, thereby reshaping the electron shells.*

- *Quarks continuously fluctuate in color. Will it matter, or will the repulsive phenomenon that occurs between adjacent, like colors simply transfer seamlessly from one state to the next? Given that the nuclear bond between quarks is unbroken during this natural process, it may be reasonable to*

*assume that changes in color will have no impact
on the mechanisms discussed in this paper.*

There is also the question of the role neutrons will play in these mechanisms. Being possessed of two down quarks and one up quark, the net electromagnetic charge of a neutron is 0e. However, the expectation is that the force of torque will be conveyed from protons to neutrons via the color force, similarly to how a car with only one driving wheel nonetheless causes all four wheels to turn simultaneously as they carry the car forward. Under normal conditions, it is impossible to detect which of the four wheels is supplying the force that causes the car to move. Likewise, the electromagnetic field used to cause the collective protons of the nucleus to rotate must be sufficiently powerful to rotate the neutrons as well, overcoming the resistance of the color force for themselves and the neutrons. This suggests that, in general, elements with lower proportions of neutrons in ratio to protons may be more efficient materials for antigravity.

Finally, nucleons are not arranged as neatly in reality as they have been depicted here. They are clusters of protons and neutrons, in which the alignment of color charges must play out in three dimensions. The efficiency of the systems discussed here will be a factor of how those nucleons are arranged.

The next question is the most obvious of all. How can this be done?

GTSC-IFDE-448449

Interstellar Format for Data Exchange

Abstract

The Interstellar Format for Data Exchange (IFDE) is a set of specifications describing the structure, content and methodologies for sharing information between parties. The entirety of the specification is defined via a set of interdependent documents that describe, in exhaustive detail, the various concerns which must be orchestrated to achieve the following goals:

1. *Universal identification of sending and receiving parties*

2. *Establishment of base linguistic elements with which numeric and logical constructs may be conveyed*

3. *Standardization of transport, encryption, time and spatially-based signing*

4. *Compliance with audit and traceability regulations established by the Galactic Technological Standards Commission (GTSC), which governs the use of Non-Relativistic Mediums of Communication (NRMC).*

This sub-specification deals with the core language elements underlying all NRMC data traffic.

Note that this document has been translated according to LA-UDA standards, with further reference to the LA-UBLA sub-documents.

Terminology

- **GTSC**: *Galactic Technological Standards Commission*

- **IFDE**: *Interstellar Format for Data Exchange*

- ***LA-UDA****: Linguistic Algorithms for Ubiquitous Data Normalization*

- ***LA-UBLA****: Linguistic Algorithms for Ubiquitous Binary Logic Normalization*

- ***NRMC****: Non-Relativistic Mediums of Communication*

Standard Encodings for Information Exchange

The base set of elements underlying all interstellar communication is described as the set of binary values between zero (0) and fifteen (15 dec), inclusive. Note that substantial extensions and derivative character sets are in widespread use.

The base element set is as follows:

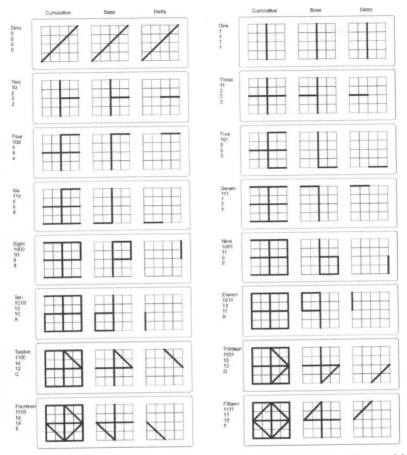

Each of the elements above represents a numerical value, along with common ways in which it may be interpreted, as described below:

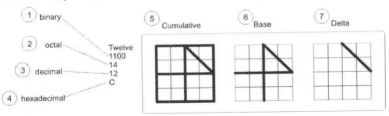

1. *Binary: the two-state value of the number (radix of 2).*

2.   *Octal: The eight-state value of the number (radix of 8).*

3.   *Decimal: The ten-state value of the number (radix of 10).*

4.   *Hexadecimal: The sixteen-state value of the number (radix 16).*

5.   *Cumulative: Each value within the IFDE is constructed via the cumulative overlay of delta (or significant) segments. The system is designed such that larger numbers are comprised of the entirety of the segments embodied within lower values, plus one differentiating segment.*

6.   *Base: Although both the cumulative and base expressions are equally correct, the base form is preferred.*

7.   *Delta: The additive segment that differentiates a value from the next lower value. The system is designed to support segment-level bitmasking. Each discrete value has a unique significant segment.*

Cumulative Segment Overlay

The following figure illustrates that the difference between the cumulative value for eight and nine, for example, is equal to the delta (or significant) segment of the value nine. As noted, mathematical addition, and the binary operators of "and", "or" and "xor" have the same effect in this example.

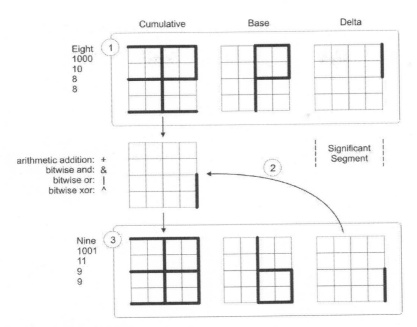

Normative References

GTSC-IFDE-933983	NRMC Signature Format
GTSC-IFDE-C-11373	Spatial Cryptography
GTSC-IFDE-C-11361	Time-based Cryptography
GTSC-IFDE-C-02234	Multi-Symmetric Data Cryptography
GTSC-IFDE-325767	NRMC Data Envelopment
GTSC-IFDE-023924	NRMC Logic Envelopment via Spatial Offsetting
GTSC-IFDE-000024	NRMC Compliance and Regulation
GTSC-IFDE-001102	Linguistic Algorithms for Ubiquitous Data Normalization
GTSC-IFDE-001103	Linguistic Algorithms for Ubiquitous Binary Logic Normalization

Assemblies of the Living

Human Assimilation

Over a period of 150 Earth years, beginning in 2024 and ending in 2174, a program of global assimilation shall be undertaken during which the human race will be guided along a path of understanding and compliance, into behavioral, social and technological governance by the Assemblies of the Living. The 150-year period is divided into 25-year phases, during which the anticipated disposition of age groups, with respect to acceptance of oversight, are monitored and guided.

Although the assimilation of Earth shall follow an exception path due to circumstances not disclosed within this decree, the 150-year journey outlined in the table below is the outcome of both precedent, and intelligence gathered about the human race.

The current behavioral and social disposition of humanity in consideration of base-most concerns related to suitability for participation in the Assembly of the Living is summarily wanting, as illustrated below.

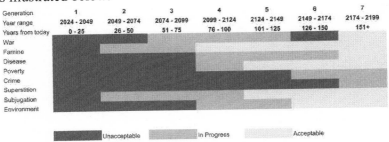

Little measurable progress is expected during the first 25 years. However, famine and subjugation will begin trending towards favorability almost immediately, with significant improvement expected within 26 to 50 years.

At the program level, assimilation shall progress via the sharing of enlightened information, clarity of expectation, the promise of improved quality of life, and the goal of acceptance as a participant in good standing within the Assemblies of the Living.

Very little shall be achieved via direct intervention. Human assimilation shall be accomplished by means of conditioning, wherein defined age groups are targeted, educated, and thereby progressed towards adherence.

The color-coded table below depicts the anticipated disposition of age groups within 25-year windows of time, which correspond to the social graph above. The darker colors indicate general unfavourability towards assimilation, as ranked on a scale from zero (0) to seven (7). Taken together, this view depicts the means by which the outcomes outlined above will be reached.

Generation	1	2	3	4	5	6
Year Range	2024 - 2049	2049 - 2074	2074 - 2099	2099 - 2124	2124 - 2149	2149 - 2174
Year Delta	0 - 25	26 - 50	51 - 75	76 - 100	101 - 125	126 - 150
						0-6: Indoctrinated [7]
					0-6: Indoctrinated [7]	7-31: Contributive [7]
				0-6: Indoctrinated [7]	7-31: Indoctrinated [6]	32-56: Assimilated [7]
			0-6: Amenable [5]	7-31: Strategic [5]	32-56: Invested [6]	57-81: Invested [6]
			7-31: Indoctrinated [5]	32-56: Progressive [5]	57-81: Stabilizing [6]	82-106: Supportive [6]
	0-6: Amenable [3]	0-6: Amenable [4]	32-56: Influential [4]	57-81: Advocative [4]	82-106: Supportive [5]	
	7-31: Adherent [2]	7-31: Disruptive [3]	57-81: Accepting [3]	82-106: Inconsequential		
	32-56: Distrustful [1]	32-56: Receptive [2]	82-106: Inconsequential			
	57-81: Resistant [0]	57-81: Compliant [1]				
	82-106: Inconsequential	82-106: Inconsequential				

Age Demographic-Targeted Assimilation

The program establishes core age-based demographic groups, generalizes their dispositions with respect to assimilation, and introduces treatments to influence them favorably.

Generation One: 2024 through 2049

Ages 0 through 6: Amenable

Overall, newborns, through the age of 6 are highly impressionable. Any new generation, that is, any person within this age group, typically has the capacity for immediate assimilation; however, the demographic is also entirely dependent upon, and therefore, influenced by its parent generation. For this reason, although the individuals themselves have the ability; in fact, the potential to reach indoctrination, they will not have the proper influences to do so.

Ages 7 through 31: Adherent

Having young individuals in their care, and being generally progressive, this age group is most influential in the initial phases of turning towards the social ideals promoted within the Assemblies of the Living. However, the group does not hold the reins of power, and is therefore, heavily influenced by its parent generation. Even so, this group is the first to adhere to the requirements of the Assemblies of the Living.

Ages 32 through 56: Distrustful

Being well into their chosen vocations, this group is most influential in terms of spending power. Although they are not, in general, in direct control of governmental or corporate policies, they nonetheless, indirectly guide trends by reason of spending habits.

Even so, they are distrustful of new influences. They will adhere to regulation and policy, but may subvert it where they do not understand or agree with it.

Ages 57 through 81: Resistant

This group is most influential in terms of governmental and corporate power. During the span of the first 25 years, the group will be unreceptive to oversight, and actively subvert the goals of the assimilation program. Changing the disposition of this group will not be possible within the span of years within which they will be in possession of their far-reaching influence. Therefore, they shall be tolerated until they age to become inconsequential.

Ages 82 through 106: Inconsequential

Although individuals within this age demographic are in possession of monetary influence, they are typically conservative in their utilization of it. With few exceptions, this age group is not materially influential in ways that are impactful to the assimilation program, and therefore, will not be actively targeted for behavioral modification.

Generation Two: 2049 through 2074

Ages 0 through 6: Amenable

Having been born into the world after the first 25-year phase is complete, this group will grow to become highly influential and contributive to the goals of assimilation. War and subjugation will have been largely arrested, but the tensions and conditions under which they could reignite, remain.

Ages 7 through 31: Disruptive

As the first generation to live almost entirely under the influence of the assimilation program, and therefore, having seen the value and promise of its objectives, this demographic will be disruptive in a positive way towards assimilation. However, it is still heavily influenced by the next-older generation, which has become receptive, but not entirely supportive of assimilation.

Ages 32 through 56: Receptive

As holder of the largest reserve of disposable income, and having lived the majority of life within the influence of the assimilation program, this group is receptive and influential, but not fully accepting of the notion of oversight. Even so, the group is less likely to subvert program goals, or act in collusion with those who do.

Ages 57 through 81: Compliant

Having been largely distrustful of oversight, and the means by which the goals of assimilation have been undertaken during the first 25-year phase, this demographic is compliant, but does not embrace or fully accept forfeiture of sovereignty. The group progresses no further in terms of adoption of the ideals promoted within the Assemblies of the Living, but will soon age into inconsequentialism, and therefore, will not be targeted for further behavioral modification.

Ages 82 through 106: Inconsequential

Having been the holder of governmental and corporate power during the first phase of assimilation, and actively resistant during that time, the passage of this demographic into inconsequentialism is significant to the program. This is a pivotal span of years for that reason.

Generation Three: 2074 through 2099

Ages 0 through 6: Amenable

Beginning with this generation, all newborn individuals have benefit of parentage that has become indoctrinated with the ideals of the assimilation program. Therefore, going forward, this demographic and its nascent influence is no longer a concern. However, at this phase (phase 3) exposure to higher age groups that have not, and in most cases, will not accept indoctrination, continues to manifest untoward, but largely ineffectual influence.

Ages 7 through 31: Indoctrinated

Having come into life under the influence of the assimilation program, this demographic is the first to achieve full indoctrination. However, though compliant, the generation is not materially progressive towards program goals. Primarily, this is due to the residual influences of higher age demographics. Even so, the demographic holds a great deal of promise for later program phases.

Ages 32 through 56: Influential

Having been the first demographic to grasp the promise of assimilation during earlier phases of the program, it has now become highly influential. Spending habits, hiring practices, choices in entertainment and behavior, bring this demographic forward to become the most influential of phase three. This is partly due to a shift forward with respect to actively rejecting residual, untoward influences of higher age generations.

Ages 57 through 81: Accepting

Having been adherent and receptive to program goals from earlier in life, this demographic has not been detractive, but never fully embraces its ideals. The influence this demographic has had during prior phases, and back to many generations beyond, is subverted by the next-younger age bracket of 32 through 56. For this reason, the typical top-down structure of power in terms of age demographic, is

disrupted for the first time. It will restore naturally as the goals of
the program are achieved and society stabilizes going forward.

Ages 82 through 106: Inconsequential

During prior phases, this demographic transitioned from distrustful
to compliant. Though never having achieved full adoption of
program ideals, it had neither been a relevant disruptive force.
Therefore, passage into inconsequentialism is not positively or
negatively significant.

Generation Four: 2099 through 2124

Ages 0 through 6: Indoctrinated

The first newborn demographic to be free of material untoward
influence. This generation shall be the first to eventually achieve
full assimilation.

Ages 7 through 31: Strategic

No longer encumbered with assimilation as a controversial concern,
this demographic is strategic in that its behavior and choices are
fully organic with respect to the ideals of the Assemblies of the
Living. Even so, the group, like all others in this age-demographic,
are not the primary holders of power. It is, therefore, nascent and
strategic in its positioning.

Ages 32 through 56: Progressive

Having become indoctrinated during the prior phase, this
demographic is pivotal in that it has achieved a position of primary
economic influence while at the same time, surrounded by higher
and lower age groups that are like minded with respect to
assimilation. The indirect effects of spending habits and investment
begin to have positive effect.

Ages 57 through 81: Advocative

During the prior phase, this demographic was influential to, but not
the holder of governmental and corporate power. Having now
become the holder of power, this group begins to affect change in
government and corporate posture that, for the first time, progresses
the assimilation program by policy.

Ages 82 through 106: Inconsequential
No material impact.

Generation Five: 2124 through 2149

Ages 0 through 6: Indoctrinated
Fully indoctrinated. Free from untoward influence.

Ages 7 through 31: Indoctrinated
Fully indoctrinated. Free from untoward influence.

Ages 32 through 56: Invested
The first age-demographic to begin building and investing in the ways of the Assemblies of the Living. It is the first point at which the path to indoctrination matures beyond simple acceptance and compliance, and towards a contributive posture.

Ages 57 through 81: Stabilizing
As the holders of governmental and corporate policy, this age-demographic begins to interlace the principles of the Assemblies of the Living into laws and regulatory requirements, which has a stabilizing effect. At this point, the possibility of achieving good-standing within the Assemblies of the Living is first realized and aspired to.

Ages 82 through 106: Supportive
A sustaining and stabilizing influence, but not progressive.

Generation Six: 2149 through 2174

Ages 0 through 6: Indoctrinated
Fully indoctrinated. Free from untoward influence.

Ages 7 through 31: Contributive
Having fully embraced the principles of the Assemblies of the Living, the goals and aspirations of this demographic align and contribute to acceptable and ubiquitous standards of behavior.

Ages 32 through 56: Assimilated
The first generation to achieve a recognized position of good-standing within the Assemblies of the Living. Going forward, this position of influence will trend back towards the tendency for power

to rest with the higher age-demographic of 57 through 81. However, first entrance, will occur due to recognition of economic, social and quality of life benefits, which will be swayed through activities and interests largely led by this age group (32 through 56).

Ages 57 through 81: Invested
A sustaining and stabilizing influence, but not progressive.

Ages 82 through 106: Supportive
A sustaining and stabilizing influence, but not progressive.

Lunar Anomaly Annotated View

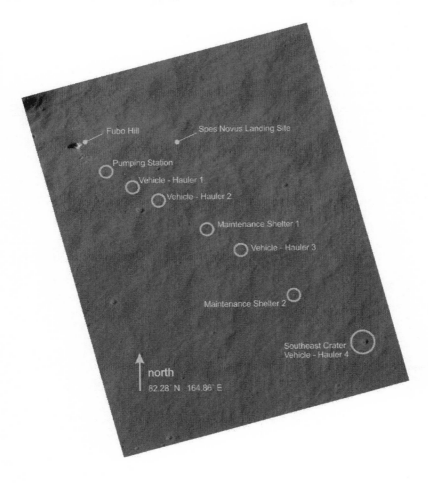

Fubo Hill

Spes Novus Landing Site

Pumping Station

Vehicle - Hauler 1

Vehicle - Hauler 2

Maintenance Shelter 1

Vehicle - Hauler 3

Maintenance Shelter 2

Southeast Crater
Vehicle - Hauler 4

north

82.28° N   164.86° E

Made in the USA
Columbia, SC
30 October 2018